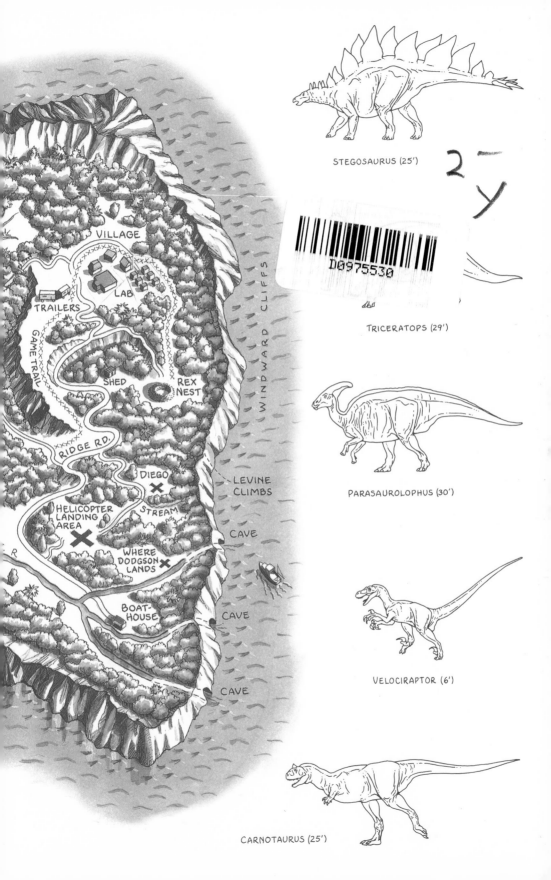

STEGOSAURUS (25')

TRICERATOPS (29')

PARASAUROLOPHUS (30')

VELOCIRAPTOR (6')

CARNOTAURUS (25')

VILLAGE

LAB

TRAILERS

GAME TRAIL

SHED

REX NEST

RIDGE RD.

DIEGO

LEVINE CLIMBS

HELICOPTER LANDING AREA

STREAM

CAVE

WHERE DODGSON LANDS

BOAT-HOUSE

CAVE

CAVE

WINDWARD CLIFFS

D0975530

THE LOST WORLD

The Lost World

A NOVEL BY

MICHAEL CRICHTON

ALFRED A. KNOPF   *New York*   1995

THIS IS A BORZOI BOOK
PUBLISHED BY ALFRED A. KNOPF, INC.

Published in the United States by Alfred A. Knopf, Inc.,
New York, and simultaneously in Canada by Random House of Canada Limited,
Toronto. Distributed by Random House, Inc., New York.

Library of Congress Cataloging-in-Publication Data

Crichton, Michael, [date]
The lost world : a novel / by Michael Crichton. — 1st ed.
p.   cm.
ISBN 0-679-41946-2
I. Title.
PS3553.R48L67   1995b
813′ .54—dc20   95-32034
CIP

Manufactured in the United States of America
First Trade Edition

To Carolyn Conger

"What really interests me is whether God had any choice in the creation of the world."

ALBERT EINSTEIN

"Deep in the chaotic regime, slight changes in structure almost always cause vast changes in behavior. Complex controllable behavior seems precluded."

STUART KAUFFMAN

"Sequelae are inherently unpredictable."

IAN MALCOLM

Introduction:
"Extinction at the K-T Boundary"

The late twentieth century has witnessed a remarkable growth in scientific interest in the subject of extinction.

It is hardly a new subject—Baron Georges Cuvier had first demonstrated that species became extinct back in 1786, not long after the American Revolution. Thus the fact of extinction had been accepted by scientists for nearly three-quarters of a century before Darwin put forth his theory of evolution. And after Darwin, the many controversies that swirled around his theory did not often concern issues of extinction.

On the contrary, extinction was generally considered as unremarkable as a car running out of gas. Extinction was simply proof of failure to adapt. How species adapted was intensely studied and fiercely debated. But the fact that some species failed was hardly given a second thought. What was there to say about it? However, beginning in the 1970s, two developments began to focus attention on extinction in a new way.

The first was the recognition that human beings were now very numerous, and were altering the planet at a very rapid rate—eliminating traditional habitats, clearing the rain forest, polluting air and water, perhaps even changing global climate. In the process, many animal species were becoming extinct. Some scientists cried out in alarm; others were quietly uneasy. How fragile was the earth's ecosystem? Was the human species engaged in behavior that would eventually lead to its own extinction?

No one was sure. Since nobody had ever bothered to study extinction in an organized way, there was little information about rates of extinction in other geological eras. So scientists began to look closely at extinction in the past, hoping to answer anxieties about the present.

The second development concerned new knowledge about the death of the dinosaurs. It had long been known that all dinosaur species had become extinct in a relatively short time at the end of the Cretaceous era, approximately sixty-five million years ago. Exactly how quickly those extinctions occurred was a subject of long-standing debate: some paleontologists believed they had been catastrophically swift, others felt the dinosaurs had died out more gradually, over a period of ten thousand to ten million years—hardly a rapid event.

Then, in 1980, physicist Luis Alvarez and three coworkers discovered high concentrations of the element iridium in rocks from the end of the Cretaceous and the start of the Tertiary—the so-called K-T boundary. (The Cretaceous was shorthanded as "K" to avoid confusion with the Cambrian and other geological periods.) Iridium is rare on earth, but abundant in meteors. Alvarez's team argued that the presence of so much iridium in rocks at the K-T boundary suggested that a giant meteorite, many miles in diameter, had collided with the earth at that time. They theorized that the resulting dust and debris had darkened the skies, inhibited photosynthesis, killed plants and animals, and ended the reign of the dinosaurs.

This dramatic theory captured the media and public imagination. It began a controversy which continued for many years. Where was the crater from this meteor? Various candidates were proposed. There were five major periods of extinction in the past—had meteors caused them all? Was there a twenty-six-million-year cycle of catastrophe? Was the planet even now awaiting another devastating impact?

After more than a decade, these questions remained unanswered. The debate raged on—until August 1993, when, at a weekly seminar of the Santa Fe Institute, an iconoclastic mathematician named Ian Malcolm announced that none of these questions mattered, and that the debate over a meteoric impact was "a frivolous and irrelevant speculation."

"Consider the numbers," Malcolm said, leaning on the podium, staring forward at his audience. "On our planet there are currently fifty million species of plants and animals. We think that is a remarkable diversity, yet it is nothing compared to what has existed before. We estimate that there have been fifty billion species on this planet since life began. That means that for every thousand species that ever existed on the planet, only one remains today. Thus 99.9 percent of all species that ever lived are extinct. And mass killings account for only five percent of that total. The overwhelming majority of species died one at a time."

The truth, Malcolm said, was that life on earth was marked by a continuous, steady rate of extinction. By and large, the average lifespan of a species was four million years. For mammals, it was a million years. Then the species vanished. So the real pattern was one of species rising, flourishing, and dying out in a few million years. On average, one species a day had become extinct throughout the history of life on the earth.

"But why?" he asked. "What leads to the rise and decline of earth's species in a four-million-year life cycle?

"One answer is that we do not recognize how continuously active our planet is. Just in the last fifty thousand years—a geological blink of an eye—the rain forests have severely contracted, then expanded again. Rain forests aren't an ageless feature of the planet; they're actually rather new. As recently as ten thousand years ago, when there were human hunters on the American continent, an ice pack extended as far down as New York City. Many animals became extinct during that time.

"So most of earth's history shows animals living and dying against a very active background. That probably explains 90 percent of extinctions. If the seas dry up, or become more salty, then of course ocean plankton will all die. But complex animals like dinosaurs are another matter, because complex animals have insulated themselves—literally and figuratively—against such changes. Why do complex animals die out? Why don't they adjust? Physically, they seem to have the capacity to survive. There appears to be no reason why they should die. And yet they do.

"What I wish to propose is that complex animals become extinct not because of a change in their physical adaptation to their environment, but because of their behavior. I would suggest that the latest thinking in chaos theory, or nonlinear dynamics, provides tantalizing hints to how this happens.

"It suggests to us that behavior of complex animals can change very rapidly, and not always for the better. It suggests that behavior can cease to be responsive to the environment, and lead to decline and death. It suggests that animals may stop adapting. Is this what happened to the dinosaurs? Is this the true cause of their disappearance? We may never know. But it is no accident that human beings are so interested in dinosaur extinction. The decline of the dinosaurs allowed mammals—including us—to flourish. And that leads us to wonder whether the disappearance of the dinosaurs is going to be repeated, sooner or later, by us as well. Whether at the deepest level the fault lies not in blind fate—in some fiery meteor from the skies—but in our own behavior. At the moment, we have no answer."

And then he smiled.

"But I have a few suggestions," he said.

THE LOST WORLD

Prologue:
"Life at the Edge of Chaos"

The Santa Fe Institute was housed in a series of buildings on Canyon Road which had formerly been a convent, and the Institute's seminars were held in a room which had served as a chapel. Now, standing at the podium, with a shaft of sunlight shining down on him, Ian Malcolm paused dramatically before continuing his lecture.

Malcolm was forty years old, and a familiar figure at the Institute. He had been one of the early pioneers in chaos theory, but his promising career had been disrupted by a severe injury during a trip to Costa Rica; Malcolm had, in fact, been reported dead in several newscasts. "I was sorry to cut short the celebrations in mathematics departments around the country," he later said, "but it turned out I was only *slightly* dead. The surgeons have done wonders, as they will be the first to tell you. So now I am back—in my next iteration, you might say."

Dressed entirely in black, leaning on a cane, Malcolm gave the impression of severity. He was known within the Institute for his unconventional analysis, and his tendency to pessimism. His talk that August, entitled "Life at the Edge of Chaos," was typical of his thinking. In it, Malcolm presented his analysis of chaos theory as it applied to evolution.

He could not have wished for a more knowledgeable audience. The Santa Fe Institute had been formed in the mid-1980s by a group of scientists interested in the implications of chaos theory. The scientists came from many fields—physics, economics, biology, computer science. What they had in common was a belief that the complexity of the world concealed an underlying order which had previously eluded science, and which would be revealed by chaos theory, now known as complexity theory. In the words of one, complexity theory was "the science of the twenty-first century."

The Institute had explored the behavior of a great variety of complex systems—corporations in the marketplace, neurons in the human brain, enzyme cascades within a single cell, the group behavior of migratory birds—systems so complex that it had not been possible to study them before the advent of the computer. The research was new, and the findings were surprising.

It did not take long before the scientists began to notice that complex systems showed certain common behaviors. They started to think of these behaviors as characteristic of all complex systems. They realized that these behaviors could not be explained by analyzing the components of the systems. The time-honored scientific approach of reductionism—taking the watch apart to see how it worked—didn't get you anywhere with complex systems, because the interesting behavior seemed to arise from the spontaneous interaction of the components. The behavior wasn't planned or directed; it just happened. Such behavior was therefore called "self-organizing."

"Of the self-organizing behaviors," Ian Malcolm said, "two are of particular interest to the study of evolution. One is adaptation. We see it everywhere. Corporations adapt to the marketplace, brain cells adapt to signal traffic, the immune system adapts to infection, animals adapt to their food supply. We have come to think that the ability to adapt is characteristic of complex systems—and may be one reason why evolution seems to lead toward more complex organisms."

He shifted at the podium, transferring his weight onto his cane. "But even more important," he said, "is the way complex systems seem to strike a balance between the need for order and the imperative to change. Complex systems tend to locate themselves at a place we call 'the edge of chaos.' We imagine the edge of chaos as a place where there is enough innovation to keep a living system vibrant, and enough stability to keep it from collapsing into anarchy. It is a zone of conflict and upheaval, where the old and the new are constantly at war. Finding the balance point must be a delicate matter—if a living system drifts too close, it risks falling over into incoherence and dissolution; but if the system moves too far away from the edge, it becomes rigid, frozen, totalitarian. Both conditions lead to extinction. Too much change is as destructive as too little. Only at the edge of chaos can complex systems flourish."

He paused. "And, by implication, extinction is the inevitable result of one or the other strategy—too much change, or too little."

In the audience, heads were nodding. This was familiar thinking to most of the researchers present. Indeed, the concept of the edge of chaos was very nearly dogma at the Santa Fe Institute.

"Unfortunately," Malcolm continued, "the gap between this theoretical construct and the fact of extinction is vast. We have no way to know if our thinking is correct. The fossil record can tell us that an animal became extinct at a certain time, but not why. Computer simulations are of limited value. Nor can we perform experiments on living organisms. Thus, we are obliged to admit that extinction—untestable, unsuited for experiment—may not be a scientific subject at all. And this may explain why the subject has been embroiled in the most intense religious and political controversy. I would remind you that there is no religious debate about Avogadro's number, or Planck's constant, or the functions of the pancreas. But about extinction, there has been perpetual controversy for two hundred years. And I wonder how it is to be solved if—Yes? What is it?"

At the back of the room, a hand had gone up, waving impatiently. Malcolm frowned, visibly annoyed. The tradition at the Institute was that questions were held until the presentation ended; it was poor form to interrupt a speaker. "You had a question?" Malcolm asked.

From the back of the room, a young man in his early thirties stood. "Actually," the man said, "an observation."

The speaker was dark and thin, dressed in khaki shirt and shorts, precise in his movements and manner. Malcolm recognized him as a paleontologist from Berkeley named Levine, who was spending the summer at the Institute. Malcolm had never spoken to him, but he knew his reputation: Levine was generally agreed to be the best paleobiologist of his generation, perhaps the best in the world. But most people at the Institute disliked him, finding him pompous and arrogant.

"I agree," Levine continued, "that the fossil record is not helpful in addressing extinction. Particularly if your thesis is that behavior is the cause of extinction—because bones don't tell us much about behavior. But I disagree that your behavioral thesis is untestable. In point of fact, it implies an outcome. Although perhaps you haven't yet thought of it."

The room was silent. At the podium, Malcolm frowned. The eminent mathematician was not accustomed to being told he had not thought through his ideas. "What's your point," he said.

Levine appeared indifferent to the tension in the room. "Just this," he said. "During the Cretaceous, *Dinosauria* were widely distributed across the planet. We have found their remains on every continent, and in every climatic zone—even in the Antarctic. Now. If their extinction

was really the result of their behavior, and not the consequence of a catastrophe, or a disease, or a change in plant life, or any of the other
broad-scale explanations that have been proposed, then it seems to me
highly unlikely that they all changed their behavior at the same time,
everywhere. And that in turn means that there may well be some remnants of these animals still alive on the earth. Why couldn't you look
for them?"

"You could," Malcolm said coldly, "if that amused you. And if you
had no more compelling use for your time."

"No, no," Levine said earnestly. "I'm quite serious. What if the dinosaurs did not become extinct? What if they still exist? Somewhere in
an isolated spot on the planet."

"You're talking about a Lost World," Malcolm said, and heads in the
room nodded knowingly. Scientists at the Institute had developed a
shorthand for referring to common evolutionary scenarios. They spoke
of the Field of Bullets, the Gambler's Ruin, the Game of Life, the Lost
World, the Red Queen, and Black Noise. These were well-defined ways
of thinking about evolution. But they were all—

"No," Levine said stubbornly. "I am speaking literally."

"Then you're badly deluded," Malcolm said, with a dismissive wave
of his hand. He turned away from the audience, and walked slowly to
the blackboard. "Now, if we consider the implications of the edge of
chaos, we may begin by asking ourselves, what is the minimal unit of
life? Most contemporary definitions of life would include the presence
of DNA, but there are two examples which suggest to us that this definition is too narrow. If you consider viruses and so-called prions, it is
clear that life may in fact exist without DNA. . . ."

At the back of the room, Levine stared for a moment. Then, reluctantly, he sat down, and began to make notes.

The Lost World
Hypothesis

The lecture ended, Malcolm hobbled across the open courtyard of the Institute, shortly after noon. Walking beside him was Sarah Harding, a young field biologist visiting from Africa. Malcolm had known her for several years, since he had been asked to serve as an outside reader for her doctoral thesis at Berkeley.

Crossing the courtyard in the hot summer sun, they made an unlikely pair: Malcolm dressed in black, stooped and ascetic, leaning on his cane; Harding compact and muscular, looking young and energetic in shorts and a tee shirt, her short black hair pushed up on her forehead with sunglasses. Her field of study was African predators, lions and hyenas. She was scheduled to return to Nairobi the next day.

The two had been close since Malcolm's surgery. Harding had been on a sabbatical year in Austin, and had helped nurse Malcolm back to health, after his many operations. For a while it seemed as if a romance had blossomed, and that Malcolm, a confirmed bachelor, would settle down. But then Harding had gone back to Africa, and Malcolm had gone to Santa Fe. Whatever their former relationship had been, they were now just friends.

They discussed the questions that had come at the end of his lecture. From Malcolm's point of view, there had been only the predictable objections: that mass extinctions *were* important; that human beings owed their existence to the Cretaceous extinction, which had wiped out the dinosaurs and allowed the mammals to take over. As one questioner had pompously phrased it, "The Cretaceous allowed our own sentient awareness to arise on the planet."

Malcolm's reply was immediate: "What makes you think human beings are sentient and aware? There's no evidence for it. Human beings never think for themselves, they find it too uncomfortable. For the most part, members of our species simply repeat what they are told—and become upset if they are exposed to any different view. The characteristic human trait is not awareness but conformity, and the characteristic result is religious warfare. Other animals fight for territory or food; but, uniquely in the animal kingdom, human beings fight for their 'beliefs.' The reason is that beliefs guide behavior, which has evolutionary importance among human beings. But at a time when our behavior may well lead us to extinction, I see no reason to assume we have any awareness at all. We are stubborn, self-destructive conformists. Any other view of our species is just a self-congratulatory delusion. Next question."

Now, walking across the courtyard, Sarah Harding laughed. "They didn't care for that."

"I admit it's discouraging," he said. "But it can't be helped." He shook his head. "These are some of the best scientists in the country, and still . . . no interesting ideas. By the way, what's the story on that guy who interrupted me?"

"Richard Levine?" She laughed. "Irritating, isn't he? He has a worldwide reputation for being a pain in the ass."

Malcolm grunted. "I'd say."

"He's wealthy, is the problem," Harding said. "You know about the Becky dolls?"

"No," Malcolm said, giving her a glance.

"Well, every little girl in America does. There's a series: Becky and Sally and Frances, and several more. They're Americana dolls. Levine is the heir of the company. So he's a smartass rich kid. Impetuous, does whatever he wants."

Malcolm nodded. "You have time for lunch?"

"Sure, I would be—"

"Dr. Malcolm! Wait up! Please! Dr. Malcolm!"

Malcolm turned. Hurrying across the courtyard toward them was the gangling figure of Richard Levine.

"Ah, shit," Malcolm said.

"Dr. Malcolm," Levine said, coming up. "I was surprised that you didn't take my proposal more seriously."

"How could I?" Malcolm said. "It's absurd."

"Yes, but—"

"Ms. Harding and I were just going to lunch," Malcolm said, gesturing to Sarah.

"Yes, but I think you should reconsider," Levine said, pressing on. "Because I believe my argument is valid—it is entirely possible, even likely, that dinosaurs still exist. You must know there are persistent rumors about animals in Costa Rica, where I believe you have spent time."

"Yes, and in the case of Costa Rica I can tell you—"

"Also in the Congo," Levine said, continuing. "For years there have been reports by pygmies of a large sauropod, perhaps even an apatosaur, in the dense forest around Bokambu. And also in the high jungles of Irian Jaya, there is supposedly an animal the size of a rhino, which perhaps is a remnant ceratopsian—"

"Fantasy," Malcolm said. "Pure fantasy. Nothing has ever been seen. No photographs. No hard evidence."

"Perhaps not," Levine said. "But absence of proof is not proof of absence. I believe there may well be a locus of these animals, survivals from a past time."

Malcolm shrugged. "Anything is possible," he said.

"But in point of fact, survival *is* possible," Levine insisted. "I keep getting calls about new animals in Costa Rica. Remnants, fragments."

Malcolm paused. "Recently?"

"Not for a while."

"Umm," Malcolm said. "I thought so."

"The last call was nine months ago," Levine said. "I was in Siberia looking at that frozen baby mammoth, and I couldn't get back in time. But I'm told it was some kind of very large, atypical lizard, found dead in the jungle of Costa Rica."

"And? What happened to it?"

"The remains were burned."

"So nothing is left?"

"That's right."

"No photographs? No proof?"

"Apparently not."

"So it's just a story," Malcolm said.

"Perhaps. But I believe it is worth mounting an expedition, to find out about these reported survivals."

Malcolm stared at him. "An expedition? To find a hypothetical Lost World? Who is going to pay for it?"

"I am," Levine said. "I have already begun the preliminary planning."

"But that could cost—"

"I don't care what it costs," Levine said. "The fact is, survival is possible, it has occurred in a variety of species from other genera, and it may be that there are survivals from the Cretaceous as well."

"Fantasy," Malcolm said again, shaking his head.

Levine paused, and stared at Malcolm. "Dr. Malcolm," he said, "I must say I'm very surprised at your attitude. You've just presented a thesis and I am offering you a chance to prove it. I would have thought you'd jump at the opportunity."

"My jumping days are over," Malcolm said.

"But instead of taking me up on this, you—"

"I'm not interested in dinosaurs," Malcolm said.

"But everyone is interested in dinosaurs."

"Not me." He turned on his cane, and started to walk off.

"By the way," Levine said. "What were you doing in Costa Rica? I heard you were there for almost a year."

"I was lying in a hospital bed. They couldn't move me out of intensive care for six months. I couldn't even get on a plane."

"Yes," Levine said. "I know you got hurt. But what were you doing there in the first place? Weren't you looking for dinosaurs?"

Malcolm squinted at him in the bright sun, and leaned on his cane. "No," he said. "I wasn't."

They were all three sitting at a small painted table in the corner of the Guadalupe Cafe, on the other side of the river. Sarah Harding drank Corona from the bottle, and watched the two men opposite her. Levine looked pleased to be with them, as if he had won some victory to be sitting at the table. Malcolm looked weary, like a parent who has spent too much time with a hyperactive child.

"You want to know what I've heard?" Levine said. "I've heard that a couple of years back, a company named InGen genetically engineered some dinosaurs and put them on an island in Costa Rica. But something went wrong, a lot of people were killed, and the dinosaurs were destroyed. And now nobody will talk about it, because of some legal angle. Nondisclosure agreements or something. And the Costa Rican government doesn't want to hurt tourism. So nobody will talk. That's what I've heard."

Malcolm stared at him. "And you believe that?"

"Not at first, I didn't," Levine said. "But the thing is, I keep hearing it. The rumors keep floating around. Supposedly you, and Alan Grant, and a bunch of other people were there."

"Did you ask Grant about it?"

"I asked him, last year, at a conference in Peking. He said it was absurd."

Malcolm nodded slowly.

"Is that what you say?" Levine asked, drinking his beer. "I mean, you know Grant, don't you?"

"No. I never met him."

Levine was watching Malcolm closely. "So it's not true?"

Malcolm sighed. "Are you familiar with the concept of a techno-myth? It was developed by Geller at Princeton. Basic thesis is that we've lost all the old myths, Orpheus and Eurydice and Perseus and Medusa. So we fill the gap with modern techno-myths. Geller listed a dozen or so. One is that an alien's living at a hangar at Wright-Patterson Air Force Base. Another is that somebody invented a carburetor that gets a hundred and fifty miles to the gallon, but the automobile companies bought the patent and are sitting on it. Then there's the story that the Russians trained children in ESP at a secret base in Siberia and these kids can kill people anywhere in the world with their thoughts. The story that the lines in Nazca, Peru, are an alien spaceport. That the CIA released the AIDS virus to kill homosexuals. That Nikola Tesla discovered an incredible energy source but his notes are lost. That in Istanbul there's a tenth-century drawing that shows the earth from space. That the Stanford Research Institute found a guy whose body glows in the dark. Get the picture?"

"You're saying InGen's dinosaurs are a myth," Levine said.

"Of course they are. They have to be. Do you think it's possible to genetically engineer a dinosaur?"

"The experts all tell me it's not."

"And they're right," Malcolm said. He glanced at Harding, as if for confirmation. She said nothing, just drank her beer.

In fact, Harding knew something more about these dinosaur rumors. Once after surgery, Malcolm had been delirious, mumbling nonsense from the anaesthesia and pain medication. And he had been seemingly fearful, twisting in the bed, repeating the names of several kinds of dinosaurs. Harding had asked the nurse about it; she said he was like that after every operation. The hospital staff assumed it was a drug-induced fantasy—yet it seemed to Harding that Malcolm was reliving some terrifying actual experience. The feeling was heightened by the slangy, familiar way Malcolm referred to the dinosaurs: he called them "raptors" and "compys" and "trikes." And he seemed especially fearful of the raptors.

Later, when he was back home, she had asked him about his delirium. He had just shrugged it off, making a bad joke — "At least I didn't mention other women, did I?" And then he made some comment about having been a dinosaur nut as a kid, and how illness made you regress. His whole attitude was elaborately indifferent, as if it were all unimportant; she had the distinct feeling he was being evasive. But she wasn't inclined to push it; those were the days when she was in love with him, her attitude indulgent.

Now he was looking at her in a questioning way, as if to ask if she was going to contradict him. Harding just raised an eyebrow, and stared back. He must have his reasons. She could wait him out.

Levine leaned forward across the table toward Malcolm and said, "So the InGen story is entirely untrue?"

"Entirely untrue," Malcolm said, nodding gravely. "Entirely untrue."

Malcolm had been denying the speculation for three years. By now he was getting good at it; his weariness was no longer affected but genuine. In fact, he had been a consultant to International Genetic Technologies of Palo Alto in the summer of 1989, and he had made a trip to Costa Rica for them, which had turned out disastrously. In the aftermath, everyone involved had moved quickly to quash the story. InGen wanted to limit its liability. The Costa Rican government wanted to preserve its reputation as a tourist paradise. And the individual scientists had been bound by nondisclosure agreements, abetted later by generous grants to continue their silence. In Malcolm's case, two years of medical bills had been paid by the company.

Meanwhile, InGen's island facility in Costa Rica had been destroyed. There were no longer any living creatures on the island. The company had hired the eminent Stanford professor George Baselton, a biologist and essayist whose frequent television appearances had made him a popular authority on scientific subjects. Baselton claimed to have visited the island, and had been tireless in denying rumors that extinct animals had ever existed there. His derisive snort, "Saber-toothed tigers, indeed!" was particularly effective.

As time passed, interest in the story waned. InGen was long since bankrupt; the principal investors in Europe and Asia had taken their losses. Although the company's physical assets, the buildings and lab equipment, would be sold piecemeal, the core technology that had been developed would, they decided, never be sold. In short, the InGen chapter was closed.

There was nothing more to say.

"So there's no truth to it," Levine said, biting into his green-corn tamale. "To tell you the truth, Dr. Malcolm, that makes me feel better."

"Why?" Malcolm said.

"Because it means that the remnants that keep turning up in Costa Rica must be real. Real dinosaurs. I've got a friend from Yale down there, a field biologist, and he says he's seen them. I believe him."

Malcolm shrugged. "I doubt," he said, "that any more animals will turn up in Costa Rica."

"It's true there haven't been any for almost a year now. But if more show up, I'm going down there. And in the interim, I am going to outfit an expedition. I've been giving a lot of thought to how it should be done. I think the special vehicles could be built and ready in a year. I've already talked to Doc Thorne about it. Then I'll assemble a team, perhaps including Dr. Harding here, or a similarly accomplished naturalist, and some graduate students. . . ."

Malcolm listened, shaking his head.

"You think I'm wasting my time," Levine said.

"I do, yes."

"But suppose—just suppose—that animals start to show up again."

"Never happen."

"But suppose they did?" Levine said. "Would you be interested in helping me? To plan an expedition?"

Malcolm finished his meal, and pushed the plate aside. He stared at Levine.

"Yes," he said finally. "If animals started showing up again, I would be interested in helping you."

"Great!" Levine said. "That's all I wanted to know."

Outside, in the bright sunlight on Guadalupe Street, Malcolm walked with Sarah toward Malcolm's battered Ford sedan. Levine climbed into a bright-red Ferrari, waved cheerfully, and roared off.

"You think it will ever happen?" Sarah Harding said. "That these, ah, animals will start showing up again?"

"No," Malcolm said. "I am quite sure they never will."

"You sound hopeful."

He shook his head, and got awkwardly in the car, swinging his bad leg under the steering wheel. Harding climbed in beside him. He glanced at her, and turned the key in the ignition. They drove back to the Institute.

The following day, she went back to Africa. During the next eighteen months, she had a rough sense of Levine's progress, since from time to time he called her with some question about field protocols, or vehicle tires, or the best anaesthetic to use on animals in the wild. Sometimes she got a call from Doc Thorne, who was building the vehicles. He usually sounded harassed.

From Malcolm she heard nothing at all, although he sent her a card on her birthday. It arrived a month late. He had scrawled at the bottom, "Have a happy birthday. Be glad you're nowhere near him. He's driving me crazy."

FIRST CONFIGURATION

"In the conservative region far from the chaotic edge, individual elements coalesce slowly, showing no clear pattern."

IAN MALCOLM

Aberrant Forms

In the fading afternoon light, the helicopter skimmed low along the coast, following the line where the dense jungle met the beach. The last of the fishing villages had flashed by beneath them ten minutes ago. Now there was only impenetrable Costa Rican jungle, mangrove swamps, and mile after mile of deserted sand. Sitting beside the pilot, Marty Guitierrez stared out the window as the coastline swept past. There weren't even any roads in this area, at least none that Guitierrez could see.

Guitierrez was a quiet, bearded American of thirty-six, a field biologist who had lived for the last eight years in Costa Rica. He had originally come to study toucan speciation in the rain forest, but stayed on as a consultant to the Reserva Biológica de Carara, the national park in the north. He clicked the radio mike and said to the pilot, "How much farther?"

"Five minutes, Señor Guitierrez."

Guitierrez turned and said, "It won't be long now." But the tall man folded up in the back seat of the helicopter didn't answer, or even acknowledge that he had been spoken to. He merely sat, with his hand on his chin, and stared frowning out the window.

Richard Levine wore sun-faded field khakis, and an Australian slouch hat pushed low over his head. A battered pair of binoculars hung around his neck. But despite his rugged appearance, Levine conveyed an air of scholarly absorption. Behind his wire-frame spectacles, his features were sharp, his expression intense and critical as he looked out the window.

"What is this place?"

"It's called Rojas."

"So we're far south?"

"Yes. Only about fifty miles from the border with Panama."

Levine stared at the jungle. "I don't see any roads," he said. "How was the thing found?"

"Couple of campers," Guitierrez said. "They came in by boat, landed on the beach."

"When was that?"

"Yesterday. They took one look at the thing, and ran like hell."

Levine nodded. With his long limbs folded up, his hands tucked under his chin, he looked like a praying mantis. That had been his nickname in graduate school: in part because of his appearance—and in part because of his tendency to bite off the head of anyone who disagreed with him.

Guitierrez said, "Been to Costa Rica before?"

"No. First time," Levine said. And then he gave an irritable wave of his hand, as if he didn't want to be bothered with small talk.

Guitierrez smiled. After all these years, Levine had not changed at all. He was still one of the most brilliant and irritating men in science. The two had been fellow graduate students at Yale, until Levine quit the doctoral program to get his degree in comparative zoology instead. Levine announced he had no interest in the kind of contemporary field research that so attracted Guitierrez. With characteristic contempt, he had once described Guitierrez's work as "collecting parrot crap from around the world."

The truth was that Levine—brilliant and fastidious—was drawn to the past, to the world that no longer existed. And he studied this world with obsessive intensity. He was famous for his photographic memory, his arrogance, his sharp tongue, and the unconcealed pleasure he took in pointing out the errors of colleagues. As a colleague once said, "Levine never forgets a bone—and he never lets you forget it, either."

Field researchers disliked Levine, and he returned the sentiment. He was at heart a man of detail, a cataloguer of animal life, and he was happiest poring over museum collections, reassigning species, rearranging display skeletons. He disliked the dust and inconvenience of life in the field. Given his choice, Levine would never leave the museum. But it was his fate to live in the greatest period of discovery in the history of paleontology. The number of known species of dinosaurs had doubled in the last twenty years, and new species were now being described at the rate of one every seven weeks. Thus Levine's worldwide reputation forced him to continually travel around the world, inspecting new finds, and rendering his expert opinion to researchers who were annoyed to admit that they needed it.

"Where'd you come from?" Guitierrez asked him.

"Mongolia," Levine said. "I was at the Flaming Cliffs, in the Gobi Desert, three hours out of Ulan Bator."

"Oh? What's there?"

"John Roxton's got a dig. He found an incomplete skeleton he thought might be a new species of *Velociraptor*, and wanted me to have a look."

"And?"

Levine shrugged. "Roxton never really did know anatomy. He's an enthusiastic fund-raiser, but if he actually uncovers something, he's incompetent to proceed."

"You told him that?"

"Why not? It's the truth."

"And the skeleton?"

"The skeleton wasn't a raptor at all," Levine said. "Metatarsals all wrong, pubis too ventral, ischium lacking a proper obturator, and the long bones much too light. As for the skull . . ." He rolled his eyes. "The palatal's too thick, antorbital fenestrae too rostral, distal carina too small—oh, it goes on and on. And the trenchant ungual's hardly present. So there we are. I don't know what Roxton could have been thinking. I suspect he actually has a subspecies of *Stenonychosaurus*, though I haven't decided for sure."

"*Stenonychosaurus*?" Guitierrez said.

"Small Triassic carnivore—two meters from pes to acetabulum. In point of fact, a rather ordinary theropod. And Roxton's find wasn't a particularly interesting example. Although there was one curious detail. The material included an integumental artifact—an imprint of the dinosaur's skin. That in itself is not rare. There are perhaps a dozen good skin impressions obtained so far, mostly among the *Hadrosauridae*. But nothing like this. Because it was clear to me that this animal's skin had some very unusual characteristics not previously suspected in dinosaurs—"

"Señores," the pilot said, interrupting them, "Juan Fernández Bay is ahead."

Levine said, "Circle it first, can we?"

Levine looked out the window, his expression intense again, the conversation forgotten. They were flying over jungle that extended up into the hills for miles, as far as they could see. The helicopter banked, circling the beach.

"There it is now," Guitierrez said, pointing out the window.

The beach was a clean, curving white crescent, entirely deserted in the afternoon light. To the south, they saw a single dark mass in the sand.

From the air, it looked like a rock, or perhaps a large clump of seaweed. The shape was amorphous, about five feet across. There were lots of footprints around it.

"Who's been here?" Levine said, with a sigh.

"Public Health Service people came out earlier today."

"Did they do anything?" he said. "They touch it, disturb it in any way?"

"I can't say," Guitierrez said.

"The Public Health Service," Levine repeated, shaking his head. "What do they know? You should never have let them near it, Marty."

"Hey," Guitierrez said. "I don't run this country. I did the best I could. They wanted to destroy it before you even got here. At least I managed to keep it intact until you arrived. Although I don't know how long they'll wait."

"Then we'd better get started," Levine said. He pressed the button on his mike. "Why are we still circling? We're losing light. Get down on the beach now. I want to see this thing firsthand."

Richard Levine ran across the sand toward the dark shape, his binoculars bouncing on his chest. Even from a distance, he could smell the stench of decay. And already he was logging his preliminary impressions. The carcass lay half-buried in the sand, surrounded by a thick cloud of flies. The skin was bloated with gas, which made identification difficult.

He paused a few yards from the creature, and took out his camera. Immediately, the pilot of the helicopter came up alongside him, pushing his hand down. "No *permitado*."

"What?"

"I am sorry, señor. No pictures are allowed."

"Why the hell not?" Levine said. He turned to Guitierrez, who was trotting down the beach toward them. "Marty, why no pictures? This could be an important—"

"No pictures," the pilot said again, and he pulled the camera out of Levine's hand.

"Marty, this is crazy."

"Just go ahead and make your examination," Guitierrez said, and then he began speaking in Spanish to the pilot, who answered sharply and angrily, waving his hands.

Levine watched a moment, then turned away. The hell with this, he thought. They could argue forever. He hurried forward, breathing through his mouth. The odor became much stronger as he approached it. Although the carcass was large he noticed there were no birds, rats, or other scavengers feeding on it. There were only flies—flies so dense they covered the skin, and obscured the outline of the dead animal.

Even so, it was clear that this had been a substantial creature, roughly the size of a cow or horse before the bloat began to enlarge it further. The dry skin had cracked in the sun and was now peeling upward, exposing the layer of runny, yellow subdermal fat beneath.

Oof, it stunk! Levine winced. He forced himself closer, directing all his attention to the animal.

Although it was the size of a cow, it was clearly not a mammal. The skin was hairless. The original skin color appeared to have been green, with a suggestion of darker striations running through it. The epidermal surface was pebbled in polygonal tubercles of varying sizes, the pattern reminiscent of the skin of a lizard. This texture varied in different parts of the animal, the pebbling larger and less distinct on the underbelly. There were prominent skin folds at the neck, shoulder, and hip joints— again, like a lizard.

But the carcass was large. Levine estimated the animal had originally weighed about a hundred kilograms, roughly two hundred and twenty pounds. No lizards grew that large anywhere in the world, except the Komodo dragons of Indonesia. *Varanus komodoensis* were nine-foot-long monitor lizards, crocodile-size carnivores that ate goats and pigs, and on occasion human beings as well. But there were no monitor lizards anywhere in the New World. Of course, it was conceivable that this was one of the *Iguanidae*. Iguanas were found all over South America, and the marine iguanas grew quite large. Even so, this would be a record-size animal.

Levine moved slowly around the carcass, toward the front of the animal. No, he thought, it wasn't a lizard. The carcass lay on its side, its left rib cage toward the sky. Nearly half of it was buried; the row of protuberances that marked the dorsal spinous processes of the backbone were just a few inches above the sand. The long neck was curved, the head hidden beneath the bulk of the body like a duck's head under feathers. Levine saw one forelimb, which seemed small and weak. The distal appendage was buried in sand. He would dig that out and have a look at it, but he wanted to take pictures before he disturbed the specimen *in situ*.

In fact, the more Levine saw of this carcass, the more carefully he thought he should proceed. Because one thing was clear—this was a very rare, and possibly unknown, animal. Levine felt simultaneously excited and cautious. If this discovery was as significant as he was beginning to think it was, then it was essential that it be properly documented.

Up the beach, Guitierrez was still shouting at the pilot, who kept shaking his head stubbornly. These banana-republic bureaucrats, Levine thought. Why shouldn't he take pictures? It couldn't harm anything. And it was vital to document the changing state of the creature.

He heard a thumping, and looked up to see a second helicopter circling the bay, its dark shadow sliding across the sand. This helicopter was ambulance-white, with red lettering on the side. In the glare of the setting sun, he couldn't read it.

He turned back to the carcass, noticing now that the hind leg of the animal was powerfully muscled, very different from the foreleg. It suggested that this creature walked upright, balanced on strong hind legs. Many lizards were known to stand upright, of course, but none so large as this. In point of fact, as Levine looked at the general shape of the carcass, he felt increasingly certain that this was not a lizard.

He worked quickly now, for the light was fading and he had much to do. With every specimen, there were always two major questions to answer, both equally important. First, what was the animal? Second, why had it died?

Standing by the thigh, he saw the epidermis was split open, no doubt from the gaseous subcutaneous buildup. But as Levine looked more closely, he saw that the split was in fact a sharp gash, and that it ran deep through the femorotibialis, exposing red muscle and pale bone beneath. He ignored the stench, and the white maggots that wriggled across the open tissues of the gash, because he realized that—

"Sorry about all this," Guitierrez said, coming over. "But the pilot just refuses."

The pilot was nervously following Guitierrez, standing beside him, watching carefully.

"Marty," Levine said. "I really need to take pictures here."

"I'm afraid you can't," Guitierrez said, with a shrug.

"It's important, Marty."

"Sorry. I tried my best."

Farther down the beach, the white helicopter landed, its whine diminishing. Men in uniforms began getting out.

"Marty. What do you think this animal is?"

"Well, I can only guess," Guitierrez said. "From the general dimensions I'd call it a previously unidentified iguana. It's extremely large, of course, and obviously not native to Costa Rica. My guess is this animal came from the Galápagos, or one of the—"

"No, Marty," Levine said. "It's not an iguana."

"Before you say anything more," Guitierrez said, glancing at the pilot, "I think you ought to know that several previously unknown species of lizard have shown up in this area. Nobody's quite sure why. Perhaps it's due to the cutting of the rain forest, or some other reason. But new species are appearing. Several years ago, I began to see unidentified species of—"

"Marty. It's not a damn lizard."

Guitierrez blinked his eyes. "What are you saying? Of course it's a lizard."

"I don't think so," Levine said.

Guitierrez said, "You're probably just thrown off because of its size. The fact is, here in Costa Rica, we occasionally encounter these aberrant forms—"

"Marty," Levine said coldly. "I am never *thrown off*."

"Well, of course, I didn't mean that—"

"And I am telling you, this is not a lizard," Levine said.

"I'm sorry," Guitierrez said, shaking his head. "But I can't agree."

Back at the white helicopter, the men were huddled together, putting on white surgical masks.

"I'm not asking you to agree," Levine said. He turned back to the carcass. "The diagnosis is settled easily enough, all we need do is excavate the head, or for that matter any of the limbs, for example this thigh here, which I believe—"

He broke off, and leaned closer. He peered at the back of the thigh.

"What is it?" Guitierrez said.

"Give me your knife."

"Why?" Guitierrez said.

"Just give it to me."

Guitierrez fished out his pocketknife, put the handle in Levine's outstretched hand. Levine peered steadily at the carcass. "I think you will find this interesting."

"What?"

"Right along the posterior dermal line, there is a—"

Suddenly, they heard shouting on the beach, and looked up to see the men from the white helicopter running down the beach toward them. They carried tanks on their backs, and were shouting in Spanish.

"What are they saying?" Levine asked, frowning.

Guitierrez sighed. "They're saying to get back."

"Tell them we're busy," Levine said, and bent over the carcass again.

But the men kept shouting, and suddenly there was a roaring sound, and Levine looked up to see flamethrowers igniting, big red jets of flame roaring out in the evening light. He ran around the carcass toward the men, shouting, "No! No!"

But the men paid no attention.

He shouted, "No, this is a priceless—"

The first of the uniformed men grabbed Levine, and threw him roughly to the sand.

"What the hell are you doing?" Levine yelled, scrambling to his feet. But even as he said it, he saw it was too late, the first of the flames had reached the carcass, blackening the skin, igniting the pockets of methane with a blue *whump!* The smoke from the carcass began to rise thickly into the sky.

"Stop it! Stop it!" Levine turned to Guitierrez. "Make them stop it!"

But Guitierrez was not moving, he was staring at the carcass. Consumed by flames, the torso crackled and the fat sputtered, and then as the skin burned away, the black, flat ribs of the skeleton were revealed, and then the whole torso turned, and suddenly the neck of the animal swung up, surrounded by flames, moving as the skin contracted. And inside the flames Levine saw a long pointed snout, and rows of sharp predatory teeth, and hollow eye sockets, the whole thing burning like some medieval dragon rising in flames up into the sky.

San José

Levine sat in the bar of the San José airport, nursing a beer, waiting for his plane back to the States. Guitierrez sat beside him at a small table, not saying much. An awkward silence had fallen for the last few minutes. Guitierrez stared at Levine's backpack, on the floor by his feet. It was specially constructed of dark-green Gore-Tex, with extra pockets on the outside for all the electronic gear.

"Pretty nice pack," Guitierrez said. "Where'd you get that, anyway? Looks like a Thorne pack."

Levine sipped his beer. "It is."

"Nice," Guitierrez said, looking at it. "What've you got there in the top flap, a satellite phone? And a GPS? Boy, what won't they think of next. Pretty slick. Must have cost you a—"

"Marty," Levine said, in an exasperated tone. "Cut the crap. Are you going to tell me, or not?"

"Tell you what?"

"I want to know what the hell's going on here."

"Richard, look, I'm sorry if you—"

"No," Levine said, cutting him off. "That was a very important specimen on that beach, Marty, and it was destroyed. I don't understand why you let it happen."

Guitierrez sighed. He looked around at the tourists at the other tables and said, "This has to be in confidence, okay?"

"All right."

"It's a big problem here."

"What is."

"There have been, uh . . . aberrant forms . . . turning up on the coast every so often. It's been going on for several years now."

"'Aberrant forms?'" Levine repeated, shaking his head in disbelief.

"That's the official term for these specimens," Guitierrez said. "No one in the government is willing to be more precise. It started about five years ago. A number of animals were discovered up in the mountains, near a remote agricultural station that was growing test varieties of soy beans."

"Soy beans," Levine repeated.

Guitierrez nodded. "Apparently these animals are attracted to beans, and certain grasses. The assumption is that they have a great need for the amino acid lysine in their diets. But nobody is really sure. Perhaps they just have a taste for certain crops—"

"Marty," Levine said. "I don't care if they have a taste for beer and pretzels. The only important question is: where did the animals come from?"

"Nobody knows," Guitierrez said.

Levine let that pass, for the moment. "What happened to those other animals?"

"They were all destroyed. And to my knowledge, no others were found for years afterward. But now it seems to be starting again. In the last year, we have found the remains of four more animals, including the one you saw today."

"And what was done?"

"The, ah, aberrant forms are always destroyed. Just as you saw. From the beginning, the government's taken every possible step to make sure nobody finds out about it. A few years back, some North American journalists began reporting there was something wrong on one island, Isla Nublar. Menéndez invited a bunch of journalists down for a special tour of the island—and proceeded to fly them to the wrong island. They never knew the difference. Stuff like that. I mean, the government's very serious about this."

"Why?"

"They're worried."

"Worried? Why should they be worried about—"

Guitierrez held up his hand, shifted in his chair, moved closer. "Disease, Richard."

"Disease?"

"Yeah. Costa Rica has one of the best health-care systems in the world," Guitierrez said. "The epidemiologists have been tracking some weird type of encephalitis that seems to be on the increase, particularly along the coast."

"Encephalitis? Of what origin? Viral?"

Guitierrez shook his head. "No causative agent has been found."

"Marty . . ."

"I'm telling you, Richard. Nobody knows. It's not a virus, because antibody titres don't go up, and white-cell differentials don't change. It's not bacterial, because nothing has ever been cultured. It's a complete mystery. All the epidemiologists know is that it seems to affect primarily rural farmers: people who are around animals and livestock. And it's a true encephalitis—splitting headaches, mental confusion, fever, delirium."

"Mortality?"

"So far it seems to be self-limited, lasts about three weeks. But even so it's got the government worried. This country is dependent on tourism, Richard. Nobody wants talk of unknown diseases."

"So they think the encephalitis is related to these, ah, aberrant forms?"

He shrugged. "Lizards carry lots of viral diseases," Guitierrez said. "They're a known vector. So it's not unreasonable, there might be a connection."

"But you said this isn't a viral disease."

"Whatever it is. They think it's related."

Levine said, "All the more reason to find out where these lizards are coming from. Surely they must have searched . . ."

"Searched?" Guitierrez said, with a laugh. "Of course they've searched. They've gone over every square inch of this country, again and again. They've sent out dozens of search parties—I've led several myself. They've done aerial surveys. They've had overflights of the jungle. They've had overflights of the offshore islands. That in itself is a big job. There are quite a few islands, you know, particularly along the west coast. Hell, they've even searched the ones that are privately owned."

"Are there privately owned islands?" Levine asked.

"A few. Three or four. Like Isla Nublar—it was leased to an American company, InGen, for years."

"But you said that island was searched . . . ."

"Thoroughly searched. Nothing there."

"And the others?"

"Well, let's see," Guitierrez said, ticking them off on his fingers. "There's Isla Talamanca, on the east coast; they've got a Club Med there. There's Sorna, on the west coast; it's leased to a German mining company. And there's Morazan, up north; it's actually owned by a wealthy Costa Rican family. And there may be another island I've forgotten about."

"And the searches found what?"

"Nothing," Guitierrez said. "They've found nothing at all. So the assumption is that the animals are coming from some location deep in the jungle. And that's why we haven't been able to find it so far."

Levine grunted. "In that case, lots of luck."

"I know," Guitierrez said. "Rain forest is an incredibly good environment for concealment. A search party could pass within ten yards of a large animal and never see it. And even the most advanced remote sensing technology doesn't help much, because there are multiple layers to penetrate—clouds, tree canopy, lower-level flora. There's just no way around it: almost anything could be hiding in the rain forest. Anyway," he said, "the government's frustrated. And, of course, the government is not the only interested party."

Levine looked up sharply. "Oh?"

"Yes. For some reason, there's been a lot of interest in these animals."

"What sort of interest?" Levine said, as casually as he could.

"Last fall, the government issued a permit to a team of botanists from Berkeley to do an aerial survey of the jungle canopy in the central highlands. The survey had been going on for a month when a dispute arose—a bill for aviation fuel, or something like that. Anyway, a bureaucrat in San José called Berkeley to complain. And Berkeley said they'd never heard of this survey team. Meantime, the team fled the country."

"So nobody knows who they really were?"

"No. Then last winter, a couple of Swiss geologists showed up to collect gas samples from offshore islands, as part of a study, they said, of volcanic activity in Central America. The offshore islands are all volcanic, and most of them are still active to some degree, so it seemed like a reasonable request. But it turned out the 'geologists' really worked for an American genetics company called Biosyn, and they were looking for, uh, large animals on the islands."

"Why would a biotech company be interested?" Levine said. "It makes no sense."

"Maybe not to you and me," Guitierrez said, "but Biosyn's got a particularly unsavory reputation. Their head of research is a guy named Lewis Dodgson."

"Oh yeah," Levine said. "I know. He's the guy who ran that rabies-vaccine test in Chile a few years back. The one where they exposed farmers to rabies but didn't tell them they were doing it."

"That's him. He also started test-marketing a genetically engineered potato in supermarkets without telling anybody they were altered. Gave kids low-grade diarrhea; couple of them ended up in the hospital. After that, the company had to hire George Baselton to fix their image."

"Seems like everybody hires Baselton," Levine said.

Guitierrez shrugged. "The big-name university professors consult, these days. It's part of the deal. And Baselton is Regis Professor of Biology. The company needed him to clean up their mess, because Dodgson has a habit of breaking the law. Dodgson has people on his payroll all around the world. Steals other companies' research, the whole bit. They say Biosyn's the only genetics company with more lawyers than scientists."

"And why were they interested in Costa Rica?" Levine asked.

Guitierrez shrugged. "I don't know, but the whole attitude toward research has changed, Richard. It's very noticeable here. Costa Rica has one of the richest ecologies in the world. Half a million species in twelve distinct environmental habitats. Five percent of all the species on the planet are represented here. This country has been a biological research center for years, and I can tell you, things have changed. In the old days, the people who came here were dedicated scientists with a passion to learn about something for its own sake—howler monkeys, or polistine wasps, or the sombrilla plant. These people had chosen their field because they cared about it. They certainly weren't going to get rich. But now, everything in the biosphere is potentially valuable. Nobody knows where the next drug is coming from, so drug companies fund all sorts of research. Maybe a bird egg has a protein that makes it waterproof. Maybe a spider produces a peptide that inhibits blood clotting. Maybe the waxy surface of a fern contains a painkiller. It happens often enough that attitudes toward research have changed. People aren't studying the natural world any more, they're mining it. It's a looter mentality. Anything new or unknown is automatically of interest, because it might have value. It might be worth a fortune."

Guitierrez drained his beer. "The world," he said, "is turned upside down. And the fact is that a lot of people want to know what these aberrant animals represent—and where they come from."

The loudspeaker called Levine's flight. Both men stood up from the table. Guitierrez said, "You'll keep all this to yourself? I mean, what you saw today."

"To be quite honest," Levine said, "I don't know what I saw today. It could have been anything."

Guitierrez grinned. "Safe flight, Richard."

"Take care, Marty."

Departure

His backpack slung over his shoulder, Levine walked toward the departure lounge. He turned to wave goodbye to Guitierrez, but his friend was already heading out the door, raising his arm to wave for a taxi. Levine shrugged, turned back.

Directly ahead was the customs desk, travelers lined up to have their passports stamped. He was booked on a night flight to San Francisco, with a long stopover in Mexico City; not many people were queuing up. He probably had time to call his office, and leave word for his secretary, Linda, that he would be on the flight; and perhaps, he thought, he should also call Malcolm. Looking around, he saw a row of phones marked ICT TELEFONOS INTERNATIONAL along the wall to his right, but there were only a few, and all were in use. He had better use the satellite phone in his backpack, he thought, as he swung the pack off his shoulder, and perhaps it would be—

He paused, frowning.

He looked back at the wall.

Four people were using the phones. The first was a blonde woman in shorts and a halter top, bouncing a young sunburned child in her arms as she talked. Next to her stood a bearded man in a safari jacket, who glanced repeatedly at his gold Rolex watch. Then there was a gray-haired, grandmotherly woman talking in Spanish, while her two full-grown sons stood by, nodding emphatically.

And the last person was the helicopter pilot. He had removed his uniform jacket, and was standing in short sleeves and tie. He was turned away, facing the wall, shoulders hunched.

Levine moved closer, and heard the pilot speaking in English. Levine set his pack down and bent over it, pretending to adjust the straps while he listened. The pilot was still turned away from him.

He heard the pilot say, "No, no, Professor. It is not that way. No." Then there was a pause. "No," the pilot said. "I am telling to you, no. I am sorry, Professor Baselton, but this is not known. It is an island, but which one . . . We must wait again for more. No, he leaves tonight. No, I think he does not know anything, and no pictures. No. I understand. *Adiós.*"

Levine ducked his head as the pilot walked briskly toward the LACSA desk at the other end of the airport.

What the hell? he thought.

It is an island, but which one . . .

How did they know it was an island? Levine himself was still not sure of that. And he had been working intensively on these finds, day and night, trying to put it together. Where they had come from. Why it was happening.

He walked around the corner, out of sight, and pulled out the little satellite phone. He dialed it quickly, calling a number in San Francisco.

The call went through, rapidly clicking as it linked with the satellite. It began to ring. There was a beep. An electronic voice said, "Please enter your access code."

Levine punched in a six-digit number.

There was another beep. The electronic voice said, "Leave your message."

"I'm calling," Levine said, "with the results of the trip. Single specimen, not in good shape. Location: BB-17 on your map. That's far south, which fits all of our hypotheses. I wasn't able to make a precise identification before they burned the specimen. But my guess is that it was an ornitholestes. As you know, this animal is not on the list—a highly significant finding."

He glanced around, but no one was near him, no one was paying attention. "Furthermore, the lateral femur was cut in a deep gash. This is extremely disturbing." He hesitated, not wanting to say too much. "And I am sending back a sample that requires close examination. I also think some other people are interested. Anyway, whatever is going on down here is new, Ian. There haven't been any specimens for over a year, and now they're showing up again. Something new is happening. And we don't understand it at all."

Or do we? Levine thought. He pressed the disconnect, turned the phone off, and replaced it in the outer pocket of his backpack. Maybe, he thought, we know more than we realize. He looked thoughtfully toward the departure gate. It was time to catch his flight.

Palo Alto

At 2 a.m., Ed James pulled into the nearly deserted parking lot of the Marie Callender's on Carter Road. The black BMW was already there, parked near the entrance. Through the windows, he could see Dodgson sitting inside at a booth, his bland features frowning. Dodgson was never in a good mood. Right now he was talking to the heavyset man alongside him, and glancing at his watch. The heavyset man was Baselton. The professor who appeared on television. James always felt relieved whenever Baselton was there. Dodgson gave him the creeps, but it was hard to imagine Baselton involved in anything shady.

James turned off the ignition and twisted the rearview mirror so he could see as he buttoned his shirt collar and pulled up his tie. He glimpsed his face in the mirror—a disheveled, tired man with a two-day stubble of beard. What the hell, he thought. Why shouldn't he look tired? It was the middle of the fucking night.

Dodgson always scheduled his meetings in the middle of the night, and always at this same damn Marie Callender restaurant. James never understood why; the coffee was awful. But then, there was a lot he didn't understand.

He picked up the manila envelope, and got out of the car, slamming the door. He headed for the entrance, shaking his head. Dodgson had been paying him five hundred dollars a day for weeks now, to follow a bunch of scientists around. At first, James had assumed it was some sort of industrial espionage. But none of the scientists worked for industry; they held university appointments, in pretty dull fields. Like that paleobotanist Sattler whose specialty was prehistoric pollen grains. James had sat through one of her lectures at Berkeley, and had barely been able to stay awake. Slide after slide of little pale spheres that looked like cotton balls, while she nattered on about polysaccharide bonding angles and the Campanian-Maastrichtian boundary. Jesus, it was boring.

Certainly not worth five hundred dollars a day, he thought. He went inside, blinking in the light, and walked over to the booth. He sat down, nodded to Dodgson and Baselton, and raised his hand to order coffee from the waitress.

Dodgson glared at him. "I haven't got all night," he said. "Let's get started."

"Right," James said, lowering his hand. "Fine, sure." He opened the envelope, began pulling out sheets and photos, handing them across the table to Dodgson as he talked.

"Alan Grant: paleontologist at Montana State. At the moment he's on leave of absence and is now in Paris, lecturing on the latest dinosaur finds. Apparently he has some new ideas about tyrannosaurs being scavengers, and —"

"Never mind," Dodgson said. "Go on."

"Ellen Sattler Reiman," James said, pushing across a photo. "Botanist, used to be involved with Grant. Now married to a physicist at Berkeley and has a young son and daughter. She lectures half-time at the university. Spends the rest of her time at home, because —"

"Go on, go on."

"Well. Most of the rest are deceased. Donald Gennaro, lawyer . . . died of dysentery on a business trip. Dennis Nedry, Integrated Computer Systems . . . also deceased. John Hammond, who started International Genetic Technologies . . . died while visiting the company's research facility in Costa Rica. Hammond had his grandchildren with him at the time; the kids live with their mother back east and —"

"Anybody contact them? Anybody from InGen?"

"No, no contact. The boy's started college and the girl is in prep school. And InGen filed for Chapter 11 protection after Hammond died. It's been in the courts ever since. The hard assets are finally being sold off. During the last two weeks, as a matter of fact."

Baselton spoke for the first time. "Is Site B involved in that sale?"

James looked blank. "Site B?"

"Yes. Has anybody talked to you about Site B?"

"No, I've never heard of it before. What is it?"

"If you hear anything about Site B," Baselton said, "we want to know."

Sitting beside Baselton in the booth, Dodgson thumbed through the pictures and data sheets, then tossed them aside impatiently. He looked up at James. "What else have you got?"

"That's all, Dr. Dodgson."

"That's all?" Dodgson said. "What about Malcolm? And what about Levine? Are they still friends?"

James consulted his notes. "I'm not sure."

Baselton frowned. "Not sure?" he said. "What do you mean, you're not sure?"

"Malcolm met Levine at the Santa Fe Institute," James said. "They spent time together there, a couple of years ago. But Malcolm hasn't gone back to Santa Fe recently. He's taken a visiting lectureship at Berkeley in the biology department. He teaches mathematical models of evolution. And he seems to have lost contact with Levine."

"They have a falling out?"

"Maybe. I was told they argued about Levine's expedition."

"What expedition?" Dodgson said, leaning forward.

"Levine's been planning some kind of expedition for a year or so. He's ordered special vehicles from a company called Mobile Field Systems. It's a small operation in Woodside, run by a guy named Jack Thorne. Thorne outfits Jeeps and trucks for scientists doing field research. Scientists in Africa and Sichuan and Chile all swear by them."

"Malcolm knows about this expedition?"

"He must. He's gone to Thorne's place, occasionally. Every month or so. And of course Levine's been going there almost every day. That's how he got thrown in jail."

"Thrown in jail?" Baselton said.

"Yeah," James said, glancing at his notes. "Let's see. February tenth, Levine was arrested for driving a hundred and twenty in a fifteen zone. Right in front of Woodside Junior High. The judge impounded his Ferrari, yanked his license, and gave him community service. Basically ordered him to teach a class at the school."

Baselton smiled. "Richard Levine teaching junior high. I'd love to see that."

"He's been pretty conscientious. Of course he's spending time in Woodside, anyway, with Thorne. That is, until he left the country."

"When did he leave the country?" Dodgson said.

"Two days ago. He went to Costa Rica. Short trip, he was due back early this morning."

"And where is he now?"

"I don't know. And I'm afraid, uh, it's going to be hard to find out."

"Why is that?"

James hesitated, coughed. "Because he was on the passenger manifest of the flight from Costa Rica—but he wasn't on the plane when it landed. My contact in Costa Rica says he checked out of his hotel in San José before the flight, and never went back. Didn't take any other flight out of the city. So, uh, for the moment, I'm afraid that Richard Levine has disappeared."

There was a long silence. Dodgson sat back in the booth, hissing between his teeth. He looked at Baselton, who shook his head. Dodgson very carefully picked up all the sheets of paper, tapped them on the table, making a neat stack. He slipped them back into the manila envelope, and handed the envelope to James.

"Now listen, you stupid son of a bitch," Dodgson said. "There's only one thing I want from you now. It's very simple. Are you listening?"

James swallowed. "I'm listening."

Dodgson leaned across the table. *"Find him,"* he said.

Berkeley

In his cluttered office, Malcolm looked up from his desk as his assistant, Beverly, came into the room. She was followed by a man from DHL, carrying a small box.

"I'm sorry to disturb you, Dr. Malcolm, but you have to sign these forms. . . . It's that sample from Costa Rica."

Malcolm stood, and walked around the desk. He didn't use his cane. In recent weeks, he had been working steadily to walk without the cane. He still had occasional pain in his leg, but he was determined to make progress. Even his physical therapist, a perpetually cheery woman named Cindy, had commented on it. "Gee, after all these years, suddenly you're motivated, Dr. Malcolm," she had said. "What's going on?"

"Oh, you know," Malcolm had said to her. "Can't rely on a cane forever."

The truth was rather different. Confronted by Levine's relentless enthusiasm for the lost-world hypothesis, his excited telephone calls at all hours of the day and night, Malcolm had begun to reconsider his own views. And he had come to believe that it was quite possible—even probable—that extinct animals existed in a remote, previously unsuspected location. Malcolm had his own reasons for thinking so, which he had only hinted at to Levine.

But the possibility of another island location was what led him to walk unaided. He wanted to prepare for a future visit to this island. And so he had begun to make the effort, day after day.

He and Levine had narrowed their search down to a string of islands along the Costa Rican coast, and Levine was as always very intense in his excitement. But to Malcolm it remained hypothetical.

He refused to get excited until there was hard evidence—photographs, or actual tissue samples—to demonstrate the existence of new animals. And so far, Malcolm had seen nothing at all. He was not sure whether he was disappointed or relieved.

But in any case, Levine's sample had arrived.

. . .

Malcolm took the clipboard from the delivery man and quickly signed the top form: "Delivery of Excluded Materials / Samples: Biological Research."

The delivery man said, "You have to check the boxes, sir."

Malcolm looked at the list of questions running down the page, with a check box beside each. Was the specimen alive. Was the specimen cultures of bacteria, fungi, viruses, or protozoa. Was the specimen registered under an established research protocol. Was the specimen contagious. Was the specimen taken from a farm or animal-husbandry site. Was the specimen plant matter, propagative seeds, or bulbs. Was the specimen insect or insect-related. . . .

He checked off "No" to everything.

"And the next page, too, sir," the delivery man said. He was looking around the office, at the stacks of papers heaped untidily about, the maps on the walls with the colored pins stuck in them. "You do medical research here?"

Malcolm flipped the page, scrawled his signature on the next form. "No."

"And one more, sir. . . ."

The third form was a release of liability to the carrier. Malcolm signed it as well. The delivery man said, "Have a good day," and left.

Immediately Malcolm sagged, resting his weight on the edge of the desk. He winced.

"Still hurt?" Beverly said. She took the specimen to the side table, pushed some papers away, and began to unwrap it.

"I'm okay." He looked over at the cane, resting beside his chair behind the desk. Then he took a breath, and crossed the room, slowly.

Beverly had the wrapping off the package, revealing a small stainless-steel cylinder the size of his fist. A triple-bladed biohazard sign was taped across the screwtop lid. Attached to the cylinder was a second small canister with a metal valve; it contained the refrigerant gas.

Malcolm swung the light over the cylinder, and said, "Let's see what he was so excited about." He broke the taped seal and unscrewed the lid. There was a hiss of gas, and a faint white puff of condensation. The exterior of the cylinder frosted over.

Peering in, he saw a plastic baggie, and a sheet of paper. He upended the cylinder, dumping the contents onto the table. The baggie contained a ragged piece of greenish flesh about two inches square, with a small green plastic tag attached to it. He held it up to the light, examined it with a magnifying glass, then set it down again. He looked at the green skin, the pebbled texture.

Maybe, he thought.

Maybe . . .

"Beverly," he said, "call Elizabeth Gelman, over at the zoo. Tell her I have something I want her to look at. And tell her it's confidential."

Beverly nodded, and went out of the room to phone. Alone, Malcolm unrolled the strip of paper that had come with the sample. It was a piece of paper torn from a yellow legal pad. In block printing, it said:

I WAS RIGHT AND YOU WERE WRONG.

Malcolm frowned. That son of a bitch, he thought. "Beverly? After you call Elizabeth, get Richard Levine at his office. I need to talk to him right away."

The Lost World

Richard Levine pressed his face to the warm rock cliff, and paused to catch his breath. Five hundred feet below, the ocean surged, waves thundering brilliant white against the black rocks. The boat that had brought him was already heading east again, a small white speck on the horizon. It had to return, for there was no safe harbor anywhere on this desolate, inhospitable island.

For now, they were on their own.

Levine took a deep breath, and looked down at Diego, twenty feet below him on the cliff face. Diego was burdened with the backpack that contained all their equipment, but he was young and strong. He smiled cheerfully, and nodded his head upward. "Have courage. It is not far now, señor."

"I hope so," Levine said. When he had examined the cliff through binoculars from the boat, this had seemed like a good place to make the ascent. But in fact, the cliff face was nearly vertical, and incredibly dangerous because the volcanic rock was crumbling and friable.

Levine raised his arms, fingers extending upward, reaching for the next handhold. He clung to the rock; small pebbles broke free and his hand slipped down. He gripped again, then pulled himself upward. He was breathing hard, from exertion and fear.

"Just twenty meters more, señor," Diego said encouragingly. "You can do it."

"I'm sure I can," Levine muttered. "Considering the alternative." As he neared the top of the cliff, the wind blew harder, whistling in his ears, tugging at his clothes. It felt as if it was trying to suck him away from the rock. Looking up, he saw the dense foliage that grew right to the edge of the cliff face.

Almost there, he thought. Almost.

And then, with a final heave, he pushed himself over the top and collapsed, rolling in soft wet ferns. Still gasping, he looked back and saw Diego come over lightly, easily; he squatted on the mossy grass, and smiled. Levine turned away, staring at the huge ferns overhead, releasing the accumulated tension of the climb in long shuddering breaths. His legs burned fiercely.

But no matter—he was here! Finally!

He looked at the jungle around him. It was primary forest, undisturbed by the hand of man. Exactly as the satellite images had shown. Levine had been forced to rely on satellite photographs, because there were no maps available of private islands such as this one. This island existed as a kind of lost world, isolated in the midst of the Pacific Ocean.

Levine listened to the sound of the wind, the rustle of the palm fronds that dripped water onto his face. And then he heard another sound, distant, like the cry of a bird, but deeper, more resonant. As he listened, he heard it again.

A sharp sizzle nearby made him look over. Diego had struck a match, was raising it to light a cigarette. Quickly, Levine sat up, pushed the younger man's hand away, and shook his head, no.

Diego frowned, puzzled.

Levine put his finger to his lips.

He pointed in the direction of the bird sound.

Diego shrugged, his expression indifferent. He was unimpressed. He saw no reason for concern.

That was because he didn't understand what they were up against, Levine thought, as he unzipped the dark-green backpack, and began to assemble the big Lindstradt rifle. The rifle had been specially manufactured for him in Sweden, and represented the latest in animal-control technology. He screwed the barrel into the stock, locked in the Fluger clip, checked the gas charge, and handed the rifle to Diego. Diego took it with another shrug.

Meanwhile, Levine removed the black anodized Lindstradt pistol in its holster, and buckled it around his waist. He removed the pistol, checked the safety twice, and put the pistol back in the holster. Levine got to his feet, gestured for Diego to follow him. Diego zipped up the backpack, and shouldered it again.

The two men started down the sloping hillside, away from the cliff. Almost immediately, their clothes were soaked from the wet foliage. They had no views; they were surrounded on all sides by dense jungle, and could see only a few yards ahead. The fronds of the ferns were enormous, as long and broad as a man's body, the plants twenty feet tall, with rough spiky stalks. And high above the ferns, a great canopy of trees blocked most of the sunlight. They moved in darkness, silently, on damp, spongy earth.

Levine paused often, to consult his wrist compass. They were heading west, down a steep slope, toward the interior of the island. He knew that the island was the remains of an ancient volcanic crater, eroded and decomposed by centuries of weathering. The interior terrain consisted of a series of ridges that led down to the floor of the crater. But particularly here on the eastern side, the landscape was steep, rugged, and treacherous.

The sense of isolation, of having returned to a primordial world, was palpable. Levine's heart pounded as he continued down the slope, across a marshy stream, and then up again. At the top of the next ridge, there was a break in the foliage, and he felt a welcome breeze. From his vantage point, he was able to see to the far side of the island, a rim of hard black cliff, miles away. Between here and the cliffs they saw nothing but gently undulating jungle.

Standing beside him, Diego said, "*Fantástico.*"

Levine quickly shushed him.

"But señor," he protested, pointing to the view. "We are alone here."

Levine shook his head, annoyed. He had gone over all this with Diego, during the boat ride over. Once on the island, no speaking. No hair pomade, no cologne, no cigarettes. All food sealed tightly in plastic bags. Everything packed with great care. Nothing to produce a smell, or make a sound. He had warned Diego, again and again, of the importance of all these precautions.

But now it was obvious that Diego had paid no attention. He didn't understand. Levine poked Diego angrily, and shook his head again.

Diego smiled. "Señor, please. There are only birds here."

At that moment, they heard a deep, rumbling sound, an unearthly cry that arose from somewhere in the forest below them. After a moment, the cry was answered, from another part of the forest.

Diego's eyes widened.

Levine mouthed: *Birds?*

Diego was silent. He bit his lip, and stared out at the forest.

To the south, they saw a place where the tops of the trees began to move, a whole section of forest that suddenly seemed to come alive, as if brushed by wind. But the rest of the forest was not moving. It was not the wind.

Diego crossed himself quickly.

They heard more cries, lasting nearly a minute, and then silence descended again.

Levine moved off the ridge and headed down the jungle slope, going deeper into the interior.

He was moving forward quickly, looking at the ground, watching for snakes, when he heard a low whistle behind him. He turned and saw Diego pointing to the left.

Levine doubled back, pushed through the fronds, and followed Diego as he moved south. In a few moments, they came upon two parallel tracks in the dirt, long since overgrown with grass and ferns, but clearly recognizable as an old Jeep trail, leading off into the jungle. Of course they would follow it. He knew their progress would be much faster on a road.

Levine gestured, and Diego took off the backpack. It was Levine's turn; he shouldered the weight, adjusted the straps.

In silence, they started down the road.

In places, the Jeep track was hardly recognizable, so thickly had the jungle grown back. Clearly, no one had used this road for many years, and the jungle was always ready to return.

Behind him, Diego grunted, swore softly. Levine turned and saw Diego lifting his foot gingerly; he had stepped to mid-ankle in a pile of green animal-droppings. Levine went back.

Diego scraped his boot clean on the stem of a fern. The droppings appeared to be composed of pale flecks of hay, mixed with green. The material was light and crumbly—dried, old. There was no smell.

Levine searched the ground carefully, until he found the remainder of the original spoor. The droppings were well formed, twelve centimeters in diameter. Definitely left behind by some large herbivore.

Diego was silent, but his eyes were wide.

Levine shook his head, continued on. As long as they saw signs of herbivora, he wasn't going to worry. At least, not too much. Even so, his fingers touched the butt of his pistol, as if for reassurance.

They came to a stream, muddy banks on both sides. Here Levine paused. He saw clear three-toed footprints in the mud, some of them quite large. The palm of his own hand, fingers spread wide, fitted easily inside one of the prints, with room to spare.

When he looked up, Diego was crossing himself again. He held the rifle in his other hand.

They waited at the stream, listening to the gentle gurgle of the water. Something shiny glinted in the stream, catching his eye. He bent over, and plucked it out. It was a piece of glass tubing, roughly the size of a pencil. One end was broken off. There were graduated markings along the side. He realized it was a pipette, of the kind used in laboratories everywhere in the world. Levine held it up to the light, turning it in his fingers. It was odd, he thought. A pipette like this implied—

Levine turned, and caught a glimpse of movement out of the corner of his eye. Something small and brown, scurrying across the mud of the riverbank. Something about the size of a rat.

Diego grunted in surprise. Then it was gone, disappearing in foliage.

Levine moved forward and crouched in the mud by the stream. He peered at the footprints left by the tiny animal. The footprints were three-toed, like the tracks of a bird. He saw more three-toed tracks, including some bigger ones, which were several inches across.

Levine had seen such prints before, in trackways such as the Purgatoire River in Colorado, where the ancient shoreline was now fossilized, the dinosaur tracks frozen in stone. But these prints were in fresh mud. And they had been made by living animals.

Sitting on his haunches, Levine heard a soft squeak coming from somewhere to his right. Looking over, he saw the ferns moving slightly. He stayed very still, waiting.

After a moment, a small animal peeked out from among the fronds. It appeared to be the size of a mouse; it had smooth, hairless skin and large eyes mounted high on its tiny head. It was greenish-brown in color, and it made a continuous, irritable squeaking sound at Levine, as if to drive him away. Levine stayed motionless, hardly daring to breathe.

He recognized this creature, of course. It was a mussaurus, a tiny prosauropod from the Late Triassic. Skeletal remains were found only in South America. It was one of the smallest dinosaurs known.

A *dinosaur*, he thought.

Even though he had expected to see them on this island, it was still startling to be confronted by a living, breathing member of the *Dinosauria*. Especially one so small. He could not take his eyes off it. He was entranced. After all these years, after all the dusty skeletons—an actual living dinosaur!

The little mussaur ventured farther out from the protection of the fronds. Now Levine could see that it was longer than he had thought at first. It was actually about ten centimeters long, with a surprisingly thick tail. All told, it looked very much like a lizard. It sat upright, squatting on its hind legs on the frond. He saw the rib cage moving as the animal breathed. It waved its tiny forearms in the air at Levine, and squeaked repeatedly.

Slowly, very slowly, Levine extended his hand.

The creature squeaked again, but did not run. If anything it seemed curious, cocking its head the way very small animals do, as Levine's hand came closer.

Finally Levine's fingers touched the tip of the frond. The mussaur stood on its hind legs, balancing with its outstretched tail. Showing no sign of fear, it stepped lightly onto Levine's hand, and stood in the creases of his palm. He hardly felt the weight, it was so light. The mussaur walked around, sniffed Levine's fingers. Levine smiled, charmed.

Then, suddenly, the little creature hissed in annoyance, and jumped off his hand, disappearing into the palms. Levine blinked, unable to understand why.

Then he smelled a foul odor, and heard a heavy rustling in the bushes on the other side. There was a soft grunting sound. More rustling.

For a brief moment, Levine remembered that carnivores in the wild hunted near streambeds, attacking animals when they were vulnerable, bending over to drink. But the recognition came too late; he heard a terrifying high-pitched cry, and when he turned he saw that Diego was screaming as his body was hauled away, into the bushes. Diego struggled; the bushes shook fiercely; Levine caught a glimpse of a single large foot, its middle toe bearing a short curving claw. Then the foot pulled back. The bushes continued to shake.

Suddenly, the forest erupted in frightening animal roars all around him. He glimpsed a large animal charging him. Richard Levine turned and fled, feeling the adrenaline surge of pure panic, not knowing where to go, knowing only that it was hopeless. He felt a heavy weight suddenly tear at his backpack, forcing him to his knees in the mud, and he realized in that moment that despite all his planning, despite all his clever deductions, things had gone terribly wrong, and he was about to die.

School

"When we consider mass extinction from a meteor impact," Richard Levine said, "we must ask several questions. First, are there any impact craters on our planet larger than nineteen miles in diameter—which is the smallest size necessary to cause a worldwide extinction event? And second, do any craters match in time a known extinction? It turns out there are a dozen craters this large around the world, of which five coincide with known extinctions. . . ."

Kelly Curtis yawned in the darkness of her seventh-grade classroom. Sitting at her desk, she propped her chin on her elbows, and tried to stay awake. She already knew this stuff. The TV set in front of the class showed a vast cornfield, seen in an aerial view, the curving outlines faintly visible. She recognized it as the crater in Manson. In the darkness, Dr. Levine's recorded voice said, "This is the crater in Manson, Iowa, dating from sixty-five million years ago, just when dinosaurs became extinct. But was this the meteor that killed the dinosaurs?"

No, Kelly thought, yawning. Probably the Yucatán peninsula. Manson was too small.

"We now think this crater is too small," Dr. Levine said aloud. "We believe it was too small by an order of magnitude, and the current candidate is the crater near Mérida, in the Yucatán. It seems difficult to imagine, but the impact emptied the entire Gulf of Mexico, causing two-thousand-foot-high tidal waves to wash over the land. It must have been incredible. But there are disputes about this crater, too, particularly concerning the meaning of the cenote ring structure, and the differential death rates of phytoplankton in ocean deposits. That may sound complicated, but don't worry about it for now. We'll go into it in more detail next time. So, that's it for today."

The lights came up. Their teacher, Mrs. Menzies, stepped to the front of the class and turned off the computer which had been running the display, and the lecture.

"Well," she said, "I'm glad Dr. Levine gave us this recording. He told me he might not be back in time for today's lecture, but he'll be with us again for sure when we return from spring break next week. Kelly, you and Arby are working for Dr. Levine, is that what he told you?"

Kelly glanced over at Arby, who was slouched low in his seat, frowning.

"Yes, Mrs. Menzies," Kelly said.

"Good. All right, everyone, the assignment for the holidays is all of chapter seven"—there were groans from the class—"including all of the exercises at the end of part one, as well as part two. Be sure to bring that with you, completed, when we return. Have a good spring break. We'll see you back here in a week."

The bell rang; the class got up, chairs scraping, the room suddenly noisy. Arby drifted over to Kelly. He looked up at her mournfully. Arby was a head shorter than Kelly; he was the shortest person in the class. He was also the youngest. Kelly was thirteen, like the other seventh-graders, but Arby was only eleven. He had already been skipped two grades, because he was so smart. And there were rumors he would be skipped again. Arby was a genius, particularly with computers.

Arby put his pen in the pocket of his white button-down shirt, and pushed his horn-rim glasses up on his nose. R. B. Benton was black; both his parents were doctors in San Jose, and they always made sure he was dressed very neatly, like a college kid or something. Which, Kelly reflected, he would probably be in a couple of years, the way he was going.

Standing next to Arby, Kelly always felt awkward and gawky. Kelly had to wear her sister's old clothes, which her mother had bought from Kmart about a million years ago. She even had to wear Emily's old Reeboks, which were so scuffed and dirty that they never came clean, even after Kelly ran them through the washing machine. Kelly washed and ironed all her own clothes; her mother never had time. Her mother was never even home, most of the time. Kelly looked enviously at Arby's neatly pressed khakis, his polished penny loafers, and sighed.

Still, even though she was jealous, Arby was her only real friend—the only person who thought it was okay that she was smart. Kelly worried that he'd be skipped to ninth grade, and she wouldn't see him any more.

Beside her, Arby still frowned. He looked up at her and said, "Why isn't Dr. Levine here?"

"I don't know," she said. "Maybe something happened."

"Like what?"

"I don't know. Something."

"But he *promised* he would be here," Arby said. "To take us on the field trip. It was all arranged. We got permission and everything."

"So? We can still go."

"But he should be here," Arby insisted stubbornly. Kelly had seen this behavior before. Arby was accustomed to adults being reliable. His parents were both very reliable. Kelly wasn't troubled by such ideas.

"Never mind, Arb," she said. "Let's just go see Dr. Thorne ourselves."

"You think so?"

"Sure. Why not?"

Arby hesitated. "Maybe I should call my mom first."

"Why?" Kelly said. "You know she'll tell you that you have to go home. Come on, Arb. Let's just go."

He hesitated, still troubled. Arby might be smart, but any change in plan always bothered him. Kelly knew from experience he would grumble and argue if she pushed for them to go alone. She had to wait, while he made up his own mind.

"Okay," he said finally. "Let's go see Thorne."

Kelly grinned. "Meet you in front," she said, "in five minutes."

As she went down the stairs from the second floor, the singsong chant began again. "Kelly is a brainer, Kelly is a brainer. . . ."

She held her head high. It was that stupid Allison Stone and her stupid friends. Standing at the bottom of the stairs, taunting her.

"Kelly is a brainer. . . ."

She swept past the girls, ignoring them. Nearby, she saw Miss Enders, the hall monitor, paying no attention as usual. Even though Mr. Canosa, the assistant principal, had recently made a special homeroom announcement about teasing kids.

Behind her, the girls called: "Kelly is a brainer. . . . She's the queen . . . of the screen . . . and it's gonna turn her green. . . ." They collapsed in laughter.

Up ahead, she saw Arby waiting by the door, a bundle of gray cables in his hand. She hurried forward.

When she got to him, he said, "Forget it."

"They're stupid jerkoffs."

"Right."

"I don't care, anyway."

"I know. Just forget it."

Behind them, the girls were giggling. "Kel-ly and Ar-by . . . going to a party . . . take a bath, in their math. . . ."

They went outside into the sunlight, the sounds of the girls thankfully drowned in the noise of everyone going home. Yellow school buses were in the parking lot. Kids were streaming down the steps to their parents' cars, which were lined up all around the block. There was a lot of activity.

Arby ducked a Frisbee that whooshed over his head, and glanced toward the street. "There he is again."

"Well, don't look at him," Kelly said.

"I'm not, I'm not."

"Remember what Dr. Levine said."

"Jeez, Kel. I remember, okay?"

Across the street was parked the plain gray Taurus sedan that they had seen, off and on, for the past two months. Behind the wheel, pretending to read a newspaper, was that same man with the scraggly growth of beard. This bearded man had been following Dr. Levine ever since he started to teach the class at Woodside. Kelly believed that man was the reason why Dr. Levine asked her and Arby to be his assistants in the first place.

Levine had told them their job would be to help him by carrying equipment, Xeroxing class assignments, collecting homework, and routine things like that. They thought it would be a big honor to work for Dr. Levine—or anyway, interesting to work for an actual professional scientist—so they had agreed to do it.

But it turned out there never was anything to be done for the class; Dr. Levine did all that himself. Instead, he sent them on lots of little errands. And he had told them to be careful to avoid this bearded man in the car. That wasn't hard; the man never paid any attention to them, because they were kids.

Dr. Levine had explained the bearded man was following him because of something to do with his arrest, but Kelly didn't believe that. Her own mother had been arrested twice for drunk driving, and there was never anybody following her. So Kelly didn't know why this man was following Levine, but clearly Levine was doing some secret research and he didn't want anybody to find out about it. She knew one thing—Dr. Levine didn't care much about this class he was teaching. He usually gave the lecture off the top of his head. Other times he would walk in the front door of the school, hand them a taped lecture, and walk out the back. They never knew where he went, on those days.

The errands he sent them on were mysterious, too. Once they went to Stanford and picked up five small squares of plastic from a professor there. The plastic was light, and sort of foamy. Another time they went downtown to an electronics store and picked up a triangular device that the man behind the counter gave them very nervously, as if it might be illegal or something. Another time they picked up a metal tube that looked like it contained cigars. They couldn't help opening it, but they were uneasy to find four sealed plastic ampoules of straw-colored liquid. The ampoules were marked EXTREME DANGER! LETHAL TOXICITY! and had the three-bladed international symbol for biohazard.

But mostly, their assignments were mundane. He often sent them to libraries at Stanford to Xerox papers on all sorts of subjects: Japanese sword-making, X-ray crystallography, Mexican vampire bats, Central American volcanoes, oceanic currents of El Niño, the mating behavior of mountain sheep, sea-cucumber toxicity, flying buttresses of Gothic cathedrals . . .

Dr. Levine never explained why he was interested in these subjects. Often he would send them back day after day, to search for more material. And then, suddenly, he would drop the subject, and never refer to it again. And they would be on to something else.

Of course, they could figure some of it out. A lot of the questions had to do with the vehicles that Dr. Thorne was building for Dr. Levine's expedition. But most of the time, the subjects were completely mysterious.

Occasionally, Kelly wondered what the bearded man would make of all this. She wondered whether he knew something they did not. But actually, the bearded man seemed kind of lazy. He never seemed to figure out that Kelly and Arby were doing errands for Dr. Levine.

Right now, the bearded man glanced over at the entrance to the school, ignoring them. They walked to the end of the street, and sat on the bench to wait for the bus.

Tag

The baby snow leopard spit the bottle out, and rolled over onto its back, paws in the air. It made a soft mewing sound.

"She wants to be petted," Elizabeth Gelman said.

Malcolm reached out his hand, to stroke the belly. The cub spun around, and sunk its tiny teeth into his fingers. Malcolm yelled.

"She does that, sometimes," Gelman said. "Dorje! Bad girl! Is that any way to treat our distinguished visitor?" She reached out, took Malcolm's hand. "It didn't break the skin, but we should clean it anyway."

They were in the white research laboratory of the San Francisco Zoo, at three o'clock in the afternoon. Elizabeth Gelman, the youthful head of research, was supposed to report on her findings, but they had to delay for the afternoon feeding in the nursery. Malcolm had watched them feed a baby gorilla, which spit up like a human baby, and a koala, and then the very cute snow-leopard cub.

"Sorry about that," Gelman said. She took him to a side basin, and soaped his hand. "But I thought it was better that you come here now, when the regular staff is all at the weekly conference."

"Why is that?"

"Because there's a lot of interest in the material you gave us, Ian. A *lot*." She dried his hand with a towel, inspected it again. "I think you'll survive."

"What have you found?" Malcolm said to her.

"You have to admit, it *is* very provocative. By the way, is it from Costa Rica?"

Keeping his voice neutral, Malcolm said, "Why do you say that?"

"Because there are all these rumors about unknown animals showing up in Costa Rica. And this is definitely an unknown animal, Ian."

She led him out of the nursery, and into a small conference room. He dropped into a chair, resting his cane on the table. She lowered the lights, and clicked on a slide projector. "Okay. Here's a close-up of your original material, before we began our examination. As you see, it consists of a fragment of animal tissue in a state of very advanced necrosis. The tissue measures four centimeters by six centimeters. Attached to it is a green plastic tag, measuring two centimeters square. Tissue cut by a knife, but not a very sharp one."

Malcolm nodded.

"What'd you use, Ian, your pocketknife?"

"Something like that."

"All right. Let's deal with the tissue sample first." The slide changed; Malcolm saw a microscopic view. "This is a gross histologic section through the superficial epidermis. Those patchy, ragged gaps are where the postmortem necrotic change has eroded the skin surface. But what is interesting is the arrangement of epidermal cells. You'll notice the density of chromatophores, or pigment-bearing cells. In the cut section you see the difference between melanophores here, and allophores, here. The overall pattern is suggestive of a lacerta or amblyrhynchus."

"You mean a lizard?" Malcolm said.

"Yes," she said. "It looks like a lizard—though the picture is not entirely consistent." She tapped the left side of the screen. "You see this one cell here, which has this slight rim, in section? We believe that's muscle. The chromatophore could open and close. Meaning that this animal could change color, like a chameleon. And over here you see this large oval shape, with a pale center? That's the pore of a femoral scent gland. There is a waxy substance in the center which we are still analyzing. But our presumption is that this animal was male, since only male lizards have femoral glands."

"I see," Malcolm said.

She changed the slide. Malcolm saw what looked like a close-up of a sponge. "Going deeper. Here we see the structure of the subcutaneous layers. Highly distorted, because of gas bubbles from the clostridia infection that bloated the animal. But you can get a sense of the vessels— see, one here—and another here—which are surrounded by smooth muscle fibers. This is not characteristic of lizards. In fact, the whole appearance of this slide is wrong for lizards, or reptiles of any sort."

"You mean it looks warm-blooded."

"Right," Gelman said. "Not really mammalian, but perhaps avian. This could be, oh, I don't know, a dead pelican. Something like that."

"Uh-huh."

"Except no pelican has a skin like that."

"I see," Malcolm said.

"And there's no feathers."

"Uh-huh."

"Now," Gelman said, "we were able to extract a minute quantity of blood from the intra-arterial spaces. Not much, but enough to conduct a microscopic examination. Here it is."

The slide changed again. He saw a jumble of cells, mostly red cells, and an occasional misshapen white cell. It was confusing to look at.

"This isn't my area, Elizabeth," he said.

"Well, I'll just give you the highlights," she said. "First of all, nucleated red cells. That's characteristic of birds, not mammals. Second, rather atypical hemoglobin, differing in several base pairs from other lizards. Third, aberrant white-cell structure. We don't have enough material to make a determination, but we suspect this animal has a highly unusual immune system."

"Whatever that means," Malcolm said, with a shrug.

"We don't know, and the sample doesn't give us enough to find out. By the way, can you get more?"

"I might be able to," he said.

"Where, from Site B?"

Malcolm looked puzzled. "Site B?"

"Well, that's what's embossed on the tag." She changed the slide. "I must say, Ian, this tag is very interesting. Here at the zoo, we tag animals all the time, and we're familiar with all the ordinary commercial brands sold around the world. Nobody's seen this tag before. Here it is, magnified ten times. The actual object is roughly the size of your thumbnail. Uniform plastic outer surface, attaches to the animal by a Teflon-coated, stainless-steel clip on the other side. It's a rather small clip, of the kind used to tag infants. The animal you saw was adult?"

"Presumably."

"So the tag was probably in place for a while, ever since the animal was young," Gelman said. "Which makes sense, considering the degree of weathering. You'll notice the pitting on the surface. That's very unusual. This plastic is Duralon, the stuff they use to make football helmets. It's extremely tough, and this pitting can't have occurred through simple wear."

"Then what?"

"It's almost certainly a chemical reaction, such as exposure to acid, perhaps in aerosol form."

"Like volcanic fumes?" Malcolm said.

"That could do it, particularly in view of what else we've learned.

You'll notice that the tag is rather thick—actually, it's nine millimeters across. And it's hollow."

"Hollow?" Malcolm said, frowning.

"Yes. It contains an inner cavity. We didn't want to open it, so we X-rayed it. Here." The slide changed. Malcolm saw a jumble of white lines and boxes, inside the tag.

"There appears to be substantial corrosion, again perhaps from acid fumes. But there's no question what this once was. It's a radio tag, Ian. Which means that this unusual animal, this warm-blooded lizard or whatever it was, was tagged and raised by somebody from birth. And that's the part that's got people around here upset. Somebody's *raising* these things. Do you know how that happened?"

"I haven't the faintest idea," Malcolm said.

Elizabeth Gelman sighed. "You're a lying son of a bitch."

He held out his hand. "May I have my sample back?"

She said, "Ian. After all I've done for you."

"The sample?"

"I think you owe me an explanation."

"And I promise, you'll have one. In about two weeks. I'll buy dinner."

She tossed a silver-foil package on the table. He picked it up, and slipped it in his pocket. "Thanks, Liz." He got up to go. "I hate to run, but I've got to make a call right away."

He started for the door, and she said, "By the way, how did it die, Ian? This animal."

He paused. "Why do you ask?"

"Because, when we teased up the skin cells, we found a few foreign cells under the outer epidermal layer. Cells belonging to another animal."

"Meaning what?"

"Well, it's the typical picture you see when two lizards fight. They rub against each other. Cells get pushed under the superficial layer."

"Yes," he said. "There were signs of a fight on the carcass. The animal had been wounded."

"And you should also know there were signs of chronic vasoconstriction in the arterial vessels. This animal was under stress, Ian. And not just from the fight that wounded it. That would have disappeared in early postmortem changes. I'm talking about chronic, continuous stress. Wherever this creature lived, its environment was extremely stressful and dangerous."

"I see."

"So. How come a tagged animal has such a stressful life?"

At the entrance to the zoo, he looked around to see if he was being followed, then stopped at a pay phone and dialed Levine. The machine picked up; Levine wasn't there. Typical, Malcolm thought. Whenever you needed him he wasn't there. Probably off trying to get his Ferrari out of impound again.

Malcolm hung up, and headed toward his car.

Thorne

"Thorne Mobile Field Systems" was stenciled in black lettering on a large rolling metal garage door, at the far end of the Industrial Park. There was a regular door to the left. Arby pushed the buzzer on a small box with a grille. A gruff voice said, "Go away."

"It's us, Dr. Thorne. Arby and Kelly."

"Oh. Okay."

There was a click as the door unlocked, and they walked inside. They found themselves in a large open shed. Workmen were making modifications on several vehicles; the air smelled of acetylene, engine oil, and fresh paint. Directly ahead Kelly saw a dark-green Ford Explorer with its roof cut open; two assistants stood on ladders, fitting a large flat panel of black solar cells over the top of the car. The hood of the Explorer was up, and the V-6 engine had been pulled out; workmen were now lowering a small, new engine in its place—it looked like a rounded shoebox, with the dull shine of aluminum alloy. Others were bringing the wide, flat rectangle of the Hughes converter that would be mounted on top of the motor.

Over to the right, she saw the two RV trailers that Thorne's team had been working on for the last few weeks. They weren't the usual trailers you saw people driving for the weekends. One was enormous and sleek, almost as big as a bus, and outfitted with living and sleeping quarters for four people, as well as all sorts of special scientific equipment. It was called "Challenger" and it had an unusual feature: once you parked it, the walls could slide outward, expanding the inside dimensions.

The Challenger trailer was made to connect up through a special accordion passageway to the second trailer, which was somewhat smaller, and was pulled by the first. This second RV contained laboratory equipment and some very high-tech refinements, though Kelly wasn't sure exactly what. Right now, the second trailer was nearly hidden by the huge stream of sparks that spit out from a welder on the roof. Despite all the activity, the trailer looked mostly finished—although she could see people working inside, and all the upholstery, the chairs and seats, were lying around on the ground outside.

Thorne himself was standing in the middle of the room, shouting at the welder on the roof of the camper. "Come on, come on, we've got to be finished today! Eddie, let's go." He turned, shouted again, "No, no, no. Look at the plans! Henry: you can't place that strut laterally. It has to be crosswise, for strength. Look at the plans!"

Doc Thorne was a gray-haired, barrel-chested man of fifty-five. Except for his wire-frame glasses, he looked as if he might be a retired prizefighter. It was hard for Kelly to imagine Thorne as a university professor; he was immensely strong, and in continuous movement. "Damn it, Henry! Henry! Henry, are you listening to me?"

Thorne swore again, and shook his fist in the air. He turned to the kids. "These guys," he said. "They're supposed to be *helping* me." From the Explorer, there was a white-hot crack like lightning. The two men leaning into the hood jumped away, as a cloud of acrid smoke rose above the car. "What'd I tell you?" Thorne shouted. "*Ground it!* Ground it before you do anything! We've got serious voltages here, guys! You're going to get fried if you're not careful!"

He looked back at the kids and shook his head. "They just don't get it," he said. "That IUD is serious defense."

"IUD?"

"Internal Ursine Deterrent—that's what Levine calls it. It's his idea of a joke," Thorne said. "Actually, I developed this system a few years back for park rangers in Yellowstone, where bears break into trailers. Flip a switch, and you run ten thousand volts across the outer skin of the trailer. Wham-o! Takes the fight out of the biggest bear. But that kind of voltage'll blow these guys right off the trailer. And then what? I get a workmen's-compensation suit. For their stupidity." He shook his head. "So? Where's Levine?"

"We don't know," Arby said.

"What do you mean? Didn't he teach your class today?"

"No, he didn't come."

Thorne swore again. "Well, I need him today, to go over the final revisions, before we do our field testing. He was supposed to be back today."

"Back from where?" Kelly said.

"Oh, he went on one of his field trips," Thorne said. "Very excited about it, before he went. I outfitted him myself—loaned him my latest field pack. Everything he could ever want in just forty-seven pounds. He liked it. Left last Monday, four days ago."

"For where?"

"How should I know?" Thorne said. "He wouldn't tell me. And I gave up asking. You know they're all the same, now. Every scientist I deal with is secretive. But you can't blame them. They're all afraid of being ripped off, or sued. The modern world. Last year I built equipment for an expedition to the Amazon, we waterproofed it—which you'd want in the Amazon rain forest—soaking-wet electronics just don't work—and the principal scientist was charged with misappropriating funds. For waterproofing! Some university bureaucrat said it was an 'unnecessary expense.' I'm telling you, it's insane. Just insane. Henry—did you hear anything I said to you? Put it *crosswise!*"

Thorne strode across the room, waving his arms. The kids followed behind him.

"But now, look at this," Thorne said. "For months we've been modifying his field vehicles, and finally we're ready. He wants them light, I build them light. He wants them strong, I build them strong—light and strong both, why not, it's just impossible, what he's asking for, but with enough titanium and honeycarbon composite, we're doing it anyway. He wants it off petroleum base, and off the grid, and we do that, too. So finally he's got what he wanted, an immensely strong portable laboratory to go where there's no gasoline and no electricity. And now that it's finished . . . I can't believe it. He really didn't show up for your class?"

"No," Kelly said.

"So he's disappeared," Thorne said. "Wonderful. Perfect. What about our field test? We were going to take these vehicles out for a week, and put them through their paces."

"I know," Kelly said. "We got permission from our parents and everything, so we could go, too."

"And now he's not here," Thorne fumed. "I suppose I should have expected it. These rich kids, they do whatever they want. A guy like Levine gives *spoiled* a bad name."

From the ceiling, a large metal cage came crashing down, landing next to them on the floor. Thorne jumped aside. "Eddie! Damn! Will you watch it?"

"Sorry, Doc," said Eddie Carr, high up in the rafters. "But specs are it can't deform at twelve thousand psi. We had to test it."

"That's fine, Eddie. But don't test it when we're under it!" Thorne bent to examine the cage, which was circular, constructed of inch-thick titanium-alloy bars. It had survived the fall without harm. And it was light; Thorne lifted it upright with one hand. It was about six feet high and four feet in diameter. It looked like an oversized bird cage. It had a swinging door, fitted with a heavy lock.

"What's that for?" Arby asked.

"Actually," Thorne said, "it's part of *that*." He pointed across the room, where a workman was putting together a stack of telescoping aluminum struts. "High observation platform, made to be assembled in the field. Scaffolding sets up into a rigid structure, about fifteen feet high. Fitted with a little shelter on top. Also collapsible."

"A platform to observe what?" Arby said.

Thorne said, "He didn't tell you?"

"No," Kelly said.

"No," Arby said.

"Well, he didn't tell me, either," Thorne said, shaking his head. "All I know is he wants everything immensely strong. Light and strong, light and strong. Impossible." He sighed. "God save me from academics."

"I thought you were an academic," Kelly said.

"Former academic," Thorne said briskly. "Now I actually make things. I don't just talk."

Colleagues who knew Jack Thorne agreed that retirement marked the happiest period in his life. As a professor of applied engineering, and a specialist in exotic materials, he had always demonstrated a practical focus and a love of students. His most famous course at Stanford, Structural Engineering 101a, was known among the students as "Thorny Problems," because Thorne continually provoked his class to solve applied-engineering challenges he set for them. Some of these had long since entered into student folklore. There was, for example, the Toilet Paper Disaster: Thorne asked the students to drop a carton of eggs from Hoover Tower without injury. As padding, they could only use the cardboard tubes at the center of toilet paper rolls. There were spattered eggs all over the plaza below.

Then, another year, Thorne asked the students to build a chair to support a two-hundred-pound man, using only paper Q-tips and thread. And another time, he hung the answer sheet for the final exam from the classroom ceiling, and invited his students to pull it down, using whatever they could make with a cardboard shoebox containing a pound of licorice, and some toothpicks.

When he was not in class, Thorne often served as an expert witness in legal cases involving materials engineering. He specialized in explosions, crashed airplanes, collapsed buildings, and other disasters. These forays into the real world sharpened his view that scientists needed the widest possible education. He used to say, "How can you design for people if you don't know history and psychology? You can't. Because your mathematical formulas may be perfect, but the people will screw it up. And if that happens, it means *you* screwed it up." He peppered his lectures with quotations from Plato, Chaka Zulu, Emerson, and Chang-tzu.

But as a professor who was popular with his students—and who advocated general education—Thorne found himself swimming against the tide. The academic world was marching toward ever more specialized knowledge, expressed in ever more dense jargon. In this climate, being liked by your students was a sign of shallowness; and interest in real-world problems was proof of intellectual poverty and a distressing indifference to theory. But in the end, it was his fondness for Chang-tzu that pushed him out the door. In a departmental meeting, one of his colleagues got up and announced that "Some mythical Chinese bullshitter means fuck-all for engineering."

Thorne took early retirement a month later, and soon after started his own company. He enjoyed his work thoroughly, but he missed contact with the students, which was why he liked Levine's two youthful assistants. These kids were smart, they were enthusiastic, and they were young enough so that the schools hadn't destroyed all their interest in learning. They could still actually use their brains, which in Thorne's view was a sure sign they hadn't yet completed a formal education.

"Jerry!" Thorne bellowed, to one of the welders on the RVs. "Balance the struts on both sides! Remember the crash tests!" Thorne pointed to a video monitor set on the floor, which showed a computer image of the RV crashing into a barrier. First it crashed end-on, then it crashed sideways, then it rolled and crashed again. Each time, the vehicle survived with very little damage. The computer program had been developed by the auto companies, and then discarded. Thorne acquired it, and modified it. "Of course the auto companies discarded it—it's a good idea. Don't want any good ideas coming out of a big company. Might lead to a good product!" He sighed. "Using this computer, we've crashed these vehicles ten thousand times: designing, crashing, modifying, crashing again. No theories, just actual testing. The way it ought to be."

Thorne's dislike of theory was legendary. In his view, a theory was nothing more than a substitute for experience put forth by someone who didn't know what he was talking about. "And now look. Jerry? Jerry! Why'd we do all these simulations, if you guys aren't going to follow the plans? Is everybody brain-dead around here?"

"Sorry, Doc . . ."

"Don't be sorry! Be right!"

"Well, we're massively overbuilt anyway—"

"Oh? Is that your decision? You're the designer now? Just follow the plans!"

Arby trotted alongside Thorne. "I'm worried about Dr. Levine," he said.

"Really? I'm not."

"But he's always been reliable. And very well organized."

"That's true," Thorne said. "He's also completely impulsive and does whatever he feels like."

"Maybe so," Arby said, "but I don't think he'd be missing without a good reason. I'm afraid he might be in trouble. Only last week, he had us go with him to visit Professor Malcolm in Berkeley, who had this map of the world in his office, and it showed—"

"Malcolm!" Thorne snorted. "Spare me! Peas in a pod, those two. Each more impractical than the other. But I'd better get hold of Levine now." He turned on his heel, and walked toward his office.

Arby said, "You going to use the satphone?"

Thorne paused. "The what?"

"The satphone," Arby said. "Didn't Dr. Levine take a satphone with him?"

"How could he?" Thorne said. "You know the smallest satellite phones are the size of a suitcase."

"Yeah, but they don't have to be," Arby said. "You could have made one very small."

"Could I? How?" Despite himself, Thorne was amused by this kid. You had to like him.

"With that VLSI com board that we picked up," Arby said. "The triangular one. It had two Motorola BSN-23 chip arrays, and they're restricted technology developed for the CIA because they allow you to make a—"

"Hey, hey," Thorne said, interrupting him. "Where did you learn all this? I've warned you about hacking systems—"

"Don't worry, I'm careful," Arby said. "But it's true about the com board, isn't it? You could use it to make a one-pound satphone. So: did you?"

Thorne stared at him for a long time.

"Maybe," he said finally. "What of it?"

Arby grinned. "Cool," he said.

Thorne's small office was located in a corner of the shed. Inside, the walls were plastered with blueprints, order forms on clipboards, and three-dimensional cutaway computer drawings. Electronic components, equipment catalogs, and stacks of faxes were scattered across his desk. Thorne rummaged through them, and finally came up with a small gray handheld telephone. "Here we are." He held it up for Arby to see. "Pretty good, huh? Designed it myself."

Kelly said, "It looks just like a cellular phone."

"Yes, but it's not. A cellular phone uses a grid in place. A satellite phone links directly to communication satellites in space. With one of these I can talk anywhere in the world." He dialed swiftly. "Used to be, they needed a three-foot dish. Then it was a one-foot dish. Now no dish at all—just the handset. Not bad, if I say so myself. Let's see if he's answering." He pushed the speakerphone. They heard the call dial through, hissing static.

"Knowing Richard," Thorne said, "he probably just missed his plane, or forgot that he was supposed to be back here today for final approvals. And we're pretty much finished here. When you see we're down to the exterior struts and the upholstery, the fact is, we're done. He's going to hold us up. It's very inconsiderate of him." The phone rang, repeated electronic beeps. "If I can't get through to him, I'll try Sarah Harding."

"Sarah Harding?" Kelly asked, looking up.

Arby said, "Who's Sarah Harding?"

"Only the most famous young animal behaviorist in the world, Arb." Sarah Harding was one of Kelly's personal heroes. Kelly had read every article she could about her. Sarah Harding had been a poor scholarship student at the University of Chicago but now, at thirty-three, she was an assistant professor at Princeton. She was beautiful and independent, a rebel, who went her own way. She had chosen the life of a scientist in the field, living alone in Africa, where she studied lions and hyenas. She was famously tough. Once, when her Land Rover broke down, she walked twenty miles across the savannah all by herself, driving away lions by throwing rocks at them.

In photographs, Sarah was usually posed in shorts and a khaki shirt, with binoculars around her neck, next to a Land Rover. With her short, dark hair and her strong, muscular body, she looked rugged but glamorous at the same time. At least, that was how she appeared to Kelly, who always studied the pictures intently, taking in every detail.

"Never heard of her," Arby said.

Thorne said, "Spending too much time with computers, Arby?"

Arby said, "No." Kelly saw Arby's shoulders hunch, and he sort of withdrew into himself, the way he always did when he felt criticized. Sulky, he said, "Animal behaviorist?"

"That's right," Thorne said. "I know Levine's talked to her several times in the last few weeks. She's helping him with all this equipment, when it finally goes into the field. Or advising him. Or something. Or maybe the connection is with Malcolm. After all, she was in love with Malcolm."

"I don't believe it," Kelly said. "Maybe *he* was in love with *her*. . . ."

Thorne looked at her. "You've met her?"

"No. But I know about her."

"I see." Thorne said no more. He could see all the signs of hero worship, and he approved. A girl could do worse than admire Sarah Harding. At least she wasn't an athlete or a rock star. In fact, it was refreshing for a kid to admire somebody who actually tried to advance knowledge. . . .

The phone continued to ring. There was no answer.

"Well, we know Levine's equipment is in order," Thorne said. "Because the call is going through. We know that much."

Arby said, "Can you trace it?"

"Unfortunately, no. And if we keep this up, we'll probably drain the field battery, which means—"

There was a click, and they heard a man's voice, remarkably distinct and clear: "Levine."

"Okay. Good. He's there," Thorne said, nodding. He pushed the button on his handset. "Richard? It's Doc Thorne."

Over the speakerphone, they heard a sustained static hiss. Then a cough, and a scratchy voice said: "Hello? Hello? It's Levine here."

Thorne pressed the button on his phone. "Richard. It's Thorne. Do you read me?"

"Hello?" Levine said, at the other end. "Hello?"

Thorne sighed. "Richard. You have to press the 'T' button, for transmit. Over."

"Hello?" Another cough, deep and rasping. "This is Levine. Hello?"

Thorne shook his head in disgust. "Obviously, he doesn't know how to work it. Damn! I went over it very carefully with him. Of course he wasn't paying attention. Geniuses never pay attention. They think they know everything. These things aren't toys." He pushed the send button. "Richard, listen to me. You must push the 'T' in order to—"

"This is Levine. Hello? Levine. Please. I need help." A kind of groan. "If you can hear me, send help. Listen, I'm on the island, I managed to get here all right, but—"

A crackle. A hiss.

"Uh-oh," Thorne said.

"What is it?" Arby said, leaning forward.

"We're losing him."

"Why?"

"Battery," Thorne said. "It's going fast. Damn. Richard: *where are you?*"

Over the speakerphone, they heard Levine's voice: "—dead already—situation got—now—very serious—don't know—can hear me, but if you—get help—"

"Richard. *Tell us where you are!*"

The phone hissed, the transmission getting steadily worse. They heard Levine say: "—have me surrounded, and—vicious—can smell them especially—night—"

"What is he talking about?" Arby said.

"—to—injury—can't—not long—please—"

And then there was a final, fading hiss.

And suddenly the phone went dead.

Thorne clicked off his own handset, and turned off the speakerphone. He turned to the kids, who were both pale. "We have to find him," he said. "Right away."

SECOND CONFIGURATION

"Self-organization elaborates in complexity as the
system advances toward the chaotic edge."

IAN MALCOLM

Clues

Thorne unlocked the door to Levine's apartment, and flicked on the lights. They stared, astonished. Arby said, "It looks like a museum!"

Levine's two-bedroom apartment was decorated in a vaguely Asian style, with rich wooden cabinets, and expensive antiques. But the apartment was spotlessly clean, and most of the antiques were housed in plastic cases. Everything was neatly labeled. They walked slowly into the room.

"Does he *live* here?" Kelly said. She found it hard to believe. The apartment seemed so impersonal to her, almost inhuman. And her own apartment was such a mess all the time. . . .

"Yeah, he does," Thorne said, pocketing the key. "It always looks like this. It's why he can never live with a woman. He can't stand to have anybody touch anything."

The living-room couches were arranged around a glass coffee table. On the table were four piles of books, each neatly aligned with the glass edge. Arby glanced at the titles. *Catastrophe Theory and Emergent Structures. Inductive Processes in Molecular Evolution. Cellular Automata. Methodology of Non-Linear Adaptation. Phase Transition in Evolutionary Systems.* There were also some older books, with titles in German.

Kelly sniffed the air. "Something cooking?"

"I don't know," Thorne said. He went into the dining room. Along the wall, he saw a hot plate with a row of covered dishes. They saw a polished wood dining table, with a place set for one, silver and cut glass. Soup steamed from a bowl.

Thorne walked over and picked up a sheet of paper on the table and read: "Lobster bisque, baby organic greens, seared ahi tuna." A yellow Post-it was attached. "Hope your trip was good! Romelia."

"Wow," Kelly said. "You mean somebody makes dinner for him every day?"

"I guess," Thorne said. He didn't seem impressed; he shuffled through a stack of unopened mail that had been set out beside the plate. Kelly turned to some faxes on a nearby table. The first one was from the

Peabody Museum at Yale, in New Haven. "Is this German?" she said, handing it to Thorne.

> Dear Dr. Levine:
>
> Your requested document:
>
>> "*Geschichtliche Forschungsarbeiten über die Geologie Zentralamerikas, 1922–1929*"
>
> has been sent by Federal Express today.
> Thank you.
>
>> (signed)
>> Dina Skrumbis, Archivist

"I can't read it," Thorne said. "But I think it's 'Something Researches on the Geology of Central America.' And it's from the twenties—not exactly hot news."

"I wonder why he wanted it?" she said.

Thorne didn't answer her. He went into the bedroom.

The bedroom had a spare, minimal look, the bed a black futon, neatly made. Thorne opened the closet doors, and saw racks of clothing, everything pressed, neatly spaced, much of it in plastic. He opened the top dresser drawer and saw socks folded, arranged by color.

"I don't know how he can live like this," Kelly said.

"Nothing to it," Thorne said. "All you need is servants." He opened the other drawers quickly, one after another.

Kelly wandered over to the bedside table. There were several books there. The one on top was very small, and yellowing with age. It was in German; the title was *Die Fünf Todesarten*. She flipped through it, saw colored pictures of what looked like Aztecs in colorful costumes. It was almost like an illustrated children's book, she thought.

Underneath were books and journal articles with the dark-red cover of the Santa Fe Institute: *Genetic Algorithms and Heuristic Networks. Geology of Central America, Tessellation Automata of Arbitrary Dimension.* The 1989 Annual Report of the InGen Corporation. And next to the telephone, she noticed a sheet of hastily scribbled notes. She recognized the precise handwriting as Levine's.

It said:

"SITE B"
Vulkanische
Tacaño?
Nublar?
1 of 5 Deaths?
in mtns? No!!!
maybe Guitierrez
<u>careful</u>

Kelly said, "What's Site B? He has notes about it."

Thorne came over to look. "*Vulkanische*," he said. "That means 'volcanic,' I think. And Tacaño and Nublar . . . They sound like place names. If they are, we can check that on an atlas. . . ."

"And what's this about one of five deaths?" Kelly said.

"Damned if I know," he said.

They were staring at the paper when Arby walked into the bedroom and said, "What's Site B?"

Thorne looked up. "Why?"

"You better see his office," Arby said.

Levine had turned the second bedroom into an office. It was, like the rest of the apartment, admirably neat. There was a desk with papers laid out in tidy stacks alongside a computer, covered in plastic. But behind the desk there was a large corkboard that covered most of the wall. And on this board, Levine had tacked up maps, charts, newspaper clippings, Landsat images, and aerial photographs. At the top of the board was a large sign that said "Site B?"

Alongside that was a blurred, curling snapshot of a bespectacled Chinese man in a white lab coat, standing in the jungle beside a wooden sign that said "Site B." His coat was unbuttoned, and he was wearing a tee shirt with lettering on it.

Alongside the photo was a large blowup of the tee shirt, as seen in the original photograph. It was hard to read the lettering, which was partly covered on both sides by the lab coat, but the shirt seemed to say:

nGen Site B
esearch Facili

In neat handwriting, Levine had noted: "InGen Site B Research Facility???? WHERE???"

Just below that was a page cut from the InGen Annual Report. A circled paragraph read:

> In addition to its headquarters in Palo Alto, where InGen
> maintains an ultra-modern 200,000 square foot research
> laboratory, the company runs three field laboratories around
> the world. A geological lab in South Africa, where amber
> and other biological specimens are acquired; a research
> farm in the mountains of Costa Rica, where exotic varieties
> of plants are grown; and a facility on the island of Isla
> Nublar, 120 miles west of Costa Rica.

Next to that Levine had written: "No B! Liars!"

Arby said, "He's really obsessed with Site B."

"I'll say," Thorne said. "And he thinks it's on an island somewhere."

Peering closely at the board, Thorne looked at the satellite images. He noticed that although they were printed in false colors, at various degrees of magnification, they all seemed to show the same general geographical area: a rocky coastline, and some islands offshore. The coastline had a beach, and encroaching jungle; it might be Costa Rica, but it was impossible to say for sure. In truth, it could be any of a dozen places in the world.

"He said he was on an island," Kelly said.

"Yes." Thorne shrugged. "But that doesn't help us much." He stared at the board. "There must be twenty islands here, maybe more."

Thorne looked at a memo, near the bottom.

> **SITE B @#$#TO ALL DEPARTMENTS OF[]****
> **MINDER OF%$#@#!PRESS AVOIDAN******
> ~~Mr. Hammond wishes to remind all~~****after^*&^marketing
> *%**Long-term marketing plan*&^&^%
> Marketing of proposed resort facilities requires that full com-
> plexity of JP technology not be ~~revealed~~ announced ~~made
> known~~. Mr. Hammond wishes to remind all departments that
> Production facility will not be ~~topic~~ subject of any press release
> ~~or discussion~~ at any time.
> Production/manufacturing facility cannot be#@#$#
> reference to production island loc
> Isla S. inhouse reference only
> strict press***^%$**guidelines

"This is weird," he said. "What do you make of this?"

Arby came over, and looked at it thoughtfully.

"All these missing letters and garbage," Thorne said. "Does it make any sense to you?"

"Yes," Arby said. He snapped his fingers, and went directly to Levine's desk. There, he pulled the plastic cover off the computer, and said, "I thought so."

The computer on Levine's desk was not the modern machine that Thorne would have expected. This computer was several years old, large and bulky, its cover scratched in many places. It had a black stripe on the box that said "Design Associates, Inc." And lower down, right by the power switch, a shiny little metal tag that said "Property International Genetics Technology, Inc., Palo Alto, CA."

"What's this?" Thorne said. "Levine has an InGen computer?"

"Yes," Arby said. "He sent us to buy it last week. They were selling off computer equipment."

"And he sent you?" Thorne said.

"Yeah. Me and Kelly. He didn't want to go himself. He's afraid of being followed."

"But this thing's a CAD-CAM machine, and it must be five years old," Thorne said. CAD-CAM computers were used by architects, graphic artists, and mechanical engineers. "Why would Levine want it?"

"He never told us," Arby said, flipping on the power switch. "But I know now."

"Yes?"

"That memo," Arby said, nodding to the wall. "You know why it looks that way? It's a recovered computer file. Levine's been recovering InGen files from this machine."

As Arby explained it, all the computers that InGen sold that day had had their hard drives reformatted to destroy any sensitive data on the disks. But the CAD-CAM machines were an exception. These machines all had special software installed by the manufacturer. The software was keyed to individual machines, using individual code references. That made these computers awkward to reformat, because the software would have to be reinstalled individually, taking hours.

"So they didn't do it," Thorne said.

"Right," Arby said. "They just erased the directory, and sold them."

"And that means the original files are still on the disk."

"Right."

The monitor glowed. The screen said:

TOTAL RECOVERED FILES: 2,387

"Jeez," Arby said. He leaned forward, staring intently, fingers poised over the keys. He pushed the directory button, and row after row of file names scrolled down. Thousands of files in all.

Thorne said, "How are you going to—"

"Give me a minute here," Arby said, interrupting him. Then he began to type rapidly.

"Okay, Arb," Thorne said. He was amused by the imperious way Arby behaved whenever he was working with a computer. He seemed to forget how young he was, his usual diffidence and timidity vanished. The electronic world was really his element. And he knew he was good at it.

Thorne said, "Any help you can give us will be—"

"Doc," Arby said. "Come on. Go and, uh, I don't know. Help Kelly or something."

And he turned away, and typed.

Raptor

The velociraptor was six feet tall and dark green. Poised to attack, it hissed loudly, its muscular neck thrust forward, jaws wide. Tim, one of the modelers, said, "What do you think, Dr. Malcolm?"

"No menace," Malcolm said, walking by. He was in the back wing of the biology department, on his way to his office.

"No menace?" Tim said.

"They never stand like this, flatfooted on two feet. Give him a book"—he grabbed a notebook from a desk, and placed it in the forearms of the animal—"and he might be singing a Christmas carol."

"Gee," Tim said. "I didn't think it was that bad."

"Bad?" Malcolm said. "This is an insult to a great predator. We should feel his speed and menace and power. Widen the jaws. Get the neck down. Tense the muscles, tighten the skin. And get that leg up. Remember, raptors don't attack with their jaws—they use their toe-claws," Malcolm said. "I want to see the claw raised up, ready to slash down and tear the guts out of its prey."

"You really think so?" Tim said doubtfully. "It might scare little kids. . . ."

"You mean it might scare you." Malcolm continued down the hallway. "And another thing: change that hissing sound. It sounds like somebody taking a pee. Give this animal a *snarl*. Give a great predator his due."

"Gee," Tim said, "I didn't know you had such personal feelings about it."

"It should be accurate," Malcolm said. "You know, there is such a thing as accurate and inaccurate. Irrespective of whatever your *feelings* are." He walked on, irritable, ignoring the momentary pain in his leg. The modeler annoyed him, although he had to admit Tim was just a representative of the current, fuzzy-minded thinking—what Malcolm called "sappy science."

Malcolm had long been impatient with the arrogance of his scientific colleagues. They maintained that arrogance, he knew, by resolutely ignoring the history of science as a way of thought. Scientists pretended that history didn't matter, because the errors of the past were now corrected by modern discoveries. But of course their forebears had believed exactly the same thing in the past, too. They had been wrong then. And modern scientists were wrong now. No episode of science history proved it better than the way dinosaurs had been portrayed over the decades.

It was sobering to realize that the most accurate perception of dinosaurs had also been the first. Back in the 1840s, when Richard Owen first described giant bones in England, he named them *Dinosauria:* terrible lizards. That was still the most accurate description of these creatures, Malcolm thought. They were indeed like lizards, and they were terrible.

But since Owen, the "scientific" view of dinosaurs had undergone many changes. Because the Victorians believed in the inevitability of progress, they insisted that the dinosaurs must necessarily be inferior—why else would they be extinct? So the Victorians made them fat, lethargic, and dumb—big dopes from the past. This perception was elaborated, so that by the early twentieth century, dinosaurs had become so weak that they could not support their own weight. Apatosaurs had to stand belly-deep in water or they would crush their own legs. The whole conception of the ancient world was suffused with these ideas of weak, stupid, slow animals.

That view didn't change until the 1960s, when a few renegade scientists, led by John Ostrom, began to imagine quick, agile, hot-blooded dinosaurs. Because these scientists had the temerity to question dogma, they were brutally criticized for years, even though it now seemed their ideas were correct.

But in the last decade, a growing interest in social behavior had led to still another view. Dinosaurs were now seen as caring creatures, living in groups, raising their little babies. They were good animals, even cute animals. The big sweeties had nothing to do with their terrible fate, which was visited on them by Alvarez's meteor. And that new sappy view produced people like Tim, who were reluctant to look at the other side of the coin, the other face of life. Of course, some dinosaurs had been social and cooperative. But others had been hunters—and killers of unparalleled viciousness. For Malcolm, the truest picture of life in the past incorporated the interplay of all aspects of life, the good and the bad, the strong and the weak. It was no good pretending anything else.

Scaring little kids, indeed! Malcolm snorted irritably, as he walked down the hall.

In truth, Malcolm was bothered by what Elizabeth Gelman had told him about the tissue fragment, and especially the tag. That tag meant trouble, Malcolm was sure of it.

But he wasn't sure what to do about it.

He turned the corner, past the display of Clovis points, arrowheads made by early man in America. Up ahead, he saw his office. Beverly, his assistant, was standing behind her desk, tidying papers, getting ready to go home. She handed him his faxes and said, "I've left word for Dr. Levine at his office, but he hasn't called back. They don't seem to know where he is."

"For a change," Malcolm said, sighing. It was so difficult working with Levine; he was so erratic, you never knew what to expect. Malcolm had been the one to post bail when Levine was arrested in his Ferrari. He riffled through the faxes: conference dates, requests for reprints . . . nothing interesting. "Okay. Thanks, Beverly."

"Oh. And the photographers came. They finished about an hour ago."

"What photographers?" he said.

"From *Chaos Quarterly*. To photograph your office."

"What are you talking about?" Malcolm said.

"They came to photograph your office," she said. "For a series about workplaces of famous mathematicians. They had a letter from you, saying it was—"

"I never sent any letter," Malcolm said. "And I've never heard of *Chaos Quarterly*."

He went into his office and looked around. Beverly hurried in after him, her face worried.

"Is it okay? Is everything here?"

"Yes," he said, scanning quickly. "It seems to be fine." He was opening the drawers to his desk, one after another. Nothing appeared to be missing.

"That's a relief," Beverly said, "because—"

He turned, and looked at the far side of the room.

The map.

Malcolm had a large map of the world, with pins stuck in it for all the sightings of what Levine kept calling "aberrant forms." By the most liberal count—Levine's count—there had now been twelve in all, from

Rangiroa in the west, to Baja California and Ecuador in the east. Few of them were verified. But now there was a tissue sample that confirmed one specimen, and that made all the rest more likely.

"Did they photograph this map?"

"Yes, they photographed everything. Does it matter?"

Malcolm looked at the map, trying to see it with fresh eyes. To see what an outsider would make of it. He and Levine had spent hours in front of this map, considering the possibility of a "lost world," trying to decide where it might be. They had narrowed it down to five islands in a chain, off the coast of Costa Rica. Levine was convinced that it was one of those islands, and Malcolm was beginning to think he was right. But those islands weren't highlighted on the map. . . .

Beverly said, "They were a very nice group. Very polite. Foreign— Swiss, I think."

Malcolm nodded, and sighed. The hell with it, he thought. It was bound to get out sooner or later.

"It's all right, Beverly."

"Are you sure?"

"Yes, it's fine. Have a good evening."

"Good night, Dr. Malcolm."

Alone in his office, he dialed Levine. The phone rang, and then the answering machine beeped. Levine was still not home.

"Richard, are you there? If you are, pick up, it's important."

He waited, nothing happened.

"Richard, it's Ian. Listen, we have a problem. The map is no longer secure. And I've had that sample analyzed, Richard, and I think it tells us the location of Site B, if my—"

There was a click as the phone lifted. He heard the sound of breathing.

"Richard?" he said.

"No," said the voice, "this is Thorne. And I think you better get over here right away."

The Five Deaths

"I knew it," Malcolm said, coming into Levine's apartment, and glancing quickly around. "I knew he would do something like this. You know how impetuous he is. I said to him, don't go until we have all the information. But I should have known. Of course, he went."

"Yes, he did."

"Ego," Malcolm said, shaking his head. "Richard has to be first. Has to figure it out first, has to get there first. I'm very concerned, he could ruin everything. This impulsive behavior: you realize it's a storm in the brain, neurons on the edge of chaos. Obsession is just a variety of addiction. But what scientist ever had self-control? They instruct them in school: it's bad form to be balanced. They forget Neils Bohr was not only a great physicist but an Olympic athlete. These days they all *try* to be nerds. It's the professional style."

Thorne looked at Malcolm thoughtfully. He thought he detected a competitive edge. He said, "Do you know which island he went to?"

"No. I do not." Malcolm was stalking around the apartment, taking things in. "The last time we talked, we had narrowed it down to five islands, all in the south. But we hadn't decided which one."

Thorne pointed to the wallboard, the satellite images. "These islands here?"

"Yes," Malcolm said, looking briefly. "They're strung out in an arc, all about ten miles offshore from the bay of Puerto Cortés. Supposedly they're all uninhabited. Local people call them the Five Deaths."

"Why?" Kelly said.

"Some old Indian story," Malcolm said. "Something about a brave warrior captured by a king who offered him his choice of deaths. Burning, drowning, crushing, hanging, decapitation. The warrior said he would take them all, and he went from island to island, experiencing the various challenges. Sort of a New World version of the labors of Hercules—"

"So *that's* what it is!" Kelly said, and ran out of the room.

Malcolm looked blank.

He turned to Thorne, who shrugged.

Kelly returned, carrying the German children's book in her hand. She gave it to Malcolm.

"Yes," he said. "*Die Fünf Todesarten.* The Five Ways of Death. Interesting that it is in German. . . ."

"He has lots of German books," Kelly said.

"Does he? That bastard. He never told me."

"That means something?" Kelly said.

"Yes, it means a lot. Hand me that magnifying glass, would you?"

Kelly gave him a magnifying glass from the desk. "What does it mean?"

"The Five Deaths are ancient volcanic islands," he said. "Which means that they are geologically very rich. Back in the twenties, the Germans wanted to mine them." He peered at the images, squinting. "Ah. Yes, these are the islands, no question. Matanceros, Muerte, Tacaño, Sorna, Pena . . . All names of death and destruction . . . All right. I think we may be close. Do we have any satellite pictures with spectrographic analyses of the cloud cover?"

Arby said, "Is that going to help you find Site B?"

"What?" Malcolm spun around. "What do you know about Site B?"

Arby was sitting at the computer, still working. "Nothing. Just that Dr. Levine was looking for Site B. And it was the name in the files."

"What files?"

"I've recovered some InGen files from this computer. And, searching through old records, I found references to Site B. . . . But they're pretty confusing. Like this one." He leaned back, to let Malcolm look at the screen.

Summary: Plan Revisions #35

PRODUCTION	(SITE B)
AIR HANDLERS	Grade 5 to Grade 7
LAB STRUCTURE	400 cmm to 510 cmm
BIO SECURITY	Level PK/3 to Level PK/5
CONVEYOR RATES	3 mpm to 2.5 mpm
HOLDING PENS	13 hectares to 26 hectares
STAFF Q	17 (4 admin) to 19 (4 admin)
COMM PROTOCOL	ET(VX) to RDT (VX)

Malcolm frowned. "Curious, but not very helpful. It doesn't tell us which island—or even if it's on an island at all. What else have you got?"

"Well . . ." Arby flicked keys. "Let's see. There's this."

SITE B ISLAND NETWORK	NODAL POINTS
ZONE 1 (RIVER)	1–8
ZONE 2 (COAST)	9–16
ZONE 3 (RIDGE)	17–24
ZONE 4 (VALLEY)	25–32

Malcolm said, "Okay, so it's an island. And Site B has a network—but a network of what? Computers?"

Arby said, "I don't know. Maybe a radio network."

"For what purpose?" Malcolm said. "What would a radio network be used for? This isn't very helpful."

Arby shrugged. He took it as a challenge. He began typing furiously again. Then said, "Wait! . . . Here's another one . . . if I can just format it. . . . There! Got it!"

He moved away from the screen, so the others could see.

Malcolm looked and said, "Very good. *Very* good!"

SITE B LEGENDS

EAST WING	WEST WING	LOADING BAY
LABORATORY	ASSEMBLY BAY	ENTRANCE
OUTLYING	MAIN CORE	GEO TURBINE
CONVENIENCE STORE	WORKER VILLAGE	GEO CORE
GAS STATION	POOL/TENNIS	PUTTING GREENS
MGRS HOUSE	JOG PATH	GAS LINES
SECURITY ONE	SECURITY TWO	THERMAL LINES
RIVER DOCK	BOATHOUSE	SOLAR ONE
SWAMP ROAD	RIVER ROAD	RIDGE ROAD
MTN VIEW ROAD	CLIFF ROAD	HOLDING PENS

"Now we're getting somewhere," Malcolm said, scanning the listing. "Can you print this out?"

"Sure." Arby was beaming. "Is it really good?"

"It really is," Malcolm said.

Kelly looked at Arby and said, "Arb. Those're the text labels that go with a map."

"Yeah, I think so. Pretty neat, huh?" He pushed a button, sending the image to the printer.

Malcolm peered at the listing some more, then turned his attention back to the satellite maps, looking closely at each one with the magnifying glass. His nose was just inches from the photographs.

"Arb," Kelly said, "don't just sit there. Come on! Recover the map! That's what we need!"

"I don't know if I can," Arby said. "It's a proprietary thirty-two-bit format. . . . I mean, it's a big job."

"Stop whining, Arb. Just do it."

"Never mind," Malcolm said. He stepped away from the satellite images pinned on the wall. "It's not important."

"It's not?" Arby said, a little wounded.

"No, Arby. You can stop. Because, from what you've already discovered, I am quite certain we can identify the island, right now."

James

Ed James yawned, and pushed the earpiece tighter into his ear. He wanted to make sure he got all this. He shifted in the driver's seat of his gray Taurus, trying to get comfortable, trying to stay awake. The small tape recorder was spinning in his lap, next to his notepad, and the crumpled papers from two Big Macs. James looked across the street at Levine's apartment building. The lights were on in the third-floor apartment.

And the bug he had placed there last week was working fine. Through his earpiece, he heard one of the kids say, "How?"

And then the crippled guy, Malcolm, said, "The essence of verification is multiple lines of reasoning that converge at a single point."

"Meaning what?" the kid said.

Malcolm said, "Just look at the Landsat pictures."

On his notepad, James wrote LANDSAT.

"We already looked at those," the girl said.

James felt foolish not to have realized earlier that these two kids were working for Levine. He remembered them well, they were in the class Levine taught. There was a short black kid and a gawky white girl. Just kids: maybe eleven or twelve. He should have realized.

Not that it mattered now, he thought. He was getting the information anyway. James reached across the dashboard and plucked out the last two French fries, and ate them, even though they were cold.

"Okay," he heard Malcolm say. "It's this island here. This is the island Levine went to."

The girl said doubtfully, "You think so? This is . . . Isla Sorna."

James wrote ISLA SORNA.

"That's our island," Malcolm said. "Why? Three independent reasons. First, it's privately owned, so it hasn't been thoroughly searched by the Costa Rican government. Second, privately owned by whom? By the Germans, who leased rights to mineral excavations, back in the twenties."

"All the German books!"

"Exactly. Third, from Arby's list—and from another independent source—it is clear that there is volcanic gas located at Site B. So, which islands have volcanic gas? Take the magnifying glass and look for your-self. Turns out, only one island does."

"You mean this here?" the girl said.

"Right. That's volcanic smoke."

"How do you know?"

"Spectrographic analysis. See this spike here? That's elementary sul-fur in the cloud cover. There aren't really any sources for sulfur except volcanic sources."

"What's this other spike?" the girl said.

"Methane," Malcolm said. "Apparently there is a fairly large source of methane gas."

"Is that also volcanic?" Thorne said.

"It might be. Methane is released from volcanic activity, but most commonly during active eruptions. The other possibility is, it might be organic."

"Organic? Meaning what?"

"Large herbivores, and—"

Then there was something that James couldn't hear, and the kid said, "Do you want me to finish this recovery, or not?" He sounded an-noyed.

"No," Thorne said. "Never mind now, Arby. We know what we have to do. Let's go, kids!"

James looked up at the apartment and saw the lights being turned off. A few minutes later, Thorne and the kids appeared at the front en-trance, on the street level. They got in a Jeep, and drove off. Malcolm went to his own car, climbed in awkwardly, and drove away in the op-posite direction.

James considered following Malcolm, but he had something else to do now. He turned on the car ignition, picked up the phone, and dialed.

Field Systems

Half an hour later, when they got back to Thorne's office, Kelly stared, stunned. Most of the workers were gone, and the shed had been cleaned up. The two trailers and the Explorer stood side by side, freshly painted dark green, and ready to go.

"They're finished!"

"I told you they would be," Thorne said. He turned to his chief foreman, Eddie Carr, a stocky young man in his twenties. "Eddie, where are we?"

"Just wrapping up, Doc," Eddie said. "Paint's still wet in a few places, but it should be dry by morning."

"We can't wait until morning. We're moving out now."

"We are?"

Arby and Kelly exchanged glances. This was news to them, too.

Thorne said, "I'll need you to drive one of these, Eddie. We've got to be at the airport by midnight."

"But I thought we were field testing. . . ."

"No time for that. We're going right to the location." The front door buzzed. "That'll be Malcolm, probably." He pushed the button to unlock the door.

"You're not going to field test?" Eddie said, with a worried look. "I think you better shake them down, Doc. We made some pretty complex modifications here, and—"

"There's no time," Malcolm said, coming in. "We have to go right away." He turned to Thorne. "I'm very worried about him."

"Eddie!" Thorne said. "Did the exit papers come in?"

"Oh sure, we've had them for the last two weeks."

"Well, get them, and call Jenkins, tell him to meet us at the airport, and do the details for us. I want to be off the ground in four hours."

"Jeez, Doc—"

"Just do it."

Kelly said, "You're going to Costa Rica?"

"That's right. We've got to get Levine. If it's not too late."

"We're coming with you," Kelly said.

"Right," Arby said. "We are."

"Absolutely not," Thorne said. "It's out of the question."

"But we earned it!"

"Dr. Levine talked to our parents!"

"We already have permission!"

"You have permission," Thorne said severely, "to go on a field test in the woods a hundred miles from here. But we're not doing that. We're going someplace that might be very dangerous, and you're not coming with us, and that's final."

"But—"

"Kids," Thorne said. "Don't piss me off. I'm going to go make a phone call. You get your stuff together. You're going home."

And he turned and walked away.

"Gee," Kelly said.

Arby stuck his tongue out at the departing Thorne and muttered, "What an asshole."

"Get with the program, Arby," Thorne said, not looking back. "You two guys are going home. Period."

He went into his office and slammed the door.

Arby stuck his hands in his pockets. "They couldn't have figured it out without our help."

"I know, Arb," she said. "But we can't make him take us."

They turned to Malcolm. "Dr. Malcolm, can you please—"

"Sorry," Malcolm said. "I can't."

"But—"

"The answer is no, kids. It's just too dangerous."

Dejected, they drifted over to the vehicles, gleaming beneath the ceiling lights. The Explorer with the black photovoltaic panels on the roof and hood, the inside crammed with glowing electronic equipment. Just looking at the Explorer gave them a sense of adventure—an adventure they would not be part of.

Arby peered into the larger trailer, cupping his eyes over the window. "Wow, look at this!"

"I'm going in," Kelly said, and she opened the door. She was momentarily surprised at how solid and heavy it was. Then she climbed up the steps into the trailer.

Inside, the trailer was fitted out with gray upholstery and much more electronic equipment. It was divided into sections, for different laboratory functions. The main area was a biological lab, with specimen trays, dissecting pans, and microscopes that connected to video monitors. The lab also included biochemistry equipment, spectrometers, and a series of automated sample-analyzers. Next to it there was an extensive computer section, a bank of processors, and a communications section. All the lab equipment was miniaturized, and built into small tables that slid into the walls, and then bolted down.

"This is *cool*," Arby said.

Kelly didn't answer. She was looking closely at the lab. Dr. Levine had designed this trailer, apparently with a very specific purpose. There was no provision for geology, or botany, or chemistry, or lots of other things that a field team might be expected to study. It wasn't a general scientific lab at all. There really seemed to be just a biology unit, and a large computer unit.

Biology, and computers.

Period.

What had this trailer been built to study?

Set in the wall was a small bookshelf, the books held in place with a Velcro strap. She scanned the titles: *Modeling Adaptive Biological Systems, Vertebrate Behavioral Dynamics, Adaptation in Natural and Artificial Systems, Dinosaurs of North America, Preadaptation and Evolution.* . . . It seemed like a strange set of books to take on a wilderness expedition; if there was a logic behind it, she didn't see it.

She moved on. At intervals along the walls, she could see where the trailer had been strengthened; dark carbon-honeycomb strips ran up the walls. She had overheard Thorne saying it was the same material used in supersonic jet fighters. Very light and very strong. And she noticed that all the windows had been replaced with that special glass with fine wire mesh inside it.

Why was the trailer so strong?

It made her a little uneasy, when she thought about it. She remembered the telephone call with Dr. Levine, earlier in the day. He had said he was surrounded.

Surrounded by what?

He had said: *I can smell them, especially at night.*

What was he referring to?

Who was *them*?

Still uneasy, Kelly moved toward the back of the trailer, where there was a homey little living area, complete with gingham curtains on the windows. Compact kitchen, a toilet, and four beds. Storage compartments above and below the beds. There was even a little walk-in shower. It was nice.

From there, she went through the accordion pleating that connected the two trailers. It was a little bit like the connection between two railway cars, a short transitional passage. She emerged inside the second trailer, which seemed to be mostly utility storage: extra tires, spare parts, more lab equipment, shelves and cabinets. All the extra supplies that meant an expedition to some far-off place. There was even a motorcycle hanging off the back of the trailer. She tried some of the cabinets, but they were locked.

But even here there were extra reinforcing strips as well. This section had also been built especially strong.

Why? she wondered. Why so strong?

"Look at this," Arby said, standing before a wall unit. It was a complex of glowing LED displays and lots of buttons, and looked to Kelly like a complicated thermostat.

"What does it do?" Kelly said.

"Monitors the whole trailer," he said. "You can do everything from here. All the systems, all the equipment. And look, there's TV. . . ." He pushed a button, and a monitor glowed to life. It showed Eddie walking toward them, across the floor.

"And, hey, what's this?" Arby said. At the bottom of the display was a button with a security cover. He flipped the cover open. The button was silver and said DEF.

"Hey, I bet this is that bear defense he was talking about."

A moment later, Eddie opened the trailer door and said, "You better stop that, you'll drain the batteries. Come on, now. You heard what the doc said. Time for you kids to go home."

Kelly and Arby exchanged glances.

"Okay," Kelly said. "We're going."

Reluctantly, they left the trailer.

They walked across the shed to Thorne's office to say goodbye. Arby said, "I wish he'd let us go."

"Me, too."

"I don't want to stay home for break," he said. "They're just going to be working all the time." He meant his parents.

"I know."

Kelly didn't want to go home, either. This idea of a field test during spring break was perfect for her, because it got her out of the house, and out of a bad situation. Her mother did data entry in an insurance company during the day, and at night she worked as a waitress at Denny's. So her mom was always busy at her jobs, and her latest boyfriend, Phil, tended to hang around the house a lot at night. It had been okay when Emily was there, too, but now Emily was studying nursing at the community college, so Kelly was alone in the house. And Phil was sort of creepy. But her mother liked Phil, so she never wanted to hear Kelly say anything bad about him. She just told Kelly to grow up.

So now Kelly went to Thorne's office, hoping against hope that at the last minute he would relent. He was on the phone, his back to them. On the screen of his computer, they saw one of the satellite images they had taken from Levine's apartment. Thorne was zooming in on the image, successive magnifications. They knocked on the door, opened it a little.

"Bye, Dr. Thorne."

"See you, Dr. Thorne."

Thorne turned, holding the phone to his ear. "Bye, kids." He gave a brief wave.

Kelly hesitated. "Listen, could we just talk to you for a minute about—"

Thorne shook his head. "No."

"But—"

"No, Kelly. I've got to place this call now," he said. "It's already four a.m. in Africa, and in a little while she'll go to sleep."

"Who?"

"Sarah Harding."

"Sarah Harding is coming, too?" she said, lingering at the door.

"I don't know." Thorne shrugged. "Have a good vacation, kids. See you in a week. Thanks for your help. Now get out of here." He looked across the shed. "Eddie, the kids are leaving. Show them to the door, and lock them out! Get me those papers! And pack a bag, you're coming with me!" Then in a different voice he said, "Yes, operator, I'm still waiting."

And he turned away.

Harding

Through the night-vision goggles, the world appeared in shades of fluorescent green. Sarah Harding stared out at the African savannah. Directly ahead, above the high grass, she saw the rocky outcrop of a kopje. Bright-green pinpoints glowed back from the boulders. Probably rock hyraxes, she thought, or some other small rodent.

Standing up in her Jeep, wearing a sweatshirt against the cool night air, feeling the weight of the goggles, she turned her head slowly. She could hear the yelping in the night, and she was trying to locate the source.

Even from her high vantage point, standing up in the vehicle, she knew the animals would be hidden from direct view. She turned slowly north, looking for movement in the grass. She saw none. She looked back quickly, the green world swirling momentarily. Now she faced south.

And she saw them.

The grass rippled in a complex pattern as the pack raced forward, yelping and barking, prepared to attack. She caught a glimpse of the female she called Face One, or F1. F1 was distinguished by a white streak between her eyes. F1 loped along, in the peculiar sideways gait of hyenas; her teeth were bared; she glanced back at the rest of the pack, noting their position.

Sarah Harding swung the glasses through the darkness, looking ahead of the pack. She saw the prey: a herd of African buffalo, standing belly-deep in the grass, agitated. They were bellowing and stamping their feet.

The hyenas yelped louder, a pattern of sound that would confuse the prey. They rushed through the herd, trying to break it up, trying to separate the calves from their mothers. African buffalo looked dull and stupid, but in fact they were among the most dangerous large African mammals, heavy powerful creatures with sharp horns and notoriously mean dispositions. The hyenas could not hope to bring down an adult, unless it was injured or sick.

But they would try to take a calf.

Sitting behind the wheel of the Jeep, Makena, her assistant, said, "You want to move closer?"

"No, this is fine."

In fact, it was more than fine. Their Jeep was on a slight rise, and they had a better-than-average view. With any luck, she would record the entire attack pattern. She turned on the video camera, mounted on a tripod five feet above her head, and dictated rapidly into the tape recorder.

"F1 south, F2 and F5 flanking, twenty yards. F3 center. F6 circling wide east. Can't see F7. F8 circling north. F1 straight through. Disrupting. Herd moving, stamping. There's F7. Straight through. F8 angling through from the north. Coming out, circling again."

This was classic hyena behavior. The lead animals ran through the herd, while others circled it, then came in from the sides. The buffalo couldn't keep track of their attackers. She listened to the herd bellowing, even as the group panicked, broke its tight clustered formation. The big animals moved apart, turning, looking. Harding couldn't see the calves; they were below the grass. But she could hear their plaintive cries.

Now the hyenas came back. The buffalo stamped their feet, lowered their big heads menacingly. The grass rippled as the hyenas circled, yelping and barking, the sounds more staccato. She caught a brief glimpse of female F8, her jaws already red. But Harding hadn't seen the actual attack.

The buffalo herd moved a short distance to the east, where it regrouped. One female buffalo now stood apart from the herd. She bellowed continuously at the hyenas. They must have taken her calf.

Harding felt frustrated. It had happened so swiftly—too swiftly—which could only mean that the hyenas had been lucky, or the calf was injured. Or perhaps very young, even newborn; a few of the buffalo were still calving. She would have to review the videotape, to try and reconstruct what had happened. The perils of studying fast-moving nocturnal animals, she thought.

But there was no question they had taken an animal. All the hyenas were clustered around a single area of grass; they yelped and jumped. She saw F3, and then F5, their muzzles bloody. Now the pups came up, squealing to get at the kill. The adults immediately made room for them, helped them to eat. Sometimes they pulled away flesh from the carcass, and held it so the young ones could eat.

Their behavior was familiar to Sarah Harding, who had become in recent years the foremost expert on hyenas in the world. When she first reported her findings, she was greeted with disbelief and even outrage from colleagues, who disputed her results in very personal terms. She was attacked for being a woman, for being attractive, for having "an overbearing feminist perspective." The university reminded her she was on tenure track. Colleagues shook their heads. But Harding had persisted, and slowly, over time, as more data accumulated, her view of hyenas had come to be accepted.

Still, hyenas would never be appealing creatures, she thought, watching them feed. They were ungainly, heads too big and bodies sloping, coats ragged and mottled, gait awkward, vocalizations too reminiscent of an unpleasant laugh. In an increasingly urban world of concrete skyscrapers, wild animals were romanticized, classified as noble or ignoble, heroes or villains. And in this media-driven world, hyenas were simply not photogenic enough to be admirable. Long since cast as the laughing villains of the African plain, they were hardly thought worth a systematic study until Harding had begun her own research.

What she had discovered cast hyenas in a very different light. Brave hunters and attentive parents, they lived in a remarkably complex social structure—and a matriarchy as well. As for their notorious yelping vocalizations, they actually represented an extremely sophisticated form of communication.

She heard a roar, and through her night-vision goggles saw the first of the lions approaching the kill. It was a large female, circling closer. The hyenas barked and snapped at the lioness, guiding their own pups off into the grass. Within a few moments, other lions appeared, and settled down to feed on the hyenas' kill.

Now, lions, she thought. There was a truly nasty animal. Although called the king of beasts, lions in truth were actually vile and—

The phone rang.

"Makena," she said.

The phone rang again. Who could be calling her now?

She frowned. Through the goggles, she saw the lionesses look up, heads turning in the night.

Makena was fumbling beneath the dashboard, looking for the phone. It rang three more times before he found it.

She heard him say, "*Jambo, mzee.* Yes, Dr. Harding is here." He handed the phone up to her. "It's Dr. Thorne."

Reluctantly, she removed her night goggles, and took the phone. She knew Thorne well; he had designed most of the equipment in her Jeep. "Doc, this better be important."

"It is," Thorne said. "I'm calling about Richard."

"What about him?" She caught his concern, but didn't understand why. Lately, Levine had been a pain in the neck, telephoning her almost daily from California, picking her brains about field work with animals. He had lots of questions about hides, and blinds, data protocols, record-keeping, it went on and on. . . .

"Did he ever tell you what he intended to study?" Thorne asked.

"No," she said. "Why?"

"Nothing at all?"

"No," Harding said. "He was very secretive. But I gathered he'd located an animal population that he could use to make some point about biological systems. You know how obsessive he is. Why?"

"Well, he's missing, Sarah. Malcolm and I think he's in some kind of trouble. We've located him on an island in Costa Rica, and we're going to get him now."

"Now?" she said.

"Tonight. We're flying to San José in a few hours. Ian's going with me. We want you to come, too."

"Doc," she said. "Even if I took a flight out of Seronera tomorrow morning to Nairobi, it'd take me almost a day to get there. And that's if I got lucky. I mean—"

"You decide," Thorne said, interrupting. "I'll give you the details, and you decide what you want to do."

He gave her the information, and she wrote it on the notepad strapped to her wrist. Then Thorne rang off.

She stood staring out at the African night, feeling the cool breeze on her face. Off in the darkness, she heard the growl of the lions at the kill. Her work was here. Her life was here.

Makena said, "Dr. Harding? What do we do?"

"Go back," she said. "I have to pack."

"You're leaving?"

"Yes," she said. "I'm leaving."

Message

Thorne drove to the airport, the lights of San Francisco disappearing behind them. Malcolm sat in the passenger seat. He looked back at the Explorer driving behind them and said, "Does Eddie know what this is all about?"

"Yes," Thorne said. "But I'm not sure he believes it."

"And the kids don't know?"

"No," Thorne said.

There was a beeping alongside him. Thorne pulled out his little black Envoy, a radio pager. A light was flashing. He flipped up the screen, and handed it to Malcolm. "Read it for me."

"It's from Arby," Malcolm said. "Says, 'Have a good trip. If you want us, call. We'll be standing by if you need our help.' And he gives his phone number."

Thorne laughed. "You got to love those kids. They never give up." Then he frowned, as a thought occurred to him. "What's the time on that message?"

"Four minutes ago," Malcolm said. "Came in via netcom."

"Okay. Just checking."

They turned right, toward the airport. They saw the lights in the distance. Malcolm stared forward gloomily. "It's very unwise for us to be rushing off like this. It's not the right way to go about it."

Thorne said, "We should be all right. As long as we have the right island."

"We do," Malcolm said.

"How do you know?"

"The most important clue was something I didn't want the kids to know about. A few days ago, Levine saw the carcass of one of the animals."

"Oh?"

"Yes. He had a chance to look at it, before the officials burned it. And he discovered that it was tagged. He cut the tag off and sent it to me."

"Tagged? You mean like—"

"Yes. Like a biological specimen. The tag was old, and it showed pitting from sulfuric acid."

"Must be volcanic," Thorne said.

"Exactly."

"And you say it was an old tag?"

"Several years," Malcolm said. "But the most interesting finding was the way the animal died. Levine concluded the animal had been injured while it was still alive—a deep slashing cut in the leg that went right down to the bone."

Thorne said, "You're saying the animal was injured by another dinosaur."

"Yes. Exactly. "

They drove a moment in silence. "Who else besides us knows about this island?"

"I don't know," Malcolm said. "But somebody's trying to find out. My office was broken into today, and photographed."

"Great." Thorne sighed. "But you didn't know where the island was, did you?"

"No. I hadn't put it together yet."

"Do you think anybody else has?"

"No," Malcolm said. "We're on our own."

Exploitation

Lewis Dodgson threw open the door marked ANIMAL QUARTERS, and immediately all the dogs began barking. Dodgson walked down the corridor between the rows of cages, stacked ten feet high on both sides. The building was large; the Biosyn Corporation of Cupertino, California, required an extensive animal-testing facility.

Walking alongside him, Rossiter, the head of the company, gloomily brushed the lapels of his Italian suit. "I hate this fucking place," he said. "Why did you want me to come here?"

"Because," Dodgson said. "We need to talk about the future."

"Stinks in here," Rossiter said. He glanced at his watch. "Get on with it, Lew."

"We can talk in here." Dodgson led him to a glass-walled superintendent's booth, in the center of the building. The glass cut down the sound of the barking. But through the windows, they could look out at the rows of animals.

"It's simple," Dodgson said, starting to pace. "But I think it's important."

Lewis Dodgson was forty-five years old, bland-faced and balding. His features were youthful, and his manner was mild. But appearances were deceiving—the baby-faced Dodgson was one of the most ruthless and aggressive geneticists of his generation. Controversy had dogged his career: as a graduate student at Hopkins, he had been dismissed for planning human gene therapy without FDA permission. Later, after joining Biosyn, he had conducted a controversial rabies-vaccine test in Chile—the illiterate farmers who were the subjects were never informed they were being tested.

In each case, Dodgson explained that he was a scientist in a hurry, and could not be held back by regulations drawn up for lesser souls. He called himself "results-oriented," which really meant he did whatever he considered necessary to achieve his goal. He was also a tireless self-promoter. Within the company, Dodgson presented himself as a researcher, even though he lacked the ability to do original research, and had never done any. His intellect was fundamentally derivative; he never conceived of anything until someone else had thought of it first.

He was very good at "developing" research, which meant stealing someone else's work at an early stage. In this, he was without scruple and without peer. For many years he had run the reverse-engineering section at Biosyn, which in theory examined competitors' products and determined how they were made. But in practice, "reverse engineering" involved a great deal of industrial espionage.

Rossiter, of course, had no illusions about Dodgson. He disliked him, and avoided him as much as possible. Dodgson was always taking chances, cutting corners; he made Rossiter uneasy. But Rossiter also knew that modern biotechnology was highly competitive. To stay competitive, every company needed a man like Dodgson. And Dodgson was very good at what he did.

"I'll come right to the point," Dodgson said, turning to Rossiter. "If we act quickly, I believe we have an opportunity to acquire the InGen technology."

Rossiter sighed. "Not again. . . ."

"I know, Jeff. I know how you feel. I admit, there is some history here."

"History? The only history is you failed—time and again. We've tried this, back door and front door. Hell, we even tried to buy the company when it was in Chapter 11, because you told us it would be available. But it turned out it wasn't. The Japanese wouldn't sell."

"I understand, Jeff. But let's not forget—"

"What I can't forget," Rossiter said, "is that we paid seven hundred and fifty thousand dollars to your friend Nedry, and have nothing to show for it."

"But Jeff—"

"Then we paid five hundred thousand to that Dai-Ichi marriage broker. Nothing to show for that, either. Our attempts to acquire InGen technology have been a complete fucking failure. That's what I can't forget."

"But the point," Dodgson said, "is that we kept trying for a good reason. This technology is vital to the future of the company."

"So you say."

"The world is changing, Jeff. I'm talking about solving one of the major problems this company faces in the twenty-first century."

"Which is?"

Dodgson pointed out the window, at the barking dogs. "Animal testing. Let's face it, Jeff: every year, we get more pressure not to use animals for testing and research. Every year, more demonstrations, more break-ins, more bad press. First it was just simple-minded zealots and Hollywood celebrities. But now it's a bandwagon: even university philosophers are beginning to argue that it's unethical for monkeys, and dogs, and even rats to be subjected to the indignities of laboratory research. We've even had some protests about our 'exploitation' of squid, even though they're on dinner tables all over the world. I'm telling you, Jeff, there's no end to this trend. Eventually, somebody's going to say we can't even exploit bacteria to make genetic products."

"Oh, come on."

"Just wait. It'll happen. And it'll shut us down. Unless we have a genuinely created animal. Consider—an animal that is extinct, and is brought back to life, is for all practical purposes not an animal at all. It can't have any rights. It's already extinct. So if it exists, it can only be something *we have made*. We made it, we patent it, we own it. And it is a perfect research testbed. And we believe that the enzyme and hormone systems of dinosaurs are identical to mammalian systems. In the future, drugs can be tested on small dinosaurs as successfully as they are now tested on dogs and rats—with much less risk of legal challenge."

Rossiter was shaking his head. "You think."

"I know. They're basically big lizards, Jeff. And nobody loves a lizard. They're not like these cute doggies that lick your hand and break your heart. Lizards have no personality. They're snakes with legs."

Rossiter sighed.

"Jeff. We're talking about real freedom, here. Because, at the moment, everything to do with living animals is tied up in legal and moral knots. Big-game hunters can't shoot a lion or an elephant—the same animals their fathers and grandfathers used to shoot, and then pose proudly for a photo. Now there are forms, licenses, expenses—and plenty of guilt. These days, you don't dare shoot a tiger and admit it afterward. In the modern world, it's a much more serious transgression to shoot a tiger than to shoot your parents. Tigers have advocates. But now imagine: a specially stocked hunting preserve, maybe somewhere in Asia, where individuals of wealth and importance could hunt tyrannosaurs and triceratops in a natural setting. It would be an incredibly desirable attraction. How many hunters have a stuffed elk head on their wall? The world's full of them. But how many can claim to have a snarling tyrannosaurus head, hanging above the wet bar?"

"You're not serious."

"I'm trying to make a point here, Jeff: *these animals are totally exploitable.* We can do anything we want with them."

Rossiter stood up from the table, put his hands in his pockets. He sighed, then looked up at Dodgson.

"The animals still exist?"

Dodgson nodded slowly.

"And you know where they are?"

Dodgson nodded.

"Okay," Rossiter said. "Do it."

He turned toward the door, then paused, looked back. "But, Lew," he said. "Let's be clear. This is it. This is absolutely the last time. Either you get the animals now, or it's over. This is the last time. Got it?"

"Don't worry," Dodgson said. "This time, I'll get them."

THIRD CONFIGURATION

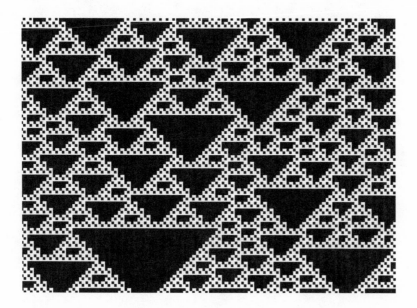

"In the intermediate phase, swiftly developing complexity within the system hides the risk of imminent chaos. But the risk is there."

IAN MALCOLM

Costa Rica

There was a drenching downpour in Puerto Cortés. Rain drummed on the roof of the little metal shed beside the airfield. Dripping wet, Thorne stood and waited while the Costa Rican official went over the papers, again and again. Rodríguez was his name, and he was just a kid in his twenties, wearing an ill-fitting uniform, terrified of making a mistake.

Thorne looked out at the runway, where, in the soft dawn light, the cargo containers were being clamped to the bellies of two big Huey helicopters. Eddie Carr was out there in the rain with Malcolm, shouting as the workmen secured the clamps.

Rodríguez shuffled the papers. "Now, Señor Thorne, according to this, your destination is Isla Sorna. . . ."

"That's right."

"And your containers have only vehicles?"

"Yes, that's right. Research vehicles."

"Sorna is a primitive place. There is no petrol, no supplies, not even any roads to speak of. . . ."

"Have you been there?"

"Myself, no. People here have no interest in this island. It is a wild spot, rock and jungle. And there is no place for a boat to land, except in very special weather conditions. For example, today one cannot go there."

"I understand," Thorne said.

"I just wish that you will be prepared," Rodríguez said, "for the difficulties you will find there."

"I think we're prepared."

"You are taking adequate petrol for your vehicles?"

Thorne sighed. Why bother to explain? "Yes, we are."

"And there are just three of you, Dr. Malcolm, yourself, and your assistant, Señor Carr?"

"Correct."

"And your intended stay is less than one week?"

"That's correct. More like two days: with any luck, we expect to be off the island sometime tomorrow."

Rodríguez shuffled the papers again, as if looking for a hidden clue. "Well . . ."

"Is there a problem?" Thorne said, glancing at his watch.

"No problem, señor. Your permits are signed by the Director General of the Biological Preserves. They are in order. . . ." Rodríguez hesitated. "But it is very unusual, that such a permit would be granted at all."

"Why is that?"

"I do not know the details, but there was some trouble on one of the islands a few years ago, and since then the Department of Biological Preserves has closed all the Pacific islands to tourists."

"We're not tourists," Thorne said.

"I understand that, Señor Thorne."

More shuffling of papers.

Thorne waited.

Out on the runway, the container clamps locked in place, and the containers lifted off the ground.

"Very well, Señor Thorne," Rodríguez said finally, stamping the papers. "I wish you good luck."

"Thank you," Thorne said. He tucked the papers in his pocket, ducked his head against the rain, and ran back out on the runway.

Three miles offshore, the helicopters broke through the coastal cloud layer, into early-morning sunlight. From the cockpit of the lead Huey, Thorne could look up and down the coast. He saw five islands at various distances offshore—harsh rocky pinnacles, rising out of rough blue sea. The islands were each several miles apart, undoubtedly part of an old volcanic chain.

He pressed the speaker button. "Which is Sorna?"

The pilot pointed ahead. "We call them the Five Deaths," he said. "Isla Muerte, Isla Matanceros, Isla Pena, Isla Tacaño, and Isla Sorna, which is the big one farthest north."

"Have you been there?"

"Never, señor. But I believe there will be a landing site."

"How do you know?"

"Some years ago, there were some flights there. I have heard the Americans would come, and fly there, sometimes."

"Not Germans?"

"No, no. There have been no Germans since . . . I do not know. The World War. They were Americans that came."

"When was that?"

"I am not sure. Perhaps ten years ago."

The helicopter turned north, passing over the nearest island. Thorne glimpsed rugged, volcanic terrain, overgrown with dense jungle. There was no sign of life, or of human habitation.

"To the local people, these islands are not happy places," the pilot said. "They say, no good comes from here." He smiled. "But they do not know. They are superstitious Indians."

Now they were over open water, with Isla Sorna directly ahead. It was clearly an old volcanic crater: bare, reddish-gray rock walls, an eroded cone.

"Where do the boats land?"

The pilot pointed to where the sea surged and crashed against the cliffs. "On the east side of this island, there are many caves, made by the waves. Some of the local people call this Isla Gemido. It means 'groan,' from the sound of the waves inside the caves. Some of the caves go all the way through to the interior, and a boat can pass through at certain times. But not in weather as you see it now."

Thorne thought of Sarah Harding. If she was coming, she would land later today. "I have a colleague who may be arriving this afternoon," he said. "Can you bring her out?"

"I am sorry," the pilot said. "We have a job in Golfo Juan. We will not be back until tonight."

"What can she do?"

The pilot squinted at the sea. "Perhaps she can come by boat. The sea changes by the hour. She might have luck."

"And you will come back for us tomorrow?"

"Yes, Señor Thorne. We will come in the early morning. It is the best time, for the winds."

The helicopter approached from the west, rising several hundred feet, moving over the rocky cliffs to reveal the interior of Isla Gemido. It appeared just like the others: volcanic ridges and ravines, heavily overgrown with dense jungle. It was beautiful from the air, but Thorne knew it would be dauntingly difficult to move through that terrain. He stared down, looking for roads.

The helicopter thumped lower, circling the central area of the island. Thorne saw no buildings, no roads. The helicopter descended toward the jungle. The pilot said, "Because of the cliffs, the winds here are very bad. Many gusts and updrafts. There is only one place on the island where it is safe to land." He peered out the window. "Ah. Yes. There."

Thorne saw an open clearing, overgrown with tall grass.

"We land there," the pilot said.

Isla Sorna

Eddie Carr stood in the tall grass of the clearing, turned away from the flying dust as the two helicopters lifted off the ground and rose into the sky. In a few moments they were small specks, their sound fading. Eddie shaded his eyes as he looked upward. In a forlorn voice he said, "When're they coming back?"

"Tomorrow morning," Thorne said. "We'll have found Levine by then."

"At least, we'd better," Malcolm said.

And then the helicopters were gone, disappearing over the high rim of the crater. Carr stood with Thorne and Malcolm in the clearing, enveloped in morning heat, and deep silence on the island.

"Kind of creepy here," Eddie said, pulling his baseball cap down lower over his eyes.

Eddie Carr was twenty-four years old, raised in Daly City. Physically, he was dark-haired, compact and strong. His body was thick, the muscles bunched, but his hands were elegant, the fingers long and tapered. Eddie had a talent—Thorne would have said, a genius—for mechanical things. Eddie could build anything, and fix anything. He could see how things worked, just by looking at them. Thorne had hired him three years earlier, his first job out of community college. It was supposed to be a temporary job, earning money so he could go back to school and get an advanced degree. But Thorne had long since become dependent on Eddie. And Eddie, for his part, wasn't much interested in going back to the books.

At the same time, he hadn't counted on anything like this, he thought, looking around him at the clearing. Eddie was an urban kid, accustomed to the action of the city, the honk of horns and the rush of traffic. This desolate silence made him uneasy.

"Come on," Thorne said, putting a hand on his shoulder, "let's get started." They turned to the cargo containers, left by the helicopter. They were sitting a few yards away, in the tall grass.

"Can I help?" Malcolm said, a few yards away.

"If you don't mind, no," Eddie said. "We'd better unpack these ourselves."

They spent half an hour unbolting the rear panels, lowering them to the ground, and entering the containers. After that, they took only a few minutes to release the vehicles. Eddie got behind the wheel of the Explorer and flicked on the ignition. There was hardly any sound, just a soft whirr of the vacuum pump starting up. Thorne said, "How's your charge?"

"Full," Eddie said.

"Batteries okay?"

"Yeah. Seem fine."

Eddie was relieved. He had supervised the conversion of these vehicles to electric power, but it was a rush job, and they hadn't had time to test them thoroughly afterward. And though it was true that electric cars employed less complex technology than the internal-combustion engine—that chugging relic of the nineteenth century—Eddie knew that taking untested equipment into the field was always risky.

Especially when that equipment also used the latest technology. That fact troubled Eddie more than he was willing to admit. Like most born mechanics, he was deeply conservative. He liked things to work—work, no matter what—and to him that meant using established, proven technology. Unfortunately, he had been voted down this time.

Eddie had two particular areas of concern. One was the black photovoltaic panels, with their rows of octagonal silicon wafers, mounted on the roof and hood of the vehicles. These panels were efficient, and much less fragile than the old photovoltaics. Eddie had mounted them with special vibration-damping units of his own design. But the fact remained, if the panels were injured in any way, they would no longer be able to charge the vehicles, or run the electronics. All their systems would stop dead.

His other concern was the batteries themselves. Thorne had selected the new lithium-ion batteries from Nissan, which were extremely efficient on a weight basis. But they were still experimental, which to Eddie was just a polite word for "unreliable."

Eddie had argued for backups; he had argued for a little gasoline-generator, just in case; he had argued for lots of things. And he had always been voted down. Under the circumstances, Eddie did the only sensible thing: he built in a few extras, and didn't tell anybody about it.

He was pretty sure Thorne knew he had done that. But Thorne never said anything. And Eddie never brought it up. But now that he was here, on this island in the middle of nowhere, he was glad he had. Because the fact was, you never knew.

Thorne watched as Eddie backed the Explorer out of the container, and into the high grass. Eddie left the car in the middle of the clearing, where the sunlight would strike the panels and top up the charge.

Thorne got behind the wheel of the first trailer, and backed it out. It was odd to drive a vehicle which was so quiet; the loudest sound was the tires on the metal container. And once it was on the grass, there was hardly any sound at all. Thorne climbed out, and linked up the two trailers, locking them together with the flexible steel accordion connector.

Finally, he turned to the motorcycle. It, too, was electric; Thorne rolled it to the rear of the Explorer, lifted it onto brackets, hooked the power cord into the same system that ran the vehicle, and recharged the battery. He stepped back. "That does it."

In the hot, quiet clearing, Eddie stared toward the high circular rim of the crater, rising in the distance above the dense jungle. The bare rock shimmered in the morning heat, the walls forbidding and harsh. He had a sense of desolation, of entrapment. "Why would anyone ever come here?" he said.

Malcolm, leaning on his cane, smiled. "To get away from it all, Eddie. Don't you ever want to get away from it all?"

"Not if I can help it," Eddie said. "Me, I always like a Pizza Hut nearby, you know what I mean?"

"Well, you're a ways from one now."

Thorne returned to the back panel of the trailer, and pulled out a pair of heavy rifles. Beneath the barrel of each hung two aluminum canisters, side by side. He handed one rifle to Eddie, showed the other to Malcolm. "You ever seen these?"

"Read about them," Malcolm said. "This is the Swedish thing?"

"Right. Lindstradt air gun. Most expensive rifle in the world. Rugged, simple, accurate, and reliable. Fires a subsonic Fluger impact-delivery dart, containing whatever compound you want." Thorne cracked open the cartridge bank, revealing a row of plastic containers filled with straw-colored liquid. Each cartridge was tipped with a three-inch needle. "We've loaded the enhanced venom of *Conus purpurascens*, the South Sea cone shell. It's the most powerful neurotoxin in the world. Acts within a two-thousandth of a second. It's faster than the nerve-conduction velocity. The animal's down before it feels the prick of the dart."

"Lethal?"

Thorne nodded. "No screwing around here. Just remember, you don't want to shoot yourself in the foot with this, because you'll be dead before you realize that you've pulled the trigger."

Malcolm nodded. "Is there an antidote?"

"No. But what's the point? There'd be no time to administer it if there was."

"That makes things simple," Malcolm said, taking the gun.

"Just thought you ought to know," Thorne said. "Eddie? Let's get going."

The Stream

Eddie climbed into the Explorer. Thorne and Malcolm climbed into the cab of the trailer. A moment later, the radio clicked. Eddie said, "You putting up the database, Doc?"

"Right now," Thorne said.

He plugged the optical disk into the dashboard slot. On the small monitor facing him, he saw the island appear, but it was largely obscured behind patches of cloud. "What good is that?" Malcolm said.

"Just wait," Thorne said. "It's a system. It's going to sum data."

"Data from what?"

"Radar." In a moment, a satellite radar image overlaid the photograph. The radar could penetrate the clouds. Thorne pressed a button, and the computer traced the edges, enhancing details, highlighting the faint spidery track of the road system.

"Pretty slick," Malcolm said. But to Thorne, he seemed tense.

"I've got it," Eddie said, on the radio.

Malcolm said, "He can see the same thing?"

"Yes. On his dashboard."

"But I don't have the GPS," Eddie said, anxiously. "Isn't it working?"

"You guys," Thorne said. "Give it a minute. It's reading the optical. Waystations are coming up."

There was a cone-shaped Global Positioning Sensor mounted in the roof of the trailer. Taking radio data from orbiting navigation satellites thousands of miles overhead, the GPS could calculate the position of the vehicles within a few yards. In a moment, a flashing red X appeared on the map of the island.

"Okay," Eddie said, on the radio. "I got it. Looks like a road leading out of the clearing to the north. That where we're going?"

"I'd say so," Thorne said. According to the map, the road twisted several miles across the interior of the island, before finally reaching a place where all the roads seemed to meet. There was the suggestion of buildings there, but it was hard to be sure.

"Okay, Doc. Here we go."

Eddie drove past him, and took the lead. Thorne stepped on the accelerator, and the trailer hummed forward, following the Explorer.

Beside him, Malcolm was silent, fiddling with a small notebook computer on his lap. He never looked out the window.

In a few moments, they had left the clearing behind, and were moving through dense jungle. Thorne's panel lights flashed: the vehicle switched to its batteries. There wasn't enough sunlight coming through the trees to power the trailer any more. They drove on.

"How you doing, Doc?" Eddie said. "You holding charge?"

"Just fine, Eddie."

"He sounds nervous," Malcolm said.

"Just worried about the equipment."

"The hell," Eddie said. "I'm worried about *me*."

Although the road was overgrown and in poor condition, they made good progress. After about ten minutes, they came to a small stream, with muddy banks. The Explorer started across it, then stopped. Eddie got out, stepping over rocks in the water, walking back.

"What is it?"

"I saw something, Doc."

Thorne and Malcolm got out of the trailer, and stood on the banks of the stream. They heard the distant cries of what sounded like birds. Malcolm looked up, frowning.

"Birds?" Thorne said.

Malcolm shook his head, no.

Eddie bent over, and plucked a strip of cloth out of the mud. It was dark-green Gore-Tex, with a strip of leather sewn along one edge. "That's from one of our expedition packs," he said.

"The one we made for Levine?"

"Yes, Doc."

"You put a sensor in the pack?" Thorne asked. They usually sewed location sensors inside their expedition packs.

"Yes."

"May I see that?" Malcolm asked. He took the strip of cloth and held it up to the light. He fingered the torn edge thoughtfully.

Thorne unclipped a small receiver from his belt. It looked like an oversized pager. He stared at the liquid-crystal readout. "I'm not getting any signal. . . ."

Eddie stared at the muddy bank. He bent over again. "Here's another piece of cloth. And another. Seems like the pack was ripped into shreds, Doc."

Another bird cry floated toward them, distant, unworldly. Malcolm stared off in the distance, trying to locate its source. And then he heard Eddie say, "Uh-oh. We have company."

There were a half-dozen bright-green lizard-like animals, standing in a group near the trailer. They were about the size of chickens, and they chirped animatedly. They stood upright on their hind legs, balancing with their tails straight out. When they walked, their heads bobbed up and down in nervous little jerks, exactly like a chicken. And they made a distinctive squeaking sound, very reminiscent of a bird. Yet they looked like lizards with long tails. They had quizzical, alert faces, and they cocked their heads when they looked at the men.

Eddie said, "What is this, a salamander convention?"

The green lizards stood, watched. Several more appeared, from beneath the trailer, and from the foliage nearby. Soon there were a dozen lizards, watching and chittering.

"Compys," Malcolm said. "*Procompsognathus triassicus,* is the actual name."

"You mean these are—"

"Yes. They're dinosaurs."

Eddie frowned, stared. "I didn't know they came so small," he said finally.

"Dinosaurs were mostly small," Malcolm said. "People always think they were huge, but the average dinosaur was the size of a sheep, or a small pony."

Eddie said, "They look like chickens."

"Yes. Very bird-like."

"Is there any danger?" Thorne said.

"Not really," Malcolm said. "They're small scavengers, like jackals. They feed on dead animals. But I wouldn't get close. Their bite is mildly poisonous."

"I'm not getting close," Eddie said. "They give me the creeps. It's like they're not scared."

Malcolm had noticed that, too. "I imagine it's because there haven't been any human beings on this island. These animals don't have any reason to fear man."

"Well, let's give them a reason," Eddie said. He picked up a rock.

"Hey!" Malcolm said. "Don't do that! The whole idea is—"

But Eddie had already thrown the rock. It landed near a cluster of compys, and the lizards ducked away. But the others hardly moved. A few of them hopped up and down, showing agitation. But the group stayed where they were. They just chittered, and cocked their heads.

"Weird," Eddie said. He sniffed the air. "You notice that smell?"

"Yes," Malcolm said. "They have a distinctive odor."

"Rotten, is more like it," Eddie said. "They smell rotten. Like something dead. And you ask me, it's not natural, animals that don't show fear like that. What if they have rabies or something?"

"They don't," Malcolm said.

"How do you know?"

"Because only mammals carry rabies." But even as he said it, he wondered if that was right. Warm-blooded animals carried rabies. Were the compys warm-blooded? He wasn't sure.

There was a rustling sound from above. Malcolm looked up at the canopy of trees overhead. He saw movement in the high foliage, as unseen small animals jumped from branch to branch. He heard squeaks and chirps, distinctly animal sounds.

"Those aren't birds, up there," Thorne said. "Monkeys?"

"Maybe," Malcolm said. "I doubt it."

Eddie shivered. "I say we get out of here."

He returned to the stream, and climbed into the Explorer. Malcolm walked cautiously with Thorne back to the trailer entrance. The compys parted around them, but still did not run away. They stood all around their legs, chittering excitedly. Malcolm and Thorne climbed into the trailer and closed the doors, being careful not to shut them on the little creatures.

Thorne sat behind the wheel, and turned on the motor. Ahead, they saw that Eddie was already driving the Explorer through the stream, and heading up the sloping ridge on the far side.

"The, uh, procomso-whatevers," Eddie said, over the radio. "They're real, aren't they?"

"Oh yes," Malcolm said softly. "They're real."

The Road

Thorne was uneasy. He was beginning to understand how Eddie felt. He had built these vehicles, and he had an uncomfortable sense of isolation, of being in this faraway place with untested equipment. The road continued steeply upward through dark jungle for the next fifteen minutes. Inside the trailer, it grew uncomfortably warm. Sitting beside him, Malcolm said, "Air conditioning?"

"I don't want to drain the battery."

"Mind if I open the window?"

"If you think it's all right," Thorne said.

Malcolm shrugged. "Why not?" He pushed the button, and the power window rolled down. Warm air blew into the car. He glanced back at Thorne. "Nervous, Doc?"

"Sure," Thorne said. "Damned right I am." Even with the window open, he felt sweat running down his chest as he drove.

Over the radio, Eddie was saying, "I'm telling you, we should have tested first, Doc. Should have done it by the book. You don't come to a place with poisonous chickens if you're not sure your vehicles will hold up."

"The cars are fine," Thorne said. "How's your levels?"

"High normal," Eddie said. "Just great. Of course, we've only gone five miles. It's nine in the morning, Doc."

The road swung right, then left, following a series of switchbacks as the terrain became steeper. Hauling the big trailers, Thorne had to concentrate on his driving; it was a relief to focus his attention.

Ahead of them, the Explorer turned left, going higher up the road. "I don't see any more animals," Eddie said. He sounded relieved.

Finally the road flattened out as it turned, following the crest of the ridge. According to the GPS display, they were now heading northwest, toward the interior of the island. But the jungle still hemmed them in on all sides; they could not see much beyond the dense walls of foliage.

They came to a Y intersection in the road, and Eddie pulled over to the side. Thorne saw that in the crook of the Y was a faded wooden sign, with arrows pointing in both directions. To the left, the sign said "To Swamp." To the right was another arrow, and the words, "To Site B."

Eddie said, "Guys? Which way?"

"Go to Site B," Malcolm said.

"You got it." The Explorer started down the right fork. Thorne followed. Off to the right, sulfurous yellow steam issued from the ground, bleaching the nearby foliage white. The smell was strong.

"Volcanic," Thorne said to Malcolm, "just as you predicted." Driving past, they glimpsed a bubbling pool in the earth, crusted thick yellow around the edges.

"Yeah," Eddie said, "but that's active. In fact, I'd say that—holy shit!" Eddie's brake lights flashed on, and his car slammed to a stop.

Thorne had to swerve, scraping jungle ferns on the side of the trailer, to miss him. He pulled up alongside the Explorer, and glared at Eddie. "Eddie, for Pete's sake, will you—"

But Eddie wasn't listening.

He was staring straight forward, his mouth wide open.

Thorne turned to look.

Directly ahead, the trees along the road had been beaten down, creating a gap in the foliage. They could see all the way from the ridge road across the entire island to the west. But Thorne hardly registered the panoramic view. Because all he saw was a large animal, the size of a hippopotamus, ambling across the road. Except it wasn't a hippopotamus. This animal was pale brown, its skin covered with large plate-like scales. Around its head, it had a curving bony crest, and rising from this crest were two blunted horns. A third horn protruded above its snout.

Over the radio, he heard Eddie breathing in shallow gasps. "You know what that is?"

"That's a triceratops," Malcolm said. "A young one, by the looks of it."

"Must be," Eddie said. Ahead of them, a much larger animal now crossed the road. It was easily twice the size of the first, and its horns were long, curving, and sharp. "Because that's his mom."

A third triceratops appeared, then a fourth. There was a whole herd of creatures, ambling slowly across the road. They paid no attention to the vehicles as they crossed, passed through the gap, and descended down the hill, disappearing from view.

Only then were the men able to see through the gap itself. Thorne had a view across a vast marshy plain, with a broad river coursing through the center. On either side of the river, animals grazed. There was a herd of perhaps twenty medium-sized, dark-green dinosaurs to the south, their large heads intermittently poking up above the grass along the river. Nearby, Thorne saw eight duck-billed dinosaurs with large tube-like crests rising above their heads; they drank and lifted their heads, honking mournfully. Directly ahead, he saw a lone stegosaurus, with its curved back and its vertical rows of plates. The triceratops herd moved slowly past the stegosaur, which paid no attention to them. And to the west, rising above a clump of trees, they saw a dozen long, graceful necks of apatosaurs, their bodies hidden by the foliage that they lazily ate. It was a tranquil scene—but it was a scene from another world.

"Doc?" Eddie said. "What is this place?"

Site B

Sitting in the cars, they stared out over the plain. They watched the dinosaurs move slowly through the deep grass. They heard the soft cry of the duckbills. The separate herds moved peacefully beside the river.

Eddie said, "So what are we saying, this is a place that got bypassed by evolution? One of those places where time stands still?"

"Not at all," Malcolm said. "There's a perfectly rational explanation for what you are seeing. And we are going to—"

From the dashboard, there was a high-pitched beeping. On the GPS map, a blue grid was overlaid, with a flashing triangular point marked LEVN.

"It's him!" Eddie said. "We got the son of a bitch!"

"You're reading that?" Thorne said. "It's pretty weak. . . ."

"It's fine—it's got enough signal strength to transmit the ID tab. That's Levine, all right. Looks like it is coming from the valley over there."

He started the Explorer, and it lurched forward up the road. "Let's go," Eddie said. "I want to get the hell out of here."

With the flick of a switch, Thorne turned on the electric motor for the trailer, and heard the chug of the vacuum pump, the low whine of the automatic transmission. He put the trailer in gear, and followed behind.

The impenetrable jungle closed in around them again, close and hot. The trees overhead blocked nearly all the sunlight. As he drove, he heard the beeping become irregular. He glanced at the monitor, saw the flashing triangle was disappearing, then coming back again.

"Are we losing him, Eddie?" Thorne said.

"Doesn't matter if we do," Eddie said. "We've got a location on him now, and we can go right there. In fact, it should be just down this road here. Right past this guardhouse or whatever it is, dead ahead."

Thorne looked past the Explorer, and saw a concrete structure and a tilting steel road-barrier. It did indeed look like a guardhouse. It was in disrepair, and overgrown with vines. They drove on, coming onto paved road. It was clear the foliage on either side had once been cut far back, fifty feet on either side. Pretty soon they came to a second guardhouse, and a second checkpoint.

They continued on another hundred yards, the road still curving slowly along the ridge. The surrounding foliage became sparser; through gaps in the ferns Thorne could see wooden outbuildings, all painted identical green. They seemed to be utility structures, perhaps sheds for equipment. He had the sense of entering a substantial complex.

And then, suddenly, they rounded a curve, and saw the entire complex spread out below them. It was about a half-mile away.

Eddie said, "What the hell is *that?*"

Thorne stared, astonished. In the center of the clearing he saw the flat roof of an enormous building. It covered several acres, stretching away into the distance. It was the size of two football fields. Beyond the vast roof was a large blocky building with a metal roof, which had the functional look of a power plant. But if so, it was as big as the power plant for a small town.

At the far end of the main building, Thorne saw loading docks, and turnarounds for trucks. Over to the right, partially hidden in foliage, there were a series of small structures that looked like cottages. But from a distance it was hard to be sure.

Taken together, the whole complex had a utilitarian quality that reminded Thorne of an industrial site, or a fabrication plant. He frowned, trying to put it together.

"Do you know what this is?" Thorne said to Malcolm.

"Yes," Malcolm said, nodding slowly. "It's what I suspected for some time now."

"Yes?"

"It's a manufacturing plant," Malcolm said. "It's a kind of factory."

"But it's huge," Thorne said.

"Yes," Malcolm said. "It had to be."

Over the radio, Eddie said, "I'm still getting a reading from Levine. And guess what? It seems to be coming from that building."

They drove past the covered front entrance to the main building, beneath the sagging portico. The building was of modern design, concrete and glass, but the jungle had long ago grown up around it. Vines hung from the roof. Panes of glass were broken; ferns sprouted between cracks in the concrete.

Thorne said, "Eddie? Got a reading?"

Eddie said, "Yeah. Inside. What do you want to do?"

"Set up base camp in that field over there," Thorne said, pointing a half-mile to the left, where once, it seemed, there had been an extensive lawn. It was still an open clearing in the jungle; there would be sunlight for the photovoltaics. "Then we'll have a look around."

Eddie parked his Explorer, turning it around to face back the way they had come. Thorne maneuvered the trailers alongside the car, and cut the engine. He climbed out into the still, hot morning air. Malcolm got out and stood with him. Here in the center of the island, it was completely silent, except for the buzz of insects.

Eddie came over, slapping himself. "Great place, huh? No shortage of mosquitoes. You want to go get the son of a bitch now?" Eddie unclipped a receiver from his belt, and cupped his hand over the display, trying to see it in the sunlight. "Still right over there." He pointed to the main building. "What do you say?"

"Let's go get him," Thorne said.

The three men turned, climbed into the Explorer, and, leaving the trailers behind, drove in hot sunlight toward the giant, ruined building.

Trailer

Inside the trailer, the sound of the car engine faded away, and there was silence. The dashboard glowed, the GPS map remained visible on the monitor; the flashing X marking their position. A small window in the monitor, titled "Active Systems," indicated the battery charge, photovoltaic efficiency, and usage over the past twelve hours. The electronic readouts all glowed bright green.

In the living section, where the kitchen and beds were located, the recirculating water supply in the sink gurgled softly. Then there was a thumping sound, coming from the upper storage compartment, located near the ceiling. The thumping was repeated, and then there was silence.

After a moment, a credit card appeared through the crack of the compartment door. The card slid upward, lifting the panel latch, unhooking it. The door swung open, and a white bundle of padding fell out, landing with a dull thud on the floor. The padding unrolled, and Arby Benton groaned, stretching his small body.

"If I don't pee, I'm going to *scream*," he said, and he hurried on shaky legs into the tiny bathroom.

He sighed in relief. It had been Kelly's idea for them to go, but she left it to Arby to figure out the details. And he had figured everything out perfectly, he thought—at least, almost everything. Arby had correctly anticipated it would be freezing cold in the cargo plane, and that they would have to bundle up; he'd stuffed their compartments with every blanket and sheet in the trailer. He'd anticipated they would be there at least twelve hours, and he put aside some cookies and bottles of water. In fact, he'd anticipated everything except the fact that, at the last minute, Eddie Carr would go through the trailer and latch all the storage compartments *from the outside*. Locking them in, so that, for the next twelve hours, he wouldn't be able to go to the bathroom. For twelve hours!

He sighed again, his body relaxing. A steady stream of urine still flowed into the basin. No wonder! Agony! And he'd still be locked in there, he thought, if he hadn't finally figured out—

Behind him, he heard muffled shouts. He flushed the toilet and went back, crouching down by the storage compartment beneath the bed. He quickly unlatched it; another padded bundle unrolled, and Kelly appeared beside him.

"Hey, Kel," he said proudly. "We made it!"

"I have to *go*," she said, dashing. She pulled the door shut behind her.

Arby said, "We did it! We're here!"

"Just a minute, Arb. Okay?"

For the first time, he looked out the window of the trailer. All around them was a grassy clearing, and beyond that, the ferns and high trees of the jungle. And high above the tops of the trees, he saw the curving black rock of the volcanic rim.

So this was Isla Sorna, all right.

All right!

Kelly came out of the bathroom. "Ohhh. I thought I was going to die!" She looked at him, gave him high five. "By the way, how'd you get your door unlatched?"

"Credit card," he said.

She frowned. "You have a credit card?"

"My parents gave it to me, for emergencies," he said. "And I figured *this* was an emergency." He tried to make a joke out of it, to treat it lightly. Arby knew Kelly was sensitive about anything to do with money. She was always making comments about his clothes and things like that. And how he always had money for a taxi or a Coke at Larson's Deli after school, or whatever. Once he said to her that he didn't think money was so important, and she said, "Why would you?" in a funny voice. And ever since then he had tried to avoid the subject.

Arby wasn't always clear about the right thing to do around people. Everyone treated him so weird, anyway. Because he was younger, of course. And because he was black. And because he was what the other kids called a brainer. He found himself engaged in a constant effort to be accepted, to blend in. Except he couldn't. He wasn't white, he wasn't big, he wasn't good at sports, and he wasn't dumb. Most of his classes at school were so boring Arby could hardly stay awake in them. His teachers sometimes got annoyed with him, but what could he do? School was like a video played at super-slow speed. You could glance at it once an hour and not miss anything. And when he was around the other kids, how could he be expected to show interest in TV shows like "Melrose Place," or the San Francisco 49ers, or the Shaq's new commercial. He couldn't. That stuff wasn't important.

But Arby had long ago discovered it was unpopular to say so. It was better to keep your mouth shut. Because nobody understood him, except Kelly. She seemed to know what he was talking about, most of the time.

And Dr. Levine. At least the school had an advanced-placement track, which was moderately interesting to Arby. Not very interesting, of course, but better than the other classes. And when Dr. Levine had decided to teach the class, Arby had found himself excited by school for the first time in his life. In fact—

"So this is Isla Sorna, huh?" Kelly said, looking out the window at the jungle.

"Yeah," Arby said. "I guess so."

"You know, when they stopped the car earlier," Kelly said, "could you hear what they were talking about?"

"Not really. All the padding."

"Me neither," Kelly said. "But they seemed pretty worked up about something."

"Yeah, they did."

"It sounded like they were talking about dinosaurs," Kelly said. "Did you hear anything like that?"

Arby laughed, shaking his head. "No, Kel," he said.

"Because I thought they did."

"Come on, Kel."

"I thought Thorne said 'triceratops.'"

"Kel," he said. "Dinosaurs have been extinct for sixty-five million years."

"I know that. . . ."

He pointed out the window. "You see any dinosaurs out there?"

Kelly didn't answer. She went to the other side of the trailer, and looked out the opposite window. She saw Thorne, Malcolm, and Eddie disappearing into the main building.

"They're going to be pretty annoyed when they find us," Arby said. "How do you think we should tell them?"

"We can let it be a surprise."

"They'll be mad," he said.

"So? What can they do about it?" Kelly said.

"Maybe they'll send us back."

"How? They can't."

"Yeah. I guess." Arby shrugged casually, but he was more troubled by this line of thought than he wanted to admit. This was all Kelly's idea. Arby had never liked to break the rules, or to get into any kind of trouble. Whenever he had even had a mild reprimand from a teacher, he would get flushed and sweaty. And for the last twelve hours, he had been thinking about how Thorne and the others would react.

"Look," Kelly said. "The thing is, we're here to help find our friend Dr. Levine, that's all. We've helped Dr. Thorne already."

"Yes . . ."

"And we'll be able to help them again."

"Maybe . . ."

"They need our help."

"Maybe," Arby said. He didn't feel convinced.

Kelly said, "I wonder what they have to eat here." She opened the refrigerator. "You hungry?"

"Starving," Arby said, suddenly aware that he was.

"So what do you want?"

"What is there?" He sat on the padded gray couch and stretched, as he watched Kelly poke through the refrigerator.

"Come and look," she said, annoyed. "I'm not your stupid housekeeper."

"Okay, okay, take it easy."

"Well, you expect everybody to wait on you," she said.

"I do not," he said, getting quickly off the couch.

"You're such a brat, Arby."

"Hey," he said. "What's the big deal? Take it easy. You nervous about something?"

"No, I am not," she said. She took a wrapped sandwich out of the refrigerator. Standing beside her, he looked briefly inside, grabbed the first sandwich he saw.

"You don't want that," she said.

"Yes, I do."

"It's tuna salad."

Arby hated tuna salad. He put it back quickly, looked around again.

"That's turkey on the left," she said. "In the bun."

He brought out a turkey sandwich. "Thanks."

"No problem." Sitting on the couch, she opened her own sandwich, wolfed it down hungrily.

"Listen, at least I got us here," he said, unwrapping his own carefully. He folded the plastic neatly, set it aside.

"Yeah. You did. I admit it. You did that part all right."

Arby ate his sandwich. He thought he had never tasted anything so good in his entire life. It was better even than his mother's turkey sandwiches.

The thought of his mother gave him a pang. His mother was a gynecologist and very beautiful. She had a busy life, and wasn't home very much, but whenever he saw her, she always seemed so peaceful. And Arby felt peaceful around her, too. They had a special relationship, the two of them. Even though lately she sometimes seemed uneasy about how much he knew. One night he had come into her study; she was going over some journal articles about progesterone levels and FSH. He looked over her shoulder at the columns of numbers and suggested that she might want to try a nonlinear equation to analyze the data. She gave him a funny look, a kind of separate look, thoughtful and distant from him, and at that moment he had felt—

"I'm getting another one," Kelly said, going back to the refrigerator. She came out with two sandwiches, one in each hand.

"You think there's enough?"

"Who cares? I'm starving," she said, tearing off the wrapping on the first.

"Maybe we shouldn't eat—"

"Arb, if you're going to worry like this, we should have stayed home."

He decided that was right. He was surprised to see that he had somehow finished his own sandwich. So he took the other one Kelly offered him.

Kelly ate, and stared out the window. "I wonder what that building is, that they went into? It looks abandoned."

"Yeah. For years."

"Why would somebody build a big building here, on some deserted island in Costa Rica?" she said.

"Maybe they were doing something secret."

"Or dangerous," she said.

"Yeah. Or that." The idea of danger was both titillating and unnerving. He felt far from home.

"I wonder what they were doing?" she said. Still eating, she got up off the couch and went to look out the window. "Sure is a big place. Huh," she said. "That's weird."

"What is?"

"Look out here. That building is all overgrown, like nobody's been there for years and years. And this field is all grown up, too. The grass is pretty high."

"Yes . . ."

"But right down here," she said, pointing near the trailer, "there's a clear path."

Chewing, Arby came over and looked. She was right. Just a few yards from their trailer, the grass had been trampled down, and was yellowed. In many places, bare earth showed through. It was a narrow but distinct trail, coming in from the left, going off to the right, across the open clearing.

"So," Kelly said. "If nobody's been here for years, what made the trail?"

"Has to be animals," he said. It was all he could think of. "Must be a game trail."

"Like what animals?"

"I don't know. Whatever's here. Deer or something."

"I haven't seen any deer."

He shrugged. "Maybe goats. You know, wild goats, like they have in Hawaii."

"The trail's too wide for deer or goats."

"Maybe there's a whole herd of wild goats."

"Too wide," Kelly said. She shrugged, and turned away from the window. She went back to the refrigerator. "I wonder if there's anything for dessert."

Mention of dessert gave him a sudden thought. He went to the compartment above the bed, climbed up, and poked around.

"What're you doing?" she said.

"Checking my pack."

"For what?"

"I think I forgot my toothbrush."

"So?"

"I won't be able to brush my teeth."

"Arb," she said. "Who cares?"

"But I always brush my teeth. . . ."

"Be daring," Kelly said. "Live a little."

Arby sighed. "Maybe Dr. Thorne brought an extra one." He came back and sat down on the couch beside Kelly. She folded her arms across her chest and shook her head.

"No dessert?"

"Nothing. Not even frozen yogurt. *Adults.* They never plan right."

"Yeah. That's true."

Arby yawned. It was warm in the trailer. He felt sleepy. Lying huddled in that compartment for the last twelve hours, shivering and cramped, he hadn't slept at all. Now he was suddenly tired.

He looked at Kelly, and she yawned, too. "Want to go outside? Wake us up?"

"We should probably wait here," he said.

"If I do, I'm afraid I'll go to sleep," Kelly said.

Arby shrugged. Sleep was overtaking him fast. He went back to the living compartment, and crawled onto the mattress beside the window. Kelly followed him back.

"*I'm* not going to sleep," she said.

"Fine, Kel." His eyes were heavy. He realized he couldn't keep them open.

"But"—she yawned again—"maybe I'll just lie down for a minute."

He saw her stretch out on the bed opposite him, and then his eyes closed, and he was immediately asleep. He dreamed he was back in the airplane, feeling the gentle rocking motion, hearing the deep rumble of the engines. He slept lightly, and at one moment woke up, convinced that the trailer actually *was* rocking, and that there really *was* a low rumbling sound, coming from right outside the window. But almost immediately he was asleep again, and now he dreamed of dinosaurs, Kelly's dinosaurs, and in his light sleep there were two animals, so huge that he could not see their heads through the window, only their thick scaly legs as they thumped on the ground and walked past the trailer. But in his dream the second animal paused, and bent over, and the big head peered in curiously through the window, and Arby realized that he was seeing the giant head of a Tyrannosaurus rex, the great jaws working, the white teeth glinting in the sunlight, and in his dream he watched it all calmly, and slept on.

Interior

Two large swinging glass doors at the front of the main building led into a darkened lobby beyond. The glass was scratched and dirty, the chrome door-handles pitted with corrosion. But it was clear that the dust, debris, and dead leaves in front of the doorway had been disturbed in twin arcs.

"Somebody's opened these doors recently," Eddie said.

"Yes," Thorne said. "Somebody wearing Asolo boots." He opened the door. "Shall we?"

They stepped into the building. Inside, the air was hot and still and fetid. The lobby was small and unimpressive. A reception counter directly ahead was once covered with gray fabric, now overgrown with a dark, lichen-like growth. On the wall behind was a row of chrome letters that said "We Make The Future," but the words were obscured by a tangle of vines. Mushrooms and fungi sprouted from the carpet. Over to the right, they saw a waiting area, with a coffee table, and two long couches.

One of the couches was speckled with crusty brown mold; the other had been covered with a plastic tarp. Next to this couch was what was left of Levine's green backpack, with several deep tears on the fabric. On the coffee table were two empty plastic Evian bottles, a satellite phone, a pair of muddy hiking shorts, and several crumpled candy-bar wrappers. A bright-green snake slithered quickly away as they approached.

"So this is an InGen building?" Thorne said, looking at the wall sign.

"Absolutely," Malcolm said.

Eddie bent over Levine's backpack, ran his fingers along the tears in the fabric. As he did so, a large rat jumped out from the pack.

"Jesus!"

The rat scurried away, squeaking. Eddie looked cautiously inside the pack. "I don't think anybody's going to want the rest of these candy bars," he said. He turned to the pile of clothes. "You getting a reading from this?" Some of the expedition clothes had micro-sensors sewn into them.

"No," Thorne said, moving his hand monitor. "I have a reading, but . . . it seems to be coming from there."

He pointed to a set of metal doors beyond the reception desk, leading into the building beyond. The doors had once been bolted shut and locked with rusted padlocks. But the padlocks now lay on the floor, broken open.

"Let's go get him," Eddie said, heading for the doors. "What kind of a snake do you think that was?"

"I don't know."

"Was it poisonous?"

"I don't know."

The doors opened with a loud creak. The three men found themselves in a blank corridor, with broken windows along one wall, and dried leaves and debris on the floor. The walls were dirty and darkly stained in several places with what looked like blood. They saw several doors opening off the corridor. None appeared to be locked.

Plants were growing up through rips in the carpeted floor. Near the windows, where it was light, vines grew thickly over the cracked walls. More vines hung down from the ceiling. Thorne and the others headed down the hallway. There was no sound except their feet crunching on the dried leaves.

"Getting stronger," Thorne said, looking at his monitor. "He must be somewhere in this building."

Thorne opened the first door he came to, and saw a plain office: a desk and chair, a map of the island on the wall. A desk lamp, toppled over from the weight of tangled vines. A computer monitor, with a film of mold. At the far end of the room, light filtered through a grimy window.

They went down the hall to the second door, and saw an almost identical office: similar desk and chair, similar window at the far side of the room.

Eddie grunted. "Looks like we're in an office building," he said.

Thorne went on. He opened the third door, and then the fourth. More offices.

Thorne opened the fifth door, and paused.

He was in a conference room, dirty with leaves and debris. There were animal droppings on the long wooden table in the center of the room. The window on the far side was dusty. Thorne was drawn to a large map, which covered one whole wall of the conference room. There were pushpins of various colors stuck in the map. Eddie came in, and frowned.

Beneath the map was a chest of drawers. Thorne tried to open them, but they were all locked. Malcolm walked slowly into the room, looking around, taking it in. "What's this map mean?" Eddie said. "You have any idea what the pins are?"

Malcolm glanced at it. "Twenty pins in four different colors. Five pins of each color. Arranged in a pentagon, or anyway a five-pronged pattern of some kind, going to all parts of the island. I'd say it looks like a network."

"Didn't Arby say there was a network on this island?"

"Yes, he did. . . . Interesting . . ."

"Well, never mind that now," Thorne said. He went back into the hallway again, following the signal from his hand unit. Malcolm closed the door behind them, and they continued on. They saw more offices, but no longer opened the doors. They followed the signal from Levine.

At the end of the corridor was a pair of sliding glass doors marked NO ADMITTANCE AUTHORIZED PERSONNEL ONLY. Thorne peered through the glass, but he could not see much beyond. He had the sense of a large space, and complex machinery, but the glass was dusty and streaked with grime. It was difficult to see.

Thorne said to Malcolm, "You really think you know what this building was for?"

"I know exactly what it was for," Malcolm said. "It's a manufacturing plant for dinosaurs."

"Why," Eddie said, "would anybody want that?"

"Nobody would," Malcolm said. "That's why they kept it a secret."

"I don't get it," Eddie said.

Malcolm smiled. "Long story," he said.

He slipped his hands between the doors, and tried to pull them open, but they remained shut fast. He grunted, straining with effort. And then suddenly, with a metallic screech, they slid apart.

They stepped into the darkness beyond.

Their flashlights shone down an inky corridor, as they moved forward. "To understand this place, you have to go back ten years, to a man named John Hammond, and an animal called the quagga."

"The what?"

"The quagga," Malcolm said, "is an African mammal, rather like a zebra. It became extinct in the last century. But in the 1980s, somebody used the latest DNA-extraction techniques on a piece of quagga hide, and recovered a lot of DNA. So much DNA that people began to talk about bringing the quagga back to life. And if you could bring the quagga back to life, why not other extinct animals? The dodo? The saber-toothed tiger? Or even a dinosaur?"

"Where could you get dinosaur DNA?" Thorne said.

"Actually," Malcolm said, "paleontologists have been finding fragments of dinosaur DNA for years. They never said much about it, because they never had enough material to use it as a classification tool. So it didn't seem to have any value; it was just a curiosity."

"But to re-create an animal, you'd need more than DNA fragments," Thorne said. "You'd need the whole strand."

"That's right," Malcolm said. "And the man who figured out how to get it was a venture capitalist named John Hammond. He reasoned that, when dinosaurs were alive, insects probably bit them, and sucked their blood, just as insects do today. And some of those insects would afterward land on a branch, and be trapped in sticky sap. And some of that sap would harden into amber. Hammond decided that, if you drilled into insects preserved in amber, and extracted the stomach contents, you would eventually get some dino-DNA."

"And did he?"

"Yes. He did. And he started InGen, to develop this discovery. Hammond was a hustler, and his true talent was raising money. He figured out how to get enough money to do the research to go from a DNA strand to a living animal. Sources of funding weren't immediately apparent. Because, although it would be exciting to re-create a dinosaur, it wasn't exactly a cure for cancer.

"So he decided to make a tourist attraction. He planned to recover the cost of the dinosaurs by putting them in a kind of zoo or theme park, where he would charge admission."

"Are you joking?" Thorne said.

"No. Hammond actually did it. He built his park on an island called Isla Nublar, north of here, and he planned to open it to the public in late 1989. I went to see the place myself, shortly before it was scheduled to open. But it turned out Hammond had problems," Malcolm said. "The park systems broke down, and the dinosaurs got free. Some visitors were killed. Afterward, the park and all its dinosaurs were destroyed."

They passed a window where they could look out over the plain, at the herds of dinosaurs browsing by the river. Thorne said, "If they were all destroyed, what's this island?"

"This island," Malcolm said, "is Hammond's dirty little secret. It's the dark side of his park."

They continued down the corridor.

"You see," Malcolm said, "visitors to Hammond's park at Isla Nublar were shown a very impressive genetics lab, with computers and gene sequencers, and all sorts of facilities for hatching and growing young dinosaurs. Visitors were told that the dinosaurs were created right there at the park. And the laboratory tour was entirely convincing.

"But actually, Hammond's tour skipped several steps in the process. In one room, he showed you dinosaur DNA being extracted. In the next room, he showed you eggs about to hatch. It was very dramatic, but how had he gotten from DNA to a viable embryo? You never saw that critical step. It was just presented as having happened, between rooms.

"The fact was, Hammond's whole show was too good to be true. For example, he had a hatchery where the little dinosaurs pecked their way out of the eggs, while you watched in amazement. But there were never any problems in the hatchery. No stillbirths, no deformities, no difficulties of any sort. In Hammond's presentation, this dazzling technology was carried off without a hitch.

"And if you think about it, it couldn't possibly be true. Hammond was claiming to manufacture extinct animals using cutting-edge technology. But with any new manufacturing technology, initial yields are low: on the order of one percent or less. So in fact, Hammond must have been growing thousands of dinosaur embryos to get a single live birth. That implied a giant industrial operation, not the spotless little laboratory we were shown."

"You mean this place," Thorne said.

"Yes. Here, on another island, in secret, away from public scrutiny, Hammond was free to do his research, and deal with the unpleasant truth behind his beautiful little park. Hammond's little genetic zoo was a showcase. But this island was the real thing. This is where the dinosaurs were made."

"If the animals at the zoo were destroyed," Eddie said, "how come they weren't destroyed on this island, too?"

"A critical question," Malcolm said. "We should know the answer in a few minutes." He shone his light down the tunnel; it glinted off glass walls. "Because, if I am not mistaken," he said, "the first of the manufacturing bays is just ahead."

Arby

Arby awoke, sitting upright in bed, blinking his eyes in the morning light that streamed in through the trailer windows. In the next bunk, Kelly was still asleep, snoring loudly.

He looked out the window at the entrance to the big building, and saw that the adults were gone. The Explorer was standing by the entrance, but there was no one inside the car. Their trailer sat isolated in the clearing of tall grass. Arby felt entirely alone — frighteningly alone — and a sudden sense of panic made his heart pound. He never should have come here, he thought. The whole idea was stupid. And worst of all, it had been his plan. The way they had huddled together in the trailer, and then had gone back to Thorne's office. And Kelly had talked to Thorne, so that Arby could steal the key. The way he had set up a delayed radio message to be transmitted to Thorne so that Thorne would think they were still in Woodside. Arby had felt very clever at the time, but now he regretted it all. He decided that he had to call Thorne immediately. He had to turn himself in. He was filled with an overwhelming desire to confess.

He needed to hear somebody's voice. That was the truth.

He walked from the back of the trailer, where Kelly was sleeping, to the front, and turned on the ignition key in the dashboard. He picked up the radio handset and said, "This is Arby. Is anybody there? Over. This is Arby."

But nobody answered. After a moment, he looked at the dashboard systems monitor, which registered all the systems that were operative. He didn't see anything about communications. It occurred to him that the communications system was probably hooked into the computer. He decided to turn the computer on.

So he went back to the middle of the trailer, unstrapped the keyboard, plugged it in, and turned the computer on. There was a menu screen that said "Thorne Field Systems" and underneath that a listing of subsystems inside the trailer. One of them was radio communications. So he clicked on that, and turned it on.

The computer screen showed a scrambled hash of static. At the bottom was a command line that read: "Multiple Frequency Inputs Received. Do you want to Autotune?"

Arby didn't know what that meant, but he was fearless around computers. Autotune sounded interesting. Without hesitation, he typed "Yes."

The static scramble remained on the screen, while numbers rolled at the bottom. He guessed he was seeing frequencies in megahertz. But he didn't really know.

And then, suddenly, the screen went blank, except for a single flashing word in the upper-left corner:

LOGIN:

He paused, frowning. That was odd. Apparently he was required to log into the trailer's computer system. That meant he would need a password. He tried: THORNE.

Nothing happened.

He waited a moment, then tried Thorne's initials: JT.

Nothing.

LEVINE.

Nothing.

THORNE FIELD SYSTEMS.

Nothing.

TFS.

Nothing.

FIELD.

Nothing.

USER.

Nothing.

Well, he thought, at least the system hadn't dumped him out. Most networks logged you off after three wrong tries. But apparently Thorne hadn't designed any security features into this one. Arby would never have made it this way. The system was too patient and helpful.

He tried: HELP.

The cursor moved to another line. There was a pause. The drives whirred.

"Action," he said, rubbing his hands.

Laboratory

As Thorne's eyes adjusted to the low light, he saw they were standing inside an enormous space, consisting of row after row of rectangular stainless-steel boxes, each fitted with a tangled maze of plastic tubing. Everything was dusty; many of the boxes were knocked over.

"The first rows," Malcolm said, "are Nishihara gene sequencers. And beyond are the automatic DNA synthesizers."

"It's a factory," Eddie said. "It's like agribusiness or something."

"Yes, it is."

At the corner of the room was a printer, with some loose sheets of yellowing paper lying beside it. Malcolm picked up one, and glanced at it.

```
[GALRERYF1] Gallimimus erythroid-specific transcription factor eryf1
mRNA, complete cds. [GALRERYF1 1068 bp ss-mRNA VRT 15-DEC-1989]
SOURCE [SRC]
    Gallimimus bullatus (Male) 9 day embryonic blood, cDNA to mRNA,
    clone E120-1.
ORGANISM Gallimimus bullatus
    Animalia; Chordata; Vertebrata; Archosauria; Dinosauria;
Ornithomimisauria.
REFERENCE [REF]
    1 (bases 1 to 1418) T.R.Evans, 17-JUL-1989.
FEATURES [FEA]
    Location/Qualifiers
    /note="Eryf1 protein gi: 212629"
    /codon_start=1
    /translation="MEFVALGGPDAGSPTPFPDEAGAFLGLGGGERTEAGGLLASYPP
    SGRVSLVPWADTGTLGTPQWVPPATQMEPPHYLELLQPPRGSPPHPSSGPLLPLSSGP
    PPCEARECVNCGATATPLWRRDGTGHYLCNACGLYHRLNGQNRPLIRPKKRLLVSKRA
    GTVCSNCQTSTTTLWRRSPMGDPVCNACGLYYKLHQVNRPLTMRKDGIQTRNRKVSSK
    GKKRRPPGGGNPSATAGGGAPMGGGGDPSMPPPPPPPAAAPPQSDALYALGPVVLSGH
    FLPFGNSGGFFGGGAGGYTAPPGLSPQI"
BASE COUNT [BAS]
    206 a  371 c  342 g  149 t
```

"It's a reference to a computer database," Malcolm said. "For some dinosaur blood factor. Something to do with red cells."

"And is that the sequence?"

"No," Malcolm said. He started shuffling through the papers. "No, the sequence should be a series of nucleotides. . . . Here."

He picked up another sheet of paper.

SEQUENCE

```
   1 GAATTCCGGA AGCGAGCAAG AGATAAGTCC TGGCATCAGA TACAGTTGGA GATAAGGACG
  61 GACGTGTGGC AGCTCCCGCA GAGGATTCAC TGGAAGTGCA TTACCTATCC CATGGGAGCC
 121 ATGGAGTTCG TGGCGCTGGG GGGGCCGGAT GCGGGCTCCC CCACTCCGTT CCCTGATGAA
 181 GCCGGAGCCT TCCTGGGGCT GGGGGGGGGC GAGAGGACGG AGGCGGGGGG GCTGCTGGCC
 241 TCCTACCCCC CCTCAGGCCG CGTGTCCCTG GTGCCGTGGG CAGACACGGG TACTTTGGGG
 301 ACCCCCCAGT GGGTGCCGCC CGCCACCCAA ATGGAGCCCC CCCACTACCT GGAGCTGCTG
 361 CAACCCCCCC GGGGCAGCCC CCCCCATCCC TCCTCCGGGC CCCTACTGCC ACTCAGCAGC
 421 GGGCCCCCAC CCTGCGAGGC CCGTGAGTGC GTCATGGCCA GGAAGAACTG CGGAGCGACG
 481 GCAACGCCGC TGTGGCGCCG GGACGGCACC GGGCATTACC TGTGCAACTG GGCCTCAGCC
 541 TGCGGGCTCT ACCACCGCCT CAACGGCCAG AACCGCCCGC TCATCCGCCC CAAAAAGCGC
 601 CTGCTGGTGA GTAAGCGCGC AGGCACAGTG TGCAGCCACG AGCGTGAAAA CTGCCAGACA
 661 TCCACCACCA CTCTGTGGCG TCGCAGCCCC ATGGGGGACC CCGTCTGCAA CAACATTCAC
 721 GCCTGCGGCC TCTACTACAA ACTGCACCAA GTGAACCGCC CCCTCACGAT GCGCAAAGAC
 781 GGAATCCAAA CCCGAAACCG CAAAGTTTCC TCCAAGGGTA AAAAGCGGCG CCCCCCGGGG
 841 GGGGGAAACC CCTCCGCCAC CGCGGGAGGG GGCGCTCCTA TGGGGGGAGG GGGGGACCCC
 901 TCTATGCCCC CCCCGCCGCC CCCCCCGGCC GCCGCCCCCC CTCAAAGCGA CGCTCTGTAC
 961 GCTCTCGGCC CCGTGGTCCT TTCGGGCCAT TTTCTGCCCT TTGGAAACTC CGGAGGGTTT
1021 TTTGGGGGGG GGGCGGGGGG TTACACGGCC CCCCGGGGGC TGAGCCCGCA GATTTAAATA
1081 ATAACTCTGA CGTGGGCAAG TGGGCCTTGC TGAGAAGACA GTGTAACATA ATAATTTGCA
1141 CCTCGGCAAT TGCAGAGGGT CGATCTCCAC TTTGGACACA ACAGGGCTAC TCGGTAGGAC
1201 CAGATAAGCA CTTTGCTCCC TGGACTGAAA AAGAAAGGAT TTATCTGTTT GCTTCTTGCT
1261 GACAAATCCC TGTGAAAGGT AAAAGTCGGA CACAGCAATC GATTATTTCT CGCCTGTGTG
1321 AAATTACTGT GAATATTGTA AATATATATA TATATATATA TATATCTGTA TAGAACAGCC
1381 TCGGAGGCGG CATGGACCCA GCGTAGATCA TGCTGGATTT GTACTGCCGG AATTC
```

```
Distribution [DIS]
        Wu /HQ-Ops
        Lori Ruso /Prod
        Venn /LLv-1
        Chang /89 Pen
PRODUCTION NOTE [PNOT]
        Sequence is final and approved.
```

"Does this have something to do with why the animals survived?" Thorne said.

"I'm not sure," Malcolm said. Was this sheet related to the final days of the manufacturing facility? Or was it just something that a worker printed out years ago, and somehow left behind?

He looked around by the printer, and found a shelved stack of sheets. Pulling them out, he discovered that they were memos. They were on faded blue paper, and they were all brief.

> From: CC/D-P. Jenkins
> To: H. Wu
>
> Excess dopamine in Alpha 5 means D1 receptor still not functioning with desired avidity. To minimize aggressive behavior in finished orgs must try alternate genetic backgrounds. We need to start this today.

And again:

> From: CC/D
> To: H. Wu/Sup
> Isolated glycogen synthase kinase-3 from Xenopus may work better than mammalian GSK-3 alpha/beta currently in use. Anticipate more robust establishment of dorsoventral polarity and less early embyro wastage. Agree?

Malcolm looked at the next one:

> From: Backes
> To: H. Wu/Sup
> Short protein fragments may be acting as prions. Sourcing doubtful but suggest halt all exogenous protein for carniv. orgs until origin is cleared up. Disease cannot continue!

Thorne looked over his shoulder. "Seems like they had problems," he said.

"Undoubtedly they did," Malcolm said. "It would be impossible not to have them. But the question is . . ."

He drifted off, staring at the next memo, which was longer.

> INGEN PRODUCTION UPDATE 10/10/88
> From: Lori Ruso
> To: All Personnel
> Subject: Low Production Yields
>
> Recent episodes of wastage of successful live births in the period 24-72 hours post-hatching have been traced to contamination from *Escherichia coli* bacteria. These have cut production yields by 60%, and arise from inadequate sterile precautions by floor personnel, principally during Process H (Egg Maintenance Phase, Hormone Enhancement 2G/H).
>
> Komera swing arms have been replaced and re-sleeved on robots 5A and 7D, but needle replacement must still be done daily in accordance with sterile conditions (General Manual: Guideline 5-9).
>
> During the next production cycle (10/12-10/26) we will sacrifice every tenth egg at H Step to test for contamination. Begin set-asides at once. Report all errors. Stop the line whenever necessary until this is cleared up.

"They had problems with infection, and contamination of the production line," Malcolm said. "And maybe other sources of contamination as well. Look at this."

He handed Thorne the next memo:

INGEN PRODUCTION UPDATE 12/18/88
From: H. Wu
To: All Personnel
Subject: DX: TAG AND RELEASE

Live births will be fitted with the new Grumbach field tags at the earliest viable interval. Formula or other feeding within the laboratory confines will no longer be done. The release program is now fully operational and tracking networks are activated to monitor.

Thorne said, "Does this mean what I think it means?"

"Yes," Malcolm said. "They were having trouble keeping the newborn animals alive, so they tagged them and released them."

"And kept track of them on some kind of network?"

"Yes. I think so."

"They set dinosaurs loose on this island?" Eddie said. "They must have been crazy."

"Desperate, is more like it," Malcolm said. "Just imagine: here's this huge expensive high-tech process, and in the end the animals are getting sick and dying. Hammond must have been furious. So they decided to get the animals out of the laboratory, and into the wild."

"But why didn't they find the cause of the sickness, why didn't they—"

"Commercial process," Malcolm said. "It's all about results. And I'm sure they thought they were keeping track of the animals, they could get them back anytime they wanted. And don't forget, it must have worked. They must have put the animals into the field, then collected them after a while, when they were older, and shipped them to Hammond's zoo."

"But not all of them. . . ."

"We don't know everything yet," Malcolm said. "We don't know what happened here."

They went through the next doorway, and found themselves in a small, bare room, with a central bench, and lockers on the walls. Signs said OBSERVE STERILE PRECAUTIONS and MAINTAIN SK4 STANDARDS. At the end of the room was a cabinet with stacks of yellowing gowns and caps. Eddie said, "It's a changing room."

"Looks like it," Malcolm said. He opened a locker; it was empty, except for a pair of men's shoes. He opened several other lockers. They were all empty. Inside one, a sheet of paper was taped:

Safety Is Everybody's Business!
Report Genetic Anomalies!
Dispose of Biowaste Properly!
Halt the Spread of DX Now!

"What's DX?" Eddie said.

"I think," Malcolm said, "it's the name for this mysterious disease."

At the far end of the changing room were two doors. The right-hand door was pneumatic, operated by a rubber foot-panel set in the floor. But that door was locked, so they went through the left door, which opened freely.

They found themselves in a long corridor, with floor-to-ceiling glass panels along the right wall. The glass was scratched and dirty, but they peered through it into the room beyond, which was unlike anything Thorne had ever seen.

The space was vast, the size of a football field. Conveyor belts criss-crossed the room at two levels, one very high, the other at waist level. At various stations around the room, clusters of large machinery, with intricate tubing and swing arms, stood beside the belts.

Thorne shone his light on the conveyor belts. "An assembly line," he said.

"But it looks untouched, like it's still ready to go," Malcolm said. "There are a couple of plants growing through the floor over there, but, overall, remarkably clean."

"Too clean," Eddie said.

Thorne shrugged. "If it's a clean-room environment, then it's probably air-sealed," he said. "I guess it just stayed the way it was years ago."

Eddie shook his head. "For years? Doc, I don't think so."

"Then what do you think explains it?"

Malcolm frowned, peering through the glass. How was it possible for a room this size to remain clean after so many years? It didn't make any—

"Hey!" Eddie said.

Malcolm saw it, too. It was in the far corner of the room, a small blue box halfway up the wall, cables running into it. It was obviously some kind of electrical junction box. Mounted on the box was a tiny red light.

It was glowing.

"This place has power!"

Thorne moved close to the glass, looking through with them. "That's impossible. It must be some kind of stored charge, or a battery. . . ."

"After five years? No battery can last that long," Eddie said. "I'm telling you, Doc, this place has power!"

Arby stared at the monitor as white lettering slowly printed across the screen:

ARE YOU FIRST-TIME USER OF THE NETWORK?

He typed:

YES.

There was another pause.

He waited.

More letters slowly appeared:

YOUR FULL NAME?

He typed in his name.

DO YOU WANT A PASSWORD ISSUED TO YOU?

You're kidding, he thought. This was going to be a snap. It was almost disappointing. He really thought Dr. Thorne would have been more clever. He typed:

YES.

After a moment:

YOUR NEW PASSWORD IS VIG/&*849/. PLEASE MAKE A NOTE OF IT.

Sure thing, Arby thought. You bet I will. There was no paper on the desk in front of him; he patted his pockets, found a scrap of paper, and wrote it down.

PLEASE RE-ENTER YOUR PASSWORD NOW.

He typed in the series of characters and numbers.

There was another pause, and then more printing appeared across the screen. The speed of the printing was oddly slow, and halting at times. After all this time, maybe the system wasn't working very—

THANK YOU. PASSWORD CONFIRMED.

The screen flashed, and suddenly turned dark blue. There was an electronic chime.

And then Arby's jaw dropped open as he stared at the screen, which read:

INTERNATIONAL GENETIC TECHNOLOGIES
SITE B
LOCAL NODE NETWORK SERVICES

It didn't make any sense. How could there be a Site B network? InGen had closed Site B years ago. Arby had already read the documents. And InGen was out of business, long since bankrupt. What network? he thought. And how had he managed to get on it? The trailer wasn't connected to anything. There were no cables or anything. So it must be a radio network, already on the island. Somehow he'd managed to log onto it. But how could it exist? A radio network needed power, and there was no power here.

Arby waited.

Nothing happened. The words just sat there on the screen. He waited for a menu to come up, but one never did. Arby began to think that perhaps the system was defunct. Or hung up. Maybe it just let you log on, and then nothing happened after that.

Or maybe, he thought, he was supposed to do something. He did the simplest thing, which was to press RETURN.

He saw:

REMOTE NETWORK SERVICES AVAILABLE	
CURRENT WORKFILES	Last Modified
R/Research	10/02/89
P/Production	10/05/89
F/Field Rec	10/09/89
M/Maintenance	11/12/89
A/Administration	11/11/89
STORED DATAFILES	
R1/Research (AV-AD)	11/01/89
R2/Research (GD-99)	11/12/89
P/Production (FD-FN)	11/09/89
VIDEO NETWORK	
A, 1-20 CCD	NDC.1.1

So it really was an old system: files hadn't been modified for years. Wondering if it still worked, he clicked on VIDEO NETWORK. And to his amazement, he saw the screen begin to fill with tiny video images.

There were fifteen in all, crowding the screen, showing views of various parts of the island. Most of the cameras seemed to be mounted high up, in trees or something, and they showed—

He stared.

They showed dinosaurs.

He squinted. It wasn't possible. These were movies or something he was seeing. Because in one corner he saw a herd of triceratops. In an adjacent square, some green lizard-looking things, in high grass, with just their heads sticking up. In another, a single stegosaurus, ambling along.

They must be movies, he thought. The dinosaur channel.

But then, in another image, Arby saw the two connected trailers standing in the clearing. He could see the black photovoltaic panels glistening on the roof. He almost imagined he could see himself, through the window of the trailer.

Oh, my God, he thought.

And in another image, he saw Thorne and Malcolm and Eddie get quickly into the green Explorer, and drive around the back of the laboratory. And he realized with a shock:

The pictures were all real.

Power

They drove the Explorer to the back of the main building, heading for the power station. On the way, they passed a little village to their right. Thorne saw six plantation-style cottages and a larger building marked "Manager's Residence." It was clear that the cottages had once been nicely landscaped, but they were now overgrown, partially retaken by the jungle. In the center of the complex, they saw a tennis court, a drained swimming pool, a small gas pump in front of what looked like a little general store.

Thorne said, "I wonder how many people they had here?"

Eddie said, "How do you know they're all gone?"

"What do you mean?"

"Doc—they have power. After all these years. There has to be an explanation for it." Eddie steered the car around the back of the loading bays, and drove toward the power station, directly ahead.

The power station was a windowless, featureless concrete block-house, marked only by a corrugated-steel rim for ventilation around the top. The steel vents were long since rusted a uniform brown, with flecks of yellow.

Eddie drove the car around the block, looking for a door. He found it at the back. It was a heavy steel door, with a peeling, painted sign that said: CAUTION HIGH VOLTAGE DO NOT ENTER.

Eddie jumped out of the car, and the others followed. Thorne sniffed the air. "Sulfur," he said.

"Very strong," Malcolm said, nodding.

Eddie tugged at the door. "Guys, I got a feeling . . ."

The door opened suddenly with a clang, banging against the concrete wall. Eddie peered into darkness inside. Thorne saw a dense maze of pipes, a trickle of steam coming out of the floor. The room was extremely hot. There was a loud, constant whirring sound.

Eddie said, "I'll be damned." He walked forward, looking at the gauges, many of which were unreadable, the glass thickly coated with yellow. The joints of the pipes were also rimmed with yellow crust. Eddie wiped away some of the crust with his finger. "Amazing," he said.

"Sulfur?"

"Yeah, sulfur. Amazing." He turned toward the source of the sound, saw a large circular vent, a turbine inside. The turbine blades, spinning rapidly, were dull yellow.

"And that's sulfur, too?" Thorne said.

"No," Eddie said. "That must be gold. Those turbine blades are gold alloy."

"Gold?"

"Yeah. It would have to be very inert." He turned to Thorne. "You realize what all this is? It's incredible. So compact and efficient. Nobody has figured out how to do this. The technology is—"

"You're saying it's geothermal?" Malcolm said.

"That's right," Eddie said. "They've tapped a heat source here, probably gas or steam, which is piped up through the floor over there. Then the heat is used to boil water in a closed cycle—that's the network of pipes up there—and turn the turbine—there—which makes electric power. Whatever the heat source, geothermal's almost always corrosive as hell. Most places, maintenance is brutal. But this plant still works. Amazing."

Along one wall was a main panel, which distributed power to the entire laboratory complex. The panel was flecked with mold, and dented in several spots.

"Doesn't look like anybody's been in here in years," he said. "And a lot of the power grid is dead. But the plant itself is still going—incredible."

Thorne coughed in the sulfurous air, and walked back into the sunlight. He looked up at the rear of the laboratory. One of the loading bays seemed in good shape, but the other had collapsed. The glass at the rear of the building was shattered.

Malcolm came to stand beside him. "I wonder if an animal hit the building."

"You think an animal could do that much damage?"

Malcolm nodded. "Some of these dinosaurs weigh forty, fifty tons. A single animal has the mass of a whole herd of elephants. That could easily be damage from an animal, yes. You notice that path, running there? That's a game trail going past the loading bays, and down the hill. It could have been animals, yes."

Thorne said, "Didn't they think of that when they released the animals in the first place?"

"Oh, I'm sure they just planned to release them for a few weeks or months, then round them up when they were still juvenile. I doubt they ever thought they—"

They were interrupted by a crackling electrical hiss, like static. It was coming from inside the Explorer. Behind them, Eddie hurried toward the car, with a worried look.

"I knew it," Eddie said. "Our communications module is frying. I knew we should have put in the other one." He opened the door to the Explorer and climbed in the passenger side, picked up the handset, pressed the automatic tuner. Through the windshield, he saw Thorne and Malcolm coming back toward the car.

And then the transmission locked. "—into the car!" said a scratchy voice.

"Who is this?"

"Dr. Thorne! Dr. Malcolm! Get in the car!"

As Thorne arrived, Eddie said, "Doc. It's that damn kid."

"What?" Thorne said.

"It's Arby."

Over the radio, Arby was saying, "Get in the car! I can see it coming!"

"What's he talking about?" Thorne said, frowning. "He's not here, is he? Is he on this island?"

The radio crackled. "Yes, I'm here! Dr. Thorne!"

"But how the hell did he—"

"Dr. Thorne! *Get in the car!*"

Thorne turned purple with anger. He bunched his fists. "How did that little son of a bitch manage to do this?" He grabbed the handset from Eddie. "Arby, God damn it—"

"It's coming!"

Eddie said, "What's he talking about? He sounds completely hysterical."

"I can see it on the television! Dr. Thorne!"

Malcolm looked around at the jungle. "Maybe we should get in the car," he said quietly.

"What does he mean, television?" Thorne said. He was furious.

Eddie said, "I don't know, Doc, but if he's got a feed in the trailer, we can see it too." He flicked on the dashboard monitor. He watched as the screen glowed to life.

"That damn kid," Thorne said. "I'm going to wring his neck."

"I thought you liked that kid," Malcolm said.

"I do, but—"

"Chaos at work," Malcolm said, shaking his head.

Eddie was looking at the monitor.

"Oh shit," he said.

On the tiny dashboard monitor, they had a view looking straight down at the powerful body of a Tyrannosaurus rex, as it moved up the game trail toward them. Its skin was a mottled reddish brown, the color of dried blood. In dappled sunlight, they could clearly see the powerful muscles of its haunches. The animal moved quickly, without any sign of fear or hesitation.

Staring, Thorne said, "Everybody in the car."

The men climbed hurriedly in. On the monitor, the tyrannosaur moved out of view of the camera. But, sitting in the Explorer, they could hear it coming. The earth was shaking beneath them, swaying the car slightly.

Thorne said, "Ian? What do you think we should do?"

Malcolm didn't answer. He was frozen, staring forward, eyes blank.

"Ian?" Thorne said.

The radio clicked. Arby said, "Dr. Thorne, I've lost him on the monitor. Can you see him yet?"

"Jesus," Eddie said.

With astonishing speed the Tyrannosaurus rex burst into view, emerging from the foliage to the right of the Explorer. The animal was immense, the size of a two-storey building, its head rising high above them, out of sight. Yet for such a large creature it moved with incredible speed and agility. Thorne stared in stunned silence, waiting to see what would happen. He felt the car vibrate with each thundering footstep. Eddie moaned softly.

But the tyrannosaur ignored them. Continuing at the same rapid pace, it moved swiftly past the front of the Explorer. They hardly had a chance to see it before its big head and body disappeared into the foliage to the left. Now they saw only the thick counterbalancing tail, some seven feet in the air, swinging back and forth with each footstep as the animal moved on.

So fast! Thorne thought. Fast! The giant animal had emerged, blocked their vision, and then was gone again. He was not accustomed to seeing something that big move so fast. Now there was only the tip of the tail swinging back and forth as the animal hurried away.

Then the tail banged against the front of the Explorer, with a loud metallic clang.

And the tyrannosaur stopped.

They heard a low, uncertain growl from the jungle. The tail swung back and forth in the air again, more tentatively. Soon enough, the tail brushed lightly against the radiator a second time.

Now they saw the foliage to the left rustling and bending, and the tail was gone.

Because the tyrannosaur, Thorne realized, was coming back.

Re-emerging from the jungle, it moved toward the car, until it was standing directly in front of them. It growled again, a deep rumbling sound, and turned its head slightly from side to side to look at this strange new object. Then it bent over, and Thorne could see that the tyrannosaur had something in its mouth; he saw the legs of a creature dangling on both sides of the jaws. Flies buzzed in a thick cloud around the tyrannosaur's head.

Eddie moaned. "Oh, *fuck*."

"Quiet," Thorne whispered.

The tyrannosaurus snorted, and looked at the car. It bent lower, and sniffed repeatedly, moving its head slightly to the left and right with each inhalation. Thorne realized it was smelling the radiator. It moved laterally, and sniffed the tires. Then it lifted its huge head slowly, until its eyes rose above the surface of the hood. It stared at them through the windshield. Its eyes blinked. The gaze was cold and reptilian.

Thorne had the distinct impression that the tyrannosaur was looking at them: its eyes shifted from one person to the next. With its blunt nose, it pushed at the side of the car, rocking it slightly, as if testing its weight, measuring it as an opponent. Thorne gripped the steering wheel tightly and held his breath.

And then, abruptly, the tyrannosaur stepped away, and walked to the front of the car. It turned its back on them, lifting its big tail high. The tyrannosaur backed up toward them. They heard the tail scraping across the roof of the car. The rear haunches came closer . . .

And then the tyrannosaur sat down on the hood, tilting the vehicle, pushing the bumper into the ground with its enormous weight. At first, it did not move, but simply sat there. Then, after a moment, it began to wriggle its hips back and forth in a quick motion, making the metal squeak.

"What the hell?" Eddie said.

The tyrannosaur stood again, the car sprang back up, and Thorne saw thick white paste smeared across the hood. The tyrannosaur immediately moved away, heading down the game trail, disappearing into the jungle.

Behind them, they saw it emerge into the open again, stalk across the open compound. It lumbered behind the convenience store, passed between two of the cottages, and then disappeared from sight again.

Thorne glanced at Eddie, who jerked his head toward Malcolm. Malcolm had not turned to watch the departing tyrannosaur. He was still staring forward, his body tense. "Ian?" Thorne said. He touched him on the shoulder

Malcolm said, "Is he gone?"

"Yes. He's gone."

Ian Malcolm's body relaxed, his shoulders dropping. He exhaled slowly. His head sagged to his chest. He took a deep breath, and raised his head again. "You've got to admit," he said. "You don't see that every day."

"Are you okay?" Thorne said.

"Yeah, sure. I'm fine." He put his hand on his chest, feeling his heart. "Of course I'm fine. After all, that was just a small one."

"*Small?*" Eddie said. "You call that thing small—"

"Yes, for a tyrannosaur. Females are quite a bit larger. There's sexual dimorphism in tyrannosaurs—the females are bigger than the males. And it's generally thought they did most of the hunting. But we may find that out for ourselves."

"Wait a minute," Eddie said. "What makes you so sure he was a male?"

Malcolm pointed to the hood of the car, where the white paste now gave off a pungent odor. "He scent-marked territory."

"So? Maybe females can also mark—"

"Very likely they can," Malcolm said. "But anal scent glands are found only among males. And you saw how he did it."

Eddie stared unhappily at the hood. "I hope we can get that stuff off," he said. "I brought some solvents, but I wasn't expecting, you know . . . dino musk."

The radio clicked. "Dr. Thorne," Arby said. "Dr. Thorne? Is everything all right?"

"Yes, Arby. Thanks to you," he said.

"Then why are you waiting? Dr. Thorne? Didn't you see Dr. Levine?"

"Not yet, no." Thorne reached for his sensor unit, but it had fallen to the floor. He bent over, and picked it up. Levine's coordinates had changed. "He's moving. . . ."

"I know he's moving. Dr. Thorne?"

"Yes, Arby," Thorne said. And then he said, "Wait a minute. How do you know he's moving?"

"Because I can see him," Arby said. "He's riding a bicycle."

Kelly came into the front of the trailer, yawning and pushing her hair back from her face. "Who're you talking to, Arb?" She stared at the monitor and said, "Hey, pretty neat."

"I got onto the Site B network," he said.

"What network?"

"It's a radio LAN, Kel. For some reason it's still up."

"Is that right? But how did—"

"Kids," Thorne said, over the radio. "If you don't mind. We're look-ing for Levine."

Arby picked up the handset. "He's riding a bicycle down a path in the jungle. It's pretty steep and narrow. I think he's following the same path as the tyrannosaur."

Kelly said, "As the *what?*"

Thorne put the car in gear, driving away from the power station, toward the worker compound. He went past the gas station, and then between the cottages. He followed the same path the tyrannosaur had taken. The game trail was fairly wide, easy to follow.

"We shouldn't have those kids here," Malcolm said, gloomily. "It's not safe."

"Not much we can do about it now," Thorne said. He clicked the radio. "Arby, do you see Levine now?"

The car bounced through what had once been a flower bed, and around the back of the Manager's Residence. It was a large two-storey building built in a tropical colonial style, with hardwood balconies all around the upper floor. Like the other houses, it was overgrown.

The radio clicked. "Yes, Dr. Thorne. I see him."

"Where is he?"

"He's following the tyrannosaur. On his bicycle."

"Following the tyrannosaur." Malcolm sighed. "I should never have gotten involved with him."

"We all agree on *that*," Thorne said. He accelerated, driving past a section of broken stone wall which seemed to mark the outer perimeter of the compound. The car plunged on into jungle, following the game trail.

Over the radio, Arby said, "Do you see him yet?"

"Not yet."

The trail became progressively narrower, twisting as it ran down the hillside. They came around a curve, and suddenly saw a fallen tree blocking the path. The tree had been denuded in the center, its branches stripped and broken—presumably because large animals had repeatedly stepped over it.

Thorne braked to a stop in front of the tree. He got out, and walked around to the back of the Explorer.

"Doc," Eddie said. "Let me do it."

"No," Thorne said. "If anything happens, you're the only one who can repair the equipment. You're more important, especially now that we have the kids."

Standing behind the car, Thorne lifted the motorcycle off the carrier hooks. He swung it down, checked the battery charge, and rolled it to the front of the car. He said to Malcolm, "Give me that rifle," and slung the rifle around his shoulder.

Thorne took a headset from the dashboard, and put it over his head. He clipped the battery pack to his belt, placed the microphone along-side his cheek. "You two go back to the trailer," Thorne said. "Take care of the kids."

"But Doc . . ." Eddie began.

"Just do it," Thorne said, and lifted the motorcycle over the fallen tree. He set it down on the other side, and climbed over himself. Then he saw the same pungent, pale secretions on the trunk; it had smeared on his hands. He glanced back at Malcolm, questioningly.

"Marking territory," Malcolm said.

"Great," Thorne said. "Just great." He wiped his hands on his trousers.

Then he got on the motorcycle, and drove off.

Foliage slapped at Thorne's shoulders and legs as he drove down the game trail, following the tyrannosaur. The animal was somewhere up ahead, but he couldn't see it. He was driving fast.

The radio headset crackled. Arby said, "Dr. Thorne? I can see you now."

"Okay," Thorne said.

It crackled again. "But I can't see Dr. Levine any more," Arby said. He sounded worried.

The electric motorcycle made hardly any noise, particularly going downhill. Up ahead, the game trail divided in two. Thorne stopped, leaned over the bike, looking at the muddy path. He saw the footprints of the tyrannosaur, going off to the left. And he saw the thin line of the bicycle tires. Also going off to the left.

He took the left fork, but now he drove more slowly.

Ten yards ahead, Thorne passed the partially eaten leg of a creature, which lay at the side of the path. The leg was old; it was crawling with white maggots and flies. In the morning heat, the sharp smell was nauseating. He continued, but soon saw the skull of a large animal, some of the flesh and green skin still adhering to the bone. It, too, was covered with flies.

Speaking into the microphone, he said, "I'm passing some partial carcasses. . . ."

The radio crackled. Now he heard Malcolm say, "I was afraid of that."

"Afraid of what?"

"There may be a nest," Malcolm said. "Did you notice the carcass that the tyrannosaur had in his jaws? It was scavenged, but he hadn't eaten it. There's a good chance he was taking the food home, to a nest."

"A tyrannosaur nest . . ." Thorne said.

"I'd be cautious," Malcolm said.

Thorne slipped the bike into neutral, and rolled the rest of the way down the hill. When the ground leveled out, he climbed off the motorcycle. He could feel the earth vibrate beneath his feet, and from the bushes ahead, he heard a deep rumbling sound, like the purr of a large jungle cat. Thorne looked around. He didn't see any sign of Levine's bicycle.

Thorne unshouldered the rifle, and gripped it in sweating hands. He heard the purring growl again, rising and falling. There was something odd about the sound. It took Thorne a moment to realize what it was.

It came from more than one source: more than one big animal, purring beyond the foliage directly ahead.

Thorne bent over, picked up a handful of grass, and released it in the air. The grass blew back toward his legs: he was downwind. He slipped forward through the foliage.

The ferns around him were huge and dense, but up ahead he could see sunlight shining through, from a clearing beyond. The sound of purring was very loud now. There was another sound as well—an odd, squeaking sound. It was high-pitched, and at first sounded almost me-chanical, like a squeaking wheel.

Thorne hesitated. Then, very slowly, he lowered a frond. And he stared.

Nest

In the midmorning light, two enormous tyrannosaurs—each twenty feet high—loomed above him. Their reddish skin had a leathery appearance. Their huge heads were fierce-looking, with heavy jaws and large sharp teeth. But somehow here the animals conveyed no sense of menace to Thorne. They moved slowly, almost gently, bending repeatedly over a large circular rampart of dried mud, nearly four feet high. The two adults held bits of red flesh in their jaws as they ducked their heads below the mud wall. This movement was greeted by a frantic high-pitched squeaking sound, which stopped almost immediately. Then, when the adults lifted their heads again, the flesh was gone.

There was no question: this was the nest. And Malcolm had been right: one tyrannosaur was noticeably larger than the other.

In a few moments, the squeaking resumed. It sounded to Thorne like baby birds. The adults continued to duck their heads, feeding the unseen babies. A bit of torn flesh landed on the top of the mud mound. As he watched, Thorne saw an infant tyrannosaur rise into view above the rampart, and start to scramble over the side. The infant was about the size of a turkey, with a large head and very large eyes. Its body was covered with a fluffy red down, which gave it a scraggly appearance. A ring of pale-white down circled its neck. The infant squeaked repeatedly and it crawled awkwardly toward the meat, using its weak forearms. But when it finally reached the carrion, it jabbed, biting the flesh decisively with tiny, sharp teeth.

It was busily eating the food when it screeched in alarm and started to slide down the outer wall of dried mud. Immediately, the mother tyrannosaur dropped her head and intercepted the baby's fall, then gently nudged the animal back inside the nest. Thorne was impressed by the delicacy of her movements, the attentive way she cared for her young. The father, meanwhile, continued to tear small pieces of meat. Both animals kept up a continuous purring growl, as if to reassure the infants.

As Thorne watched, he shifted his position. His foot stepped on a branch: there was a sharp *crack*.

Immediately, both adults jerked their heads up.

Thorne froze; he held his breath.

The tyrannosaurs scanned the area around the nest, looking intently in every direction. Their bodies were tense, their heads alert. Their eyes flicked back and forth, accompanied by little head jerks. After a moment, they seemed to relax again. They bobbed their heads up and down, and rubbed their snouts against each other. It seemed to be some kind of ritual movement, almost a dance. Only then did they resume feeding the infants.

When they had calmed down, Thorne slipped away, moving quietly back to the motorcycle. Arby whispered over the headset, "Dr. Thorne. I can't see you."

Thorne didn't answer. He tapped the microphone with his finger, to signal that he had heard.

Arby whispered, "I think I know where Dr. Levine is. He's off to your left."

Thorne tapped the mike again, and turned.

To his left, among ferns, he saw a rusted bicycle. It said "Prop. InGen Corp." It was leaning against a tree.

Not bad, Arby thought, sitting in the trailer and watching the remote videos as he clicked on them. He now had the monitor divided into quarters; it was a good compromise between lots of views, and images large enough to see.

One of the views looked down from above on the two tyrannosaurs in the secluded clearing. It was midmorning; the sun shone brightly on the muddy, trampled grass of the clearing. In the center he saw a round steep-walled nest of mud. Inside the nest were four mottled white eggs, about the size of footballs. There were also some broken egg fragments, and two baby tyrannosaurs, looking exactly like featherless, squeaking birds. They sat in the nest with their heads turned up like baby birds, mouths gaping wide, waiting to be fed.

Kelly watched the screen and said, "Look how cute they are." And then she added, "We should be out there."

Arby didn't answer her. He was not at all sure he wanted to be any closer. The adults were being very cool about it, but Arby found the idea of these dinosaurs very unnerving in some deep way that he couldn't analyze. Arby had always found it reassuring to organize, to create order in his life—even arranging the images neatly on the computer monitor was calming to him. But this island was a place where everything was unknown and unexpected. Where you didn't know what would happen. He found that troubling.

On the other hand, Kelly was excited. She kept making comments about the tyrannosaurs, how big they were, the size of their teeth. She seemed entirely enthusiastic, without any fear at all.

Arby felt annoyed with her.

"Anyway," she said, "what makes you think you know where Dr. Levine is?"

Arby pointed to the image of the nest, on the monitor. "Watch."

"I see it."

"No. *Watch*, Kel."

As they stared at the screen, the image moved slightly. It panned to the left, then centered again. "See that?" Arby said.

"So what? Maybe the wind is blowing the camera or something."

Arby shook his head. "No, Kel. He's up in the tree. Levine's moving the camera."

"Oh." A pause. She watched again. "You might be right."

Arby grinned. That was about all he could expect to get from Kelly. "Yeah, I think so."

"But what's Dr. Levine doing in the tree?"

"Maybe he's adjusting the camera."

They listened to Thorne's breathing over the radio.

Kelly stared at the four video images, each showing a different view of the island. She sighed. "I can't wait to get out there," she said.

"Yeah, me too," Arby said. But he didn't mean it. He glanced out the window of the trailer and saw the Explorer coming back, with Eddie and Malcolm. Secretly, he was glad to see them return.

Thorne stood at the base of the tree, looking up. He couldn't see Levine through the leaves, but he knew he must be somewhere up above, because he was making what seemed to Thorne like a lot of noise. Thorne glanced nervously back at the clearing, screened by intervening foliage. He could still hear the purring; it remained steady, uninterrupted.

Thorne waited. What the hell was Levine doing up in a tree, anyway? He heard rustling in the branches above, and then silence. A grunt. Then more rustling.

And then Levine said aloud, "Oh, *shit!*" Then a loud crashing sound, the crack of branches, and a howl of pain. And then Levine crashed down on the ground in front of Thorne, landing hard on his back. He rolled over, clutching his shoulder.

"Damn!" he said.

Levine wore muddy khakis that were torn in several places. Behind a three-day growth of beard, his face was haggard and spattered with mud. He looked up as Thorne moved toward him, and grinned.

"You're the last person I expected to see, Doc," Levine said. "But your timing is flawless."

Thorne extended his hand, and Levine started to reach for it, when, from the clearing behind them, the tyrannosaurs gave a deafening roar.

"Oh, no!" Kelly said. On the monitor, the tyrannosaurs were agitated, moving swiftly in circles, raising their heads and bellowing.

"Dr. Thorne! What's happening?" Arby said.

They heard Levine's voice, tinny and scratchy on the radio, but they couldn't make out the words. Eddie and Malcolm came into the trailer. Malcolm took one look at the monitor and said, "Tell them to get out of there *right now!*"

On the monitor, the two tyrannosaurs had turned their backs to each other, so they were facing outward in a posture of defense. The babies were protected in the center. The adults swung their heavy tails back and forth over the nest, above the babies' heads. But the tension was palpable.

And then one of the adults bellowed, and charged out of the clearing.

"Dr. Thorne! Dr. Levine! Get out of there!"

Thorne swung his leg over the bike and gripped the rubber handles. Levine jumped on behind, clutched him around the waist. Thorne heard a chilling roar, and looked back to see one of the tyrannosaurs crash through the foliage and charge them. The animal was running at full speed—head low, jaws open, in an unmistakable posture of attack.

Thorne twisted the throttle. The electric motor whirred, the back wheel spun in the mud, not moving.

"Go!" Levine shouted. "Go!"

The tyrannosaur rushed toward them, roaring. Thorne could feel the ground shake. The roar was so loud it hurt his ears. The tyrannosaur was nearly on them, the big head lunging forward, jaws wide open —

Thorne kicked back with his heels, pushing the bike forward. Suddenly the rear wheel caught, throwing up a plume of mud, and the bike roared up the muddy track. He accelerated fast. The motorcycle fished and swerved treacherously on the trail.

Behind him Levine was shouting something, but Thorne didn't listen. His heart was pounding. The bike jumped across a rut in the path and they almost lost their balance, then regained it, accelerating again. Thorne did not dare look back. He could smell the odor of rotten flesh, could hear the rasping breath of the giant animal in pursuit. . . .

"Doc! Take it easy!" Levine shouted.

Thorne ignored him. The bike roared up the hill. The foliage slapped at them; mud spit up on their faces and chests. He was pulled over into a rut, then brought the bike back to the center of the trail. He heard another roar, and imagined it was a bit fainter, but—

"Doc!" Levine shouted, leaning close to his ear. "What're you trying to do, kill us? Doc! We're alone!"

Thorne came to a flat part of the path, and risked a glance back over his shoulder. Levine was right. They were alone. He saw no sign of the pursuing tyrannosaur, though he still heard it roaring, somewhere in the distance.

He slowed the bike.

"Take it easy," Levine said, shaking his head. His face was ashen, frightened. "You're a terrible driver, do you know that? You ought to take some lessons. You almost got us killed there."

"He was attacking us," Thorne said angrily. He was familiar with Levine's critical manner, but right now—

"That's absurd," Levine said. "He wasn't attacking at all."

"It sure as hell looked like it," Thorne said.

"No, no, no," Levine said. "He *wasn't* attacking us. The rex was defending his nest. There's a big difference."

"I didn't see any difference," Thorne said. He pulled the bike to a stop, and glared at Levine.

"In point of fact," Levine said, "if the rex had decided to chase you, we'd be dead right now. But he stopped almost immediately."

"He did?" Thorne said.

"There's no question about it," Levine said, in his pedantic manner. "The rex only intended to scare us off, and defend his territory. He'd never leave the nest unguarded, unless we took something, or disrupted the nest. I'm sure he's back there with his mate right now, hovering over the eggs, not going anywhere."

"Then I guess we're lucky he's a good parent," Thorne said, gunning the motor.

"Of course he's a good parent," Levine continued. "Any fool could tell that. Didn't you see how thin he was? He's been neglecting his own nourishment to feed his offspring. Probably been doing it for weeks. A Tyrannosaurus rex is a complex animal, with complex hunting behavior. And he has complex childrearing behavior as well. I wouldn't be surprised if adult tyrannosaurs have an extended parenting role that lasts for months. He may teach his offspring to hunt, for example. Start by bringing in small wounded animals, and letting the youngsters finish them off. That kind of thing. It'll be interesting to find out exactly what he does. Why are we waiting here?"

Through Thorne's earpiece, the radio crackled. Malcolm said, "It would never occur to him to thank you for saving his life."

Thorne grunted. "Evidently not," he said.

Levine said, "Who are you talking to? Is it Malcolm? Is he here?"

"Yes," Thorne said.

"He's agreeing with me, isn't he," Levine said.

"Not exactly," Thorne said, shaking his head.

"Look, Doc," Levine said, "I'm sorry if you got upset. But there was no reason for it. The truth is, we were never in danger—except from your bad driving."

"Fine. That's fine." Thorne's heart was still pounding in his chest. He took a deep breath, swung the bike to the left, and headed down a wider path, back toward their camp.

Sitting behind him, Levine said, "I'm very glad to see you, Doc. I really am."

Thorne didn't answer. He followed the path downward, through foliage. They descended to the valley, picking up speed. Soon they saw the trailers in the clearing below. Levine said, "Good. You brought everything. And the equipment's working? Everything in good condition?"

"It all seems to be fine."

"Perfect," Levine said. "Then this is just perfect."

"Maybe not," Thorne said.

Through the back window of the trailer, Kelly and Arby were waving cheerfully through the glass.

"You're kidding," Levine said.

FOURTH CONFIGURATION

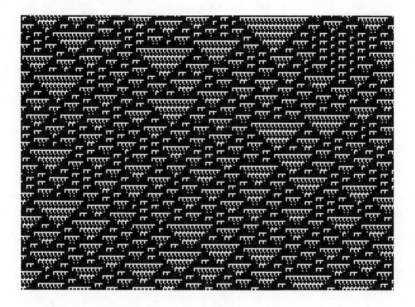

"Approaching the chaotic edge, elements show internal conflict. An unstable and potentially lethal region."

IAN MALCOLM

Levine

They came running across the clearing, shouting, "Dr. Levine! Dr. Levine! You're safe!" They hugged Levine, who smiled despite himself. He turned to Thorne.

"Doc," Levine said. "This was very unwise."

"Why don't you explain that to them?" Thorne said. "They're your students."

Kelly said, "Don't be mad, Dr. Levine."

"It was our decision," Arby explained to Levine. "We came on our own."

"On your own?" Levine said.

"We thought you'd need help," Arby said. "And you did." He turned to Thorne.

Thorne nodded. "Yes. They've helped us."

"And we promise, we won't get in the way," Kelly said. "You go ahead and do whatever you have to do, and we will just—"

"The kids were worried about you," Malcolm said, coming up to Levine. "Because they thought you were in trouble."

"Anyway, what's the big rush?" Eddie said. "I mean, you build all these vehicles, and then you leave without them—"

"I had no choice," Levine said. "The government has an outbreak of some new encephalitis on its hands. They've decided it's related to the occasional dinosaur carcass that washes up there. Of course, the whole idea is idiotic, but that won't stop them from destroying every animal on this island the minute they find out about it. I had to get here first. Time is short."

"So you came here alone," Malcolm said.

"Nonsense, Ian. Stop pouting. I was going to call you, as soon as I verified this was the island. And I didn't come here alone. I had a guide named Diego, a local man who swore he had been on this island as a kid, years before. And he seemed entirely knowledgeable. He led me up the cliff without any problem. And everything was going just fine, until we were attacked at the stream, and Diego—"

"Attacked?" Malcolm said. "By what?"

"I didn't really see what it was," Levine said. "It happened extremely fast. The animal knocked me down, and tore the backpack, and I don't really know what happened after that. Possibly the shape of my pack confused it, because I got up and started running again, and it didn't chase me."

Malcolm was staring at him. "You were damn lucky, Richard."

"Yes, well, I ran for a long time. When I looked back, I was alone in the jungle. And lost. I didn't know what to do, so I climbed a tree. That seemed like a good idea—and then, around nightfall, the velociraptors showed up."

"Velociraptors?" Arby said.

"Small carnivores," Levine said. "Basic theropod body shape, long snout, binocular vision. Roughly two meters tall, weighing perhaps ninety kilos. Very fast, intelligent, nasty little dinosaurs, and they travel in packs. And last night there were eight of them, jumping all around my tree, trying to get to me. All night long, jumping and snarling, jumping and snarling . . . I didn't get any sleep at all."

"Aw, that's a shame," Eddie said.

"Look," Levine said crossly. "It's not my problem if—"

Thorne said, "You spent the night in the tree?"

"Yes, and in the morning the raptors had gone. So I came down and started looking around. I found the lab, or whatever it is. Clearly, they abandoned it in a hurry, leaving some animals behind. I went through the building, and discovered that there is still power—some systems are still going, all these years later. And, most important, there is a network of security cameras. That's a very lucky break. So I decided to check on those cameras, and I was hard at work when you people barged in—"

"Wait a minute," Eddie said. "We came here to rescue you."

"I don't know why," Levine said. "I certainly never asked you to."

Thorne said, "It sounded like you did, over the phone."

"That is a misunderstanding," Levine said. "I was momentarily upset, because I couldn't work the phone. You've made that phone too complicated, Doc. That's the problem. So: shall we get started?"

Levine paused. He looked at the angry faces all around him. Malcolm turned to Thorne. "A great scientist," he said, "and a great human being."

"Look," Levine said, "I don't know what your problem is. The expedition was going to come to this island sooner or later. In this instance, sooner is better. Everything has turned out quite well, and, frankly, I don't see any reason to discuss it further. This is not the time for petty bickering. We have important things to do—and I think we should get started. Because this island is an extraordinary opportunity, and it isn't going to last forever. "

Dodgson

Lewis Dodgson sat hunched in a dark corner of the Chesperito Cantina in Puerto Cortés, nursing a beer. Beside him, George Baselton, the Regis Professor of Biology at Stanford, was enthusiastically devouring a plate of huevos rancheros. The egg yolks ran yellow across green salsa. It made Dodgson sick just to look at it. He turned away, but he could still hear Baselton licking his lips, noisily.

There was no one else in the bar, except for some chickens clucking around the floor. Every so often, a young boy would come to the door, throw a handful of rocks at the chickens, and run away again, giggling. A scratchy stereo played an old Elvis Presley tape through corroded speakers above the bar. Dodgson hummed "Falling in Love With You," and tried to control his temper. He had been sitting in this dump for damn near an hour.

Baselton finished his eggs, and pushed the plate away. He brought out the small notebook he carried everywhere with him. "Now Lew," he said. "I've been thinking about how to handle this."

"Handle what?" Dodgson said irritably. "There's nothing to handle, unless we can get to that island." While he spoke, he tapped a small photograph of Richard Levine on the edge of the bar table. Turned it over. Looked at the image upside down. Then right side up.

He sighed. He looked at his watch.

"Lew," Baselton said patiently, "getting to the island is not the important part. The important part is how we present our discovery to the world."

Dodgson paused. "Our *discovery*," he repeated. "I like that, George. That's very good. Our discovery."

"Well, that's the truth, isn't it?" Baselton said, with a bland smile. "InGen is bankrupt, its technology lost to mankind. A tragic, tragic loss, as I have said many times on television. But under the circumstances, anyone who finds it again has made a discovery. I don't know what else you would call it. As Henri Poincaré put it—"

"Okay," Dodgson said. "So we make a discovery. And then what? Hold a press conference?"

"Absolutely not," Baselton said, looking horrified. "A press conference would appear extremely crass. It would open us up to all sorts of criticism. No, no. A discovery of this magnitude must be treated with decorum. It must be reported, Lew."

"Reported?"

"In the literature: *Nature,* I imagine. Yes."

Dodgson squinted. "You want to announce this in an academic publication?"

"What better way to make it legitimate?" Baselton said. "It's entirely proper to present our findings to our scholarly peers. Of course it will start a debate—but what will that debate consist of? An academic squabble, professors sniping at professors, which will fill the science pages of the newspapers for three days, until it is pushed aside by the latest news on breast implants. And in those three days, we will have staked our claim."

"You'll write it?"

"Yes," Baselton said. "And later, I think, an article in *American Scholar,* or perhaps *Natural History.* A human-interest piece, what this discovery means for the future, what it tells us about the past, all that. . . ."

Dodgson nodded. He could see that Baselton was correct, and he was reminded once again how much he needed him, and how wise he had been to add him to the team. Dodgson never thought about public reaction. And Baselton thought about nothing else.

"Well, that's fine," Dodgson said. "But none of it matters, unless we get to that island." He glanced at his watch again.

He heard a door open behind him, and Dodgson's assistant Howard King came in, pulling a heavyset Costa Rican man, with a mustache. The man had a weathered face and a sullen expression.

Dodgson turned on his stool. "Is this the guy?"

"Yes, Lew."

"What's his name?"

"Gandoca."

"Señor Gandoca." Dodgson held up the photo of Levine. "You know this man?"

Gandoca hardly glanced at the photo. He nodded. "*Sí.* Señor Levine."

"That's right. Señor fucking Levine. When was he here?"

"A few days ago. He left with Dieguito, my cousin. They are not back yet."

"And where did they go?" Dodgson asked.

"Isla Sorna."

"Good." Dodgson drained his beer, pushed the bottle away. "You have a boat?" He turned to King. "Does he have a boat?"

King said, "He's a fisherman. He has a boat."

Gandoca nodded. "A fishing boat. *Sí.*"

"Good. I want to go to Isla Sorna, too."

"*Sí*, señor, but today the weather—"

"I don't care about the weather," Dodgson said. "The weather will get better. I want to go now."

"Perhaps later—"

"Now."

Gandoca spread his hands. "I am very sorry, señor—"

Dodgson said, "Show him the money, Howard."

King opened a briefcase. It was filled with five thousand colon notes. Gandoca looked, picked up one of the bills, inspected it. He put it back carefully, shifted on his feet a little.

Dodgson said, "I want to go *now.*"

"*Sí*, señor," Gandoca said. "We leave when you are ready."

"That's more like it," Dodgson said. "How long to get to the island?"

"Perhaps two hours, señor."

"Fine," Dodgson said. "That'll be fine."

The High Hide

"Here we go!"

There was a click as Levine connected the flexible cable to the Explorer's power winch, and flicked it on. The cable turned slowly in the sunlight.

They had all moved down onto the broad grassy plain at the base of the cliff. The midday sun was high overhead, glaring off the rocky rim of the island. Below, the valley shimmered in midday heat.

There was a herd of hypsilophodons a short distance away; the green gazelle-like animals raised their heads occasionally above the grass to look toward them, every time they heard the clink of metal, as Eddie and the kids laid out the aluminum strut assembly which had been the subject of so much speculation back in California. That assembly now looked like a jumble of thin struts—an oversized version of pickup sticks—lying in the grass of the plain.

"Now we will see," Levine said, rubbing his hands together.

As the motor turned, the aluminum struts began to move, and slowly lifted into the air. The emerging structure appeared spidery and delicate, but Thorne knew that the cross-bracing would give it surprising strength. Struts unfolding, the structure rose ten feet, then fifteen feet, and finally it stopped. The little house at the top was now just beneath the lowest branches of the nearby trees, which almost concealed it from view. But the scaffolding itself gleamed bright and shiny in the sun.

"Is that it?" Arby said.

"That's it, yes." Thorne walked around the four sides, slipping in the locking pins, to hold it upright.

"But it's much too shiny," Levine said. "We should have made it matte black."

Thorne said, "Eddie, we need to hide this."

"Want to spray it, Doc? I think I brought some black paint."

Levine shook his head. "No, then it'll smell. How about those palms?"

"Sure, we can do that." Eddie walked to a stand of nearby palms, and began to hack away big fronds with his machete.

Kelly stared up at the aluminum strut assembly. "It's great," she said. "But what is it?"

"It's a high hide," Levine said. "Come on." And he began to climb the scaffolding.

The structure at the top was a little house, its roof supported by aluminum bars spaced four feet apart. The floor of the house was also made of aluminum bars, but these were closer together, about six inches apart. Their feet threatened to slip through, so Levine took the first of the bundles of fronds that Eddie Carr was raising on a rope, and used them to make a more complete floor. The remaining fronds he tied to the outside of the house, concealing its structure.

Arby and Kelly stared out at the animals. From their vantage point, they could look across the whole valley. There was a distant herd of apatosaurs, on the other side of the river. A cluster of triceratops browsed to the north. Nearer the water, some duck-billed dinosaurs with long crests rising above their heads moved forward to drink. A low, trumpeting cry from the duckbills floated across the valley toward them: a deep, unearthly sound. A moment later, there was an answering cry, from the forest at the opposite side of the valley.

"What was that?" Kelly said.

"Parasaurolophus," Levine said. "It's trumpeting through its nuchal crest. Low-frequency sound carries a long distance."

To the south, there was a herd of dark-green animals, with large curved protruding foreheads, and a rim of small knobby horns. They looked a little like buffalo. "What do you call those?" Kelly said.

"Good question," Levine said. "They are either *Gravitholus albertae,* or more likely *Pachycephalosaurus wyomingensis.* But it's difficult to say for sure, because a full skeleton for these animals has never been recovered. Their foreheads are very thick bone, so we've found many domed cranial fragments. But this is the first time I've ever seen the whole animal."

"And those heads? What are they for?" Arby said.

"Nobody knows," Levine said. "Everyone has assumed they're used for butting, for intraspecies fighting among males. Competition for females, that sort of thing."

Malcolm climbed up into the hide. "Yes, butting heads," he said sourly. "Just as you see them now."

"All right," Levine said, "so they're not butting heads at the moment. Perhaps their breeding season is concluded."

"Or perhaps they don't do it at all," Malcolm said, staring at the green animals. "They look pretty peaceful to me."

"Yes," Levine said, "but of course that doesn't mean a thing. African buffalo appear peaceful most of the time, too—in fact, they usually just stand motionless. Yet they're unpredictable and dangerous animals. We have to presume those domes exist for a reason—even if we're not seeing it now."

Levine turned to the kids. "That's why we made this structure. We want to make round-the-clock observations on the animals," he said. "To the extent possible, we want a full record of their activities."

"Why?" Arby said.

"Because," Malcolm said, "this island presents a unique opportunity to study the greatest mystery in the history of our planet: extinction."

"You see," Malcolm said, "when InGen shut down their facility, they did it hastily, and they left some live animals behind. That was five or six years ago. Dinosaurs mature rapidly; most species attain adulthood in four or five years. By now, the first generation of InGen dinosaurs—bred in a laboratory—has attained maturity, and has begun to breed a new generation, entirely in the wild. There is now a complete ecological system on this island, with a dozen or so dinosaur species living in social groups, for the first time in sixty-five million years."

Arby said, "So why is that an opportunity?"

Malcolm pointed across the plain. "Well, think about it. Extinction is a very difficult research topic. There are dozens of competing theories. The fossil record is incomplete. And you can't perform experiments. Galileo could climb the tower of Pisa and drop balls to test his theory of gravity. He never actually did it, but he could have. Newton used prisms to test his theory of light. Astronomers observed eclipses to test Einstein's theory of relativity. Testing occurs throughout science. But how can you test a theory of extinction? You can't."

Arby said, "But here . . ."

"Yes," Malcolm said. "What we have here is a population of extinct animals artificially introduced into a closed environment, and allowed to evolve all over again. There's never been anything like it in all history. We already know these animals became extinct once. But nobody knows why."

"And you expect to find out? In a few days?"

"Yes," Malcolm said. "We do."

"How? You don't expect them to become extinct again, do you?"

"You mean, right before our eyes?" Malcolm laughed. "No, no. Nothing like that. But the point is, for the first time we aren't just studying bones. We're seeing live animals, and observing their behavior. I have a theory, and I think that even in a short time, we will see evidence for that theory."

"What evidence?" Kelly said.

"What theory?" Arby said.

Malcolm smiled at them. "Wait," he said.

The Red Queen

The apatosaurs had come down to the river in the heat of the day; their graceful curving necks were reflected in the water as they bent to drink. Their long, whip-like tails swung back and forth lazily. Several younger apatosaurs, much smaller than the adults, scampered about in the center of the herd.

"Beautiful, isn't it?" Levine said. "The way it all fits together. Just beautiful." He leaned over the side and shouted to Thorne, "Where's my mount?"

"Coming up," Thorne said.

The rope now brought up a heavy wide-based tripod, and a circular mount on top. There were five video cameras atop the mount, and dangling wires leading to solar panels. Levine and Malcolm began to set it up.

"What happens to the video?" Arby said.

"The data gets multiplexed, and we uplink it back to California. By satellite. We'll also hook into the security network. So we'll have lots of observation points."

"And we don't have to be here?"

"Right."

"And this is what you call a high hide?"

"Yes. At least, that's what scientists like Sarah Harding call it."

Thorne climbed up to join them. The little shelter was now quite crowded, but Levine didn't seem to notice. He was entirely focused on the dinosaurs; he turned a pair of binoculars on the animals spread across the plain. "Just as we thought," he said to Malcolm. "Spatial organization. Infants and juveniles in the center of the herd, protective adults on the periphery. The apatosaurs use their tails as defense."

"That's the way it looks."

"Oh, there's no question about it," Levine said. He sighed. "It's so agreeable to be proven right."

On the ground below, Eddie unpacked the circular aluminum cage, the same one they had seen in California. It was six feet tall and four feet in diameter, constructed of one-inch titanium bars. "What do you want me to do with this?" Eddie said.

"Leave it down there," Levine said. "That's where it belongs."

Eddie set the cage upright in the corner of the scaffolding. Levine climbed down.

"And what's that for?" Arby said, looking down. "Catching a dinosaur?"

"In point of fact, just the opposite." Levine clipped the cage to the side of the scaffolding. He swung the door open and shut, testing it. There was a lock in the door. He checked the lock, too, leaving the key in place, with its dangling elastic loop. "It's a predator cage, like a shark cage," Levine said. "If you're down here walking around and anything happens, you can climb in here, and you'll be safe."

"In case what happens?" Arby said, with a worried look.

"Actually, I don't think anything will happen," Levine said. "Because I doubt the animals will pay any attention to us, or to this little house, once the structure's been concealed."

"You mean they won't see it?"

"Oh, they'll see it," Levine said, "but they'll ignore it."

"But if they smell us . . ."

Levine shook his head. "We sited the hide so the prevailing wind is toward us. And you may have noticed these ferns have a distinct smell." It was a mild, slightly tangy odor, almost like eucalyptus.

Arby fretted. "But suppose they decide to eat the ferns?"

"They won't," Levine said. "These are *Dicranopterus cyatheoides*. They're mildly toxic and cause a rash in the mouth. In point of fact, there's a theory that their toxicity first evolved back in the Jurassic, as a defense against dinosaur browsers."

"That's not a theory," Malcolm said. "It's just idle speculation."

"There's some logic behind it," Levine said. "Plant life in the Mesozoic must have been severely challenged by the arrival of very large dinosaurs. Herds of giant herbivores, each animal consuming hundreds of pounds of plant matter each day, would have wiped out any plants that didn't evolve some defense—a bad taste, or nettles, or thorns, or chemical toxicity. So perhaps *cyatheoides* evolved its toxicity back then. And it's very effective, because contemporary animals don't eat these ferns, anywhere on earth. That's why they're so abundant. You may have noticed."

"Plants have defenses?" Kelly said.

"Of course they do. Plants evolve like every other form of life, and they've come up with their own forms of aggression, defense, and so on. In the nineteenth century, most theories concerned animals—nature red in tooth and claw, all that. But now scientists are thinking about nature green in root and stem. We realize that plants, in their ceaseless struggle to survive, have evolved everything from complex symbiosis with other animals, to signaling mechanisms to warn other plants, to outright chemical warfare."

Kelly frowned. "Signaling? Like what?"

"Oh, there are many examples," Levine said. "In Africa, acacia trees evolved very long, sharp thorns—three inches or so—but that only provoked animals like giraffes and antelope to evolve long tongues to get past the thorns. Thorns alone didn't work. So in the evolutionary arms race, the acacia trees next evolved toxicity. They started to produce large quantities of tannin in their leaves, which sets off a lethal metabolic reaction in the animals that eat them. Literally kills them. At the same time, the acacias also evolved a kind of chemical warning system among themselves. If an antelope begins to eat one tree in a grove, that tree releases the chemical ethylene into the air, which causes other trees in the grove to step up the production of leaf tannin. Within five or ten minutes, the other trees are producing more tannin, making themselves poisonous."

"And then what happens to the antelope? It dies?"

"Well, not any more," Levine said, "because the evolutionary arms race continued. Eventually, antelopes learned that they could only browse for a short time. Once the trees started to produce more tannin, they had to stop eating it. And the browsers developed new strategies. For example, when a giraffe eats an acacia tree, it then avoids all the trees downwind. Instead, it moves on to another tree that is some distance away. So the animals have adapted to this defense, too."

"In evolutionary theory, this is called the Red Queen phenomenon," Malcolm said. "Because in *Alice in Wonderland* the Red Queen tells Alice she has to run as fast as she can just to stay where she is. That's the way evolutionary spirals seem. All the organisms are evolving at a furious pace just to stay in the same balance. To stay where they are."

Arby said, "And this is common? Even with plants?"

"Oh yes," Levine said. "In their own way, plants are extremely active. Oak trees, for example, produce tannin and phenol as a defense when caterpillars attack them. A whole grove of trees is alerted as soon as one tree is infested. It's a way to protect the entire grove—a kind of cooperation among trees, you might say."

Arby nodded, and looked out from the high hide at the apatosaurs, still by the river below. "So," Arby said, "is that why the dinosaurs haven't eaten all the trees off this island? Because those big apatosaurs must eat a lot of plants. They have long necks to eat the high leaves. But the trees hardly look touched."

"Very good," Levine said, nodding. "I noticed that myself."

"Is that because of these plant defenses?"

"Well, it might be," Levine said. "But I think there is a very simple explanation for why the trees are preserved."

"What's that?"

"Just look," Levine said. "It's right before your eyes."

Arby picked up the binoculars and stared at the herds. "What's the simple explanation?"

"Among paleontologists," Levine said, "there's been an interminable debate about why sauropods have long necks. Those animals you see have necks twenty feet long. The traditional belief has been that sauropods evolved long necks to eat high foliage that could not be reached by smaller animals."

"So?" Arby said. "What's the debate?"

"Most animals on this planet have short necks," Levine said, "because a long neck is, well, a pain in the neck. It causes all sorts of problems. Structural problems: how to arrange muscles and ligaments to support a long neck. Behavioral problems: nerve impulses must travel a long way from the brain to the body. Swallowing problems: food has to go a long way from the mouth to the stomach. Breathing problems: air has to be pulled down a long windpipe. Cardiac problems: blood has to be pumped way up to the head, or the animal faints. In evolutionary terms, all this is very difficult to do."

"But giraffes do it," Arby said.

"Yes, they do. Although giraffe necks are nowhere near this long. Giraffes have evolved large hearts, and very thick fascia around the neck. In effect, the neck of a giraffe is like a blood-pressure cuff, going all the way up."

"Do dinosaurs have the same cuff?"

"We don't know. We assume apatosaurs have huge hearts, perhaps three hundred pounds or more. But there is another possible solution to the problem of pumping blood in a long neck."

"Yes?"

"You're looking at it right now," Levine said.

Arby clapped his hands. "They don't raise their necks!"

"Correct," Levine said. "At least, not very often, or for long periods. Of course, right now the animals are drinking, so their necks are down, but my guess is that if we watch them for an extended period we'll find they don't spend much time with their necks raised high."

"And that's why they don't eat the leaves on the trees!"

"Right."

Kelly frowned. "But if their long necks aren't used for eating, then why did they evolve them in the first place?"

Levine smiled. "There must be a good reason," he said. "I believe it has to do with defense."

"Defense? Long necks?" Arby stared. "I don't get it."

"Keep looking," Levine said. "It's really rather obvious."

Arby peered through binoculars. He said to Kelly, "I hate it when he tells us it's obvious."

"I know," she said, with a sigh.

Arby glanced over at Thorne, and caught his eye. Thorne made a V with his fingers, and then pushed one finger, tilting it over. The movement forced the second finger to shift, too. So the two fingers were connected. . . .

If it was a clue, he didn't get it. He didn't get it. He frowned.

Thorne mouthed: *Bridge.*

Arby looked, and watched the whip-like tails swing back and forth over the younger animals. "I get it!" Arby said. "They use their tails for defense. And they need long necks to counterbalance the long tails. It's like a suspension bridge!"

Levine squinted at Arby. "You did that very fast," he said.

Thorne turned away, hiding a smile.

"But I'm right . . ." Arby said.

"Yes," Levine said, "your view is essentially correct. Long necks exist because the long tails exist. It's a different situation in theropods, which stand on two legs. But in quadrupeds, there needs to be a counterbalance for the long tail, or the animal would simply tip over."

Malcolm said, "Actually, there is something much more puzzling about this apatosaur herd."

"Oh?" Levine said. "What's that?"

"There are no true adults," Malcolm said. "Those animals we see are very large by our standards. But in fact, none of them has attained full adult size. I find that perplexing."

"Do you? It doesn't trouble me in the least," Levine said. "Unquestionably, it is simply because they haven't had enough time to reach maturity. I'm sure apatosaurs grow more slowly than the other dinosaurs. After all, large mammals like elephants grow more slowly than small ones."

Malcolm shook his head. "That's not the explanation," he said.

"Oh? Then what?"

"Keep looking," Malcolm said, pointing out over the plain. "It's really rather obvious."

The kids giggled.

Levine gave a little shiver of displeasure. "What is obvious to me," he said, "is that none of the species appear to have attained full adulthood. The triceratops, the apatosaurs, even the parasaurs are a bit smaller than one would expect. This argues for a consistent factor: some element of diet, the effects of confinement on a small island, perhaps even the way they were engineered. But I don't consider it particularly remarkable or worrisome."

"Maybe you're right," Malcolm said. "And then again, maybe you're not."

Puerto Cortés

"No flights?" Sarah Harding said. "What do you mean, there are no flights?" It was eleven o'clock in the morning. Harding had been flying for the last fifteen hours, much of it spent on a U.S. military transport that she'd caught from Nairobi to Dallas. She was exhausted. Her skin felt grimy; she needed a shower and a change of clothes. Instead she found herself arguing with this very stubborn official in a ratty little town on the west coast of Costa Rica. Outside, the rain had stopped, but the sky was still gray, with low-hanging clouds over the deserted airfield.

"I am sorry," Rodríguez said. "No flights can be arranged."

"But what about the helicopter that took the men earlier?"

"There is a helicopter, yes."

"Where is it?"

"The helicopter is not here."

"I can see that. But where is it?"

Rodríguez spread his hands. "It has gone to San Cristóbal."

"When will it be back?"

"I do not know. I think tomorrow, or perhaps the day after."

"Señor Rodríguez," she said firmly, "I must get to that island today."

"I understand your wish," Rodríguez said. "But I cannot do anything to help this."

"What do you suggest?"

Rodríguez shrugged. "I could not make a suggestion."

"Is there a boat that will take me?"

"I do not know of a boat."

"This is a harbor," Harding said. She pointed out the window. "I see all sorts of boats out there."

"I know. But I do not believe one will go to the islands. The weather is not so favorable."

"But if I were to go down to—"

"Yes, of course." Rodríguez sighed. "Of course you may ask."

Which was how she found herself, shortly after eleven o'clock on a rainy morning, walking down the rickety wooden dock, with her backpack on her shoulder. Four boats were tied up to the dock, which smelled strongly of fish. But all the boats seemed to be deserted. All the activity was at the far end of the dock, where a much larger boat was tied up. Beside the boat, a red Jeep Wrangler was being strapped for loading, along with several large steel drums and wooden crates of supplies. She admired the car in passing; it had been specially modified, enlarged to the size of the Land Rover Defender, the most desirable of all field vehicles. Changing this Jeep must have been an expensive alteration, she thought: only for researchers with lots of money.

Standing on the dock, a pair of Americans in wide-brimmed sun hats were shouting and pointing as the Jeep lifted lopsidedly into the air, and was swung onto the deck of the boat with an ancient crane. She heard one of the men shout "Careful! Careful!" as the Jeep thudded down hard on the wooden deck. "Damn it, be careful!" Several workmen began to carry the boxes onto the ship. The crane swung back to pick up the steel drums.

Harding went over to the nearest man and said politely, "Excuse me, but I wonder if you could help me."

The man glanced at her. He was medium height, with reddish skin and bland features; he looked awkward in new khaki safari clothes. His manner was preoccupied and tense. "I'm busy now," he said, and turned away. "Manuel! Watch it, that's sensitive equipment!"

"I'm sorry to bother you," she continued, "but my name is Sarah Harding, and I'm trying—"

"I don't care if you're Sarah Bernhardt, the— Manuel! Damn it!" The man waved his arms. "You there! Yes, you! Hold that box *upright!*"

"I'm trying to get to Isla Sorna," she said, finishing.

At this, the man's entire demeanor changed. He turned back to her slowly. "Isla Sorna?" he said. "You're not associated with Dr. Levine by any chance, are you?"

"Yes, I am."

"Well, I'll be damned," he said, suddenly breaking into a warm smile. "What do you know!" He extended his hand. "I'm Lew Dodgson, from the Biosyn Corporation, back in Cupertino. This is my associate, Howard King."

"Hi," the other man said, nodding. Howard King was younger and taller than Dodgson, and he was handsome in a clean-cut California way. Sarah recognized his type: a classic beta male animal, subservient to the core. And there was something odd about his behavior toward her: he moved a little away, and seemed as uncomfortable around her as Dodgson now seemed friendly.

"And up there," Dodgson continued, pointing onto the deck, "is our third, George Baselton."

Harding saw a heavyset man on the deck, bent over the boxes as they came on board. His shirtsleeves were soaked in sweat. She said, "Are you all friends of Richard?"

"We're on our way over to see him right now," Dodgson said, "to help him out." He hesitated, frowning at her. "But, uh, he didn't tell us about you. . . ."

She was suddenly aware then of how she must appear to him: a short woman in her thirties, wearing a rumpled shirt, khaki shorts, and heavy boots. Her clothes dirty, her hair unkempt after all the flights.

She said, "I know Richard through Ian Malcolm. Ian and I are old friends."

"I see. . . ." He continued to stare at her, as if he was unsure of her in some way.

She felt compelled to explain. "I've been in Africa. I decided to come here at the last minute," she said. "Doc Thorne called me."

"Oh, of course. Doc." The man nodded, and seemed to relax, as if everything now made sense to him.

She said, "Is Richard all right?"

"Well, I certainly hope so. Because we're taking all this equipment to him."

"You're going to Sorna now?"

"We are, if this weather holds," Dodgson said, glancing at the sky. "We should be ready to go in five or ten minutes. You know, you're welcome to join us, if you need a ride," he said cheerfully. "We could use the company. Where's your stuff?"

"I've only got this," she said, lifting her small backpack.

"Traveling light, eh? Well, good, Ms. Harding. Welcome to the party."

He seemed entirely open and friendly now. It was such a marked change from his earlier behavior. But she noticed that the handsome man, King, remained distinctly uneasy. King turned his back to her, and acted very busy, shouting at the workmen to be careful with the last of the wooden crates, which were marked "Biosyn Corporation" in stenciled lettering. She had the impression he was avoiding looking at her. And she still hadn't gotten a good look at the third man, on deck. It made her hesitate.

"You're sure it's all right. . . ."

"Of course it's all right! We'd be delighted!" Dodgson said. "Besides, how else are you going to get there? There's no planes, the helicopter is gone."

"I know, I checked. . . ."

"Well, then, you know. If you want to get to the island, you'd better go with us."

She looked at the Jeep on the boat, and said, "I think Doc must already be there, with his equipment."

At the mention of that, the second man, King, snapped his head around in alarm. But Dodgson just nodded calmly and said, "Yes, I think so. He left last night, I believe."

"That's what he said to me."

"Right." Dodgson nodded. "So he's already there. At least, I hope he is."

From on deck, there were shouts in Spanish, and a captain in greasy overalls came and looked over the side. "Señor Dodgson, we are ready."

"Good," Dodgson said. "Excellent. Climb aboard, Ms. Harding. Let's get going!"

King

Spewing black smoke, the fishing boat chugged out of the harbor, heading toward open sea. Howard King felt the rumble of the ship's engines beneath his feet, heard the creak of the wood. He listened to the shouts of the crewmen in Spanish. King looked back at the little town of Puerto Cortés, a jumble of little houses clustered around the water's edge. He hoped this damn boat was seaworthy—because they were out in the middle of nowhere.

And Dodgson was cutting corners. Taking chances again.

It was the situation King feared most.

Howard King had known Lewis Dodgson for almost ten years, ever since he had joined Biosyn as a young Berkeley Ph.D., a promising researcher with the energy to conquer the world. King had done his doctoral thesis on blood-coagulation factors. He had joined Biosyn at a time of intense interest in those factors, which seemed to hold the key to dissolving clots in patients with heart attacks. There was a race among biotech companies to develop a new drug that would save lives, and make a fortune as well.

Initially, King worked on a promising substance called Hemaggluttin V-5, or HGV-5. In early tests it dissolved platelet aggregation to an astonishing degree. King became the most promising young researcher at Biosyn. His picture was prominently featured in the annual report. He had his own lab, and an operating budget of nearly half a million dollars.

And then, without warning, the bottom fell out. In preliminary tests on human subjects, HGV-5 failed to dissolve clots in either myocardial infarctions or pulmonary embolisms. Worse, it produced severe side effects: gastrointestinal bleeding, skin rashes, neurological problems. After one patient died from convulsions, the company halted further testing. Within weeks, King lost his lab. A newly arrived Danish researcher took it over; he was developing an extract from the saliva of the Sumatran yellow leech, which showed more promise.

King moved to a smaller lab, decided he was tired of blood factors, and turned his attention to painkillers. He had an interesting compound, the L-isomer of a protein from the African horny toad, which seemed to have narcotic effects. But he had lost his former confidence, and when the company reviewed his work, they concluded that his research was insufficiently documented to warrant seeking FDA approvals for testing. His horny-toad project was summarily canceled.

King was then thirty-five, and twice a failure. His picture no longer graced the annual report. It was rumored that the company would probably let him go at the next review period. When he proposed a new research project, it was rejected at once. It was a dark time in his life.

Then Lewis Dodgson suggested they have lunch.

Dodgson had an unsavory reputation among the researchers; he was known as "The Undertaker," because of the way he took over the work of others, and prettied it up as his own. In earlier years, King never would have been seen with him. But now he allowed Dodgson to take him to an expensive seafood restaurant in San Francisco.

"Research is hard," Dodgson said, sympathetically.

"You can say that again," King said.

"Hard, and *risky*," Dodgson said. "The fact is, innovative research rarely pans out. But does management understand? No. If the research fails, you're the one who's blamed. It's not fair."

"Tell me," King said.

"But that's the name of the game." Dodgson shrugged, and speared a leg of soft-shell crab.

King said nothing.

"Personally, I don't like risk," Dodgson continued. "And original work is risky. Most new ideas are bad, and most original work fails. That's the reality. If you feel compelled to do original research, you can expect to fail. That's all right if you work in a university, where failure is praised and success leads to ostracism. But in industry . . . no, no. Original work in industry is not a wise career choice. It's only going to get you into trouble. Which is where you are right now, my friend."

"What can I do?" King said.

"Well," Dodgson said. "I have my own version of the scientific method. I call it focused research development. If only a few ideas are going to be good, why try to find them yourself? It's too hard. Let other people find them — let them take the risk — let them go for the so-called glory. I'd rather wait, and develop ideas that already show promise. Take what's good, and make it better. Or at least, make it different enough so that I can patent it. And then I own it. Then, it's mine."

King was amazed at the straightforward way that Dodgson admitted he was a thief. He didn't seem in the least embarrassed. King poked at his salad for a while. "Why are you telling me this?"

"Because I see something in you," Dodgson said. "I see ambition. Frustrated ambition. And I'm telling you, Howard, you don't have to be frustrated. You don't even have to be fired from the company at the next performance review. Which is exactly what's going to happen. How old is your kid?"

"Four," King said.

"Terrible, to be out of work, with a young family. And it won't be easy to get another job. Who's going to give you a chance now? By thirty-five, a research scientist has already made his mark, or he's not likely to. I don't say that's right, but that's how they think."

King knew that's how they thought. At every biotechnology company in California.

"But Howard," Dodgson said, leaning across the table, lowering his voice, "a wonderful world awaits you, if you choose to look at things differently. There's a whole other way to live your life. I really think you should consider what I'm saying."

Two weeks later, King became Dodgson's personal assistant in the Department of Future Biogenic Trends, which was how Biosyn referred to its efforts at industrial espionage. And in the years that followed, King had once again risen swiftly at Biosyn—this time because Dodgson liked him.

Now King had all the accoutrements of success: a Porsche, a mortgage, a divorce, a kid he saw on weekends. All because King had proven to be the perfect second in command, working long hours, handling the details, keeping his fast-talking boss out of trouble. And in the process, King had come to know all the sides of Dodgson—his charismatic side, his visionary side, and his dark, ruthless side. King told himself that he could handle the ruthless side, that he could keep it in check, that over the years he had learned how to do that.

But sometimes, he was not so sure.

Like now.

Because here they were, in some rickety stinking fishing boat, heading out into the ocean off some desolate village in Costa Rica, and in this tense moment Dodgson had suddenly decided to play some kind of game, meeting this woman and deciding to take her along.

King didn't know what Dodgson intended, but he could see the intense gleam in Dodgson's eyes that he had seen only a few times before, and it was a look that always alarmed him.

The woman Harding was now up on the foredeck, standing near the bow. She was looking off at the ocean. King saw Dodgson walking around the Jeep, and beckoned to him nervously.

"Listen," King said, "we have to talk."

"Sure," Dodgson said, easily. "What's on your mind?"

And he smiled. That charming smile.

Harding

Sarah Harding stared at the gray, menacing sky. The boat rolled in the heavy offshore swell. The deckhands scrambled to tie down the Jeep, which threatened repeatedly to break free. She stood in the bow, fighting seasickness. On the far horizon, dead ahead, she could just see the low black line that was their first glimpse of Isla Sorna.

She turned and looked back, and saw Dodgson and King were huddled by the railing amidships, in intense conversation. King seemed to be upset, gesticulating rapidly. Dodgson was listening, and shaking his head. After a moment, he put his arm on King's shoulder. He seemed to be trying to calm the younger man down. Both men ignored the activity around the Jeep. Which was odd, she thought, considering how worried they had been earlier about the equipment. Now they didn't seem to care.

As for the third man, Baselton, she had of course recognized him, and she was surprised to find him here on this little fishing boat. Baselton had shaken her hand in a perfunctory way, and he had disappeared belowdecks as soon as the ship pulled away from the dock. He had not reappeared. But perhaps he was seasick, too.

As she continued to watch, she saw Dodgson break away from King, and hurry over to supervise the deckhands. Left alone, King went to check on the straps that lashed the boxes and barrels to the deck farther aft. The boxes marked "Biosyn."

Harding had never heard of the Biosyn Corporation. She wondered what connection Ian and Richard had with it. Whenever Ian was around her, he had always been critical, even contemptuous, of biotechnology companies. And these men seemed to be unlikely friends. They were too rigid, too . . . geeky.

But then, she reflected, Ian did have strange friends. They were always showing up unexpectedly at his apartment—the Japanese calligrapher, the Indonesian gamalan troupe, the Las Vegas juggler in a shiny bolero jacket, that weird French astrologer who thought the earth was hollow. . . . And then there were his mathematician friends. They were *really* crazy. Or so they seemed to Sarah. They were so wild-eyed, so wrapped up in their proofs. Pages and pages of proofs, sometimes hundreds of pages. It was all too abstract for her. Sarah Harding liked to touch the dirt, to see the animals, to experience the sounds and the smells. That was real to her. Everything else was just a bunch of theories: possibly right, possibly wrong.

Waves began to crash over the bow, and she moved a little astern, to keep dry. She yawned; she hadn't slept much in the last twenty-four hours. Dodgson finished working on the Jeep, and came over to her.

She said, "Everything all right?"

"Oh yes," Dodgson said, smiling cheerfully.

"Your friend King seemed upset."

"He doesn't like boats," Dodgson said. He nodded to the waves. "But we're making better time. It'll only be an hour or so, until we land."

"Tell me," she said. "What is the Biosyn Corporation? I've never heard of it."

"It's a small company," Dodgson said. "We make what are called consumer biologicals. We specialize in recreational and sports organisms. For example, we engineered new kinds of trout, and other game fish. We're making new kinds of dogs—smaller pets for apartment dwellers. That sort of thing."

Exactly the sort of thing that Ian hated, she thought. "How do you know Ian?"

"Oh, we go way back," Dodgson said.

She noticed his vagueness. "How far?"

"Back to the days of the park."

"The park," she said.

He nodded. "Did he ever tell you how he hurt his leg?"

"No," she said. "He would never talk about it. He just said it happened on a consulting job that had . . . I don't know. Some sort of trouble. Was it a park?"

"Yes, in a way," Dodgson said, staring out at the ocean. After a moment, he shrugged. "And what about you? How do you know him?"

"He was one of my thesis readers. I'm an ethologist. I study large mammals in African grassland ecosystems. East Africa. Carnivores, in particular."

"Carnivores?"

"I've been studying hyenas," she said. "Before that, lions."

"For a long time?"

"Almost ten years, now. Six years continuously, since my doctorate."

"Interesting," Dodgson said, nodding. "And so did you come here all the way from Africa?"

"Yes, from Seronera. In Tanzania."

Dodgson nodded vaguely. He looked past her shoulder toward the island. "What do you know. Looks like the weather may clear, after all."

She turned and saw streaks of blue in the thinning clouds overhead. The sun was trying to break through. The sea was calmer. And she was surprised to see the island was much closer. She could clearly see the cliffs, rising above the seas. The cliffs were reddish-gray volcanic rock, very sheer.

"In Tanzania," Dodgson said. "You run a large research team?"

"No. I work alone."

"No students?" he said.

"I'm afraid not. It's because my work just isn't very glamorous. The big savannah carnivores in Africa are primarily nocturnal. So my research is mostly conducted at night."

"Must be hard on your husband."

"Oh, I'm not married," she said, with a little shrug.

"I'm surprised," he said. "After all, a beautiful woman like you . . ."

"I never had time," she said quickly. To change the subject, she said, "Where do you land on this island?"

Dodgson turned to look. They were now close enough to the island to see the waves crashing, high and white, against the base of the cliffs. They were only a mile or two away.

"It's an unusual island," Dodgson said. "This whole region of central America is volcanic. There are something like thirty active volcanoes between Mexico and Colombia. All these offshore islands were at one time active volcanoes, part of the central chain. But unlike the mainland, the islands are now dormant. Haven't erupted for a thousand years or so."

"So we're seeing the outside of the crater?"

"Exactly. The cliffs are all the result of erosion from rainfall, but the ocean erodes the base of the cliffs, too. Those flat sections on the cliff you see are where the ocean cut in at the bottom, and huge areas of the cliff face were undermined, and just cleaved, falling straight down into the sea. It's all soft volcanic rock."

"And so you land . . ."

"There are several places on the windward side where the ocean has cut caves into the cliff. And at two of those places, the caves meet rivers flowing out from the interior. So they're passable." He pointed ahead. "You see there, you can just now see one of the caves."

Sarah Harding saw a dark irregular opening cut into the base of the cliff. All around it, the waves crashed, plumes of white water rising fifty feet up into the air.

"You're going to take this boat into that cave there?"

"If the weather holds, yes." Dodgson turned away. "Don't worry, it's not as bad as it looks. Anyway, you were saying. About Africa. When did you leave Africa?"

"Right after Doc Thorne called. He said he was going with Ian to rescue Richard, and asked if I wanted to come."

"And what did you say?"

"I said I'd think about it."

Dodgson frowned. "You didn't tell him you were coming?"

"No. Because I wasn't sure I wanted to. I mean, I'm busy. I have my work. And it's a long way."

"For an old lover," Dodgson said, nodding sympathetically.

She sighed. "Well. You know. Ian."

"Yes, I know Ian," Dodgson said. "Quite a character."

"That's one way to put it," she said.

There was an awkward silence. Dodgson cleared his throat. "I'm confused," he said. "Who exactly did you tell you were coming here?"

"Nobody," she said. "I just jumped on the next plane and came."

"But what about your university, your colleagues . . ."

She shrugged. "There wasn't time. And as I said, I work alone." She looked again at the island. The cliffs rose high above the boat. They were only a few hundred yards away. The cave appeared much larger now, but the waves crashed high on either side. She shook her head. "It looks pretty rough."

"Don't worry," Dodgson said. "See? The captain's already making for it. We'll be perfectly safe, once we're passing through. And then . . . It should be very exciting."

The boat rolled and dipped in the sea, an uncertain motion. She gripped the railing. Beside her, Dodgson grinned. "See what I mean? Exciting, isn't it?" He seemed suddenly energized, almost agitated. His body became tense; he rubbed his hands together. "No need to worry, Ms. Harding, I can't allow anything to happen to—"

She didn't know what he was talking about, but before she could reply, the nose of the boat dipped again, kicking up spray, and she stumbled a little. Dodgson bent over quickly—apparently to steady her—but it seemed as if something went wrong—his body struck against her legs, then lifted—and then another wave crashed over them and she felt her body twist and she screamed and clutched at the railing. But it was all happening too fast, the world upended and swirled around her, her head clanged once on the railing and then she was tumbling, falling through space. She saw the peeling paint on the hull of the boat sliding past her, she saw the green ocean rush up toward her, and then she was shocked with the sudden stinging cold as she plunged into the rough, heaving sea, and sank beneath the waves, into darkness.

The Valley

"This is going extremely well," Levine said, rubbing his hands together. "Far beyond my expectations, I must say. I couldn't be more pleased."

He was standing in the high hide with Thorne, Eddie, Malcolm, and the kids, looking down on the valley floor below. Everyone was sweating inside the little observation hut; the midday air was still and hot. Around them, the grassy meadow was deserted; most of the dinosaurs had moved beneath the trees, into the cool of the shade.

The exception was the herd of apatosaurs, which had left the trees to return to the river, where they were now drinking once again. The huge animals clustered fairly tightly around the water's edge. In the same vicinity, but more spread out, were the high-crested parasaur-olophasaurs; these somewhat smaller dinosaurs positioned themselves near the apatosaur herd.

Thorne wiped sweat out of his eyes and said, "Why, exactly, are you pleased?"

"Because of what we're seeing here," Malcolm said. He glanced at his watch, and wrote an entry in his notebook. "We're getting the data that I hoped for. It's very exciting."

Thorne yawned, sleepy in the heat. "Why is it exciting? The dinosaurs are drinking. What's the big deal?"

"Drinking *again*," Levine corrected him. "For the second time in an hour. At midday. Such fluid intake is highly suggestive of the thermoregulatory strategies these large creatures employ."

"You mean they drink a lot to stay cool," Thorne said, always impatient with jargon.

"Yes. Clearly they do. Drink a lot. But in my view, their return to the river may have another significance entirely."

"Which is?"

"Come, come," Levine said, pointing. "Look at the herds. Look how they are arranged spatially. We are seeing something that no one has witnessed before, or even suspected, for dinosaurs. We're seeing nothing less than inter-species symbiosis."

"We are?"

"Yes," Levine said. "The apatosaurs and the parasaurs are together. I saw them together yesterday, too. I'll bet that they're always together, when they're out on the open plain. Undoubtedly you are wondering why."

"Undoubtedly," Thorne said.

"The reason," Levine said, "is that the apatosaurs are very strong but weak-sighted, whereas the parasaurs are smaller, but have very sharp vision. So the two species stay together because they provide a mutual defense. Just the way zebras and baboons stay together on the African plain. Zebras have a good sense of smell, and baboons have good eyesight. Together they're more effective against predators than either is alone."

"And you think this is true of the dinosaurs because . . ."

"It's rather obvious," Levine said. "Just look at the behavior. When the two herds were alone, each clustered tightly among themselves. But when they're together, the parasaurs spread out, abandoning their former herd arrangement, to form an outer ring around the apatosaurs. Just as you see them now. That can only mean that individual paras are going to be protected by the apatosaur herd. And vice versa. It can only be a mutual predator defense."

As they watched, one of the parasaurs lifted its head, and stared across the river. It honked mournfully, a long musical sound. All the other parasaurs looked up and stared, too. The apatosaurs continued to drink at the river, although one or two adults raised their long necks.

In the midday heat, insects buzzed around them. Thorne said, "So where are the predators?"

"Right there," Malcolm said, pointing toward a stand of trees on the other side of the river, not far from the water.

Thorne looked, and saw nothing.

"Don't you see them?"

"No."

"Keep looking. They're small, lizard-like animals. Dark brown. Raptors," he said.

Thorne shrugged. He still saw nothing. Standing beside him, Levine began to eat a power bar. Preoccupied with holding the binoculars, he dropped the wrapper on the floor of the hide. Bits of paper fluttered to the ground below.

"How are those things?" Arby said.

"Okay. A little sugary."

"Got any more?" he said.

Levine rummaged in his pockets and gave him one. Arby broke it in half, and gave half to Kelly. He began to unwrap his half, carefully folding the paper, putting it neatly in his pocket.

"You realize this is all highly significant," Malcolm said. "For the question of extinction. Already it's obvious that the extinction of the dinosaurs is a far more complex problem than anyone has recognized."

"It is?" Arby said.

"Well, consider," Malcolm said. "All extinction theories are based on the fossil record. But the fossil record doesn't show the sort of behavior we're seeing here. It doesn't record the complexity of groups interacting."

"Because fossils are just bones," Arby said.

"Right. And bones are not behavior. When you think about it, the fossil record is like a series of photographs: frozen moments from what is really a moving, ongoing reality. Looking at the fossil record is like thumbing through a family photo album. You know that the album isn't complete. You know life happens between the pictures. But you don't have any record of what happens in between, you only have the pictures. So you study them, and study them. And pretty soon, you begin to think of the album not as a series of moments, but as reality itself. And you begin to explain everything in terms of the album, and you forget the underlying reality.

"And the tendency," Malcolm said, "has been to think in terms of physical events. To assume that some external physical event caused the extinctions. A meteor hits the earth, and changes the weather. Or volcanoes erupt, and change the weather. Or a meteor causes the volcanoes to erupt and change the weather. Or vegetation changes, and species starve and become extinct. Or a new disease arises, and species become extinct. Or a new plant arises, and poisons all the dinosaurs. In every case, what is imagined is some external event. But what nobody imagines is that the animals themselves might have changed—not in their bones, but their behavior. Yet when you look at animals like these, and see how intricately their behavior is interrelated, you realize that a change in group behavior could easily lead to extinction."

"But why would group behavior change?" Thorne said. "If there wasn't some external catastrophe to force it, why should the behavior change?"

"Actually," Malcolm said, "behavior is always changing, all the time. Our planet is a dynamic, active environment. Weather is changing. The land is changing. Continents drift. Oceans rise and fall. Mountains thrust up and erode away. All the organisms on the planet are constantly adapting to those changes. The best organisms are the ones that can adapt most rapidly. That's why it's hard to see how a catastrophe that produces a large change could cause extinction, since so much change is occurring all the time, anyway."

"In that case," Thorne said, "what causes extinction?"

"Certainly not rapid change alone," Malcolm said. "The facts tell us that clearly."

"What facts?"

"After every major environmental change, a wave of extinctions has usually followed—but not right away. Extinctions only occur thousands, or millions of years later. Take the last glaciation in North America. The glaciers descended, the climate changed severely, but animals didn't die. Only after the glaciers receded, when you'd think things would go back to normal, did lots of species become extinct. That's when giraffes and tigers and mammoths vanished on this continent. And that's the usual pattern. It's almost as if species are weakened by the major change, but die off later. It's a well-recognized phenomenon."

"It's called Softening Up the Beachhead," Levine said.

"And what's the explanation for it?"

Levine was silent.

"There is none," Malcolm said. "It's a paleontological mystery. But I believe that complexity theory has a lot to tell us about it. Because if the notion of life at the edge of chaos is true, then major change pushes animals closer to the edge. It destabilizes all sorts of behavior. And when the environment goes back to normal, it's not really a return to normal. In evolutionary terms, it's another big change, and it's just too much to keep up with. I believe that new behavior in populations can emerge in unexpected ways, and I think I know why the dinosaurs—"

"What's that?" Thorne said.

Thorne was looking at the trees, and saw a single dinosaur hop out into view. It was rather slender, agile on its hind legs, balancing with a stiff tail. It was six feet tall, green-brown with dark-red stripes, like a tiger.

"That," Malcolm said, "is a velociraptor."

Thorne turned to Levine. "That's what chased you up in the tree? It looks ugly."

"Efficient," Levine said. "Those animals are brilliantly constructed killing machines. Arguably the most efficient predators in the history of the planet. The one that just stepped out will be the alpha animal. It leads the pack."

Thorne saw other movement beneath the trees. "There's more."

"Oh yes," Levine said. "This particular pack is very large." He picked up binoculars, and peered through them. "I'd like to locate their nest," he said. "I haven't been able to find it anywhere on the island. Of course they're secretive, but even so . . ."

The parasaurs were all crying loudly, moving closer to the apatosaur herd as they did so. But the big apatosaurs seemed relatively indifferent; the adults nearest the water actually turned their backs to the approaching raptor.

"Don't they care?" Arby said. "They're not even looking at him."

"Don't be fooled," Levine said, "the apatosaurs care very much. They may look like gigantic cows, but they're nothing of the sort. Those whiptails are thirty or forty feet long, and weigh several tons. Notice how fast they can swing them. One smack from those tails would snap an attacker's back."

"So turning away is part of their defense?"

"Unquestionably, yes. And you can see now how the long necks balance their tails."

The tails of the adults were so long, they reached entirely across the river, to the other shore. As they swung back and forth, and the parasaurs cried out, the lead raptor turned away. Moments later, the entire pack began to slink off, following the edge of the trees, heading up into the hills.

"Looks like you're right," Thorne said. "The tails scared them off."

"How many do you count?" Levine said.

"I don't know. Ten. No, wait—fourteen. Maybe more. I might have missed a few."

"Fourteen." Malcolm scribbled in his notebook.

"You want to follow them?" Levine said.

"Not now."

"We could take the Explorer."

"Maybe later," Malcolm said.

"I think we need to know where their nest is," Levine said. "It's essential, Ian, if we're going to settle predator-prey relationships. Nothing is more important than that. And this is a perfect opportunity to follow—"

"Maybe later," Malcolm said. He checked his watch again.

"That's the hundredth time you've checked your watch today," Thorne said.

Malcolm shrugged. "Getting to be lunchtime," he said. "By the way, what about Sarah? Shouldn't she be arriving soon?"

"Yes. I imagine she'll show up any time now," Thorne said.

Malcolm wiped his forehead. "It's hot up here."

"Yes, it's hot."

They listened to the buzzing of insects in the midday sun, and watched the raptors retreat.

"You know, I'm thinking," Malcolm said. "Maybe we ought to go back."

"Go back?" Levine said. "Now? What about our observations? What about the other cameras we want to place and—"

"I don't know, maybe it'd be good to take a break."

Levine stared at him in disbelief. He said nothing.

Thorne and the kids looked at Malcolm silently.

"Well, it seems to me," Malcolm said, "that if Sarah's coming all the way from Africa, we should be there to greet her." He shrugged. "I think it's simple politeness."

Thorne said, "I didn't realize that, uh . . ."

"No, no," Malcolm said quickly. "It's nothing like that. I just, uh . . . You know, maybe she's not even coming." He looked suddenly uncertain. "Did she say she was coming?"

"She said she'd think about it."

Malcolm frowned. "Then she's coming. If Sarah said that, she's coming. I know her. So. What do you say, want to go back?"

"Certainly not," Levine said, peering through binoculars. "I wouldn't dream of leaving here now."

Malcolm turned. "Doc? Want to go back?"

"Sure," Thorne said, wiping his forehead. "It's hot."

"If I know Sarah," Malcolm said, climbing down the scaffolding, "she's going to show up on this island just looking *great*."

Cave

She struggled upward, and her head broke the surface, but she saw only water—great swells rising fifteen feet above her, on all sides. The power of the ocean was immense. The surge dragged her forward, then back, and she was helpless to resist. She could not see the boat anywhere, only foaming sea, on all sides. She could not see the island, only water. Only water. She fought a sense of overwhelming panic.

She tried to kick against the current, but her boots were leaden. She sank down again, and struggled back, gasping for air. She had to get her boots off, somehow. She gulped a breath and ducked her head under the water, and tried to unlace the boots. Her lungs burned as she fumbled with the knots. The ocean swept her back and forth, ceaselessly.

She got one boot off, gulped air, and ducked down again. Her fingers were stiff with cold and fright, as she worked on the other boot. It seemed to take hours. Finally her legs were free, light, and she dogpaddled, catching her breath. The surge lifted her high, dropped her again. She could not see the island. She felt panic again. She turned, and felt the surge lift once more. And then she saw the island.

The sheer cliffs were close, frighteningly close. The waves boomed as they smashed against the rocks. She was no more than fifty yards offshore, being swept inexorably toward the crashing surf. On the next crest, she saw the cave, a hundred yards to her right. She tried to swim toward it, but it was hopeless. She had no power at all to move in this gigantic surf. She felt only the strength of the sea, sweeping her to the cliffs.

Panic made her heart race. She knew she would be instantly killed. A wave crested over her; she gulped sea water, and coughed. Her eyes blurred. She felt nausea and deep, deep terror.

She put her head down and began to swim, arm over arm, kicking as hard as she could. She had no sense of movement, only the sideways pull of the surge. She dared not look up. She kicked harder. When she raised her head for another breath, she saw she had moved a little—not much, but a little—to the north. She was a little nearer to the cave.

She was encouraged, but she was terrified. She had so little strength! Her arms and legs ached with her effort. Her lungs burned. Her breath came in short ragged heaving gasps. She coughed again, grabbed another breath, put her head down and kicked onward.

Even with her head in the water, she heard the deep boom of the surf against the cliffs. She kicked with all her might. The currents and surge moved her left and right, forward and back. It was hopeless. But still she tried.

Gradually, the ache in her muscles became a steady dull pain. She felt she had lived with this pain all her life. She did not notice it any more. She kicked on, oblivious.

When she felt the surge lift her up again, she raised her head for a breath. She was startled to see that the cave was very close. A few more strokes and she would be swept inside it. She had thought the current might be less severe around the cave. But it wasn't; on either side of the opening, the waves crashed high, climbing the cliff walls, and then falling back. The boat was nowhere in sight.

She ducked her head down again, kicked forward, using the last of her strength. She could feel her entire body weakening. She could not last much longer. She knew she was being carried toward the cliffs. She heard the boom of the surf louder now, and she kicked again, and suddenly a huge swell swept her up, lifting her, carrying her toward the cliffs. She was powerless to resist it. She raised her head to look, and saw darkness, inky darkness.

In her exhaustion and pain, she realized that she was inside the cave. She had been swept into the cave! The booming sound was hollow, reverberating. It was too dark to see the walls on either side. The current was intense, sweeping her ever deeper. She gasped for breath and paddled ineffectually. Her body scraped against rock; she felt a moment of searing pain, and then she was swept farther into the depths of the cave. But now there was a difference. She saw faint light on the ceiling, and the water around her seemed to glow. The surge lessened. She found it easier to keep her head above water. She saw hot light ahead, brilliantly hot—the end of the cave.

And suddenly, astonishingly, she was carried through, and burst into sunlight and open air. She found herself in the middle of a broad muddy river, surrounded by dense green foliage. The air was hot and still; she heard the distant cries of jungle birds.

Up ahead, around a bend in the river, she saw the stern of Dodgson's boat, already tied up to the shore. She could not see any of the people, and she didn't want to see them.

Summoning her remaining strength, she kicked toward shore, and clutched at a stand of mangroves, growing thickly along the water's edge. Too weak to hold on, she hooked her arm around a root, and lay on her back in the gentle current, looking up at the sky, gasping for breath. She did not know how much time passed, but finally she felt strong enough to haul herself arm over arm along the mangrove roots at the water's edge, until she came to a narrow break in the foliage, leading to a patch of muddy shore beyond. As she dragged herself out of the water, and up on the slippery bank, she noticed several rather large animal footprints in the mud. They were curious, three-toed footprints, with each toe ending in a large claw . . .

She bent to examine them more closely, and then she felt the earth vibrating, trembling beneath her hands. A large shadow fell over her and she looked up in astonishment at the leathery, pale underbelly of an enormous animal. She was too weak to react, even to raise her head.

The last thing she saw was a huge leathery foot landing beside her, squishing in the mud, and a soft snorting sound. And then suddenly, abruptly, exhaustion overtook her, and Sarah Harding collapsed, and fell onto her back. Her eyes rolled up into her head, and she lost consciousness.

Dodgson

A few yards up from the shore of the river, Lewis Dodgson climbed into the custom-made Jeep Wrangler and slammed the door shut. Beside him in the passenger seat, Howard King was wringing his hands. He said, "How could you have done that to her?"

"Done what?" George Baselton said, from the back seat.

Dodgson did not reply. He turned the key in the ignition. The engine rumbled to life. He popped the four-wheel drive into gear and headed up the hill into the jungle, away from the boat at the shore.

"How could you?" King said again, agitated. "I mean, Jesus."

"What happened was an accident," Dodgson said.

"An accident? An *accident*?"

"That's right, an accident," Dodgson said calmly. "She fell overboard."

"I didn't see anything," Baselton said.

King was shaking his head. "Jesus, what if somebody comes to investigate and—"

"What if they do?" Dodgson said, interrupting him. "We were in rough seas, she was standing at the bow, a big wave hit us and she was washed overboard. She couldn't swim very well. We circled and looked for her, but there was no hope. A very unfortunate accident. So what are you concerned about?"

"What am I concerned about?"

"Yes, Howard. Exactly what the fuck are you concerned about?"

"I *saw* it, for Christ's sake—"

"No, you didn't," Dodgson said.

"I didn't see anything," Baselton said. "I was down below, the whole time."

"That's fine for you," Howard King said. "But what if there's an investigation?"

The Jeep bounced up the dirt track, moving deeper into the jungle. "There won't be," Dodgson said. "She left Africa in a hurry, and she didn't tell anybody where she was going."

"How do you know?" King whined.

"Because she *told* me, Howard. That's how I know. Now get the map out and stop moaning. You knew the deal when you joined me."

"I didn't know you were going to kill somebody, for Christ's sake."

"Howard," Dodgson said, with a sigh. "Nothing's going to happen. Get the map out."

"How do you know?" King said.

"Because I know what I'm doing," Dodgson said. "That's why. Unlike Malcolm and Thorne, who are somewhere on this island, screwing around, doing fuck knows what in this damned jungle."

Mention of the others caused a new worry. Fretting, King said, "Maybe we'll run into them. . . ."

"No, Howard, we won't. They'll never even know we're here. We're only going to be on this island for four hours, remember? Land at one. Back on the boat by five. Back at the port by seven. Back in San Francisco by midnight. Bang. Done. *Finito.* And finally, after all these years, I'll have what I should have had long ago."

"Dinosaur embryos," Baselton said.

"Embryos?" King asked, surprised.

"Oh, I'm not interested in embryos any more," Dodgson said. "Years ago, I tried to get frozen embryos, but there's no reason to bother with embryos now. I want fertilized eggs. And in four hours, I'll have them from every species on this island."

"How can you do that in four hours?"

"Because I already know the precise location of every dinosaur breeding site on the island. The map, Howard."

King opened the map. It was a large topographical chart of the island, two feet by three feet, showing terrain elevations in blue contours. At several places in lowland valleys, there were dense red concentric circles. In some places, clusters of circles. "What's this?" King said.

"Why don't you read what it says," Dodgson said.

King turned the map, and looked at the legend. " 'Sigma data Landsat/Nordstat mixed spectra VSFR/FASLR/IFFVR.' And then a bunch of numbers. No, wait. Dates."

"Correct," Dodgson said. "Dates."

"Pass dates? This is a summary chart, combining data from several satellite passes?"

"Correct."

King frowned. "And it looks like . . . visible spectrum, and false aperture radar, and . . . what?"

"Infrared. Broadband thermal VR." Dodgson smiled. "I did all this in about two hours. Downloaded all the satellite data, summarized it, and had the answers I wanted."

"I get it," King said. "These red circles are infrared signatures!"

"Yes," Dodgson said. "Big animals leave big signatures. I got all the satellite flybys over this island for the last few years, and mapped the location of heat sources. And the locations overlapped from pass to pass, which is what makes these red concentric marks. Meaning that the animals tend to be located in these particular places. Why?" He turned to King. "Because these are the nesting sites."

"Yes. They must be," Baselton said.

"Maybe that's where they eat," King said.

Dodgson shook his head irritably. "Obviously, those circles can't be feeding sites."

"Why not?"

"Because these animals average twenty tons apiece, that's why. You get a herd of twenty-ton dinos, and you're talking a combined biomass of more than half a million pounds moving through the forest. That many big animals are going to eat a lot of plant matter in the course of a day. And the only way they can do that is by moving. Right?"

"I guess . . ."

"You guess? Look around you, Howard. Do you see any denuded sections of forest? No, you don't. They eat a few leaves from the trees, and move on. Trust me, these animals have to move to eat. But what they don't move is their nesting sites. So these red circles must be nesting sites." He glanced at the map. "And unless I'm wrong, the first of the nests is just over this rise, and down the hill on the other side."

The Jeep fishtailed in a patch of mud, and ground forward, lurching up the hill.

Mating Calls

Richard Levine stood in the high hide, staring at the herds through binoculars. Malcolm had gone back to the trailer with the others, leaving Levine alone. In fact, Levine was relieved to have him gone. Levine was quite content to make observations on these extraordinary animals, and he was aware that Malcolm did not share his boundless enthusiasm. Indeed, Malcolm always seemed to have other considerations on his mind. And Malcolm was notably impatient with the act of observation — he wanted to analyze the data, but he did not want to collect it.

Of course, among scientists, that represented a well-known difference in personality. Physics was a perfect example. The experimentalists and the theorists lived in utterly different worlds, passing papers back and forth but sharing little else in common. It was almost as if they were in different disciplines.

And for Levine and Malcolm, the difference in their approach had surfaced early, back in the Santa Fe days. Both men were interested in extinction, but Malcolm approached the subject broadly, from a purely mathematical standpoint. His detachment, his inexorable formulas, had fascinated Levine, and the two men began an informal exchange over frequent lunches: Levine taught Malcolm paleontology; Malcolm taught Levine nonlinear mathematics. They began to draw some tentative conclusions which both found exciting. But they also began to disagree. More than once they were asked to leave the restaurant; then they would go out into the heat of Guadelupe Street, and walk back toward the river, still shouting at each other, while approaching tourists hurried to the other side of the street.

In the end, their differences came down to personalities. Malcolm considered Levine pedantic and fussy, preoccupied with petty details. Levine never saw the big picture. He never looked at the consequences of his actions. For his own part, Levine did not hesitate to call Malcolm imperious and detached, indifferent to details.

"God is in the details," Levine once reminded him.

"Maybe your God," Malcolm shot back. "Not mine. Mine is in the *process.*"

. . .

Standing in the high hide, Levine thought that answer was exactly what you would expect from a mathematician. Levine was quite satisfied that details were everything, at least in biology, and that the most common failing of his biological colleagues was insufficient attention to detail.

For himself, Levine lived for the details, and he could not ever let them go. Like the animal that had attacked him with Diego. Levine thought of it often, turning it over and over again, reliving the events. Because there was something troubling, some impression that he could not get right.

The animal had attacked quickly, and he had sensed it was a basic theropod form—hind legs, stiff tail, large skull, the usual—but in the brief flash in which he had seen the creature, there seemed to be a peculiarity around the orbits, which made him think of *Carnotaurus sastrei*. From the Gorro Frigo formation in Argentina. And in addition, the skin was extremely unusual, it seemed to be a sort of bright mottled green, but there was something about it . . .

He shrugged. The troubling idea hung in the back of his mind, but he couldn't get to it. He just couldn't get it.

Reluctantly, Levine turned his attention to the parasaur herd, browsing by the river, alongside the apatosaurs. He listened as the parasaurs made their distinctive, low trumpeting sounds. Levine noticed that most often the parasaurs made a sound of short duration, a kind of rumbling honk. Sometimes, several animals made this sound at once, or very nearly overlapping; so it seemed to be an audible way of indicating to the herd where all the members were. Then there was a much longer, more dramatic trumpeting call. This sound was made infrequently, and only by the two largest animals in the herd, which raised their heads and trumpeted loud and long. But what did the sound mean?

Standing there in the hot sun, Levine decided to perform a little experiment. He cupped his hands around his mouth, and imitated the parasaur's trumpeting cry. It wasn't a very good imitation, but immediately the lead parasaur looked up, turning its head this way and that. And it gave a low cry, answering Levine.

Levine gave a second call.

Again, the parasaur answered.

Levine was pleased by this response, and made an entry in his notebook. But when he looked up again, he was surprised to see that the parasaur herd was drifting away from the apatosaurs. They collected together, formed a single line, and began to walk directly toward the high hide.

Levine started to sweat.

What had he done? In some bizarre corner of his mind, he wondered if he had imitated a mating cry. That was all he needed, to attract a randy dinosaur. Who knew how these animals behaved in mating? With growing anxiety, he watched them march forward. Probably, he should call Malcolm, and ask his advice. But as he thought about it, he realized that by imitating that cry he had interfered with the environment, introduced a new variable. He had done exactly what he had told Thorne he did not intend to do. It was thoughtless, of course. And surely not very important in the scheme of things. But Malcolm was certain to give him hell about it.

Levine lowered his binoculars and stared. A deep trumpeting sound reverberated through the air, so loud it hurt his ears. The ground began to shake, making the high hide sway back and forth precariously.

My God, he thought. *They're coming right for me.* He bent over, and with fumbling fingers, searched his backpack for the radio.

Problems of Evolution

In the trailer, Thorne took the rehydrated meals out of the microwave, and passed the plates around the little table. Everyone unwrapped them, and began to eat. Malcolm poked his fork into the food. "What is this stuff?"

"Herb-baked chicken breast," Thorne said.

Malcolm took a bite, and shook his head. "Isn't technology wonderful?" he said. "They manage to make it taste just like cardboard."

Malcolm looked at the two kids seated opposite him, who were eating energetically. Kelly glanced up at him, and gestured with her fork at the books strapped into a shelf beside the table. "One thing I don't understand."

"Only one?" Malcolm said.

"All this business about evolution," she said. "Darwin wrote his book a long time ago, right?"

"Darwin published the *Origin of Species* in 1859," Malcolm said.

"And by now, everybody believes it, isn't that right?"

"I think it's fair to say that every scientist in the world agrees that evolution is a feature of life on earth," Malcolm said. "And that we are descended from animal ancestors. Yes."

"Okay," Kelly said. "So, what's the big deal now?"

Malcolm smiled. "The big deal," he said, "is that everybody agrees evolution occurs, but nobody understands how it works. There are big problems with the theory. And more and more scientists are admitting it."

Malcolm pushed his plate away. "You have to track the theory," he said, "over a couple of hundred years. Start with Baron Georges Cuvier: the most famous anatomist in the world in his day, living in the intellectual center of the world, Paris. Around 1800, people began digging up old bones, and Cuvier realized that they belonged to animals no longer found on earth. That was a problem, because back in 1800, everybody believed that all the animal species ever created were still alive. The idea seemed reasonable because the earth was thought to be only a few thousand years old. And because God, who had created all the animals, would never let any of his creations become extinct. So extinction was agreed to be impossible. Cuvier agonized over these dug-up bones, but he finally concluded that God or no God, many animals had become extinct—as a result, he thought, of worldwide catastrophes, like Noah's flood."

"Okay . . ."

"So Cuvier reluctantly came to believe in extinction," Malcolm said, "but he never accepted evolution. In Cuvier's mind, evolution didn't occur. Some animals died and some survived, but none evolved. In his view, animals didn't change. Then along came Darwin, who said that animals did evolve, and that the dug-up bones were actually the extinct predecessors of living animals. The implications of Darwin's idea upset lots of people. They didn't like to think of God's creations changing, and they didn't like to think of monkeys in their family trees. It was embarrassing and offensive. The debate was fierce. But Darwin amassed a tremendous amount of factual data—he had made an overwhelming case. So gradually his idea of evolution was accepted by scientists, and by the world at large. But the question remained: how does evolution happen? For that, Darwin didn't have a good answer."

"Natural selection," Arby said.

"Yes, that was Darwin's explanation. The environment exerts pressure which favors certain animals, and they breed more often in subsequent generations, and that's how evolution occurs. But as many people realized, natural selection isn't really an explanation. It's just a definition: if an animal succeeds, it must have been selected for. But what in the animal is favored? And how does natural selection actually operate? Darwin had no idea. And neither did anybody else for another fifty years."

"But it's genes," Kelly said.

"Okay," Malcolm said. "Fine. We come to the twentieth century. Mendel's work with plants is rediscovered. Fischer and Wright do population studies. Pretty soon we know genes control heredity—whatever genes are. Remember, through the first half of the century, all during World War I and World War II, nobody had any idea what a gene was. After Watson and Crick in 1953, we knew that genes were nucleotides arranged in a double helix. Great. And we knew about mutation. So by the late twentieth century, we have a theory of natural selection which says that mutations arise spontaneously in genes, that the environment favors the mutations that are beneficial, and out of this selection process evolution occurs. It's simple and straightforward. God is not at work. No higher organizing principle involved. In the end, evolution is just the result of a bunch of mutations that either survive or die. Right?"

"Right," Arby said.

"But there are problems with that idea," Malcolm said. "First of all, there's a time problem. A single bacterium—the earliest form of life— has two thousand enzymes. Scientists have estimated how long it would take to randomly assemble those enzymes from a primordial soup. Estimates run from forty billion years to one hundred billion years. But the earth is only four billion years old. So, chance alone seems too slow. Particularly since we know bacteria actually appeared only four hundred million years after the earth began. Life appeared very fast—which is why some scientists have decided life on earth must be of extraterrestrial origin. Although I think that's just evading the issue."

"Okay . . ."

"Second, there's the coordination problem. If you believe the current theory, then all the wonderful complexity of life is nothing but the accumulation of chance events—a bunch of genetic accidents strung together. Yet when we look closely at animals, it appears as if many elements must have evolved simultaneously. Take bats, which have echolocation—they navigate by sound. To do that, many things must evolve. Bats need a specialized apparatus to make sounds, they need specialized ears to hear echoes, they need specialized brains to interpret the sounds, and they need specialized bodies to dive and swoop and catch insects. If all these things don't evolve simultaneously, there's no advantage. And to imagine all these things happen purely by chance is like imagining that a tornado can hit a junkyard and assemble the parts into a working 747 airplane. It's very hard to believe."

"Okay," Thorne said. "I agree."

"Next problem. Evolution doesn't always act like a blind force should. Certain environmental niches don't get filled. Certain plants don't get eaten. And certain animals don't evolve much. Sharks haven't changed for a hundred and sixty million years. Opossums haven't changed since dinosaurs became extinct, sixty-five million years ago. The environments for these animals have changed dramatically, but the animals have remained almost the same. Not exactly the same, but almost. In other words, it appears they haven't responded to their environment."

"Maybe they're still well adapted," Arby said.

"Maybe. Or maybe there's something else going on that we don't understand."

"Like what?"

"Like other rules that influence the outcome."

Thorne said, "Are you saying evolution is directed?"

"No," Malcolm said. "That's Creationism and it's wrong. Just plain wrong. But I am saying that natural selection acting on genes is probably not the whole story. It's too simple. Other forces are also at work. The hemoglobin molecule is a protein that is folded like a sandwich around a central iron atom that binds oxygen. Hemoglobin expands and contracts when it takes on and gives up oxygen—like a tiny molecular lung. Now, we know the sequence of amino acids that make up hemoglobin. But we don't know how to fold it. Fortunately, we don't need to know that, because if you make the molecule, it folds all by itself. It organizes itself. And it turns out, again and again, that living things seem to have a self-organizing quality. Proteins fold. Enzymes interact. Cells arrange themselves to form organs and the organs arrange themselves to form a coherent individual. Individuals organize themselves to make a population. And populations organize themselves to make a coherent biosphere. From complexity theory, we're starting to have a sense of how this self-organization may happen, and what it means. And it implies a major change in how we view evolution."

"But," Arby said, "in the end, evolution still must be the result of the environment acting on genes."

"I don't think it's enough, Arb," Malcolm said. "I think more is involved—I think there has to be more, even to explain how our own species arose."

"About three million years ago," Malcolm said, "some African apes that had been living in trees came down to the ground. There was nothing special about these apes. Their brains were small and they weren't especially smart. They didn't have claws or sharp teeth for weapons. They weren't particularly strong, or fast. They were certainly no match for a leopard. But because they were short, they started standing upright on their hind legs, to see over the tall African grass. That's how it began. Just some ordinary apes, looking out over the grass.

"As time went on, the apes stood upright more and more of the time. That left their hands free to do things. Like all apes, they were tool-users. Chimps, for example, use twigs to fish for termites. That sort of thing. As time went on, our ape ancestors developed more complex tools. That stimulated their brains to grow in size and complexity. It began a spiral: more complex tools provoked more complex brains which provoked more complex tools. And our brains literally exploded, in evolutionary terms. Our brains more than doubled in size in about a million years. And that caused problems for us."

"Like what?"

"Like getting born, for one thing. Big brains can't pass through the birth canal—which means that both mother and child die in childbirth. That's no good. What's the evolutionary response? To make human infants born very early in development, when their brains are still small enough to pass through the pelvis. It's the marsupial solution—most of the growth occurs outside the mother's body. A human child's brain doubles during the first year of life. That's a good solution to the problem of birth, but it creates other problems. It means that human children will be helpless long after birth. The infants of many mammals can walk minutes after they're born. Others walk in a few days, or weeks. But human infants can't walk for a full year. They can't feed themselves for even longer. So one price of big brains was that our ancestors had to evolve new, stable social organizations to permit long-term child care, lasting many years. These big-brained, totally helpless children changed society. But that's not the most important consequence."

"No?"

"No. Being born in an immature state means that human infants have unformed brains. They don't arrive with a lot of built-in, instinctive behavior. Instinctively, a newborn infant can suck and grasp, but that's about all. Complex human behavior is not instinctive at all. So human societies had to develop education to train the brains of their children. To teach them how to act. Every human society expends tremendous time and energy teaching its children the right way to behave. You look at a simpler society, in the rain forest somewhere, and you find that every child is born into a network of adults responsible for helping to raise the child. Not only parents, but aunts and uncles and grandparents and tribal elders. Some teach the child to hunt or gather food or weave; some teach them about sex or war. But the responsibilities are clearly defined, and if a child does not have, say, a mother's brother's sister to do a specific teaching job, the people get together and appoint a substitute. Because raising children is, in a sense, the reason the society exists in the first place. It's the most important thing that happens, and it's the culmination of all the tools and language and social structure that has evolved. And eventually, a few million years later, we have kids using computers.

"Now, if this picture makes sense, where does natural selection act? Does it act on the body, enlarging the brain? Does it act on the developmental sequence, pushing the kids out early? Does it act on social behavior, provoking cooperation and child-caring? Or does it act everywhere all at once—on bodies, on development, and on social behavior?"

"Everywhere at once," Arby said.

"I think so," Malcolm said. "But there may also be parts of this story that happen automatically, the result of self-organization. For example, infants of all species have a characteristic appearance. Big eyes, big heads, small faces, uncoordinated movements. That's true of kids and puppies and baby birds. And it seems to provoke adults of all species to act tenderly toward them. In a sense, you might say infant appearance seems to self-organize adult behavior. And in our case, a good thing, too."

Thorne said, "What does that have to do with dinosaur extinction?"

"Self-organizing principles can act for better or worse. Just as self-organization can coordinate change, it can also lead a population into decline, and cause it to lose its edge. On this island, my hope is we'll see self-organizing adaptations in the behavior of real dinosaurs—and it'll tell us why they became extinct. In fact, I'm pretty sure we already know why the dinosaurs became extinct."

The radio clicked. "Bravo," Levine said, over the intercom. "I couldn't have put it better myself. But perhaps you better see what is happening out here. The parasaurs are doing something very interesting, Ian."

"What's that?"

"Come and look."

"Kids," Malcolm said, "you stay here and watch the monitors." He pressed the radio button. "Richard? We're on our way."

Parasaurs

Richard Levine gripped the railing of the high hide, and watched tensely. Directly ahead, coming into view over a low rise, he saw the magnificent head of a Parasaurolophus walkeri. The duck-billed hadrosaur's skull was three feet long, but it was made larger by a long horned crest that extended backward high in the air.

As the animal approached, Levine could see the green mottling on the head. He saw the long powerful neck, the heavy body with its light-green underbelly. The parasaurolophus was twelve feet tall, and roughly the size of a large elephant. Its head was almost as high as the floor of the high hide. The animal moved steadily toward him, its footsteps thumping on the ground. Moments later, he saw a second head appear over the rise—then a third, and a fourth. The animals trumpeted, and walked in single file directly toward him.

Within moments, the lead animal was abreast of the hide. Levine held his breath as it passed. The animal stared at him, its large brown eye rolling to watch him. It licked its lips with a dark-purple tongue. The hide shook with its footsteps. And then it had passed, continuing on toward the jungle behind. Soon after, the second animal passed.

The third animal brushed against the structure, rocking it slightly. But the dinosaur did not seem to notice; it continued steadily on. So did the others. One by one, they disappeared, into the dense foliage behind the high hide. The earth ceased to vibrate. It was then that he saw the game trail, running past the high hide and into the jungle.

Levine sighed.

His body relaxed slowly. He picked up his binoculars and took a deep breath, calming himself. His panic faded. He began to feel better.

And then he thought: What are they doing? Where are they going? Because, as he considered it, the behavior of the parasaurs seemed extremely strange. They had been in a defensive cluster while they fed, but in movement they had shifted to single file, which broke the usual clumped herd pattern, and made every animal vulnerable to predation. Yet the behavior was clearly organized. Moving in single file must serve some purpose.

But what?

Now that they were within the jungle, the animals had begun making low trumpeting sounds of short duration. Again, he had the sense that this was some sort of vocalization to convey position. Perhaps for members to keep track of each other while they moved through the jungle, while they changed locations.

But why were they changing locations?

Where were they going? What were they doing?

He certainly couldn't tell here, standing up in the high hide. He hesitated, listening to them. Then, in a decisive moment, he swung his leg over the railing and climbed quickly down the scaffolding.

Heat

She felt heat, and wet. Something rough scraped along her face, like sandpaper. It happened again, this roughness on her cheek. Sarah Harding coughed. Something dripped on her neck. She smelled an odd, sweetish odor, like fermenting African beer. There was a deep hissing sound. Then the rough scraping again, starting at her neck, moving up her cheek.

Slowly, she opened her eyes and stared up into the face of a horse. The big, dull eye of the horse peered down at her, with soft eyelashes. The horse was licking her with its tongue. It was almost pleasant, she thought, almost reassuring. Lying on her back in the mud, with a horse—

It wasn't a horse.

The head was too narrow, she suddenly saw, the snout too tapered, the proportions all wrong. She turned to look and saw that it was a small head, leading to a surprisingly thick neck, and a heavy body—

She jumped up, scrambling to her knees. "Oh my God!"

Her sudden movement startled the big animal, which snorted in alarm, and moved slowly away. It walked a few steps down the muddy shore and then turned back, looking at her reproachfully.

But she could see it now: small head, thick neck, huge lumbering body, with a double row of pentagonal plates running along the crest of the back. A dragging tail, with spikes in it.

Harding blinked.

It couldn't be.

Confused and dazed, her brain fumbled for the name of this creature, and it came back to her, all the way from childhood.

Stegosaurus.

It was a God damn stegosaurus.

In her astonishment, her mind went back to the glaring white hospital room, when she had visited Ian Malcolm in his delirium, when he mumbled the names of several dinosaurs. She had always had her suspicions. But even now, confronted by a living stegosaur, her immediate reaction was that it must be some kind of a trick. Sarah squinted at the animal, looking for the seam in the costume, the mechanical joints beneath the skin. But the skin was seamless, and the animal moved in an integrated, organic way. The eyes blinked again, slowly. Then the stegosaurus turned away from her, moved to the water's edge, and lapped it with its large rough tongue.

The tongue was dark blue.

How could that be? Dark blue from venous blood? Was it cold-blooded? No. This animal moved much too smoothly; it had the assurance—and indifference—of a warm-blooded creature. Lizards and reptiles always seemed to be paying attention to the temperature of their surroundings. This creature didn't behave that way at all. It stood in the shade, and lapped up the cold water, indifferent to it all.

She looked down at her shirt, saw the foamy spittle running down from her neck. It had drooled on her. She touched it with her fingers. It was warm.

It was warm-blooded, all right.

A stegosaurus.

She stared.

The stegosaurus's skin had a pebbled texture, but it was not scaly, like a reptile's. It was more like the skin of a rhino, she thought. Or of a warthog. Except it was entirely hairless, without the bristles of a pig.

The stegosaurus moved slowly. It had a peaceful, rather stupid air. And it probably was stupid, she thought, looking again at the head. The braincase was much smaller than that of a horse. Very small for the body weight.

She got to her feet, and groaned. Her body ached. Every limb and muscle was sore. Her legs trembled. She took a breath.

A few yards away, the stegosaurus paused, glanced at her, taking in her new upright appearance. When she did not move, it became indifferent once again, and returned to drinking from the river.

"I'll be damned," she said.

She looked at her watch. It was one-thirty in the afternoon, the sun still high overhead. She couldn't use the sun to navigate, and the afternoon was very hot. She decided she had better start walking, and try and find Malcolm and Thorne. Barefooted, moving stiffly, her muscles aching, she headed into the jungle, away from the river.

After walking half an hour, she was very thirsty, but she had trained herself to go without water for long periods in the African savannah. She continued on, indifferent to her own discomfort. As she approached the top of a ridge, she came to a game trail, a wide muddy track through the jungle. It was easier walking along the trail, and she had been following it for about fifteen minutes when she heard an excited yelping from somewhere ahead. It reminded her of dogs, and she proceeded cautiously.

Moments later, there was a crashing sound in the underbrush, coming from several directions at once, and suddenly a dark-green, lizard-like animal about four feet high burst through the foliage at terrific speed, shrieked, and leapt over her. She ducked instinctively, and hardly had time to recover before a second animal appeared and raced past her. Within instants, a whole herd of animals was running past her on all sides, yelping in fear, and then the next one brushed against her and knocked her over. She fell in the mud as other animals leapt and crashed around her.

A few feet ahead on the trail she saw a large tree with low-hanging branches. She acted without thinking, jumping to her feet, grabbing the branch, and swinging up. She reached safety just as a new dinosaur, with sharp-clawed feet, rushed through the mud beneath her, and chased after the fleeing green creatures. As this animal went away from her, she glimpsed a dark body, six feet tall, with reddish stripes like a tiger. Soon after, a second striped animal appeared, then a third—a pack of predators, hissing and snarling, as they pursued the green dinosaurs.

From her years in the field, she found herself automatically counting the animals that rushed past her. By her count, there were ten striped predators, and that immediately piqued her interest. It made no sense, she thought. As soon as the last of the predators was gone, she dropped down to the ground and hurried to follow them. It occurred to her that it might be foolish to do so, but her curiosity overcame her.

She chased the tiger-dinosaurs up a hill, but even before she reached the crest she could tell from the snarls and growls that they had already brought an animal down. At the crest, she looked down on their kill.

But it was like no kill she had ever seen in Africa. On the Seronera plain, a kill site had its own organization which was quite predictable, and in a way was almost stately. The biggest predators, lions or hyenas, were closest to the carcass, feeding with their young. Farther out, waiting their turn, were the vultures and marabou storks, and still farther out, the jackals and other small scavengers circled warily. After the big predators finished, the smaller animals moved in. Different animals ate different parts of the bodies: the hyenas and vultures ate bones; the jackals nibbled the carcass clean. This was the pattern at any kill, and as a result there was very little squabbling or fighting around the food.

But here, she saw pandemonium—a feeding frenzy. The fallen animal was thickly covered with striped predators, all furiously ripping the flesh of the carcass, with frequent pauses to snarl and fight with each other. Their fights were openly vicious—one predator bit the adjacent animal, inflicting a deep flank wound. Immediately, several other predators snapped at the same animal, which limped away, hissing and bleeding, badly wounded. Once at the periphery, the wounded animal retaliated by biting the tail of another creature, again causing a serious wound.

A young juvenile, about half the size of the others, kept pushing forward, trying to get at a bit of the carcass, but the adults did not make room for it. Instead, they snarled and snapped in fury. The youngster was frequently obliged to hop back nimbly, keeping its distance from the razor-sharp fangs of the grownups. Harding saw no infants at all. This was a society of vicious adults.

As she watched the big predators, their heads and bodies smeared in blood, she noticed the crisscross pattern of healed scars on their flanks and necks. These were obviously quick, intelligent animals, yet they fought continually. Was that the way their social organization had evolved? If so, it was a rare event.

Animals of many species fought for food, territory, and sex, but these fights most often involved display and ritual aggression; serious injury seldom occurred. There were exceptions, of course. When male hippos fought to take over a harem, they often severely wounded other males. But in any case, nothing matched what she saw now.

As she watched, the wounded animal at the edge of the kill slunk forward and bit another adult, which snarled and leapt at it, slashing with its long toe-claw. In a flash, the injured predator was eviscerated, coils of pale intestine slipping out through a wide gash. The animal fell howling to the ground, and immediately three adults turned away from the kill and jumped onto its newly fallen body, and began to tear the animal's flesh with rapacious intensity.

Harding closed her eyes, and turned away. This was a different world, and one she did not understand at all. In a daze, she headed back down the hill, moving quietly, carefully away from the kill.

Noise

The Ford Explorer glided quietly forward along the jungle path. They were following a game trail on the ridge above the valley, heading down toward the high hide, in the valley below.

Thorne drove. He said to Malcolm, "You were saying earlier that you knew why the dinosaurs became extinct. . . ."

"Well, I'm pretty sure I do," Malcolm said. "The basic situation is simple enough." He shifted in his seat. "Dinosaurs arose in the Triassic, about two hundred million years ago. They proliferated throughout the Jurassic and the Cretaceous periods that followed. They were the dominant life form on this planet for about a hundred and fifty million years—which is a very long time."

"Considering we've been here for only three million," Eddie said.

"Let's not put on airs," Malcolm said. "Some puny apes have been here for three million years. We haven't. Recognizable human beings have only been on this planet for thirty-five thousand years," he said. "That's how long it's been since our ancestors painted caves in France and Spain, drawing pictures of game to invoke success in the hunt. Thirty-five thousand years. In the history of the earth, that's nothing at all. We've just arrived."

"Okay . . ."

"And of course, even thirty-five thousand years ago, we were already making species extinct. Cavemen killed so much game that animals became extinct on several continents. There used to be lions and tigers in Europe. There used to be giraffes and rhinos in Los Angeles. Hell, ten thousand years ago, the ancestors of Native Americans hunted the woolly mammoth to extinction. This is nothing new, this human tendency—"

"Ian."

"Well, it's a fact, although your modern airheads think it's all so brand-new—"

"Ian. You were talking about dinosaurs."

"Right. Dinosaurs. Anyway, during a hundred and fifty million years on this planet, dinosaurs were so successful that by the Cretaceous there were twenty-one major groups of them. A few groups, like the camarasaurs and fabrosaurs, had died out. But the overwhelming majority of dinosaur groups were still active throughout the Cretaceous. And then, suddenly, about sixty-five million years ago, every single group became extinct. And only the birds remained. So. The question is— What was that?"

"I thought you knew," Thorne said.

"No. I mean, what was that sound? Did you hear something?"

"No," Thorne said.

"Stop the car," Malcolm said.

Thorne stopped the car, and clicked off the engine. They rolled down the windows and felt the still, midday heat. There was almost no breeze. They listened for a while.

Thorne shrugged. "I don't hear anything. What did you think you—"

"Sssh," Malcolm said. He cupped his hand to his ear and put his head out the window, listening intently. After a moment, he came back in. "I could have sworn I heard an engine."

"An engine? You mean an internal-combustion engine?"

"Right." He pointed to the east. "It sounded like it was coming from over there."

They listened again, and heard nothing.

Thorne shook his head. "I can't imagine a gas engine here, Ian. There's no gas to run one."

The radio clicked. "Dr. Malcolm?" It was Arby, in the trailer.

"Yes, Arby."

"Who else is here? On the island?"

"What do you mean?"

"Turn on your monitor."

Thorne flicked on the dashboard monitor. They saw a view from one of the security cameras. The view looked down into the narrow, steep east valley. They saw the slope of a hillside, dark beneath the trees. A tree branch blocked much of the frame. But the view was still, silent. There was no sign of activity.

"What did you see, Arby?"

"Just watch."

Through the leaves, Thorne saw a flash of khaki, then another. He realized it was a person, half-walking, half-sliding, down the steep jungle slope toward the floor below. Small compact frame, short dark hair.

"I'll be damned," Malcolm said, smiling.

"You know who that is?"

"Yes, of course. It's Sarah."

"Well, we better go get her." Thorne reached for the radio, pressed the button. "Richard," he said.

There was no answer.

"Richard? Are you reading?"

There was no answer.

Malcolm sighed. "Great. He's not answering. Probably decided to go for a walk. Pursuing his research . . ."

"That's what I'm afraid of," Thorne said. "Eddie, unhook the motorcycle and go see what Levine's doing now. Take a Lindstradt with you. We'll go pick up Sarah."

Trail

Levine followed the game trail, moving deeper into the darkness of the jungle. The parasaurs were somewhere up ahead, making a lot of noise as they crashed through the ferns and palms on the jungle floor. At least now he understood why they had formed into a single file: there was no other practical way to move through the dense growth of the rain forest.

Their vocalizations had never stopped, but Levine noticed they were taking on a different character—more high-pitched, more excited. He hurried forward, pushing past wet palm fronds taller than he was, following the beaten trail. As he listened to the cries of the animals ahead, he also began to notice a distinctive odor, pungent and sweet-sour. He had the feeling the odor was growing stronger.

But up ahead, something was happening, there was no doubt about it. The parasaur vocalizations were now clipped, almost barking sounds. He sensed in them an agitated quality. But what could agitate an animal twelve feet high and thirty feet long?

His curiosity overwhelmed him. Levine began to run through the jungle, shoving aside palms, leaping over fallen trees. In the foliage ahead, he heard a hissing sound, a sort of spattering, and then one of the parasaurs gave a long, low trumpeting cry.

Eddie Carr drove the motorcycle up to the high hide, and stopped. Levine was gone. He looked at the ground around the hide, and saw many deep animal footprints in the ground. The prints were large, about two feet in diameter, and they seemed to be going off into the jungle behind the hide.

He scanned the ground, and saw fresh bootmarks as well. They had an Asolo tread; he recognized them as Levine's. In some places the bootmarks disrupted the edge of the animal footprints, which meant that they had been made afterward. The bootmarks also led into the forest.

Eddie Carr swore. The last thing he wanted to do was to go into that jungle. The very idea gave him the creeps. But what choice was there?

He had to get Levine back. That guy, he thought, was getting to be a real problem. Eddie unshouldered the rifle, and set it laterally across the handlebars of the motorcycle. Then he twisted the grips, and silently, the bike moved forward, into darkness.

Heart pounding with excitement, Levine pushed past the last of the big palms. He stopped abruptly. Directly ahead of him, the tail of a parasaur swung back and forth above his head. The animal's hindquarters were turned toward him. And a thick stream of urine gushed from the posterior pubis, spattering on the ground below. Levine jumped back, avoiding the stream. Beyond the nearest animal, he saw a clearing in the jungle, trampled flat by countless animal feet. The parasaurs had located themselves at various positions within this clearing, and they were all urinating together.

So they were latrine animals, he thought. That was fascinating, and totally unexpected.

Many contemporary animals, including rhinos and deer, preferred to relieve themselves at particular spots. And many times, the behavior of herds was coordinated. Latrine behavior was generally considered to be a method of marking territory. But whatever the reason, no one had ever suspected that dinosaurs acted in this way.

As Levine watched, the parasaurs finished urinating, and each moved a few feet to the side. Then they defecated, again in unison. Each parasaur produced a large mound of straw-colored spoor. This was accompanied by low trumpeting from each animal in the herd—along with an enormous quantity of expelled flatus, redolent of methane.

Behind him, a voice whispered, "*Very* nice."

He turned, and saw Eddie Carr sitting on the motorcycle. He was waving his hand in front of his face. "Dino farts," he said. "Better not light a match around here, you'll blow the place up. . . ."

"Ssssh," Levine hissed angrily, shaking his head. He turned back to the parasaurs. This was no time to be interrupted by a vulgar young fool. Several of the animals bent their heads down, and began to lick the puddles of urine. No doubt they wanted to recover lost nutrients, he thought. Perhaps salt. Or perhaps hormones. Or perhaps it was something seasonal. Or perhaps—

Levine edged forward.

They knew so little about these creatures. They didn't even know the most basic facts about their lives—how they ate, how they eliminated, how they slept and bred. A whole world of intricate, interlocking behaviors had evolved in these long-vanished animals. Understanding them now could be the work of a lifetime for dozens of scientists. But that would probably never happen. All he could hope to do was make a few conjectures, a few simple deductions that skimmed the surface of the complexity of their lives.

The parasaurs trumpeted, and headed deeper into the forest. Levine moved forward to follow them.

"Dr. Levine," Eddie said quietly. "Get on the bike. *Now.*"

Levine ignored him, but as the big animals departed, he saw dozens of tiny green dinosaurs leap chittering out into the clearing. He realized at once what they were: *Procompsognathus triassicus.* Small scavenger, found by Fraas in 1913, in Bavaria. Levine stared, fascinated. Of course he knew the animal well, but only from reconstructions, because there were no complete skeletons of *Procompsognathus* anywhere in the world. Ostrom had done the most complete studies, but he had to work with a skeleton that was badly crushed, and fragmentary. The tail, neck, and arms were all missing from the animals Ostrom described. Yet here the procompsognathids were, fully formed and active, hopping around like so many chickens. As he watched, the compys began to eat the fresh dung, and drink what was left of the urine. Levine frowned. Was that part of ordinary scavenger behavior?

Levine wasn't sure. . . .

He edged forward, to look at them more closely.

"Dr. Levine!" Eddie whispered.

It was interesting that the compys only ate fresh dung, not the dried remnants that were everywhere in the clearing. Whatever nutrients they were obtaining from the dung, it must only be present in fresh specimens. That suggested a protein or hormone that would degrade over time. Probably he should obtain a fresh sample for analysis. He reached into his shirt pocket, and withdrew a plastic baggie. He moved among the compys, which seemed indifferent to his presence.

He crouched down by the nearest dung pile, and reached slowly forward.

"*Dr. Levine!*"

He glanced back, annoyed, and in that moment one of the compys leapt forward and bit his hand. Another jumped onto his shoulder and bit his ear. Levine yelled, and stood up. The compys hopped onto the ground and scampered away.

"Damn it!" he said.

Eddie drove up on the motorcycle. "That's enough," he said. "Get on the damn bike. We're getting out of here."

Nest

The red Jeep Wrangler came to a stop. Directly ahead, the game trail they had been following continued through the foliage, to a clearing beyond. The game trail was wide and muddy, trampled flat by large animals. They could see large, deep footprints in the mud.

From the clearing, they heard a low honking noise, like the sound of very large geese. Dodgson said, "Okay. Give me the box."

King didn't answer.

Baselton said, "What box?"

Without taking his eyes off the clearing, Dodgson said, "There's a black box on the seat beside you, and a battery pack. Give them to me."

Baselton grunted. "It's heavy."

"That's because of the cone magnets." Dodgson reached back, took the box, which was made of black anodized metal. It was the size of a shoebox, except it ended in a flaring cone. Underneath was mounted a pistol grip. Dodgson clipped a battery pack to his belt, and plugged it into the box. Then he picked the box up by the pistol grip. There was a knob at the back, facing him, and a graduated dial.

Dodgson said, "Batteries charged?"

"They're charged," King said.

"Okay," Dodgson said. "I'll go first, into the nest area. I'll adjust the box, and get rid of the animals. You two follow behind me, and once the animals are gone, you each take an egg from the nest. Then you leave, and bring them back to the car. I'll come back last. Then we all drive off. Got it?"

"Right," Baselton said.

"Okay," King said. "What kind of dinosaurs are these?"

"I have no fucking idea," Dodgson said, climbing out of the car. "And it doesn't make any difference. Just follow the procedure." He closed the door softly.

The others got out quietly, and they started forward, down the wet trail. Their feet squished in the mud. The sound from the clearing continued. To Dodgson, it sounded like a lot of animals.

He pushed aside the last of the ferns and saw them.

It was a large nesting site, with perhaps four or five low earthen mounds, covered in grasses. The mounds were about seven feet wide, and three feet deep. There were twenty beige-colored adults around the mounds—a whole herd of dinosaurs, surrounding the nesting site. And the adults were big, thirty feet long and ten feet high, all honking and snorting.

"Oh, my God," Baselton said, staring.

Dodgson shook his head. "They're maiasaurs," he whispered. "This is going to be a piece of cake."

Maiasaurs had been named by paleontologist Jack Horner. Before Horner, scientists assumed that dinosaurs abandoned their eggs, as most reptiles did. Those assumptions fitted the old picture of dinosaurs as cold-blooded, reptilian creatures. Like reptiles, they were thought to be solitary; murals on museum walls rarely showed more than one example from each species—a brontosaurus here, a stegosaurus or a triceratops there, wading through the swamps. But Horner's excavations in the badlands of Montana provided clear, unambiguous evidence that at least one species of hadrosaurs had engaged in complex nesting and parenting behavior. Horner incorporated that behavior in the name he gave these creatures: maiasaur meant "good-mother lizard."

Watching them now, Dodgson could see the maiasaurs were indeed attentive parents, the big adults circling the nests, moving carefully to step outside the shallow earthen mounds. The beige maiasaurs were duck-billed dinosaurs; they had large heads that ended in a broad, flattened snout, rather like the bill of a duck.

They were taking mouthfuls of grass, and dropping it on the eggs in the mounds. This was, he knew, a way to regulate the temperature of the eggs. If the huge animals sat on the eggs, they would crush them. So instead they put a layer of grass over the eggs, which trapped heat and kept the eggs at a more constant temperature. The animals worked steadily.

"They're huge," Baselton said.

"They're nothing but oversized cows," Dodgson said. Although the maiasaurs were large, they were plant-eaters, and they had the docile, slightly stupid manner of cows. "Ready? Here we go."

He lifted the box like a gun, and stepped forward, into view.

. . .

Dodgson expected a big reaction when the maiasaurs saw him, but there was none at all. They hardly seemed to notice him. One or two adults looked over, stared with dumb eyes, and then looked away. The animals continued to drop grass on the eggs, which were pale white, oval, and nearly two feet long. Each was about twice the size of an ostrich egg. About the size of a small beach ball. No animals had hatched yet.

King and Baselton stepped out, and stood beside him in the clearing. Still the maiasaurs ignored them.

"Amazing," Baselton said.

"Fine for us," Dodgson said. And he turned on the box.

A continuous, high-pitched shriek filled the clearing. The maiasaurs immediately turned toward the sound, honking and lifting their heads. They seemed agitated, confused. Dodgson twisted the dial, and the shriek became higher, ear-splitting.

The maiasaurs bobbed their heads, and moved away from the painful sound. They clustered at the far end of the clearing. Several of the animals urinated in alarm. A few of them moved away into the foliage, abandoning the nest. They were agitated, but they stayed away.

"Go now," Dodgson said.

King stepped into the nearest nest, and grunted as he picked up an egg. His arms hardly reached around the huge oval. The maiasaurs honked at him, but none of the adults moved forward. Then Baselton went into the nest, took an egg, and followed King back to the car.

Dodgson walked backward, holding the box on the adults. At the edge of the clearing, he turned the sound off.

At once the maiasaurs came back, honking loudly and repeatedly. But as they returned to the nests, it seemed as if the adults forgot what had just happened. Within a few moments, they ceased honking, and went back to dropping grass over the eggs. They ignored Dodgson as he left and headed back along the game trail.

Stupid animals, Dodgson thought, as he went to the car. Baselton and King were setting the eggs into big Styrofoam containers in the back, and fitting the foam packing around them carefully. Both men were grinning like kids.

"That was amazing!"

"Great! Fantastic!"

"What'd I tell you?" Dodgson said. "Nothing to it." He glanced at his watch. "At this rate, we'll finish in less than four hours."

He climbed behind the steering wheel and turned on the engine. Baselton got into the back seat. King got in the passenger seat and took out the map.

"Next," Dodgson said.

The High Hide

"I tell you, it's fine," Levine said irritably. He was sweating in the stifling heat beneath the aluminum roof of the high hide. "Look, it didn't even break the skin." He held out his hand. There was a red semicircle where the compy had pressed its teeth into the skin, but that was all.

Beside him, Eddie said, "Yeah, well, your ear is bleeding a little."

"I don't feel anything. It can't be bad."

"No, it's not bad, " Eddie said, opening the first-aid kit. "But I better clean it up."

"I prefer," Levine said, "to get on with my observations." The dinosaurs were barely a quarter-mile away from him, and he could see them well. In the still midday air, he could hear them breathe.

He could hear them breathe.

Or at least he could, if this young man would leave him alone. "Look," Levine said, "I know what I'm doing here. You came in at the end of a very interesting and successful experiment. I actually called the dinosaurs to me, by imitating their cry."

"You did?" Eddie said.

"Yes, I did. That was what led them into the forest in the first place. So I hardly think that I need your assistance—"

"The thing is," Eddie said, "you got some of that dino shit on your ear and there's a couple of little punctures. I'll just clean it off for you." He soaked a gauze pad with disinfectant. "May sting a little."

"I don't care, I have other—Ow!"

"Stop moving," Eddie said. "It'll only take a second."

"It's absolutely unnecessary."

"If you just stand still, it'll be done. There." He took the gauze away. Levine saw brown and a faint streak of red. Just as he suspected, the injury was trivial. He reached up and touched his ear. It didn't hurt at all.

Levine squinted out at the plain, as Eddie packed up the first-aid case.

"Jeez, it's hot up here," Eddie said.

"Yes," Levine said, shrugging.

"Sarah Harding arrived, and I think they took her back to the trailer. You want to go back now?"

"I can't imagine why," Levine said.

"I just thought you might want to say hello or something," Eddie said.

"My work is here," Levine said. He turned away, raised his binoculars to his eyes.

"So," Eddie said. "You don't want to come back?"

"Wouldn't dream of it," Levine said, staring through binoculars. "Not in a million years. Not in sixty-five million years."

Trailer

Kelly Curtis listened to the sound of the shower. She couldn't believe it. She stared at the muddy clothes tossed casually on the bed. Shorts and a khaki short-sleeve shirt.

Sarah Harding's actual clothes.

She couldn't help it. Kelly reached out and touched them. She noticed how the fabric was worn and frayed. Buttons sewn back on; they didn't match. And there were some reddish streaks near the pocket that she thought must be old bloodstains. She reached down and touched the fabric—

"Kelly?"

Sarah was calling to her, from the shower.

She remembered my name.

"Yes?" Kelly said, her voice betraying her nervousness.

"Is there any shampoo?"

"I'll look, Dr. Harding," Kelly said, opening drawers hastily. The men had all gone into the next compartment, leaving her alone with Sarah while she washed. Kelly searched desperately, opening the drawers, slamming them shut again.

"Listen," Sarah called, "it's okay if you can't find any."

"I'm looking. . . ."

"Is there any dishwashing liquid?"

Kelly paused. There was a green plastic bottle by the sink. "Yes, Dr. Harding, but—"

"Give it to me. It's all the same stuff. I don't care." The hand reached out, past the shower curtain. Kelly handed it to her. "And my name is Sarah."

"Okay, Dr. Harding."

"Sarah."

"Okay, Sarah."

Sarah Harding was a regular person. Very informal and normal.

Entranced, Kelly sat on the seat in the kitchen and waited, swinging her feet, in case Dr. Harding—Sarah—needed anything else. She listened to Sarah humming "I'm Gonna Wash That Man Right Out of My Hair." After a few moments, the shower turned off, and her hand reached out and took the towel on the hook. And then she came out, wrapped in the towel.

Sarah ran her fingers through her short hair, which seemed to be all the attention she gave to her appearance. "That feels better. Boy, this is a plush field trailer. Doc really did a great job."

"Yes," she said. "It's nice."

She smiled at Kelly. "How old are you, Kelly?"

"Thirteen."

"What is that, eighth grade?"

"Seventh."

"Seventh grade," Sarah said, thoughtfully.

Kelly said, "Dr. Malcolm left some clothes for you. He said he thought they'd fit." She pointed to a clean pair of shorts and a tee shirt.

"Whose are these?"

"I think they're Eddie's."

Sarah held them up. "Might work." She took them around the corner, into the sleeping area, and started getting dressed. She said, "What are you going to do when you grow up?"

"I don't know," Kelly said.

"That's a very good answer."

"It is?" Kelly's mother was always pushing her to get a part-time job, to decide what she wanted to do with her life.

"Yes," Sarah said. "Nobody smart knows what they want to do until they get into their twenties or thirties."

"Oh."

"What do you like to study?"

"Actually, uh, I like math," she said, in a sort of guilty voice.

Sarah must have heard her tone, because she said, "What's wrong with math?"

"Well, girls aren't good at it. I mean, you know."

"No, I don't know." Sarah's voice was flat.

Kelly felt panic. She had been experiencing this warm feeling with Sarah Harding, but now she sensed it was dissolving away, as if she had given a wrong answer to a disapproving teacher. She decided not to say anything else. She waited in silence.

After a moment Sarah came out again, wearing Eddie's baggy clothes. She sat down and started putting on a pair of boots. She moved in a very normal, matter-of-fact way. "What did you mean, girls aren't good at mathematics?"

"Well, that's what everybody says."

"Everybody like who?"

"My teachers."

Sarah sighed. "Great," she said, shaking her head. "Your teachers . . ."

"And the other kids call me a brainer. Stuff like that. You know." Kelly just blurted it out. She couldn't believe that she was saying all this to Sarah Harding, whom she hardly knew at all except from articles and pictures, but here she was, telling her all this personal stuff. All these things that upset her.

Sarah just smiled cheerfully. "Well, if they say that, you must be pretty good at math, huh?"

"I guess."

She smiled. "That's wonderful, Kelly."

"But the thing is, boys don't like girls who are too smart."

Sarah's eyebrows went up. "Is that so?"

"Well, that's what everybody says. . . ."

"Like who?"

"Like my mom."

"Uh-huh. And she probably knows what she's talking about."

"I don't know," Kelly admitted. "My mom only dates jerks, actually."

"So she could be wrong?" Sarah asked, glancing up at Kelly as she tied her laces.

"I guess."

"Well, in my experience, some men like smart women, and some don't. It's like everything else in the world." She stood up. "You know about George Schaller?"

"Sure. He studied pandas."

"Right. Pandas, and before that, snow leopards and lions and gorillas. He's the most important animal researcher in the twentieth century—and you know how he works?"

Kelly shook her head.

"Before he goes into the field, George reads everything that's ever been written about the animal he's going to study. Popular books, newspaper accounts, scientific papers, everything. Then he goes out and observes the animal for himself. And you know what he usually finds?"

She shook her head, not trusting herself to speak.

"That nearly everything that's been written or said is wrong. Like the gorilla. George studied mountain gorillas ten years before Dian Fossey ever thought of it. And he found that what was believed about gorillas was exaggerated, or misunderstood, or just plain fantasy—like the idea that you couldn't take women on gorilla expeditions, because the gorillas would rape them. Wrong. Everything . . . just . . . wrong."

Sarah finished tying her boots, and stood.

"So, Kelly, even at your young age, there's something you might as well learn now. All your life people will tell you things. And most of the time, probably ninety-five percent of the time, what they'll tell you will be wrong."

Kelly said nothing. She felt oddly disheartened to hear this.

"It's a fact of life," Sarah said. "Human beings are just stuffed full of misinformation. So it's hard to know who to believe. I know how you feel."

"You do?"

"Sure. My mom used to tell me I'd never amount to anything." She smiled. "So did some of my professors."

"Really?" It didn't seem possible.

"Oh yes," Sarah said. "As a matter of fact—"

From the other section of the trailer, they heard Malcolm say, "No! No! Those idiots! They could ruin everything!"

Sarah immediately turned, and went into the other section. Kelly jumped off the seat, and hurried after her.

The men were all clustered around the monitor. Everyone was talking at once, and they seemed to be upset. "This is terrible," Malcolm was saying. "Terrible!"

Thorne said, "Is that a Jeep?"

"They had a red Jeep," Harding said, coming up to look.

"Then it's Dodgson," Malcolm said. "Damn!"

"What's he doing here?"

"I can guess."

Kelly pushed through to get a look. On the screen, she saw foliage, and intermittent flashes of a red-and-black vehicle.

"Where are they now?" Malcolm said to Arby.

"I think they're in the east valley," Arby said. "Near where we found Dr. Levine."

The radio clicked. Levine's voice said, "Do you mean there are now other people on the island?"

"Yes, Richard."

"Well, you better go stop them, before they mess everything up."

"I know. Do you want to come back?"

"Not without a compelling reason. Inform me if one arises." And his radio clicked off.

Harding stared at the screen, watching the Jeep. "That's them, all right," she said. "That's your friend Dodgson."

"He's not my friend," Malcolm said. He got up, wincing in pain from his leg. "Let's go," he said. "We have to stop these bastards. There's no time to waste."

Nest

The red Jeep Wrangler rolled softly to a stop. Directly ahead was a wall of dense foliage. But through it they could see sunlight, from the clearing beyond.

Dodgson sat quietly in the car, listening. King turned to him, about to speak, but Dodgson held up his hand, gesturing to him to be silent.

Then he heard it clearly—a low rumbling growl, almost a purr. It was coming from beyond the foliage ahead. It sounded like the biggest jungle cat he had ever heard. And intermittently, he felt a slight vibration, hardly anything, but enough to make the car keys clink against the steering column. As he felt that vibration, it slowly dawned on him: *It's walking.*

Something very big. Walking.

Beside him, King was staring forward in astonishment; his mouth hung open. Dodgson glanced back at Baselton; the professor was gripping the seat with white fingers, as he listened to the sound.

A shadow moved across the ferns directly ahead. Judging by the shadow, the animal was twenty feet high, and forty feet long. It walked on its hind legs, and had a large body, a short neck, a very big head.

A tyrannosaur.

Dodgson hesitated, staring at the shadow. His heart was pounding in his chest. He considered going on to the next nest, but he was confident that the box would work here, too. He said, "Let's get this over with. Give me the box."

Baselton handed him the box, just as he had done before.

Dodgson said, "Charged?"

"Batteries are charged," King said.

"Okay," he said. "Here we go. Exactly the same as before. I'll go first, you two follow, and bring the eggs back to the car. Ready?"

"Ready," Baselton said.

King did not answer. He was still staring at the shadow. "What kind of a dinosaur is that?"

"That's a tyrannosaurus."

"Oh Jesus," King said.

"A tyrannosaurus?" Baselton said.

"It doesn't matter what it is," Dodgson said irritably. "Just follow the plan, like before. Everybody ready?"

"Just a minute," Baselton said.

King said, "What if it doesn't work?"

"We already know it works," Dodgson said.

"There's a rather curious fact about tyrannosaurs that was recently reported," Baselton said. "A paleontologist named Roxton did a study of the tyrannosaur braincase, and concluded that they have a brain not much different from a frog's, although of course much bigger. The implication was their nervous systems were adapted to motion only. They can't see you if you stand still. Stationary objects become invisible to them."

"Are you sure about that?" King said.

Baselton said, "That was the report. And it makes perfect sense. One can't forget that dinosaurs, for all their intimidating size, were actually rather primitive intellects. It's quite logical that a tyrannosaur would have the mental equipment of a frog."

"I don't see why we're rushing into this," King said, nervously. He stared forward. "It's much bigger than the other ones."

"So what?" Dodgson said. "You heard what George said. It's just a big frog. Let's get it done. Get out of the fucking car. And don't slam the doors."

George Baselton had felt quite good and authoritative, recalling that obscure article from the journals. He had been in his accustomed role, dispensing information to people who lacked it. Now that he approached the nest, he was astonished to notice that his knees had begun to tremble. His legs felt like rubber. He had always thought that was a figure of speech. He was alarmed to realize it could be literally true. He bit his lip, and forced himself under control. He was not, he told himself, going to show fear. He was the master of this situation.

Dodgson was already moving ahead, holding the black box like a gun in his hand. Baselton glanced over at King, who was deathly pale and sweating. He looked on the verge of collapse; he moved forward slowly. Baselton walked alongside him. Making sure he was all right.

Up ahead, Dodgson gave a final glance back, waved to Baselton and King to catch up. He glared at both of them, and then he stepped through the foliage into the clearing.

Baselton saw the tyrannosaur. No—there were two! They stood on both sides of a mud mound, two adults, twenty feet high on their hind legs, powerful, dark red, with big vicious jaws. Like the maiasaurs, the animals stared at Dodgson for a moment, a dumb stare, as if amazed to see an intruder. And then the tyrannosaurs roared in fury. An incredible, bellowing, air-shaking roar.

Dodgson lifted the box, pointed it at the animals. Immediately, a continuous, high-pitched shriek filled the clearing.

The tyrannosaurs roared in response, and lowered their heads, extending their necks forward, snapping their jaws, preparing to attack. They were huge—and they were unaffected by the sound. They started to come around the mound, toward Dodgson. The earth shook as they moved.

"Oh fuck," King said.

But Dodgson stayed cool. He twisted the dial. Baselton clapped his hands over his ears. The shriek became higher, louder, ear-splitting, incredibly painful. The response was immediate: the tyrannosaurs stepped back as if they had received a physical blow. They ducked their heads. They blinked their eyes rapidly. The sound seemed to vibrate in the air. They roared again, but weakly now, without conviction. A terrible screaming came from inside the mud nest.

Dodgson moved forward, pointing the box in the air, directly at the animals. The tyrannosaurs backed away, looking into the nest, then to Dodgson. They swung their heads back and forth rapidly, as if trying to clear their ears. Dodgson calmly adjusted the dial. The sound went higher. It was now excruciating.

Dodgson began to climb the mud mound of the nest. Baselton and King scrambled up, following him. Baselton found himself looking down into a nest with four mottled white eggs, and two young babies that looked for all the world like scrawny oversized turkeys. Anyway, some kind of gigantic baby birds.

The two tyrannosaurs were at the far end of the clearing, held away by the sound. Like the maiasaurs, they urinated in agitation. They stomped their feet. But they did not come closer.

Over the ear-splitting shriek of the box, Dodgson shouted, "Get the eggs!" In a daze, King stumbled down into the nest, grabbing the nearest egg. He fumbled it in his shaking hands; the egg flew into the air; he caught it again, and lurched back. He stepped on the leg of one of the babies, which screamed in fear and pain.

At this, the parents tried to come forward again, drawn by the infant's cries. King hastily clambered out of the nest, ducked away through the foliage. Baselton watched him go.

"George!" Dodgson shouted, still aiming the box at the tyrannosaurs. "Get the other egg!"

Baselton turned to look at the adult tyrannosaurs, seeing their agitation and their anger, watching their jaws snap open and closed, and he had the sudden feeling that sound or no sound, these animals would not allow anyone to enter the nest again. King had been lucky but Baselton would not be lucky, he could feel it, and—

"George! *Now!*"

Baselton said, "I can't!"

"You dumb fuck!" Holding the gun high, Dodgson began to climb down into the nest himself. But as he started, he twisted his body—and the battery plug pulled out of the box.

The sound abruptly died.

In the clearing, there was silence.

Baselton moaned.

The tyrannosaurs shook their heads a final time, and roared.

Baselton saw Dodgson go rigidly still, his body frozen. Baselton also stood still. Somehow, he forced his body to stay where he was. He forced his knees to stop trembling. He held his breath.

And he waited.

On the far side of the clearing, the tyrannosaurs began to move toward him.

"What are they doing?" Arby cried, in the trailer. He was so close to the monitor his nose almost touched the screen. "Are they crazy? They're just standing there."

Beside him, Kelly said nothing. She watched the screen silently.

"Want to be out there now, Kel?" Arby said.

"Shut up," Kelly said.

"No, they're not crazy," Malcolm said over the radio, as he stared at the dashboard monitor. The Explorer lurched down the trail, heading toward the eastern sector of the island. Thorne was driving. Sarah and Malcolm were in the back seat.

Sarah said, "He should be trying to put his sound machine together again. Are they really just going to stand there?"

"Yes," Malcolm said.

"Why?"

"They are misinformed," Malcolm said.

Dodgson

Dodgson watched the lead tyrannosaur come toward him. For such big animals, they were cautious. Only one of the two parents approached them, and although it paused to roar fiercely every few paces, it seemed oddly tentative, as if it was perplexed by the fact that the men were staying there. Or perhaps it could not see them. Perhaps he and Baselton had vanished from their view.

The other parent hung back, remaining toward the other side of the nest. Bobbing and ducking its head, agitated.

Agitated but not attacking.

Of course, the roars of the approaching dinosaur were terrifying, blood-chilling. Dodgson didn't dare glance at Baselton, just a few yards away. Baselton was probably peeing in his pants right now. Just so he didn't turn and run, Dodgson thought. If he ran, he was a dead man. If he stayed perfectly still, everything would be all right.

Standing stiffly, keeping his body rigid, Dodgson held the anodized box at waist level in his left hand, near his belt buckle. With his right hand, he slowly, ever so slowly, pulled up the disconnected power cord. In a few moments he would feel the end plug in his hands, and then he would slip it back into the box.

Meanwhile, he never took his eyes off the approaching tyrannosaur. He felt the ground shake beneath his feet. He heard the cries of the infant that King had stepped on. Those cries seemed to bother the parents, to arouse them.

No matter. Just a few seconds more, and he would have the plug back in the power pack. And then . . .

The tyrannosaur was very close now. Dodgson could smell the rotten odor of the carnivore. The animal roared, and he felt hot breath. It was standing right by Baselton. Dodgson turned his head fractionally, to watch.

Baselton stood entirely still. The tyrannosaur came close, and lowered his big head. He snorted at Baselton. He raised his head again, as if perplexed.

He really can't see him, Dodgson thought.

The tyrannosaur bellowed, a ferocious sound. Somehow Baselton stayed unmoving. The tyrannosaur bent over, bringing his huge head down again. The jaws opened and closed. Baselton stared straight forward, not blinking. With huge flaring nostrils, the tyrannosaur smelled him, a long snuffling inhalation that fluttered Baselton's trouser legs.

Then the tyrannosaur nudged Baselton tentatively with his snout. And in that moment Dodgson realized that the animal could see him after all, and then the tyrannosaur swung his head laterally, striking Baselton in the side and easily knocking him to the earth. Baselton yelled as the tyrannosaur's big foot came down, pinning him to the ground. Baselton raised his arms and shouted "You son of a bitch!" just as the head came down, jaws wide, and closed on him. The movement was gentle, almost delicate, but in the next instant the head snapped high, tearing the body, and Dodgson heard a scream and saw something small and floppy hanging from the jaws, and realized it was Baselton's arm. Baselton's hand swung freely, the metal band of his wristwatch glinting beneath the tyrannosaur's huge eye.

Baselton was screaming, a continuous undifferentiated sound, and hearing it, Dodgson broke into a dizzying sweat. Then he turned and ran, back toward the car, back toward safety, back toward anything.

He ran.

Kelly and Arby turned away from the monitor at the same moment. Kelly felt sick. She couldn't watch. But through the radio they could still hear the tinny screams of the man lying on his back, while the tyrannosaur tore him apart.

"Turn it off," Kelly said.

A moment later, the sound stopped.

Kelly sighed, let her shoulders drop. "Thank you," she said.

"I didn't do anything," Arby said.

She glanced back at the screen, and quickly looked away again. The tyrannosaur was tearing at something red. She shivered.

It was silent in the trailer. Kelly heard the tick of electronic counters, and the thumping of the water pumps under the floor. Outside, there was the faint sound of wind rustling the tall grass. Kelly suddenly felt very alone, very isolated on this island.

"Arby," she said, "what are we going to do?"

Arby didn't answer her.

He bolted for the bathroom.

"I knew it," Malcolm said, staring at the dashboard monitor. "I knew that would happen. They tried to steal eggs. Now look—the tyrannosaurs are leaving! Both of them!" He pushed the radio transmitter. "Arby. Kelly. Are you there?"

"We can't talk," Kelly said.

The Explorer continued down the hillside, toward the area of the tyrannosaur nest. Thorne gripped the wheel grimly as he drove. "What a damn mess."

"Kelly. Are you listening? We can't see what's happening down there. The tyrannosaurs have left the nest! Kelly? What's happening?"

Dodgson sprinted for the Jeep. The battery pack fell off his belt as he ran, but he didn't care. Up ahead in the Jeep, he saw King waiting, tense and pale.

Dodgson got behind the wheel, started the engine. The tyrannosaurs roared.

"Where's Baselton?" King asked.

"Didn't make it," Dodgson said.

"What do you mean?"

"*I mean he fucking didn't make it!*" Dodgson yelled, and slammed the car into gear. The Jeep took off, bouncing up the hill. They heard the tyrannosaurs bellowing behind them.

King was holding the egg, looking back down the road. "Maybe we should get rid of this," he said.

"Don't you fucking dare!" Dodgson said.

King was rolling down the window. "Maybe he just wants the egg back."

"No," Dodgson said. "No!" He reached across the passenger seat, struggling with King as he drove. The trail was narrow, with deep ruts. The Jeep lurched forward.

Suddenly, one of the tyrannosaurs burst from the trees in the road ahead. The animal stood there, snarling, blocking the road.

"Oh Christ," Dodgson said, slamming on the brakes. The car slid sickeningly in the muddy track, came to a stop.

The tyrannosaur lumbered toward them, bellowing.

"Turn around!" King screamed. "Turn around!"

But Dodgson didn't turn around. He slammed the car into reverse, and started backing down the trail. He was driving fast, and the road was narrow.

"You're crazy!" King said. "You're going to kill us!"

Dodgson swung his arm, smacked King with his hand. "Shut the fuck up!" he shouted. It took all his attention to maneuver the car back down the winding trail. Even going as fast as he could, he was sure the tyrannosaur would be faster. It wasn't going to work. They were in a fucking Jeep with a fucking cloth top, and they were going to get killed and—

"No!" King shouted.

Behind them, Dodgson saw the second tyrannosaur, charging up the road toward them. He looked forward, saw the first tyrannosaur bearing down on them. They were trapped.

He twisted the wheel in panic and the car ran off the road, crashing backward into dense underbrush and surrounding trees, and he felt a jolting impact. Then the rear of the car dropped sickeningly, and he realized the back wheels were hanging over the edge of a hill. He gunned the engine frantically, but the wheels just spun in the air. It was hopeless. And slowly, the car sank backward, deeper into foliage so dense he could not see through it. But they were over the edge. Beside him, King was sobbing. He heard the tyrannosaurs roaring, very near now.

Dodgson flung open the car door, and jumped out into space. He plunged through the foliage, fell, hit a tree trunk, and tumbled down a steep jungle hill. Somewhere along the way he felt a sharp pain in his forehead, and saw stars for the brief moment before blackness enveloped him, and he lost consciousness.

Decision

They sat in the Explorer, on top of the ridge overlooking the jungle-covered east valley. The windows were down. They listened to the bellowing of the tyrannosaurs, as the huge animals crashed through the underbrush.

"They both left the nest," Thorne said.

"Yeah. Those guys must have taken something." Malcolm sighed.

They were silent a while, listening.

They heard a soft buzzing, and then Eddie pulled up alongside them, in the motorcycle. "I thought you might need help. Are you going to go down?"

Malcolm shook his head. "No, absolutely not. It's too dangerous—we don't know where they are."

Sarah Harding said, "Why did Dodgson just stand there like that? That's not the way to act around predators. You get caught around lions, you make a lot of noise, wave your hands, throw things at them. Try to scare them off. You don't just stand there."

"He probably read the wrong research paper," Malcolm said, shaking his head. "There's been a theory going around that tyrannosaurs can only see movement. A guy named Roxton made casts of rex braincases, and concluded that tyrannosaurs had the brain of a frog."

The radio clicked. Levine said, "Roxton is an idiot. He doesn't know enough anatomy to have sex with his wife. His paper was a joke."

"What paper?" Thorne said.

The radio clicked again. "Roxton," Levine said, "believed that tyrannosaurs had a visual system like an amphibian: like a frog. A frog sees motion but doesn't see stillness. But it is quite impossible that a predator such as a tyrannosaur would have a visual system that worked that way. Quite impossible. Because the most common defense of prey animals is to freeze. A deer or something like that, it senses danger, and it freezes. A predator has to be able to see them anyway. And of course a tyrannosaur could."

Over the radio, Levine snorted with disgust. "It's just like the other idiotic theory put forth by Grant a few years back that a tyrannosaur could be confused by a driving rainstorm, because it was not adapted to wet climates. That's equally absurd. The Cretaceous wasn't particularly dry. And in any case, tyrannosaurs are North American animals — they've only been found in the U.S. or Canada. Tyrannosaurs lived on the shores of the great inland sea, east of the Rocky Mountains. There are lots of thunderstorms on mountain slopes. I'm quite sure tyrannosaurs saw plenty of rain, and they evolved to deal with it."

"So is there any reason why a tyrannosaur might not attack somebody?" Malcolm said.

"Yes, of course. The most obvious one," Levine said.

"Which is?"

"If it wasn't hungry. If it had just eaten another animal. Anything larger than a goat would take care of its hunger for hours to come. No, no. The tyrannosaur sees fine, moving or still."

They listened to the roaring, coming up from the valley below. They saw thrashing in the underbrush, about half a mile away, to the north. More bellowing. The two rexes seemed to be answering each other.

Sarah Harding said, "What are we carrying?"

Thorne said, "Three Lindstradts. Fully loaded."

"Okay," she said. "Let's go."

The radio crackled. "I'm not there," Levine said, over the radio. "But I'd certainly advise waiting."

"The hell with waiting," Malcolm said. "Sarah's right. Let's go down there and see how bad it is."

"Your funeral," Levine said.

Arby came back to the monitor, wiping his chin. He still looked a little green. "What are they doing now?"

"Dr. Malcolm and the others are going to the nest."

"Are you kidding?" he said, alarmed.

"Don't worry," Kelly said. "Sarah can handle it."

"You hope," Arby said.

Nest

Just beyond the clearing, they parked the Explorer. Eddie pulled up in the motorcycle, and leaned it against the trunk of a tree and waited while the others climbed out of the Explorer.

Sarah Harding smelled the familiar sour odor of rotting flesh and excrement that always marked a carnivore nesting site. In the afternoon heat, it was faintly nauseating. Flies buzzed in the still air. Harding took one of the rifles, slung it over her shoulder. She looked at the three men. They were all standing very still, tense, not moving. Malcolm's face was pale, particularly around the lips. It reminded her of the time that Coffmann, her old professor, had visited her in Africa. Coffmann was one of those hard-drinking Hemingway types, with lots of affairs at home, and lots of tales of his adventures with the orangs in Sumatra, the ring-tailed lemurs in Madagascar. So she took him with her to a kill site in the savannah. And he promptly passed out. He weighed more than two hundred pounds, and she had to drag him out by the collar while the lions circled and snarled at her. It had been a good lesson for her.

Now she leaned close to the three men and whispered, "If you've got any qualms about this, don't go. Just wait here. I don't want to worry about you. I can do this myself." She started off.

"Are you sure—"

"Yes. Now keep quiet." She moved directly toward the clearing. Malcolm and the others hurried to catch up with her. She pushed aside the palm fronds, and stepped out into the open. The tyrannosaurs were gone, and the mud cone was deserted. Over to the right, she saw a shoe, with a bit of torn flesh sticking out above the ragged sock. That was all there was left of Baselton.

From within the nest, she heard a plaintive, high-pitched squeal. Harding climbed up the mud bank, with Malcolm struggling to follow. She saw two infant tyrannosaurs there, mewling. Nearby were three large eggs. They saw heavy footprints all around, in the mud.

"They took one of the eggs," Malcolm said. "Damn."

"You didn't want anything to disrupt your little ecosystem?"

Malcolm smiled crookedly. "Yeah. I was hoping."

"Too bad," she said, and moved quickly around the edge of the pit.

She bent over, looking at the baby tyrannosaurs. One of the babies was cowering, its downy neck pulled into its body. But the second one behaved very differently. It did not move as they approached, but remained lying sprawled on its side, breathing shallowly, eyes glazed.

"This one's been hurt," she said.

Levine was standing in the high hide. He pressed the headset to his ear, and spoke into the microphone near his cheek. "I need a description," he said.

Thorne said, "There's two of them, roughly two feet long, weighing maybe forty pounds. About the size of small cassowary birds. Large eyes. Short snouts. Pale-brown color. And there's a ring of down around the necks."

"Can they stand?"

"Uh . . . if they can, not very well. They're kind of flopping around. Squeaking a lot."

"Then they're infants," Levine said, nodding. "Probably only a few days old. Never been out of the nest. I'd be very careful."

"Why is that?"

"With offspring that young," Levine said, "the parents won't leave them for long."

Harding moved closer to the injured infant. Still mewling, the baby tried to crawl toward her, dragging its body awkwardly. One leg was bent at an odd angle. "I think the left leg's hurt."

Eddie came closer, standing alongside her to see. "Is it broken?"

"Yeah, probably, but—"

"Hey!" Eddie said. The baby lunged forward, and clamped its jaws around the ankle of his boot. He pulled his foot away, dragging the baby, which held its grip tightly. "Hey! Let go!"

Eddie lifted his leg up, shook it back and forth, but the baby refused to let go. He pulled for a moment longer, then stopped. Now the baby just lay there on the ground, breathing shallowly, jaws still locked around Eddie's boot. "Jeez," Eddie said.

"Aggressive little guy, isn't he," Sarah said. "Right from birth . . ."

Eddie looked down at the tiny, razor-sharp jaws. They hadn't penetrated the leather. The baby held on firmly. With the butt of his rifle, he poked the infant's head a couple of times. It had no effect at all. The baby lay on the ground, breathing shallowly. Its big eyes blinked slowly as they stared up at Eddie, but it did not release its grip.

They heard the distant roars of the parents, somewhere to the north. "Let's get out of here," Malcolm said. "We've seen what we came here to see. We've got to find where Dodgson went."

Thorne said, "I think I saw a track up the trail. They might have gone off there."

"We better have a look."

They all started back to the car.

"Wait a minute," Eddie said, looking down at his foot. "What am I going to do about the baby?"

"Shoot it," Malcolm said, over his shoulder.

"You mean kill it?"

Sarah said, "It's got a broken leg, Eddie, it's going to die anyway."

"Yeah, but—"

Thorne called, "We're going back up the trail, Eddie, and if we don't find Dodgson, we'll take the ridge road going toward the laboratory. Then down to the trailer again."

"Okay, Doc. I'm right behind you." Eddie lifted his rifle, turned it in his hands.

"Do it now," Sarah said, climbing into the Explorer. "Because you don't want to be here when Momma and Poppa get back."

Gambler's Ruin

Driving up the trail, Malcolm stared at the dashboard monitor, as the image flicked from one camera view to another. He was looking for Dodgson and the rest of his party.

Over the radio, Levine said, "How bad was it?"

"They took one egg," Malcolm said. "And we had to shoot one of the babies."

"So, a loss of two. Out of a total hatching brood of what, six?"

"That's right."

"Frankly, I'd say it's a minor matter," Levine said. "As long as you stop those people from doing anything more."

"We're looking for them now," Malcolm said morosely.

Harding said, "It was bound to happen, Ian. You know you can't expect to observe the animals without changing anything. It's a scientific impossibility."

"Of course it is," Malcolm said. "That's the greatest single scientific discovery of the twentieth century. You can't study anything without changing it."

Since Galileo, scientists had adopted the view that they were objective observers of the natural world. That was implicit in every aspect of their behavior, even the way they wrote scientific papers, saying things like "It was observed . . ." As if nobody had observed it. For three hundred years, that impersonal quality was the hallmark of science. Science was objective, and the observer had no influence on the results he or she described.

This objectivity made science different from the humanities, or from religion—fields where the observer's point of view was integral, where the observer was inextricably mixed up in the results observed.

But in the twentieth century, that difference had vanished. Scientific objectivity was gone, even at the most fundamental levels. Physicists now knew you couldn't even measure a single subatomic particle without affecting it totally. If you stuck your instruments in to measure a particle's position, you changed its velocity. If you measured its velocity, you changed its position. That basic truth became the Heisenberg uncertainty principle: that whatever you studied you also changed. In the end, it became clear that all scientists were participants in a participatory universe which did not allow anyone to be a mere observer.

"I know objectivity is impossible," Malcolm said impatiently. "I'm not concerned about that."

"Then what are you concerned about?"

"I'm concerned about the Gambler's Ruin," Malcolm said, staring at the monitor.

Gambler's Ruin was a notorious and much-debated statistical phenomenon that had major consequences both for evolution, and for everyday life. "Let's say you're a gambler," he said. "And you're playing a coin-toss game. Every time the coin comes up heads, you win a dollar. Every time it comes up tails, you lose a dollar."

"Okay . . ."

"What happens over time?"

Harding shrugged. "The chances of getting either heads or tails is even. So maybe you win, maybe you lose. But in the end, you'll come out at zero."

"Unfortunately, you don't," Malcolm said. "If you gamble long enough, you'll always lose—the gambler is always ruined. That's why casinos stay in business. But the question is, what happens over time? What happens in the period before the gambler is finally ruined?"

"Okay," she said. "What happens?"

"If you chart the gambler's fortunes over time, what you find is the gambler wins for a period, or loses for a period. In other words, everything in the world goes in streaks. It's a real phenomenon, and you see it everywhere: in weather, in river flooding, in baseball, in heart rhythms, in stock markets. Once things go bad, they tend to stay bad. Like the old folk saying that bad things come in threes. Complexity theory tells us the folk wisdom is right. Bad things cluster. Things go to hell together. That's the real world."

"So what are you saying? That things are going to hell now?"

"They could be, thanks to Dodgson," Malcolm said, frowning at the monitor. "What happened to those bastards, anyway?"

King

There was a buzzing, like the sound of a distant bee. Howard King was dimly aware of it, as he came slowly back to consciousness. He opened his eyes, and saw the windshield of a car, and the branches of trees beyond.

The buzzing was louder.

King didn't know where he was. He couldn't remember how he got here, what had happened. He felt pain in his shoulders, and at his hips. His forehead throbbed. He tried to remember but the pain distracted him, prevented him from thinking clearly. The last thing he remembered was the tyrannosaur in front of him on the road. That was the last thing. Then Dodgson had looked back and—

King turned his head, and cried out as sudden, sharp pain ran up his neck to his skull. The pain made him gasp, took his breath away. He closed his eyes, wincing. Then he slowly opened them again.

Dodgson was not in the car. The driver's door hung wide open, a dappled shadow across the door panel. The keys were still in the ignition.

Dodgson was gone.

There was a streak of blood across the top of the steering wheel. The black box was on the floor by the gearshift. The open driver's door creaked a little, moved a little.

In the distance, King heard the buzzing again, like a giant bee. It was a mechanical sound, he now realized. Something mechanical.

It made him think of the boat. How long would the boat wait at the river? What time was it, anyway? He looked at his watch. The crystal was smashed, the hands fixed at 1:54.

He heard the buzzing again. It was coming closer.

With an effort, King pushed himself away from the seat, toward the dashboard. Streaks of electric pain shot up his spine, but quickly subsided. He took a deep breath.

I'm all right, he thought. At least, I'm still here.

King looked at the open driver's door, in the sunlight. The sun was still high. It must still be sometime in the afternoon. When was the boat leaving? Four o'clock? Five o'clock? He couldn't remember any more. But he was certain that those Spanish fishermen wouldn't hang around once it started to get dark. They'd leave the island.

And Howard King wanted to be on the boat when they did. It was the only thing he wanted in the world. Wincing, he raised himself up, and painfully slid over to the driver's seat. He settled himself in, took a deep breath, and then leaned over, and looked out the open door.

The car was hanging over empty space, supported by trees. He saw a steep jungle hillside, falling away beneath him. It was dark beneath the canopy of trees. He felt dizzy, just looking down. The ground must be twenty or thirty feet below him. He saw scattered green ferns, and a few dark boulders. He twisted his body to look more.

And then he saw him.

Dodgson lay on his back, head downward, on the slope of the hill. His body was crumpled, arms and legs thrown out in awkward positions. He was not moving. King couldn't see him very well, in the dense foliage on the hillside, but Dodgson looked dead.

The buzzing was suddenly very loud, building rapidly, and King looked forward and saw, through the foliage that blocked the windshield, a car driving by, not ten yards away. A car!

And then the car was gone. From the sound of it, he thought, it was an electric car. So it must be Malcolm.

Howard King was somehow encouraged by the thought that other people were on this island. He felt new strength, despite the pain in his body. He reached forward, and turned the key in the ignition. The engine rumbled.

He put the car in gear, and gently stepped on the accelerator.

The rear wheels spun. He engaged the front-wheel drive. At once, the Jeep rumbled forward, lurching through the branches. A moment later, he was out on the road.

He remembered this road now. To the right, it led down to the tyrannosaurus nest. Malcolm's car had gone to the left.

King turned left, and headed up the road. He was trying to remember how to get back to the river, back to the boat. He vaguely recalled that there was a Y-fork in the road at the top of the hill. He would take that fork, he decided, drive down the hill, and get the hell off this island.

That was his only goal.

To get off this island, before it was too late.

Bad News

The Explorer came to the top of the hill, and Thorne drove onto the ridge road. The road curved back and forth, cut into the rock face of the cliff. In many places, the dropoff was precipitous, but they had views over the entire island. Eventually they came to a place where they could look over the valley. They could see the high hide off to the left, and closer by, the clearing with the two trailers. Off to the right was the laboratory complex, and the worker complex beyond.

"I don't see Dodgson anywhere," Malcolm said unhappily. "Where could he have gone?"

Thorne pushed the radio button. "Arby?"

"Yes, Doc."

"Do you see them?"

"No, but . . ." He hesitated.

"What?"

"Don't you want to come back here now? It's pretty amazing."

"What is?" Thorne said.

"Eddie," Arby said. "He just got back. And he brought the baby with him."

Malcolm leaned forward. "He did *what?*"

FIFTH CONFIGURATION

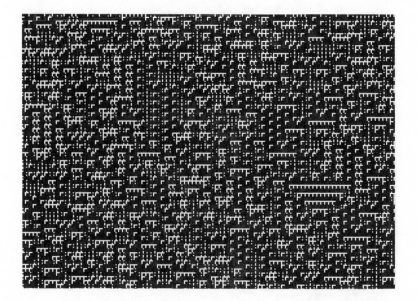

"At the edge of chaos, unexpected outcomes occur.
The risk to survival is severe."

IAN MALCOLM

Baby

In the trailer, they were clustered around the table where the baby Tyrannosaurus rex now lay unconscious on a stainless-steel pan, his large eyes closed, his snout pushed into the clear plastic oval of an oxygen mask. The mask almost fitted the baby's blunt snout. The oxygen hissed softly.

"I couldn't just leave him," Eddie said. "And I figured we can fix his leg. . . ."

"But Eddie," Malcolm said, shaking his head.

"So I shot him full of morphine from the first-aid kit, and brought him back. You see? The oxygen mask almost fits him."

"Eddie," Malcolm said, "this was the wrong thing to do."

"Why? He's okay. We just fix him and take him back."

"But you're interfering with the system," Malcolm said.

The radio clicked. "This is extremely unwise," Levine said, over the radio. "Extremely."

"Thank you, Richard," Thorne said.

"I am entirely opposed to bringing any animal back to the trailer."

"Too late to worry about that now," Sarah Harding said. She had moved forward alongside the baby, and began strapping cardiac leads to the animal's chest; they heard the thump of the heartbeat. It was very fast, over a hundred and fifty beats a minute. "How much morphine did you give him?"

"Gee," Eddie said. "I just . . . you know. The whole syringe."

"What is that? Ten cc's?"

"I think. Maybe twenty."

Malcolm looked at Harding. "How long before it wears off?"

"I have no idea," she said. "I've sedated lions and jackals in the field, when I tagged them. With those animals, there's a rough correlation between dose and body weight. But with young animals, it's unpredictable. Maybe a few minutes, maybe a few hours. And I don't know a thing about baby tyrannosaurs. Basically, it's a function of metabolism, and this one seems to be rapid, bird-like. The heart's pumping very fast. All I can say is, let's get him out of here as quickly as possible."

Harding picked up the small ultrasound transducer and held it to the baby's leg. She looked over her shoulder at the monitor. Kelly and Arby were blocking the view. "Please, give us a little room here," she said, and they moved away. "We don't have much time. Please."

As they moved away, Sarah saw the green-and-white outlines of the leg and its bones. Surprisingly like a large bird, she thought. A vulture or a stork. She moved the transducer. "Okay . . . there's the metatarsals . . . and there's the tibia and fibula, the two bones of the lower leg. . . ."

Arby said, "Why are the bones different shades like that?" The legs had some dense white sections within paler-green outlines.

"Because it's an infant," Harding said. "His legs are still mostly cartilage, with very little calcified bone. I'd guess this baby probably can't walk yet—at least, not very well. There. Look at the patella. . . . You can see the blood supply to the joint capsule. . . ."

"How come you know all this anatomy?" Kelly said.

"I have to. I spend a lot of time looking through the scat of predators," she said. "Examining pieces of bones that are left behind, and figuring out which animals have been eaten. To do that, you have to know comparative anatomy very well." She moved the transducer along the baby's leg. "And my father was a vet."

Malcolm looked up sharply. "Your father was a vet?"

"Yes. At the San Diego Zoo. He was a bird specialist. But I don't see . . . Can you magnify this?"

Arby flicked a switch. The image doubled in size.

"Ah. Okay. All right. There it is. You see it?"

"No."

"It's mid-fibula. See it? A thin black line. That's a fracture, just above the epiphysis."

"That little black line there?" Arby said.

"That little black line means death for this infant," Sarah said. "The fibula won't heal straight, so the ankle joint can't pivot when he stands on his hind feet. The baby won't be able to run, and probably can't even walk. It'll be crippled, and a predator will pick it off before it gets more than a few weeks old."

Eddie said, "But we can set it."

"Okay," Sarah said. "What were you going to use for a cast?"

"Diesterase," Eddie said. "I brought a kilo of it, in hundred-cc tubes. I packed lots, for glue. The stuff's polymer resin, it solidifies hard as steel."

"Great," Harding said. "That'll kill him, too."

"It will?"

"He's *growing*, Eddie. In a few weeks he'll be much larger. We need something that's rigid, but biodegradeable," she said. "Something that will wear off, or break off, in three to five weeks, when his leg's healed. What have you got?"

Eddie frowned. "I don't know."

"Well, we haven't got much time," Harding said.

Eddie said, "Doc? This is like one of your famous test questions. How to make a dinosaur cast with only Q-tips and superglue."

"I know," Thorne said. The irony of the situation was not lost on him. He had given problems such as these to his engineering students for three decades. Now he was faced with one himself.

Eddie said, "Maybe we could degrade the resin—mix it with something like table sugar."

Thorne shook his head. "Hydroxy groups in the sucrose will make the resin friable. It'll harden okay, but it'll shatter like glass as soon as the animal moves."

"What if we mix it with cloth that's been soaked in sugar?"

"You mean, to get bacteria to decay the cloth?"

"Yeah."

"And then the cast breaks?"

"Yeah."

Thorne shrugged. "That might work, " he said. "But without testing, we can't know how long the cast will last. Might be a few days, it might be a few months."

"That's too long," Sarah said. "This animal is growing rapidly. If growth is constricted, it'll end up being crippled by the cast."

"What we need," Eddie said, "is an organic resin that will form a decaying binder. Like a gum of some kind."

"Chewing gum?" Arby said. "Because I have plenty of—"

"No, I was thinking of a different kind of gum. Chemically speaking, the diesterase resin—"

"We'll never solve it chemically," Thorne said. "We don't have the supplies."

"What else can we do? There's no choice but—"

"What if you make something that's different in different directions?" Arby said. "Strong one way and weak in another?"

"You can't," Eddie said. "It's a homogeneous resin. It's all the same stuff, goopy glue that turns rock-hard when it dries, and—"

"No, wait a minute," Thorne said, turning to the boy. "What do you mean, Arby?"

"Well," Arby said, "Sarah said the leg is growing. That means it's going to grow longer, which doesn't matter for a cast, and wider, which does, because it'll start to squeeze the leg. But if you made it weak in the diameter—"

"He's right," Thorne said. "We can solve it structurally."

"How?" Eddie said.

"Just build in a split-line. Maybe using aluminum foil. We have some for cooking."

"That'd be much too weak," Eddie said.

"Not if we coat it with a layer of resin." Thorne turned to Sarah. "What we can do is make a cast that is very strong for vertical stresses, but weak for lateral stresses. It's a simple engineering problem. The baby can walk around on its cuff, and everything is fine, as long as the stresses are vertical. But when its leg grows, it will pop the split-line open, and the cuff will fall away."

"Yes," Arby said, nodding.

"Is that hard to do?" she said.

"No. It should be pretty easy. You just build a cuff of aluminum foil, and coat it with resin."

Eddie said, "And what'll hold the cuff together while you coat it?"

"How about chewing gum?" Arby said.

"You got it," Thorne said, smiling.

At that moment, the baby rex stirred, its legs twitching. It raised its head, the oxygen mask dropping away, and gave a low, weak squeak.

"Quickly," Sarah said, grabbing the head. "More morphine."

Malcolm had a syringe ready. He jabbed it into the animal's neck.

"Just five cc's now," Sarah said.

"What's wrong with more? Keep him out longer?"

"He's in shock from the injury, Ian. You can kill him with too much morphine. You'll put him into respiratory arrest. His adrenal glands are probably stressed, too."

"If he even has adrenals," Malcolm said. "Does a Tyrannosaurus rex have hormones at all? The truth is, we don't know anything about these animals."

The radio clicked, and Levine said, "Speak for yourself, Ian. In point of fact, I suspect we will find that dinosaurs have hormones. There are compelling reasons to imagine they do. As long as you have gone to the misguided trouble of taking the baby, you might draw some tubes of blood. Meanwhile, Doc, could you pick up the phone?"

Malcolm sighed. "That guy," he said, "is starting to get on my nerves."

Thorne moved down the trailer to the communications module near the front. Levine's request was odd; there was a perfectly good system of microphones throughout the trailer. But Levine knew that; he had designed the system himself.

Thorne picked up the phone. "Yes?"

"Doc," Levine said, "I'll get right to the point. Bringing the baby to the trailer was a mistake. It's asking for trouble."

"What sort of trouble?"

"We don't know, is the point. And I don't want to alarm anybody. But why don't you bring the kids out to the high hide for a while? And why don't you and Eddie come, too?"

"You're telling me to get the hell out of here. You really think it's necessary?"

"In a word," Levine said, "yes. I do."

As the morphine was injected into the baby, he gave a sighing wheeze, and collapsed back onto the steel pan. Sarah adjusted the oxygen mask around his face. She glanced back at the monitor, checking the heart rate, but once again Arby and Kelly were blocking her view. "Kids, please."

Thorne stepped forward, clapped his hands. "Okay, kids! Field trip! Let's get moving."

Arby said, "Now? But we want to watch the baby—"

"No, no," Thorne said. "Dr. Malcolm and Dr. Harding need room to work. This is the time for a field trip to the high hide. We can watch the dinosaurs for the rest of the afternoon."

"But Doc—"

"Don't argue. We're just in the way here, and we're going," Thorne said. "Eddie, you come, too. Leave these two lovebirds to do their work."

In a few moments, they left. The trailer door slammed shut behind them. Sarah Harding heard the soft whirr of the Explorer as it drove away. Bent over the baby, adjusting the oxygen mask, she said, "Lovebirds?"

Malcolm shrugged. "Levine . . ."

"Was this Levine's idea? Clearing everybody out?"

"Probably."

"Does he know something we don't?"

Malcolm laughed. "I'm sure he thinks he does."

"Well, let's start the cast," she said. "I want to get it done quickly, and take this baby home again."

The High Hide

The sun had disappeared behind low-hanging clouds by the time they reached the high hide. The entire valley was bathed in a soft reddish glow as Eddie parked the Explorer beneath the aluminum scaffolding, and they all climbed up to the little shelter above. Levine was there, binoculars to his eyes. He did not seem glad to see them. "Stop moving around so much," he said irritably.

From the shelter, they had a magnificent view over the valley. Somewhere in the north, thunder rumbled. The air was cooling, and felt electric.

"Is there going to be a storm?" Kelly asked.

"Looks like it," Thorne said.

Arby glanced doubtfully at the metal roof of the shelter. "How long are we staying out here?"

"For a while," Thorne said. "This is our only day here. The helicopters are taking us away tomorrow morning. I thought you kids deserved a chance to see the dinosaurs in the field one more time."

Arby squinted at him. "What's the real reason?"

"I know," Kelly said, in a worldly tone.

"Yeah? What?"

"Dr. Malcolm wants to be alone with Sarah, stupid."

"Why?"

"They're old friends," Kelly said.

"So? We were just going to watch."

"No," Kelly said. "I mean, they're *old friends.*"

"I know what you're talking about," Arby said. "I'm not stupid, you know."

"Knock it off," Levine said, staring through the binoculars. "You're missing the interesting stuff."

"What's that?"

"Those triceratops, down at the river. Something's bothering them."

The triceratops herd had been drinking peacefully from the river, but now they were beginning to make noise. For such huge animals, their vocalizations were incongruously high-pitched: they sounded more like yelping dogs.

Arby turned to look. "There's something in the trees," he said, "across the river." There was some hint of dark movement, beneath the trees.

The triceratops herd shifted, and began backing toward each other until they formed a sort of rosette, with their curved horns facing outward, against the unseen menace. The solitary baby was in the center, yelping in fear. One of the animals, presumably its mother, turned and nuzzled it. Afterward, the baby was silent.

"I see them," Kelly said, staring at the trees. "They're raptors. Over there."

The triceratops herd faced the raptors, the adults barking as they swung their sharp horns up and down. They created a kind of barrier of moving spikes. There was an unmistakable sense of coordination, of group defense against predators.

Levine was smiling happily. "There's never been any evidence for this," he said, suddenly cheerful. "In fact, most paleontologists don't believe it happens."

"Don't believe what happens?" Arby said.

"This kind of group defensive behavior. Especially with trikes—they look a bit like rhinos, so they've been assumed to be solitary, like rhinos. But now we will see. . . . Ah. Yes."

From beneath the trees, a single velociraptor hopped out into view. It moved quickly on its hind legs, balancing with a stiff tail.

The triceratops herd barked noisily at the appearance of the raptor. The other raptors remained hidden beneath the trees. The solitary velociraptor in full view moved in a slow semicircle around the herd, entering the water on the far side. It crossed, swimming easily, and came out on the other bank. It was now about fifty yards upstream from the barking triceratops herd, which wheeled to present a united front. All their attention was focused on the single velociraptor.

Slowly, other raptors began to slink out of their hiding place. They moved low, bodies hidden in the tall grass.

"Jeez," Arby said. "They're hunting."

"In a pack," Levine said, nodding. He picked up a bit of candy bar wrapper from the floor of the shelter, and dropped it, watching it flutter off in the wind. "The main pack is downwind, so the trikes can't smell them." He raised the binoculars to his eyes again. "I think," he said, "that we're about to see a kill."

They watched as the raptors closed in around the herd. And then suddenly, lightning cracked on the island rim, brilliantly lighting the valley floor. One of the stalking raptors stood up in surprise. Its head was briefly visible above the grass.

Immediately, the triceratops herd wheeled again, regrouping to face the new menace. All the raptors stopped, as if to reconsider their plan.

"What happened?" Arby said. "Why are they stopping?"

"They're in trouble."

"Why?"

"Look at them. The main pack is still across the river. They're too far away to mount an attack."

"You mean they're giving up? Already?"

"Looks like it," Levine said.

One by one, the raptors in the grass raised their heads, making their positions known. As each new predator appeared, the triceratops barked loudly. The raptors seemed to know the situation was hopeless. They slunk away, moving back toward the trees. Seeing them retreat, the triceratops barked even louder.

And then the single raptor by the water's edge charged. It moved in-credibly fast—astonishingly fast—streaking like a cheetah across the fifty yards that separated it from the herd. The adult triceratops had no time to re-form. The baby was exposed. It squealed in fright as it saw the approaching animal.

The velociraptor leapt into the air, raising both its hind legs. Light-ning cracked again, and in the brilliant light they saw the twin curved claws high in the air. At the last moment, the nearest adult turned, swiveling its big horned head with the wide bony crest, and it knocked the raptor a glancing blow, sending the animal sprawling on the muddy bank. Immediately the adult triceratops charged forward, its head high. When it reached the raptor it stopped abruptly and swung its big head down, lowering its horns toward the fallen animal. But the raptor was quick; hissing, it leapt to its feet, and the triceratops horns slashed harm-lessly into the mud. The raptor spun sideways, and kicked the adult on the snout, drawing blood with its big curved claw. The adult bellowed, but by then two other adults were charging forward, while the others re-mained behind with the baby. The raptor scrambled away, back into the grass.

"Wow," Arby said. "That was something!"

The Herd

King gave a long sigh of relief as he came to the Y-fork in the road, and drove the red Jeep left, coming onto a wide dirt road. He recognized it at once: this was the ridge road that led back to the boat. As he looked off to his left, he could see down across the east valley. The boat was still there! All right! He gave a shout and accelerated sharply, relief flooding through him. On the deck, he could see the Spanish fishermen, staring up at the sky. Despite the threatening storm, they didn't seem to be preparing to leave. Probably they were waiting for Dodgson.

Well, he thought, that was fine. King would be there in a few minutes. After working his way through dense jungle, he could finally see exactly where he was. The ridge road was high, following the crest of one of the volcanic spines. There was almost no foliage up here, and as the road twisted and turned, he had views across the entire island. To the east, he could look down into the ravine, and the boat at the shore. To the west, he could look straight across at the laboratory, and Malcolm's twin trailers parked near the far edge of the clearing.

They never did find out what the hell Malcolm was doing here, he thought. Not that it mattered now. King was getting off the island. That was the only thing that mattered. He could almost feel the deck beneath his feet. Maybe one of the fishermen would even have a beer. A nice cold beer, while they chugged down the river, and pulled out of this damned island. He'd toast Dodgson, is what he'd do.

Maybe, he thought, I'll have two beers.

King came around a curve, and saw a herd of animals standing thickly in the road. They were some kind of green dinosaurs, about four feet tall, with big domed heads and a bunch of little horns. They reminded him of green water buffalo. But there were a lot of them. He braked sharply; the car swerved to a stop.

The green dinosaurs looked at his car, but they did not move. The herd just stood there in a lazy, contented way. King waited, drumming his fingers on the steering wheel. When nothing happened, he honked the horn, and flashed his headlights.

The animals just stared.

They were funny-looking creatures, with that smooth bulging curve on the forehead and all those little horns around it. They just stared at him, with a stupid cow-like look. He slipped the car into gear and edged it forward slowly, expecting that he could push his way through the animals. They didn't move aside. Finally his front bumper nudged the nearest animal, which grunted, took a couple of steps back, lowered its head, and butted the front of the car, hard, with a metallic clang!

Christ, he thought. It could puncture the radiator, if he wasn't careful. He stopped the car again and waited, the motor idling. The animals settled down again.

Several of them lay down on the road. He couldn't drive over them. He looked ahead toward the river and saw the boat, not more than a quarter of a mile away. He hadn't realized it was so near. As he watched, he realized that the fishermen were very busy on the deck. They were swinging the crane back, lashing it down. They were getting ready to leave!

The hell with waiting, he thought. He opened the door, and climbed out, leaving the car in the center of the road. Immediately, the animals jumped to their feet, and the nearest one charged him. He had the door open; the animal smashed into it, slamming it shut, leaving a deep dent in the metal. King scrambled toward the edge of the hill, only to find he was at the top of a steep vertical descent of more than a hundred feet. He'd never make it down, at least not here. Farther along, the slope was not so steep. But now more animals were charging him. He had no choice. He ran around the back of the car, just as another animal smashed into the rear taillight, shattering the plastic.

A third animal charged the back of the car directly. King scrambled up onto the spare tire, as the animal slammed into the bumper. The jolt knocked him off, and he fell to the ground, rolling, while the buffaloes snorted all around him. He got to his feet and ran to the opposite side of the road, where there was a slight rise; he scrambled up it, moving into foliage. The animals did not pursue him. Not that it did him any good—now he was on the wrong side of the road!

Somehow he had to get back to the other side.

He climbed to the top of the rise and started down, swearing to himself. He decided to work his way forward a hundred yards or so, until he was beyond the butting animals, and then cross the road. If he could do that, then he could get to the boat.

Almost immediately, he was surrounded by dense jungle. He tripped, tumbled down a muddy slope, and when he got to his feet was no longer sure which way to go. He was at the bottom of a ravine, and the palm trees were ten feet tall, and very thick. He couldn't see more than a few feet in any direction. In a moment of panic, he realized he didn't know which way to go. He pushed forward through the wet leaves, hoping to get his bearings back.

The kids were still peering over the railing, looking at the departing raptors. Thorne pulled Levine to one side, and said quietly, "Why did you want us to come here?"

"Just a precaution," Levine said. "Bringing the infant to the trailer is asking for trouble."

"What sort of trouble?"

Levine shrugged. "We don't know, is the point. But in general, parents don't like it when their babies are taken away. And that baby has some very big parents."

From the other side of the shelter Arby said, "Look! Look!"

"What is it?" Levine said.

"It's a man."

Gasping for breath, King emerged from the jungle and walked out onto the plain. At last he could see where he was! He paused, soaked and muddy, to get his bearings.

He was disappointed to find that he was nowhere near the boat. In fact, he still seemed to be on the wrong side of the road. He was facing a broad grassy plain, with a river coursing through it. The plain was mostly deserted, although there were several dinosaurs farther down the banks. They were the horned ones: triceratops. And they looked a little agitated. The big adults were raising their heads up and down, making barking sounds.

Obviously, he would have to follow the river, until it brought him to the boat. But he'd have to be careful getting past these triceratops. He reached in his pocket and pulled out a candy bar. He ripped the wrapping while he watched the triceratops, wishing they would go away. How long would it take him to reach the boat? That was the only question on his mind. He decided to move, triceratops or not. He began walking through the tall grass.

Then he heard a reptilian hiss. It was coming from the grass, somewhere to his left. And he noticed a smell, a peculiar rotten smell. He paused, waiting. The candy bar didn't taste so good, any more.

Then, behind him, he heard splashing. It was coming from the river. King turned to look.

"It's one of those men from the Jeep," Arby said, standing in the high hide. "But why is he waiting?"

From their vantage point, they could see the dark shapes of the raptors, moving through the grass on the other side of the river. Now two of the raptors came forward, splashing in the water. Moving toward the man.

"Oh no," Arby said.

King saw two dark, striped lizards moving across the river. They walked on their hind legs, with a sort of hopping motion. Their bodies were reflected in the flowing water of the river. They snapped their long jaws, and hissed menacingly at King.

He glanced upstream, and saw another lizard crossing, and another beyond that. Those other animals were already deep in the water, and had begun to swim.

Howard King backed away from the river, moving deeper into the tall grass. Then he turned, and ran. He was chest-deep in grass and running hard, gasping for breath, when suddenly another lizard head rose up in front of him, hissing and snarling. He dodged, changed direction, but suddenly the nearest lizard leapt in the air. It jumped so high its body cleared the grass; he could see the entire animal flying through the air, its two hind legs raised to pounce. He glimpsed curved, dagger-like claws.

King turned again and the lizard shrieked as it landed on the ground behind him, and tumbled away in the grass. King ran on. He was energized by pure fear. Behind him he heard the lizard snarling. He ran hard: ahead was another twenty yards of grassy clearing, and then the jungle began again. He saw trees—big trees. He could climb one and get away.

Off to the left, he saw another lizard moving diagonally across the clearing toward him. King could only see the head above the grass. The lizard seemed to be moving incredibly fast. He thought: *I'm not going to make it.*

But he would try.

Panting, lungs searing, he sprinted for the trees. Only ten more yards now. His arms pumped, his legs churned. His breath came in ragged gasps.

And then something heavy struck him from behind, forcing him to the ground, and he felt searing pain down his back and he knew it was the claws, they dug into the flesh of his back as he was knocked down. He hit the dirt hard, and tried to roll, but the animal on his back held on, he could not move. He was pinned down on his stomach, hearing the animal snarl behind him. The pain in his back was excruciating, dizzying.

And then he felt the animal's hot breath on the back of his neck, and he heard the snorting breath, and his terror was extreme. Then suddenly a kind of lassitude, a deep and welcome sleepiness, took him. Everything became slow. As if in a dream, he could see all the blades of grass in the ground in front of his face. He saw them with a kind of languid intensity, and he almost did not mind the sharp pain on his neck, and he almost did not care that his neck was within the animal's hot jaws. It seemed to be happening to someone else. He was many miles away. He had a moment of surprise when he felt the bones of his neck crunching loudly—

And then blackness.

Nothing.

"Don't look," Thorne said, turning Arby away from the railing in the high hide. He drew the boy toward his chest, but Arby impatiently pushed away again, to watch what was happening. Thorne reached for Kelly, but she stepped away from him, and stared out at the plain.

"Don't look," Thorne kept saying. "Don't look."

The kids watched, in silence.

Levine focused his binoculars on the kill. There were now five raptors snarling around the man's body, tearing viciously at the carcass. As he watched, one of the raptors jerked its head up, tearing away a piece of blood-soaked shirt, the ragged edge of the collar. Another was shaking the man's severed head in its jaws, before finally dropping it on the ground. Thunder rumbled, and lightning flashed in the distant sky. It was growing dark, and Levine was having difficulty seeing exactly what was happening. But it was clear that whatever hierarchical organization they had adopted for hunting was abandoned for a kill.

Here it was every animal for itself; the frenzied raptors hopped and ducked their heads as they tore the body to pieces; and there was plenty of nipping and fighting among themselves. One animal came up, with something brown hanging from its jaws. The animal got an odd expression on its face as it chewed. Then it turned away from the rest of the pack, and held the brown object carefully in its forearms. In the growing darkness, it took Levine a moment to recognize what it was doing: it was eating a candy bar. And it seemed to be enjoying it.

The raptor turned back, and buried its long nose in the bloody carcass again. From across the plain, other raptors were racing to join the feast, half-running, half-bounding in great forward leaps. Snarling and furious, they threw themselves into the fray.

Levine lowered his glasses, and looked at the two kids. They were staring silently and calmly at the kill.

Dodgson

Dodgson was awakened by a noisy chittering, like the sound of a hundred tiny birds. It seemed to be coming from all around him. Slowly, he realized that he was lying on his back, on damp sloping ground. He tried to move, but his body felt painful and heavy. Some sort of weight pressed down on his legs, his stomach, his arms. The weight on his chest made it difficult to breathe.

And he was sleepy, incredibly sleepy. He wanted nothing more in all the world than to go back to sleep. Dodgson started to drift off to unconsciousness, but something was pulling at his hand. Tugging at his fingers, one by one. As if pulling him back to consciousness. Slowly, slowly, pulling him back.

Dodgson opened his eyes.

There was a little green dinosaur standing beside his hand. It leaned over, and bit his finger in its tiny jaws, tugging at the flesh. His fingers were bleeding; ragged chunks of flesh had already been bitten away.

He pulled his hand away in surprise, and suddenly the chittering grew louder. He turned and saw that he was surrounded by these little dinosaurs; they were standing on his chest and legs as well. They were the size of chickens and they pecked at him like chickens, quick darting bites on his stomach, his thighs, his crotch—

Revolted, Dodgson jumped to his feet, scattering the lizards, which hopped away, chirping in annoyance. The little animals moved a few feet away, then stopped. They turned back, and stared at him, showing no sign of fear. On the contrary, they seemed to be waiting.

That was when he realized what they were. They were procompsognathids. Compys.

Scavengers.

Christ, he thought. *They thought I was dead.*

He staggered back, almost losing his balance. He felt pain and a wave of dizziness. The little animals chittered, watched his every move.

"Go on," he said, waving his hand. "Get out of here."

They did not leave. They stood there, cocking their heads to one side quizzically, and waited.

He bent his head, stared down at himself. His shirt, his trousers were torn in a hundred places. Blood dribbled from a hundred tiny wounds down his clothes. He felt a wave of dizziness and put his hands on his knees. He took a deep breath, and watched his blood drip onto the leaf-strewn ground.

Christ, he thought. He took another deep breath.

When he did not move, the animals began to inch forward. He stood up, and they backed away. But a moment later, they began to come forward again.

One came close. Dodgson kicked it viciously, sending the little body flying through the air. The animal squealed in alarm, but it landed like a cat, upright and uninjured.

The others remained where they were.

Waiting.

He looked around, realized it was getting dark. He looked at his watch: 6:40. There were only a few minutes more of daylight. Beneath the jungle canopy, it was already quite dark.

He had to get to safety, and soon. He checked the compass on his watch strap, and headed south. He was pretty sure the river was to the south. He had to get back to the boat. He would be safe at the boat.

As he started walking, the compys chittered and followed after him. They stayed about five or ten feet behind, making a lot of noise as they hopped and crashed through the low foliage. There were dozens of them, he realized. As darkness descended, their eyes glowed bright green.

His body was a mass of pain. Every step hurt. His balance was not good. He was losing blood, and he was very, very sleepy. He would never make it all the way to the river. He would not make it more than another couple of hundred yards. He fell, tripping over a root. He got up slowly, dirt clinging to his blood-soaked clothes.

He looked back at the green eyes behind him, and forced himself onward. He could go a little farther, he thought. And then, directly ahead, he saw a light through the foliage. Was it the boat? He moved faster, hearing the compys behind him.

He pushed through the foliage and then saw a little shed, like a tool-shed or a guardhouse, made of concrete, with a tin roof. It had a square window, and light was shining through the window. He fell again, got to his knees, and crawled the rest of the way to the house. He reached the door, pulled himself up on the doorknob, and opened the door.

Inside, the shed was empty. Some pipes came up through the floor. Some time in the past, they had connected to machinery, but the machinery was gone; there were only the rust spots where it had once been bolted to the concrete floor.

In a corner of the room was an electric light. It was fitted with a timer, so that it came on at night. That was the light he had seen. Did they have electricity on this island? How? He didn't care. He staggered into the room, closed the door firmly behind him, and sank down onto the bare concrete. Through the dirty windowpanes, he saw the compys outside, banging against the glass, hopping in frustration. But he was safe for the moment.

He would have to go on, of course. He would somehow have to get off this fucking island. But not now, he thought.

Later.

He'd worry about everything later.

Dodgson laid his cheek on the damp concrete floor, and slept.

Trailer

Sarah Harding placed the aluminum-foil cuff around the baby's injured leg. The baby was still unconscious, breathing easily, not moving. Its body was relaxed. The oxygen hissed softly.

She finished shaping the aluminum foil into a cuff six inches long. Using a small brush, she began to paint resin over it, to make a cast.

"How many raptors are there?" she said. "I couldn't tell for sure, when I saw them. I thought nine."

"I think there's more," Malcolm said. "I think eleven or twelve in all."

"Twelve?" she said, glancing up at him. "On this little island?"

"Yes."

The resin had a sharp odor, like glue. She brushed it evenly on the aluminum. "You know what I'm thinking," she said.

"Yes," he said. "There are too many."

"Far too many, Ian." She worked steadily. "It doesn't make sense. In Africa, active predators like lions are very spread out. There's one lion for every ten square kilometers. Sometimes every fifteen kilometers. That's all the ecology can support. On an island like this, you should have no more than five raptors. Hold this."

"Uh-huh. But don't forget, the prey here is huge. . . . Some of those animals are twenty, thirty tons."

"I'm not convinced that's a factor," Sarah said, "but for the sake of argument, let's say it is. I'll double the estimate, and give you ten raptors for the island. But you tell me there are twelve. And there are other major predators, as well. Like the rexes . . ."

"Yes. There are."

"That's too many," she said, shaking her head.

"The animals are pretty dense here," Malcolm said.

"Not dense enough," she said. "In general, predator studies—whether tigers in India, or lions in Africa—all seem to show that you can support one predator for every two hundred prey animals. That means to support twenty-five predators here, you need at least five thousand prey on this island. Do you have anything like that?"

"No."

"How many animals in total do you think are here?"

He shrugged. "A couple of hundred. Maybe five hundred at most."

"So you're off by an order of magnitude, Ian. Hold this, and I'll get the lamp."

She swung the heat lamp over the baby, to harden the resin. She adjusted the oxygen mask over the baby's snout.

"The island can't support all those predators," she said. "And yet they're here."

He said, "What could explain it?"

She shook her head. "There has to be a food source that we don't know about."

"You mean, an artificial source?" he said. "I don't think there is one."

"No," she said. "Artificial food sources make animals tame. And these animals aren't tame. The only other possibility I can think of is that there's a differential death rate among prey. If they grow very fast, or die young, then that might represent a larger food supply than expected."

Malcolm said, "I've noticed, the largest animals seem small. It's as if they don't seem to reach maturity. Maybe they're being killed off early."

"Maybe," she said. "But if there's a differential death rate large enough to support this population, you should see evidence of carcasses, and lots of skeletons of dead animals. Have you seen that?"

Malcolm shook his head. "No. In fact, now that you mention it, I haven't seen any skeletons at all."

"Me neither." She pushed the light away. "There's something funny about this island, Ian."

"I know," Malcolm said.

"You do?"

"Yes," he said. "I've suspected it from the beginning."

Thunder rumbled. From the high hide, the plain below them was dark and silent, except for the distant snarling of the raptors. "Maybe we should go back," Eddie said anxiously.

"Why?" Levine said. Levine had switched to his night-vision glasses, pleased with himself that he had thought to bring them. Through the goggles, the world was shades of pale green. He clearly saw the raptors at the kill site, the tall grass trampled and bloody all around. The carcass was long since finished, though they could still hear the cracking of bones as the animals gnawed on them.

"I just think," Eddie said, "that now that it's night, we'd be safer in the trailer."

"Why?" Levine said.

"Well, it's reinforced, it's strong, and very safe. It has everything that we need. I just think we should be there. I mean, you're not planning on staying out here all night, are you?"

"No," Levine said. "What do you think I am, a fanatic?"

Eddie grunted.

"But let's stay for a while longer," Levine said.

Eddie turned to Thorne. "Doc? What do you say? It's going to start raining soon."

"Just a little longer," Thorne said. "And then we'll all go back together."

"There have been dinosaurs on this island for five years, maybe more," Malcolm said, "but none have appeared elsewhere. Suddenly, in the last year, carcasses of dead animals are showing up on the beaches of Costa Rica, and according to reports, on islands of the Pacific as well."

"Carried by currents?"

"Presumably. But the question is, why now? Why all of a sudden, after five years? Something has changed, but we don't know—wait a minute." He moved away from the table, over to the computer console. He turned toward the screen.

"What are you doing?" she said.

"Arby got us into the old network," he said, "and it still has research files from the eighties." He moved the mouse across the screen. "We haven't looked at them. . . ." He saw the menu come up, showing work files and research files. He began to scroll through screens of text.

"Years ago, they had trouble with some disease," he said. "There were a lot of notes about it in the laboratory."

"What kind of disease?"

"They didn't know," Malcolm said.

"In the wild, there are some very slow-acting illnesses," she said. "May take five or ten years to show up. Caused by viruses, or prions. You know, protein fragments—like scrapie or mad-cow disease."

"But," Malcolm said, "those diseases only come from eating contaminated food."

There was a silence.

"What do you suppose they fed them, back then?" she asked. "Because if I was growing baby dinosaurs, I'd wonder. What do they eat? Milk, I suppose, but—"

"Milk, yes," Malcolm said, reading the screens. "First six weeks, goat's milk."

"That's the logical choice," she said. "Goat's milk is what they always use in zoos, because it's so hypoallergenic. But what about later?"

"Give me a minute here," Malcolm said.

Harding held the baby's leg in her hand, waiting for the resin to harden. She looked at the cast, sniffed it. It was still strong-smelling. "I hope that's all right," she said. "Sometimes if there's a distinctive smell, the animals won't allow infants to return. But maybe this will dissipate after the compound hardens. How long has it been?"

Malcolm glanced at his watch. "Ten minutes. Another ten minutes and it'll set."

She said, "I'd like to take this guy back to the nest."

Thunder rumbled. They looked out the window at the black night.

"Probably too late to return him tonight," Malcolm said. He was still typing, peering at the screen.

"So . . . what did they feed them? Okay. In the period from 1988 to 1989 . . . the herbivores got a macerated plant matter on a feeding schedule three times a day . . . and the carnivores got . . ."

He stopped.

"What'd the carnivores get?"

"Looks like a ground-up extract of animal protein. . . ."

"From what? The usual source is turkey or chicken, with some antibiotics added."

"Sarah," he said. "They used sheep extract."

"No," she said. "They wouldn't do that."

"Yeah, they did. Came from their supplier, who used ground-up sheep."

"You're kidding," she said.

Malcolm said, "I'm afraid so. Now, let me see if I can find out—"

A soft alarm sounded. On the wall panel above him, a red light began to flash. A moment later, the exterior lights above the trailer turned on, bathing the grassy clearing around them in bright halogen glare.

"What's that?" Harding said.

"The sensors—something set them off." Malcolm moved away from the computer, peered out the window. He saw nothing but tall grass, and the dark trees at the perimeter. It was silent, still.

Sarah, still intent on the baby, said, "What happened?"

"I don't know. I don't see anything."

"But something triggered the sensors?"

"I guess."

"Wind?"

"There's no wind," he said.

In the high hide, Kelly said, "Hey, look!"

Thorne turned. From their location in the valley, they could look north to the high cliff behind them and the two trailers above, in the grassy clearing.

The exterior lights on the trailers had come on.

Thorne unclipped the radio at his belt. "Ian? Are you there?"

A momentary crackle: "I'm here, Doc."

"What's happening?"

"I don't know," Malcolm said. "The perimeter lights just turned on. I think the sensor was activated. But we don't see anything out there."

Eddie said, "Air's cooling off fast now. Might have been convection currents, set it off."

Thorne said, "Ian? Everything okay?"

"Yes. Fine. Don't worry."

Eddie said, "I always figured we set the sensitivity too high. That's all it is."

Levine frowned, and said nothing.

Sarah finished with the baby, and wrapped him in a blanket, and gently strapped him down to the table with cloth restraint straps. She came over and stood beside Malcolm. She looked out the window.

"What do you think?"

Malcolm shrugged. "Eddie says the system's too sensitive."

"Is it?"

"I don't know. It's never been tested before." He scanned the trees at the edge of the clearing, looking for any movement. Then he thought he heard a snorting sound, almost a growl. It seemed like it was answered from somewhere behind him. He went to look out the other side of the trailer, at the trees on the other side.

Malcolm and Harding looked out, straining to see something in the night. Malcolm held his breath, tensely. After a moment, Harding sighed. "I don't see anything, Ian."

"No. Me neither."

"Must be a false alarm."

Then he felt the vibration, a deep resonant thumping in the ground, that was carried to them through the floor of the trailer. He glanced at Sarah. Her eyes widened.

Malcolm knew what it was. The vibration came again, unmistakably this time.

Sarah stared out the window. She whispered, "Ian: *I see it.*"

Malcolm turned, and joined her. She was pointing out the window toward the nearest trees.

"What?"

And then he saw the big head emerge from the foliage midway up one tree. The head turned slowly from side to side, as if listening. It was an adult Tyrannosaurus rex.

"Ian," she whispered. "Look — there are two of them."

Over to the right, he saw a second animal step from behind the trees. It was larger, the female of the pair. The animals growled, a deep rumble in the night. They emerged slowly from the cover of the trees, stepping into the clearing. They blinked in the harsh light.

"Are those the parents?"

"I don't know. I think so."

He glanced over at the baby. It was still unconscious, breathing steadily, the blanket rising and falling regularly.

"What are they doing here?" she said.

"I don't know."

The animals were still standing at the edge of the clearing, near the cover of the trees. They seemed hesitant, waiting.

"Are they looking for the baby?" she said.

"Sarah, please."

"I'm serious."

"That's ridiculous."

"Why? They must have tracked it here."

The tyrannosaurs raised their heads, lifting their jaws. Then they turned their heads left and right, in slow arcs. They repeated the movement, then took a step forward, toward the trailer.

"Sarah," he said. "We're miles from the nest. There isn't any way for them to track it."

"How do you know?"

"Sarah—"

"You said yourself, we don't know anything about these animals. We don't know anything about their physiology, their biochemistry, their nervous systems, their behavior. And we don't know anything about their sensory equipment, either."

"Yes, but—"

"They're *predators*, Ian. Good sense of vision, good sense of hearing and smell."

"I assume so, yes."

"But we don't know what else," Sarah said.

"What else?" Malcolm said.

"Ian. There *are* other sensory modalities. Snakes sense infrared. Bats have echolocation. Birds and turtles have magnetosensors—they can detect the earth's magnetic field, which is how they migrate. Dinosaurs may have other sensory modalities that we can't imagine."

"Sarah, this is ridiculous."

"Is it? Then you tell me. What are they doing out there?"

Outside, near the trees, the tyrannosaurs had become silent. They were no longer growling, but they were still moving their heads back and forth in slow arcs, turning left and right.

Malcolm frowned. "It looks like . . . they're looking around. . . ."

"Straight into bright lights? No, Ian. They're blinded."

As soon as she said it, he realized she was right. But the heads were turning back and forth in that regular way. "Then what are they doing? Smelling?"

"No. Heads are high. Nostrils aren't moving."

"Listening?"

She nodded. "Possibly."

"Listening to what?"

"Maybe to the baby."

He glanced over again. "Sarah. The baby is out cold."

"I know."

"It isn't making any noise."

"None that we can hear." She stared at the tyrannosaurs. "But they're doing *something*, Ian. That behavior we're seeing has meaning. We just don't know what it is."

From the high hide, Levine stared through his night-vision glasses at the clearing. He saw the two tyrannosaurs standing at the edge of the forest. They were moving their heads in an odd, synchronized way.

They took a few hesitant steps toward the trailer, lifted their heads, turned right and left, and then seemed finally to make up their minds. The animals moved quickly, almost aggressively, across the clearing.

Over the radio, they heard Malcolm say, "It's the lights! The lights are drawing them."

A moment later, the exterior lights were turned off, and the clearing went black. They all squinted in the darkness. They heard Malcolm say, "That did it."

Thorne said to Levine, "What do you see?"

"Nothing."

"What're they doing?"

"They're just standing there."

Through the night-vision goggles, he saw that the tyrannosaurs had paused, as if confused by this change in light. Even from a distance, he could hear their growls, but they were uneasy. They swung their great heads up and down, and snapped their jaws. But they did not move closer.

Kelly said, "What is it?"

"They're waiting," Levine said. "At least for the moment."

Levine had the distinct impression that the tyrannosaurs were unsettled. The trailer must represent a large and fearsome change in their environment. Perhaps they would turn away, he thought, and leave. Despite their enormous size, they were cautious, almost timid animals.

They growled again. And then he saw them move forward, toward the darkened trailer.

"Ian: what do we do?"

"Damned if I know," Malcolm whispered.

They were crouched down side by side in the passageway, trying to stay out of sight in the windows. The tyrannosaurs moved implacably forward. They could feel each step as a distinct vibration now—two ten-ton animals, moving toward them.

"They're coming right at us!"

"I noticed," he said.

The first of the animals reached the trailer, coming so close that the body blocked the entire window. All Malcolm could see was powerfully muscled legs and underbelly. The head was far above them, out of view.

Then the second tyrannosaur came up on the opposite side. The two animals began to circle the trailer, growling and snorting. Heavy footsteps shook the floor beneath them. They smelled the pungent predator odor. One of the tyrannosaurs brushed against the side of the trailer and they heard a scraping sound, scaly flesh on metal.

Malcolm felt sudden panic. It was the smell that did it, the smell that he suddenly remembered, from before. He began to sweat. He glanced over at Sarah, and saw that she was intent, watching the movements of the animals. "This isn't hunting behavior," she whispered.

"I don't know," Malcolm said. "Maybe it is. They aren't lions, you know."

One of the tyrannosaurs bellowed in the night, a frightening, ear-splitting sound.

"Not hunting," she said. "They're *searching*, Ian."

A moment later, the second tyrannosaur bellowed in reply. Then the big head swung down, and peered in through the window in front of them. Malcolm ducked down, flattening himself on the trailer floor, and Sarah collapsed on top of him. Her shoe pressed on his ear.

"It's going to be fine, Sarah."

Outside, they heard the tyrannosaurs snorting and growling.

Malcolm whispered, "Would you mind moving?"

She edged to one side, and he eased up slowly, peering cautiously over the seat cushions. He had a glimpse of the big eye of the rex staring in at him. The eye swiveled in the socket. He saw the jaws open and close. The hot breath of the animal fogged the glass.

The tyrannosaur's head swung away, moving back from the trailer, and for a moment Malcolm breathed more easily. But then the head swung back, and slammed with a heavy thud into the trailer, rocking it hard.

"Don't worry, Sarah. The trailer's very strong."

She whispered, "I can't tell you how relieved I am."

From the opposite side, the other rex bellowed and struck the trailer with its snout. The suspension creaked with the impact.

The two tyrannosaurs now began an alternating, rhythmic pounding of the trailer from either side. Malcolm and Harding were thrown back and forth. Sarah tried to steady herself, but was knocked away at the next impact. The floor tilted crazily under each blow. Lab equipment flew off the tables. Glass shattered.

And then, abruptly, the pounding stopped. There was silence.

Grunting, Malcolm got up on one knee. He peered out the window, and saw the hindquarters of one of the tyrannosaurs, as it moved forward.

"What do we do?" he whispered.

The radio crackled. Thorne said, "Ian, are you there? Ian!"

"For God's sake, turn that off," Sarah whispered.

Malcolm reached for his belt, whispered, "We're okay," and clicked the radio off.

Sarah was crawling on her hands and knees forward through the trailer, into the biology lab. He followed her, and saw the big tyrannosaur peering in through the window, at the baby, strapped down. The tyrannosaur made a soft grunting sound.

Then it paused, looking in the window.

It grunted again.

"*She wants her baby, Ian,*" Sarah whispered.

"Well, God knows," Malcolm said, "it's all right with me." They were huddled on the floor, trying to stay out of sight.

"How are we going to get it to her?"

"I don't know. Maybe push it out the door?"

"I don't want them to step on it," Sarah said.

"*Who cares?*" Malcolm said.

The tyrannosaur at the window made a series of soft grunts, followed by a long, menacing growl. It was the big female.

"Sarah—"

But she was already standing up, facing the tyrannosaur. She immediately began to speak, her voice soft, soothing. "It's okay. . . . It's all right now. . . . The baby is fine. . . . I'm just going to loosen these straps here. . . . You can watch me. . . ."

The head outside the window was so huge it filled the entire glass frame. Sarah saw the powerful muscles of the neck ripple beneath the skin. The jaws moved slightly. Her hands trembled as she undid the straps.

"That's right. . . . Your baby is fine. . . . See, it's just fine. . . ."

Crouched below at her feet, Malcolm whispered, "What are you doing?"

She did not change her soft, soothing tone. "I know it sounds crazy. . . . But it works with lions . . . sometimes. . . . There we are. . . . Your baby is free. . . . "

Sarah unwrapped the blanket, and took away the oxygen mask, all the while speaking calmly. "Now . . . all I have to do . . . " She lifted the baby up in her hands. " . . . is get it to you. . . ."

Suddenly, the female's head swung back, and smashed side-on into the glass, which shattered into a white spiderweb with a harsh crack. Sarah couldn't see through it, but she saw a shadow move and then the second impact broke the glass free. Sarah dropped the baby on the tray and jumped back as the head crashed through, and pushed several feet into the trailer. Streams of blood ran down the adult's snout, from the shards of glass. But after the initial violence it stopped, and became delicate in its movements. It sniffed the baby, starting at the head, moving slowly down the body. It sniffed the cast, too, and licked it briefly with its tongue. Finally, it rested its lower jaw lightly on the baby's chest. It stayed that way for a long time, not moving. Only the eyes blinked slowly, staring at Sarah.

Malcolm, lying on the floor, saw blood dripping over the edge of the counter. He started to get up, but she pushed his head back down with her hand. She whispered, "Ssssh."

"What's happening?"

"It's feeling the heartbeat."

The tyrannosaur grunted, opened its mouth, and gently gripped the infant between its jaws. Then it moved slowly back, out through the broken glass, carrying the baby outside.

It set the baby on the ground, below their vision. It bent over, the head disappearing from view.

Malcolm whispered, "Did it wake up? Is the baby awake?"

"Ssssh!"

There was a repetitive slurping sound, coming from outside the trailer. It was interspersed with soft, guttural growls. Malcolm saw Sarah leaning forward, trying to see out the window. He whispered, "What's happening?"

"She's licking him. And pushing him with her snout."

"And?"

"That's all. She just keeps doing it."

"What about the baby?"

"Nothing. It keeps rolling over, like it's dead. How much morphine did we give him, the last time?"

"I don't know," he said. "How should I know?"

Malcolm remained on the floor, listening to the slurping and the growling. And finally, after what seemed like an eternity, he heard a soft high-pitched squeak.

"He's waking up! Ian! The baby's waking up!"

Malcolm crawled up on his knees, and looked out the window in time to see the adult carrying the baby in its jaws, walking away toward the perimeter of the clearing.

"What's it doing?"

"I guess, taking it back."

The second adult came into view, following the first. Malcolm and Sarah watched the two tyrannosaurs move away from the trailer, across the clearing.

Malcolm's shoulders dropped. "That was close," he said.

"Yes. That was close." She sighed, and wiped blood from her forearm.

In the high hide, Thorne pressed the radio button. "Ian! Are you there? Ian!"

Kelly said, "Maybe they turned the radio off."

A light rain began to fall, pattering on the metal roof of the shed. Levine was staring through his night-vision glasses toward the cliff. Lightning flashed, and Thorne said, "Can you see what the animals are doing?"

"I can," Eddie said. "It looks . . . it looks like *they're going away.*"

They all began to cheer.

Only Levine remained silent, watching through the glasses. Thorne turned to him. "Is that right, Richard? Is everything okay?"

"Actually, I think not," Levine said. "I'm afraid we have made a serious error."

Malcolm watched the retreating tyrannosaurs through the shattered glass window. Beside him, Sarah said nothing. She never took her eyes off the animals.

Rain started to fall; water dripped from the shards of glass. Thunder rumbled in the distance, and lightning cracked harshly down, illuminating the giant animals as they moved away.

At the nearest of the big trees, the adults stopped, and placed the baby on the ground.

"Why are they doing that?" Sarah said. "They should be going back to the nest."

"I don't know, maybe they're —"

"Maybe the baby is dead," she said.

But no, in the next flash of lightning they could see the baby moving. It was still alive. They could hear its high-pitched squeaking as one of the adults took the baby in its jaws, and gently placed it in a fork among the high branches of a tree.

"Oh no," Sarah said, shaking her head. "This is wrong, Ian. This is all wrong."

The female tyrannosaur remained with the baby for some moments, moving it, positioning it. Then the female turned, opened its jaws, and roared.

The male tyrannosaur roared in response.

And then both animals charged the trailer at full speed, racing across the clearing toward them.

"Oh, my God," Sarah said.

"Brace yourself, Sarah!" Malcolm shouted. "It's going to be bad!"

The impact was stunning, knocking them sideways through the air. Sarah screamed as she tumbled away. Malcolm hit his head and fell to the floor, seeing stars. Beneath him, the trailer rocked on its suspension, with a metallic scream. The tyrannosaurs roared, and slammed into it again.

He heard her shouting, "Ian! Ian!" and then the trailer crashed over onto its side. Malcolm turned away; glassware and lab equipment smashed all around him. When he looked up, everything was cockeyed. Directly above him was the broken window the tyrannosaur had smashed. Rain dripped through onto Malcolm's face. Lightning flashed, and then he saw a big head peering down at him and snarling. He heard the harsh scratching of the tyrannosaurs' claws on the metal side of the trailer, then the face disappeared. A moment later, he heard them bellowing as they pushed the trailer through the dirt.

He called "Sarah!" and he saw her, somewhere behind him, just as the world spun crazily again, and the trailer was upended with a crash. Now the trailer was lying on its roof; Malcolm started crawling along the ceiling, trying to reach Sarah. He looked up at the lab equipment, locked down on the lab benches, above his head. Liquid dripped onto him from a dozen sources. Something stung his shoulder. He heard a hiss, and realized it must be acid.

Somewhere in the darkness ahead, Sarah was groaning. Lightning flashed again, and Malcolm saw her, lying crumpled near the accordion junction that connected the two trailers. That junction was twisted almost shut, which must mean that the second trailer was still upright. It was crazy. Everything was crazy.

Outside, the tyrannosaurs roared, and he heard a muffled explosion. They were biting the tires. He thought: Too bad they don't bite into the battery cable. That'd give them a real surprise.

Suddenly, the tyrannosaurs slammed into the trailer again, knocking it laterally along the clearing. As soon as it stopped, they slammed again. The trailer lurched sideways.

By then he had reached Sarah. She threw her arms around him. "Ian," she said. The whole left half of her face was dark. When the lightning flashed, he saw it was covered in blood.

"Are you okay?"

"I'm fine," she said. With the back of her hand, she wiped blood out of her eye. "Can you see what it is?"

In another lightning flash, he saw the glint of a large chunk of glass, embedded near her hairline. He pulled it out, and pressed his hand against the sudden gush of blood. They were in the kitchen; he reached up toward the stove, and pulled down a dishtowel. He held it against her head, and watched the cloth darken.

"Does it hurt?"

"It's okay."

"I think it's not too bad," he said. Outside, the tyrannosaurs roared in the night.

"What are they doing?" she said. Her voice was dull.

The tyrannosaurs slammed into the trailer again. With this impact, the trailer seemed to move a lot more than before, sliding sideways — and down.

Sliding down.

"They're pushing us," he said.

"Where, Ian?"

"To the edge of the clearing." The tyrannosaurs slammed again, and the trailer moved farther. "They're pushing us over the cliff." The cliff was five hundred feet of sheer rock, straight down to the valley below.

They'd never survive the fall.

She held the dishtowel with her own hand, pushing his hand away. "Do something."

"Yeah, okay," he said.

He moved away from her, bracing for the next impact. He didn't know what to do. He had no idea what to do. The trailer was upside down, and everything was crazy. His shoulder burned and he could smell the acid eating his shirt. Or maybe it was his flesh. It burned a lot. The whole trailer was dark, all the power was out, there was glass everywhere, and he—

All the power was out.

Malcolm started to get to his feet, but the next impact flung him sideways, and he fell hard, slamming his head against the refrigerator. The door swung open and cartons of cold milk, glass bottles, crashed down on him. But there was no light from the refrigerator.

Because all the power was out.

Lying on his back, Malcolm looked out the window and saw the big foot of a tyrannosaur standing in the grass. Lightning flashed as the foot raised to kick, and immediately the trailer moved again, sliding easily now, metal screeching, and then tilting downward.

"Oh, shit," he said.

"Ian . . ."

But it was too late, the whole trailer was groaning and creaking in metallic protest, and then Malcolm saw the far end sink down, as the trailer slid over the cliff. It started slowly, and then gathered speed, the ceiling they were lying on falling away, everything falling, Sarah falling, clutching at him as she went, and the tyrannosaurs bellowing in triumph.

We're going over the cliff, he thought.

Not knowing what else to do, he grabbed the refrigerator door, hanging on tightly. The door was cold, and slippery with moisture. The trailer tilted and fell, the metal creaking loudly. Malcolm felt his hands sliding off the white enamel, sliding . . . sliding. . . . And then he lost his grip and fell free, dropping helplessly straight down toward the far end of the trailer. He saw the driver's seat rushing up to him, but before he got there he struck something in the darkness, felt a moment of searing pain, and bent double.

And slowly, gently, everything around him went black.

Rain drummed on the roof of the shed, and poured in a continuous sheet down the sides. Levine wiped the lenses of his glasses, then lifted them again to his eyes. He stared at the cliffs in the darkness.

Arby said, "What is it? What happened?"

"I can't tell," Levine said. It was hard to see anything in this downpour. Moments before, they had watched in horror as the two tyrannosaurs pushed the trailer toward the cliff. The large animals had done it with ease: Levine guessed the tyrannosaurs had a combined mass of twenty tons, and the trailer only weighed about two tons. Once they had turned it over, it slid easily over the wet grass as they pushed it with their underbellies, and kicked it with their powerful leg muscles.

"Why are they doing that?" Thorne said to Levine, standing beside him.

"I suspect," he said, "that we have changed the perceived territory."

"How's that again?"

"You have to remember what we're dealing with," Levine said. "Tyrannosaurs may show complex behavior, but most of it is instinctual. It's unthinking behavior, wired in. And territoriality is part of that instinct. The tyrannosaurs mark territory, they defend territory. It's not thinking behavior—they don't have very large brains—but they do it from instinct. All instinctive behavior has triggers, releasers for the behavior. And I'm afraid that, by moving the baby, we redefined their territory to include the clearing where the baby was found. So now they're going to defend their territory, by driving out the trailers."

Then lightning flashed, and they all saw it in the same horrifying moment. The first trailer had gone over the cliff. It was hanging upside down in space, still connected by the accordion connector to the second trailer in the clearing above.

"That connector won't hold!" Eddie shouted. "Not long!"

In the glare of lightning, they saw the tyrannosaurs up in the clearing. Methodically, they were now pushing the second trailer toward the cliff.

Thorne turned to Eddie. "I'm going!" he said.

"I'll come with you!" Eddie said.

"No! Stay with the kids!"

"But you need—"

"Stay with the kids! We can't leave them alone!"

"But Levine can—"

"No, you stay!" Thorne said. He was already climbing down the scaffolding, slippery in drenching rain, toward the Explorer below. He saw Kelly and Arby looking down at him. He jumped in the car, clicked on the ignition. He was already thinking of the distance to the clearing. It was three miles, maybe more. Even driving fast, it would take him seven or eight minutes to get there.

And by then it would be too late. He'd never make it in time.

But he had to try.

Sarah Harding heard a rhythmic creaking, and opened her eyes.

Everything was dark; she was disoriented. Then lightning flashed, and she stared straight down toward the valley, five hundred feet below. The view swung gently, back and forth.

She was looking through the windshield of the trailer, hanging down the side of the cliff. They were not falling any more. But they were hanging precariously in space.

She herself was lying across the driver's seat, which had broken free of its mounting, and shattered a control panel in the wall; loose wires hung out, panel indicators flickered.

She was having trouble seeing, from the blood in her left eye. She pulled out the tail of her shirt, and ripped two strips of cloth. She folded one to make a compress, and pressed it against the gash on her forehead. Then she tied the second strip around her head, to hold the compress down. The pain was intense for a moment; she gritted her teeth until it faded.

From somewhere above her, she felt a thumping vibration. She turned, and looked straight up. She saw the whole length of the trailer, suspended vertically. Malcolm was ten feet above her, bent over a lab table, not moving.

"Ian," she said.

He didn't answer. He didn't move.

The trailer shuddered again, creaking under a dull impact. And then

Harding realized what was happening. The first trailer was dangling straight down the cliff face, swinging freely in space. But it was still connected to the second trailer, up on the clearing. The first trailer now hung from the accordion connector. And the tyrannosaurs, up above, were now pushing the second trailer off the cliff.

"Ian," she said. "Ian."

She scrambled to her feet, ignoring the pain in her body. She felt a wave of dizziness, and wondered how much blood she had lost. She began to climb straight up, standing first on the back of the driver's seat, grabbing for the nearest biology table. She pulled herself upward, until she could reach a handle mounted in the wall. The trailer swayed beneath her.

From the handle, she managed to grab the refrigerator door, putting her fingers through a wire shelf. She tested it, it held, and she gave it her full weight. She raised her leg, until she got her shoe into the refrigerator itself. Then she swung her body still higher, until she was standing up and could reach the handle to the oven.

It was like mountain climbing through a damn kitchen, she thought.

Soon she was alongside Malcolm. Lightning flashed again, and she saw his battered face. He groaned. She crawled over to him, trying to see how badly he was hurt.

"Ian," she said.

His eyes were closed. "Sorry."

"Never mind."

"I got you into this."

"Ian. Can you move? Are you okay?"

He groaned. "My leg."

"Ian. We have to do something."

From the clearing above them, she heard the tyrannosaurs roaring. It seemed to her that they had been roaring her whole life. The trailer lurched and swung; her legs slid out of the refrigerator and she was hanging free in space from the oven door. The far end of the trailer was some twenty feet below.

The oven handle wouldn't hold her weight, she knew. Not for long.

Harding swung her legs, kicking wildly, finally touched something solid. She felt with her feet, then stepped down. Looking back, she saw she was standing on the side of the stainless-steel sink. She moved her foot and the faucet turned on, soaking her feet.

The tyrannosaurs roared, pounding hard. The trailer moved farther out into space, swinging.

"Ian. There's not much time. We have to do something."

He raised his head, stared at her with blank eyes. Lightning flashed again. His lips moved. "Power," he said.

"What about it?"

"Power is off."

She didn't know what he was talking about. Of course the power was off. Then she remembered: he had turned it off earlier. When the tyrannosaurs were approaching. The light had bothered them before, maybe it would bother them again.

"You want me to turn the power on?"

His head nodded fractionally. "Yes. Turn it on."

"How, Ian?" She looked around in the darkness.

"There's a panel."

"Where?"

He didn't answer her. She reached out, shook his shoulder. "Ian: where is the panel?"

He pointed downward.

She looked down, saw the loose wires from the panel. "I can't. It's broken."

"Up . . ."

She could hardly hear him. Vaguely, she remembered that there was another control panel just inside the second trailer. If she could get in, she might be able to turn the power on. "Okay, Ian," she said. "I'll do it."

She moved on, going higher. The floor of the trailer was now thirty feet below her. The tyrannosaurs roared, and kicked again. She swung in space. She moved on.

She intended to go through the accordion passage into the second trailer, but as she came closer to the top, she saw that it was not possible. In the harsh flare of lightning, she saw the accordion passage was twisted tightly shut.

She was trapped in the first trailer.

She heard the tyrannosaurs bellowing, and slamming the second trailer above. "Ian!"

She looked down. He wasn't moving.

Hanging there, she realized with a sick feeling that she was defeated. Another kick, another two kicks, and it would be all over. They would fall. There was nothing they could do. There was no time left. She was hanging suspended in blackness, the power was out, and there was nothing—

Or was there? She heard an electrical hum, not far away in the darkness. Was there a panel up here, at this end of the trailer? Did they design it to have panels at both ends?

Hanging near the top of the trailer, her shoulders and forearms burning with strain, she looked around for a second power panel. She was up near the far end. If there was a panel, it should be nearby. But where? In the glare of lightning, she looked over one shoulder, then the other.

She saw no panel.

Her arms ached.

"Ian, please . . ."

No panel.

It wasn't possible. She kept hearing that hum. There had to be a panel. She just wasn't seeing it. There had to be a panel. She swung left and right, and lightning flashed again, casting crazy shadows, and then at last she saw it.

It was just six inches above her head. It was upside down, but she could see all the buttons and switches. They were dark now. If she could just figure out which was which—

The hell with it.

She released her right hand, and hanging from her left, pressed every button on the panel she could touch. Immediately, the trailer began to light up, every interior light coming on.

She kept pressing the buttons, one after another. Some shorted out; there were sparks and smoke.

She kept pressing more.

Suddenly the side monitor came on, just inches from her face, a streaky video blur. Then it came into focus. Although she was looking at it sideways, she could see the tyrannosaurs up on the clearing, standing over the second trailer, their forearms touching it, their powerful legs kicking and pushing at it. She pressed more buttons. The final one had a silver protective cover; she flipped the cover open, and pressed that button, too.

On the monitor she saw the tyrannosaurs disappear in a sudden flaring burst of incandescent sparks, and she heard them roar in rage. And then the video monitor went off, and there was a crackling explosion of sparks all around Harding, stinging her face and hands, and then everything in the trailer went off, and it was dark again.

There was silence for a long moment.

Then, inexorably, the pounding began again.

Thorne

The windshield wipers flicked back and forth. Thorne took the curves fast, despite the driving rain. He glanced at his watch. Two minutes gone, perhaps three.

Perhaps more. He wasn't sure.

The road was a muddy track, slippery and dangerous. He splashed through deep puddles, holding his breath each time. The car had been waterproofed back in his shop, but you were never sure about these things. Each puddle was another test. So far, so good.

Three minutes gone.

At least three.

The road curved, opened out, and in a flash of lightning he saw a deep puddle ahead. He accelerated through it, the car kicking up plumes of water on both side windows. And then he was through it, still going. Still going! As he headed up a hill, he saw the dashboard needles swing wildly, and he heard the sizzle that he knew meant a fatal electrical short. There was an explosion under the hood, and acrid smoke poured out from the radiator, and the car stopped dead.

Four minutes.

He sat in the car, hearing the rain pound on the metal roof. He turned the ignition key. Nothing happened.

Dead.

Rain poured in sheets down the windshield. He sat back in his seat, sighed, and stared at the road ahead. The radio crackled on the seat beside him. "Doc? Are you almost there?"

Thorne stared at the road, trying to guess where he was. He estimated that he must still be more than a mile from the trailer in the clearing, maybe more. Too far to try it on foot. He swore, and pounded the seat.

"No, Eddie. I shorted."

"You what?"

"Eddie, the car's dead. I'm—"

Thorne broke off.

He noticed something.

From around the curve ahead, he saw a faint, flashing red glow.

Thorne squinted, trying to be sure. Yes, his eyes were not playing tricks on him. It was there, all right: a flashing red glow.

Eddie said: "Doc? You there?"

Thorne didn't answer; he grabbed the radio and the Lindstradt rifle, jumped out of the car, and ducking his head against the rain, began to run up the hill toward the junction of the ridge road. Coming around a curve, he saw the red Jeep, standing in the middle of the ridge road, its tail lights flashing. One of the lights was broken, glaring white.

He ran forward, trying to see inside. In a flash of lightning he could see there was no driver. The driver's door was not even closed; the side was deeply dented. Thorne climbed inside, reaching down with his hand for the steering wheel. . . . Yes, the keys were there! He turned the ignition. The motor rumbled to life.

He shoved the Jeep in gear, backed it around, and headed up the ridge toward the clearing. It was only another few curves before he saw the green roof of the laboratory and turned left, his headlights swinging across the grassy clearing, and shining onto the dinosaurs pushing the trailer.

Confronted by these new lights, the tyrannosaurs turned in unison, and bellowed at Thorne's Jeep. They abandoned the trailer, and charged. Thorne threw the Jeep into reverse and was backing away frantically before he realized the animals were not coming toward him.

Instead, they were running diagonally across the clearing, toward a tree near Thorne. Beneath the tree they paused, their heads turned upward. Thorne doused his lights, and waited. Now he saw the animals only intermittently, in the flashes of lightning. In one crackling burst, he saw them take down the baby from the tree. Then he saw them nuzzling the baby. Obviously his sudden arrival had made them anxious about the infant.

The next time lightning flashed, the tyrannosaurs were gone. The clearing was empty. Were they really gone? Or were they just hiding? He rolled down the window, stuck his head out in the rain. That was when he heard an odd, low, continuous squealing sound. It sounded like the extended cry of an animal, but it was too steady, too continuous. As he listened, he realized it was something else. It was metal.

Thorne turned on his lights again, and drove forward slowly. The tyrannosaurs were gone. In the pale beam of the headlamps, he saw the second trailer.

With a continuous metallic squeal, it was still sliding slowly across the wet grass, toward the edge of the cliff.

"What is he doing now?" Kelly yelled, over the rain.

"He's driving," Levine said, looking through goggles. From the high hide, they could see Thorne's headlamps cross the clearing. "He's driving to the trailer. And he's . . ."

"He's what?" Kelly said. "What is he doing now?"

"He's driving around and around a tree," Levine said. "A big tree by the clearing."

"Why?"

"He must be running the cable around the tree," Eddie said. "That's the only possible reason."

There was a moment of silence.

"What's he doing now?" Arby said.

"He's gotten out of the Jeep. Now he's running toward the trailer."

Thorne was down on his hands and knees in the mud, holding the big hook of the Jeep winch in his hands. The trailer was sliding away from him, but he managed to crawl beneath it, and get the hook around the rear axle. He pulled his fingers clear just as the hook slammed tight against the brake cover, and he rolled his body away. Newly restrained, the trailer jumped sideways in the grass, the tires slamming down where his body had been moments before.

The metal cable from the winch was pulled taut. The whole underbelly of the trailer creaked in protest.

But it held.

Thorne crawled out from beneath the trailer, and squinted at it in the rain. He looked carefully at the wheels of the Jeep, to see if they were moving at all. No. With the cable wrapped around the tree, the counterbalancing weight of the Jeep was enough to hold the second trailer on the rim of the cliff.

He went back to the Jeep, climbed inside, and set the brake. He heard Eddie saying, "Doc. Doc."

"I'm here, Eddie."

"You manage to stop it?"

"Yeah. It's not moving any more."

The radio crackled. "That's great. But listen. Doc. You know that connector is just five-mil mesh over stainless rod. It was never intended to—"

"I know, Eddie. I'm working on it." Thorne climbed out of the car again. He ran quickly through the rain toward the trailer.

He opened the side door, and went inside. The interior was inky black. He could see nothing at all. Everything was overturned. His feet crunched on glass. All the windows were shattered. He held the radio in his hand. "Eddie!"

"Yes, Doc."

"I need rope." He knew that Eddie had all sorts of supplies squirreled away.

"Doc . . ."

"Just tell me."

"It's in the other trailer, Doc."

Thorne crashed against a table in the darkness. "Great."

"There might be some nylon line in the utility locker," Eddie said. "But I don't know how much." He didn't sound hopeful. Thorne pushed his way down the trailer, came to the wall cabinets. They were jammed shut. He tugged at them in the darkness, then turned away. The utility locker was just beyond. Maybe there would be rope there. And right now, he needed rope.

Trailer

Sarah Harding, still hanging by her arms from the top of the trailer, stared up at the twisted accordion connector, leading to the second trailer. The pounding from the dinosaurs had stopped, and the other trailer was no longer moving. But now she felt water, dripping cold onto her face. And she knew what that meant.

The accordion connector was beginning to leak.

She looked up, and saw a tear had begun to open in the mesh fabric, revealing the twisted coils of steel that formed the connector. The tear was small now, but it would rapidly widen. And as the mesh broke, the steel would begin to uncoil, to lengthen, and finally snap.

They had only minutes before the hanging trailer broke free and fell to the ground below.

She climbed back down to Malcolm, bracing herself to stand beside him. "Ian."

"I know," he said, shaking his head.

"Ian, we have to get out of here." She grabbed him under his armpits, and pulled him upright. "And you're coming with me."

He shook his head, defeated. She had seen that gesture before in her life, that futile shake, giving up. She hated to see it. Harding never gave up. Not ever.

Malcolm grunted. "I can't. . . ."

"You have to," she said.

"Sarah . . ."

"I don't want to hear it, Ian. There's nothing to talk about. Now let's go." She was pulling him, and he groaned, but he straightened his body. She pulled hard, and got him up off the table. Lightning flashed, and he seemed to find some energy. He managed to stand on the edge of the seat, facing the table. He was unsteady, but standing. "What do we do?"

"I don't know, but we're going to get out of here. . . . Is there any rope?"

He nodded, weakly.

"Where?"

He pointed straight down, toward the nose of the trailer, now hanging in space. "Down there. Under the dash."

"Come on."

She leaned out into space, and spread her legs so she was braced against the floor opposite her. She was standing like a rock climber in a chimney. Twenty feet below her to the dashboard.

"Okay, Ian. Let's go."

Malcolm said, "I can't do it, Sarah. Seriously."

"Then lean on me. I'll carry you."

"But—"

"Now, damn it!"

Malcolm hoisted himself up, grasped a wall fitting, his arm trembling. He was dragging his right leg. Then she felt his weight on her, sudden and heavy, almost knocking her free. His arms locked around her neck, choking her. She gasped, reached back with both arms, grabbed his thighs, and lifted him while he adjusted his arms better around her neck. Finally she could breathe.

"Sorry," he said.

"It's okay," she said. "Here we go."

She started to make her way down the vertical passageway, grabbing at whatever she could. In places there were handholds, and when there were no handholds, she clutched at drawer handles, table legs, window latches, even the carpeting on the floor, her fingers tearing the cloth. At one point, the carpet came away in a big strip, and she slipped before her legs tightened wider, and she halted her downward slide. Hanging behind her, Malcolm wheezed; his arms around her neck were trembling. He said, "You're very strong."

"But still feminine," she said, grimly.

She was only ten feet from the dashboard. Then five. She found a wall grip, hung, dangling her legs. Her feet touched the steering wheel. She lowered herself down, easing Malcolm onto the dashboard. He lay back, gasping.

The trailer creaked and swayed. She fumbled under the dashboard, found a utility box, popped it open. Metal tools spilled out, clattering. And she found a rope. Half-inch nylon, easily fifty feet of it.

She got up, staring down through the windshield at the bottom of the valley hundreds of feet below. Directly to her side, she saw the driver's door to the trailer. She twisted the handle, pushed it open.

It clanged against the outer surface of the trailer, and she felt rain on her face.

She leaned out and looked up the side of the trailer. She saw smooth metal paneling, with no hand grips. But underneath the trailer, there must be axles and boxes and other things to stand on. Gripping the wet metal of the doorjamb, she bent over, trying to look at the underside of the trailer. She heard a metallic clanking, and she heard someone say, "Finally!" And a bulky shape suddenly loomed in front of her. It was Thorne, hanging on the undercarriage.

"For Christ's sake," Thorne said. "What are you waiting for, an engraved invitation? Let's go!"

"It's Ian," she said. "He's hurt."

Typical, Kelly thought, looking at Arby in the high hide. When things got tough, he just couldn't handle it. Too much emotion, too much tension, and he got all trembly and weird. Arby had long since turned away from the cliff, and now was looking out the other side of the shelter, toward the river. Almost as if nothing was going on. Typical.

Kelly turned back to Levine. "What's happening now?" she said.

"Thorne just went in," Levine said, peering through the goggles.

"He went in? You mean, in the trailer?"

"Yes. And now . . . someone's coming out."

"Who?"

"I think Sarah. She's getting everybody out."

Kelly strained in the night, trying to see. The rain had almost stopped; there was only a light drizzle now. Across the valley, the trailer still swung free in space. She thought she could make out a figure, clinging to the undercarriage. But she couldn't be sure.

"What's she doing?"

"Climbing."

"Alone?"

"Yes," Levine said. "Alone."

Sarah Harding came out through the door, twisting her body in the rain. She did not look down. She knew the valley was five hundred feet below her. She could feel the trailer swinging. She had the rope slung around her shoulder. She edged around, lowered her leg, and stood on a gear-box. She felt with her hand, gripped a cable. Swung around.

Thorne was inside the trailer, talking to her. "We'll never get Malcolm up without a rope," he said. "Can you climb it?"

Lightning flashed. She stared straight up at the underside of the trailer, glistening wet with rain. She saw the slick gleam of grease. Then blackness again.

"Sarah: can you do it?"

"Yes," she said. She reached up, and started to climb.

In the high hide, Kelly was saying, "Where is she? What's happening? Is she all right?"

Levine watched through the glasses. "She's climbing," he said.

Arby listened to their voices distantly. He was turned away, staring off at the river in the darkened plain. He waited impatiently for the next lightning flash. Waited to see if it was true, what he had seen earlier.

She did not know how, but slipping and sliding, she somehow got to the top of the cliff, and flung herself over the side. There was no time to waste; she uncoiled the rope, and crawled beneath the second trailer. She looped the rope through a metal bracket, quickly knotted it. Then she went back to the edge of the cliff, and threw the rope down.

"Doc!" she shouted.

Standing at the trailer door, Thorne caught the rope, and tied it around Malcolm. Malcolm groaned. "Let's go," Thorne said. He put his arm around Malcolm and swung them both out, until they were standing on the gearbox.

"Christ," Malcolm said, looking upward. But Sarah was already pulling him, the rope tightening.

"Just use your arms," Thorne said. Malcolm started to rise; in a few moments, he was ten feet above Thorne. Sarah was up on the cliff, but Thorne couldn't see her; Ian's body blocked his view. Thorne began to climb, his legs struggling for purchase. The underside of the trailer was slippery. He thought: I should have made it nonskid. But who would ever make the undercarriage of a vehicle nonskid?

In his mind's eye, he saw the accordion connector, tearing . . . slowly tearing . . . opening wider. . . .

He climbed upward. Hand over hand. Foot by foot.

Lightning flashed, and he realized that they were close to the top.

Sarah was standing on the edge of the cliff, reaching down for Malcolm. Malcolm was pulling himself up with his arms; his legs swung limp, free. But he was still going. Another few feet . . . Sarah grabbed Malcolm by the shirt collar, and hauled him up the rest of the way. Malcolm flopped over, out of sight.

Thorne continued up. His feet slipped. His arms ached.

He climbed.

Sarah was reaching down to him.

"Come on, Doc," she said.

Her hand was extended.

Fingers reaching toward him.

With a metallic *whang!* the mesh ripped on the connector, and the trailer dropped down ten feet, the coils widening.

Thorne climbed faster. Looking up toward Sarah.

Her hand still reached down.

"You can do it, Doc. . . ."

He climbed, closing his eyes, just climbing, holding the rope, gripping it tightly. His arms ached, his shoulders ached, and the rope seemed to become smaller in his hands. He twisted it around his fist, trying to hold on. But at the last moment he began to slip, and then he felt a sudden burning pain in his scalp.

"Sorry about that," Sarah said, and she pulled him up by his hair. The pain was intense but he didn't care, he hardly noticed, because now he was alongside the accordion connector, watching the coils pop free like a bursting corset, and the trailer dropped lower but she still pulled him, she was immensely strong, and then his fingers touched wet grass, and he was over the side. Safe.

Beneath them, there was a sharp series of metallic sounds—*whang! whang! whang!*—as the coiled metal rods snapped one after another, and then, with a final groan, the trailer broke all connection, and fell free down the cliff face, growing smaller and smaller, until it smashed on the rocks far below. In the glare of lightning, it looked like a crumpled paper bag.

Thorne turned, and looked up at Sarah. "Thanks," he said.

Sarah sat heavily on the ground beside him. Blood dripped from her bandaged head. She opened her fingers, and released a handful of his gray hair, which fell in a wet clump onto the grass.

"Hell of a night," she said.

The High Hide

Watching through the night-vision glasses, Levine said, "They made it!"

Kelly said, "All of them?"

"Yes! They made it!"

Kelly began to jump and cheer.

Arby turned, and grabbed the glasses out of Levine's hand.

"Hey," Levine said. "Just a minute—"

"I need them," Arby said. He spun back around and looked out at the dark plain. For a moment, he couldn't see anything, just a green blur. His fingers found the focus knob, he twisted it quickly, and the image came into view.

"What the hell is so important?" Levine said irritably. "That's an expensive piece of equipment—"

And then they all heard the snarling. It was coming closer.

In pale shades of luminous green, Arby saw the raptors clearly. There were twelve of them, moving in a loose cluster through the grass, heading in the direction of the high hide. One animal was a few yards ahead and seemed to be the leader; but it was hard to discern any organization in the pack. The raptors were all snarling and licking the blood off their snouts, wiping their faces with their clawed forearms, a gesture oddly intelligent, almost human. In the night-vision glasses, their eyes glowed bright green.

They did not seem to have noticed the high hide. They never looked up toward it. But they were certainly headed in that direction.

Abruptly, the glasses were yanked out of Arby's hands. "Excuse me," Levine said. "I think I'd better handle this."

Arby said, "You wouldn't even know about it, if it wasn't for me."

"Be quiet," Levine said. He brought the glasses to his eyes, focused them, and sighed at what he saw. Twelve animals, about twenty yards away.

Eddie said quietly, "Do they see us?"

"No. And we're downwind of them, so they won't smell us. My guess is they're following the game trail that runs past the hide. If we're quiet, they'll go right past us."

Eddie's radio crackled. He hastily reached to turn it down.

They all stared out at the plain. The night was now calm and still. The rain had stopped, and the moon was breaking through thinning clouds. Faintly, they saw the approaching animals, dark against the silver grass.

Eddie whispered, "Can they get up here?"

"I don't see how," Levine whispered. "We're almost twenty feet above the ground. I think we'll be fine."

"But you said they can climb trees."

"Ssssh. This isn't a tree. Now, everybody down, and *quiet.*"

Malcolm winced in pain as Thorne stretched him out on a table in the second trailer. "I don't seem to have much luck on these expeditions, do I?"

"No, you don't," Sarah said. "Just take it easy, Ian." Thorne held a flashlight while she cut away Malcolm's trouser. He had a deep gash on his right leg, and he had lost a lot of blood. She said, "We have a medical kit?"

Thorne said, "I think there's one outside, where we store the bike."

"Get it."

Thorne went outside to get it. Malcolm and Harding were alone in the trailer. She shone the light into the wound, peering closely. Malcolm said, "How bad is it?"

"It could be worse," she said lightly. "You'll survive." In fact, the wound cut deep, almost to the bone. Somehow it had missed the artery; that was lucky. But the gash was filthy — she saw grease and bits of leaves mashed into the ragged red muscle. She'd have to clean it out, but she'd wait for the morphine to take effect first.

"Sarah," Malcolm said, "I owe you my life."

"Never mind, Ian."

"No, no, I do."

"Ian," she said, looking at him. "This sincerity is not like you."

"It'll pass," he said, and smiled a little. She knew he must be in pain. Thorne returned with the medical kit, and she filled the syringe, tapped out the bubbles, and injected it into Malcolm's shoulder.

He grunted. "Ow. How much did you give me?"

"A lot."

"Why?"

"Because I have to clean the wound out, Ian. And you're not going to like it when I do."

Malcolm sighed. He turned to Thorne. "It's always something, isn't it? Go on, Sarah, do your damnedest."

Levine watched the approaching raptors through the night glasses. They moved in a loose group, with their characteristic hopping gait. He watched, hoping to see some organization in the pack, some structure, some sign of a dominance hierarchy. Velociraptors were intelligent and it made sense that they would organize themselves hierarchically, and that this would appear in their spatial configuration. But he could see nothing. They were like a band of marauders, shapeless, hissing and snapping at one another.

Near Levine in the high hide, Eddie and the kids were crouched down. Eddie had his arms around the kids, comforting them. The boy especially was panicky. The girl seemed to be okay. She was calmer.

Levine didn't understand why anyone was afraid. They were perfectly secure, high up here. He watched the approaching pack with academic detachment, trying to discern a pattern in their rapid movements.

There was no doubt they were following the game trail. Their path exactly matched the paras earlier in the day: up from the river, then over the slight rise, and along the back of the high hide. The raptors paid no attention to the hide itself. They seemed mostly to interact with each other.

The animals came around the side of the structure, and were about to continue on, when the nearest animal paused. It fell behind the rest of the pack, sniffing the air. Then it bent over, and began to poke its snout through the grass around the bottom of the hide.

What was it doing? Levine wondered.

The solitary raptor growled. It continued to root in the grass. And then it came up with something in its hand, something it held in its clawed fingers. Levine squinted, trying to see it.

It was a piece of wrapping paper from a candy bar.

The raptor looked up at the high hide, its eyes glowing. It stared right at Levine. And it snarled.

Malcolm

"You feel okay?" Thorne said.

"Better all the time," Malcolm said. He sighed. His body relaxed. "You know, there's a reason why people like morphine," he said.

Sarah Harding adjusted the inflatable plastic splint around Malcolm's leg. She said to Thorne, "How long until the helicopter comes?"

Thorne glanced at his watch. "Less than five hours. Dawn tomorrow."

"For sure?"

"Yes, absolutely."

Harding nodded. "Okay. He'll be okay."

"I'm fine," Malcolm said, in a dreamy voice. "I'm just sad that the experiment is over. And it was such a good experiment, too. So elegant. So unique. Darwin never knew."

Harding said to Thorne, "I'm going to clean this out now. Hold his leg for me." More loudly, she said, "What didn't Darwin know, Ian?"

"That life is a complex system," he said, "and everything that goes along with that. Fitness landscapes. Adaptive walks. Boolean nets. Self-organizing behavior. Poor man. Ouch! What are you doing there?"

"Just tell us," Harding said, bent over the wound. "Darwin had no idea . . ."

"That life is so unbelievably complex," Malcolm said. "Nobody realizes it. I mean, a single fertilized egg has a hundred thousand genes, which act in a coordinated way, switching on and off at specific times, to transform that single cell into a complete living creature. That one cell starts to divide, but the subsequent cells are different. They specialize. Some are nerve. Some are gut. Some are limb. Each set of cells begins to follow its own program, developing, interacting. Eventually there are two hundred and fifty different kinds of cells, all developing together, at exactly the right time. Just when the organism needs a circulatory system, the heart starts pumping. Just when hormones are needed, the adrenals start to make them. Week after week, this unimaginably complex development proceeds perfectly—perfectly. It's incredible. No human activity comes close.

"I mean, you ever build a house? A house is simple in comparison. But even so, workmen build the stairs wrong, they put the sink in backward, the tile man doesn't show up when he's supposed to. All kinds of things go wrong. And yet the fly that lands on the workman's lunch is perfect. Ow! Take it easy."

"Sorry," she said, continuing to clean his wound.

"But the point," Malcolm said, "is that this intricate developmental process in the cell is something we can barely describe, let alone understand. Do you realize the limits of our understanding? Mathematically, we can describe two things interacting, like two planets in space. Three things interacting—three planets in space—well, that becomes a problem. Four or five things interacting, we can't really do it. And inside the cell, there's *one hundred thousand* things interacting. You have to throw up your hands. It's so complex—how is it even possible that life ever happens at all? Some people think the answer is that living forms organize themselves. Life creates its own order, the way crystallization creates order. Some people think life crystallizes into being, and that's how the complexity is managed.

"Because, if you didn't know any physical chemistry, you could look at a crystal and ask all the same questions. You'd see those beautiful spars, those perfect geometric facets, and you could ask, What's controlling this process? How does the crystal end up so perfectly formed—and looking so much like other crystals? But it turns out a crystal is just the way molecular forces arrange themselves in solid form. No one controls it. It happens on its own. To ask a lot of questions about a crystal means you don't understand the fundamental nature of the processes that led to its creation.

"So maybe living forms are a kind of crystallization. Maybe life just happens. And maybe, like crystals, there's a characteristic order to living things that is generated by their interacting elements. Okay. Well, one of the things that crystals teach us is that order can arise very fast. One minute you have a liquid, with all the molecules moving randomly. The next minute, a crystal forms, and all the molecules are locked in order. Right?"

"Right . . ."

"Okay. Now. Think of the interaction of life forms on the planet to make an ecosystem. That's even more complex than a single animal. All the arrangements are very complicated. Like the yucca plant. You know about that?"

"Tell me."

"The yucca plant depends on a particular moth which gathers

pollen into a ball, and carries the ball to a different plant—not a different flower on the same plant—where it rubs the ball on the plant, fertilizing it. Only then does the moth lay its eggs. The yucca plant can't survive without the moth. The moth can't survive without the plant. Complex interactions like that make you think maybe behavior is a kind of crystallization, too."

"You're speaking metaphorically?" Harding said.

"I'm talking about all the order in the natural world," Malcolm said. "And how perhaps it can emerge fast, through crystallization. Because complex animals can evolve their behavior rapidly. Changes can occur very quickly. Human beings are transforming the planet, and nobody knows whether it's a dangerous development or not. So these behavioral processes can happen faster than we usually think evolution occurs. In ten thousand years human beings have gone from hunting to farming to cities to cyberspace. Behavior is screaming forward, and it might be nonadaptive. Nobody knows. Although personally, I think cyberspace means the end of our species."

"Yes? Why is that?"

"Because it means the end of innovation," Malcolm said. "This idea that the whole world is wired together is mass death. Every biologist knows that small groups in isolation evolve fastest. You put a thousand birds on an ocean island and they'll evolve very fast. You put ten thousand on a big continent, and their evolution slows down. Now, for our own species, evolution occurs mostly through our behavior. We innovate new behavior to adapt. And everybody on earth knows that innovation only occurs in small groups. Put three people on a committee and they may get something done. Ten people, and it gets harder. Thirty people, and nothing happens. Thirty million, it becomes impossible. That's the effect of mass media—it keeps anything from happening. Mass media swamps diversity. It makes every place the same. Bangkok or Tokyo or London: there's a McDonald's on one corner, a Benneton on another, a Gap across the street. Regional differences vanish. All differences vanish. In a mass-media world, there's less of everything except the top ten books, records, movies, ideas. People worry about losing species diversity in the rain forest. But what about intellectual diversity—our most necessary resource? That's disappearing faster than trees. But we haven't figured that out, so now we're planning to put five billion people together in cyberspace. And it'll freeze the entire species. Everything will stop dead in its tracks. Everyone will think the same thing at the same time. Global uniformity. Oh, that hurts. Are you done?"

"Almost," Harding said. "Hang on."

"And believe me, it'll be fast. If you map complex systems on a fitness landscape, you find the behavior can move so fast that fitness can drop precipitously. It doesn't require asteroids or diseases or anything else. It's just behavior that suddenly emerges, and turns out to be fatal to the creatures that do it. My idea was that dinosaurs—being complex creatures—might have undergone some of these behavioral changes. And that led to their extinction."

"What, all of them?"

"It just takes a few," Malcolm said. "Some dinosaur roots in the swamps around the inland sea, changes the water circulation, and destroys the plant ecology that twenty other species depend on. Bang! They're gone. That causes still more dislocations. A predator dies off, and its prey grow unchecked. The ecosystem becomes unbalanced. More things go wrong. More species die. And suddenly it's over. It could have happened that way."

"Just behavior . . ."

"Yes," Malcolm said. "Anyway, that was the idea. And I had this nice thought that we might prove it. . . . But now it's finished. We have to get out of here. You better tell the others."

Thorne clicked on the radio. "Eddie? It's Doc."

There was no answer.

"Eddie?"

The radio crackled. And then they heard a noise that at first sounded like static. It was a moment before they realized it was a high-pitched human scream.

The High Hide

The first of the raptors hissed as it began jumping up, clattering against the high hide, shaking the structure. Its claws raked against the metal, and it fell down again. Eddie was astonished at how high it jumped— the animal could leap eight feet straight up, again and again, without apparent effort. Its jumps attracted the other animals, which slowly came back to circle the hide.

Soon the hide was surrounded by leaping, snarling raptors. It swayed back and forth as the animals slammed into it, clawed for purchase, and fell back again. But more ominously, Levine saw, *they were learning.* Already, some of them had begun to use their clawed forearms to grip the structure, holding on while their legs got footing. One of the raptors came within a few feet of their little shelter before finally falling back. The falls never seemed to hurt the animals. They immediately leapt up, and jumped again.

Eddie and the kids scrambled to their feet. Levine said, "Get back! Don't look out," and he pushed the kids into the center of the shelter.

Eddie was bent over his knapsack, and held up an incandescent flare. He popped it and flung it over the side; two of the raptors fell away. The flare sputtered on the wet ground, casting harsh red shadows. But the raptors kept coming. Eddie pulled up one of the aluminum bars from the floor, leaned over the side railing brandishing the bar like a club.

One of the raptors had already climbed high enough to dart forward, jaws gaping, at Eddie's neck. Surprised, Eddie shouted and jerked his head back; the raptor narrowly missed him, but its jaws closed on his shirt. Then the raptor fell back, jaws clenched tight, and its weight pulled Eddie forward over the railing.

He yelled "Help me! Help!" as he started to topple over the side; Levine threw his arms around him, dragging him back. Levine looked past Eddie's shoulder at the raptor, which was now dangling in space, hissing furiously, still gripping the shirt. Eddie pounded the raptor on the snout with his bar. But the raptor held on like a bulldog. Eddie was bent precariously over the railing; he might fall at any moment.

He jabbed the bar into the animal's eye, and abruptly the raptor released its grip. The two men fell back into the shelter. When they got to their feet, they saw raptors climbing up the sides of the hide. As they appeared at the rail, Eddie swung at them with the strut, knocking them back.

"Quick!" he shouted to the kids. "Up on the roof! Quick!" Kelly started climbing one of the struts, then pushed herself easily up onto the roof. Arby stood there, his expression blank. She looked back down and said, "Come on, Arb!"

The boy was frozen, his eyes wide with fear. Levine ran to help him, lifted him up. Eddie was swinging the strut in wide arcs, the metal smacking against the raptors.

One of the raptors caught the strut in its jaws and jerked it hard. Eddie lost his balance, twisted, and fell backward, toppling over the side. He cried "Nooo!" as he fell. Immediately all the animals dropped down to the ground. They heard Eddie screaming in the night. The raptors snarled.

Levine was terrified. He was still holding Arby in his arms, pushing him up to the roof. "Go on," he kept saying. "Go on. Go on."

From the roof, Kelly was saying, "You can do it, Arb."

The boy gripped the roof, pulling himself up, his legs churning in panic. He kicked Levine hard in the mouth and Levine dropped him. He saw the boy slide away, and drop backward to the ground.

"Oh Christ," Levine said. "Oh Christ."

Thorne was underneath the trailer, unhooking the cable. He released it, crawled out, and sprinted for the Jeep. He heard the whirr of a motor and saw that Sarah had gotten onto the motorbike, and was already racing off, a Lindstradt rifle slung across her shoulder.

He got behind the wheel, turned on the engine, and waited impatiently while the cable winched in, the hook sliding across the grass. It seemed to take forever. Now the cable was snaking around the tree. He waited. He looked over and saw the light from Sarah's bike moving off through the foliage, heading down toward the high hide.

At last the winch motor stopped. Thorne threw the car in gear, and roared away from the clearing. The radio clicked. "Ian," he said.

"Don't worry about me," Malcolm said, in a dreamy voice. "I'm just fine."

· · ·

Kelly was lying flat on the angled roof of the shed, looking down over the side. She saw Arby hit the ground, on the other side of the structure from Eddie. He seemed to hit hard. But she didn't know what happened to him, because she had turned away to grip the wet roof, and when she looked back down again, Arby was gone.

Gone.

Sarah Harding drove fast on the muddy jungle road. She wasn't sure where she was, but she thought by following the terrain downward she would eventually come out onto the plain. At least that was her hope.

She accelerated, came around a curve, and suddenly saw a big tree blocking the road. She braked to a stop, spun the bike around, and headed back again. Farther up the road, she saw Thorne's twin headlights, turning off to the right. She followed his Jeep, racing her engine in the night.

Levine stood in the center of the high hide, frozen with terror. The raptors were no longer jumping, no longer trying to climb the structure. He heard them down on the ground, snarling. He heard the sharp crunch of bones. The boy had never made a sound.

Cold sweat broke out all over his body.

Then he heard Arby shout, "Back! Get back!"

Up on the roof, Kelly twisted around, trying to see down on the other side. In the dying light of the flare, she saw that Arby was inside the cage. He had managed to close the door, and was reaching his hand back through the bars, to turn the key in the lock. There were three raptors near him; they leapt forward when they saw his hand, and he pulled it back quickly. He shouted, "Get back!" The raptors began to bite the cage, turning their heads sideways to gnaw the bars. One of the animals got its lower jaw tangled up in the looped elastic band that hung from the key. The raptor pulled its head away, stretching the elastic, and suddenly the key snapped out of the lock, smacking against its neck.

The raptor squealed in surprise and stepped backward. The elastic was now looped tight around the lower jaw, the key glinting in the light. The raptor scratched at it with its forearms, trying to pull the elastic loop off, but it was caught around the curved back teeth, and the animal's efforts just made the elastic snap on the skin. Soon it gave up, and began rubbing its snout in the dirt, trying to get the key off.

Meanwhile the other raptors managed to pull the cage free from the superstructure, and knock it over onto the ground. They ducked their heads, slashing Arby behind the bars. When they realized that wouldn't work, they kicked and stomped the cage repeatedly. More animals joined them. Soon seven raptors were clustered over the cage. They kicked it and it rolled away from the hide. Their bodies blocked her view of Arby.

She heard a faint sound, and looked up to see two headlights in the distance. It was a car.

Someone was coming.

Arby was in hell. Inside the cage, he was surrounded by black snarling shapes. The raptors couldn't get their jaws through the spaces in the bars, but their hot saliva dripped down on him, and when they kicked their claws came through, slashing his arms and shoulders as he rolled. His body was bruised. His head hurt from banging against the bars. His world was swirling, terrifying pandemonium. He knew only one thing with certainty.

The raptors were rolling him away from the hide.

As the car came closer, Levine went to the railing and looked down. In the light of the red flare, he saw three raptors dragging what remained of Eddie's body toward the jungle. They paused frequently to fight over it, snapping at each other, but they still managed to haul it away.

Then he saw that another group of raptors were kicking and pushing the cage. They rolled it down the game trail, and into the forest.

Now he could hear the rumble of the Jeep engine, as the car came closer. He saw Thorne's silhouette behind the wheel.

He hoped he had a gun. Levine wanted to kill every one of these damned animals. He wanted to kill them all.

Up on the roof, Kelly watched the raptors kicking the cage, rolling it away. One raptor remained behind, turning around and around in circles, like a frustrated dog. Then she saw it was the raptor that had caught its jaw in the elastic loop. The key still dangled along its cheek, glinting in the red light. The raptor jerked its head up and down, trying to get free.

The Jeep came roaring forward, and the raptor seemed confused by the sudden bright lights. Thorne accelerated, trying to hit it with his car. The raptor turned and ran off, out into the plain.

Kelly scrambled off the roof, and headed down.

Thorne threw open the door as Levine jumped into the car. "They got the kid," Levine said, pointing along the trail.

Kelly was still coming down, shouting, "Wait!"

Thorne said, "Get back up there. Sarah's coming! We'll get Arby!"

"But—"

"We can't lose them!" Thorne gunned the engine, and started to drive down the game trail, chasing the raptors.

In the trailer, Ian Malcolm listened to the voices shouting over the radio. He heard the panic, the confusion.

Black noise, he thought. Everything going to hell at once.

A hundred thousand things interacting.

He sighed, and closed his eyes.

Thorne drove fast. The jungle was dense around them. The trail ahead began to narrow, the big palms edging closer, slapping the car. He said, "Can we make it?"

"It's wide enough," Levine said. "I walked it earlier today. Paras use this trail."

"How could this happen?" Thorne said. "The cage was attached to the scaffolding."

"I don't know," Levine said. "It broke off."

"How? *How?*"

"I didn't see. A lot happened."

"And Eddie?" Thorne said grimly.

"It was fast," Levine said.

The Jeep plunged through the jungle, bouncing hard as it followed the game trail; they banged their heads on the cloth roof. Thorne drove recklessly. Up ahead, the raptors were moving fast; he could hardly see the last of the animals, sprinting in the darkness up ahead.

"They wouldn't listen to me!" Kelly shouted, as Sarah pulled up on the motorcycle.

"About what?"

"The raptor took the key! Arby's locked in the cage and the raptor took the key!"

"Where?" Sarah said.

"There!" she said, pointing across the plain. In the moonlight they could just see the dark shape of the fleeing raptor. "We need the key!"

"Get on," Sarah said, unshouldering her rifle. Kelly climbed behind her on the bike. Sarah thrust the gun into her hands. "Can you shoot?"

"No. I mean, I never—"

"Can you drive a bike?"

"No, I—"

"Then you have to shoot," Sarah said. "Now, look: trigger's here. Okay? Safety's here. Twist it like this. Okay? It'll be a rough ride, so don't release it until we get close."

"Close to what?"

But Sarah didn't hear her. She gunned the engine, and the bike accelerated, heading out into the plain, chasing the fleeing raptor. Kelly put one arm around Sarah, and tried to hold on.

The Jeep bounced along the jungle trail, splashing through muddy pools. "I don't remember it this rough," Levine said, clutching the armhold. "Maybe you should slow down—"

"Hell no," Thorne said. "If we lose sight of him, it's over. We don't know where the raptor nest is. And in this jungle, at night . . . Ah, hell."

Up ahead, the raptors were leaving the trail, running off into the underbrush. The cage was gone. Thorne could not see the terrain very well, but it looked like a sheer hill, going almost straight down.

"You can't do it," Levine said. "It's too steep."

"I have to do it, " Thorne said.

"Don't be crazy," Levine said. "Face facts. We've lost the kid, Doc. It's too bad, but we've lost him."

Thorne glared at Levine. "He didn't give up on you," he said. "And we're not giving up on him."

Thorne spun the wheel and drove the Jeep over the edge. The car nosed down sickeningly, gained speed, and began a steep descent.

"Shit!" Levine yelled. "You'll kill us all!"

"Hang on!"

Bouncing, they plunged downward into darkness.

SIXTH CONFIGURATION

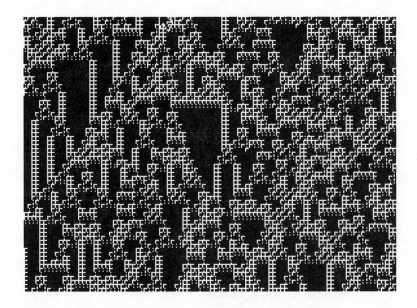

"Order collapses in simultaneous regions. Survival is
now unlikely for individuals and groups."

IAN MALCOLM

Chase

The motorcycle raced forward across the grassy plain. Kelly clutched Sarah with one hand, and held the rifle with the other; the rifle was heavy; her arm was getting tired. The motorcycle jolted over the terrain. The wind blew her hair around her face.

"Hold on!" Sarah shouted.

The moon broke through the clouds, and the grass before them was silver in the moonlight. The raptor was forty yards ahead of them, the animal just within range of their headlamp. They were gaining steadily. Kelly saw no other animals on the plain, except for the apatosaur herd in the far distance.

They came closer to the raptor. The animal ran swiftly, its tail stiff, barely visible above the grass. Sarah angled the bike to the right, as they came alongside the raptor. They moved steadily closer. She leaned back, her mouth close to Kelly's ear.

"Get ready!" she shouted.

"What do I do?"

They were running parallel to the raptor, back by its tail. Sarah accelerated, passing the legs, moving toward the head.

"The neck!" she shouted. "Shoot it in the neck!"

"Where?"

"Anywhere! The neck!"

Kelly fumbled with the gun. "Now?"

"No! Wait! Wait!"

The raptor panicked as the motorcycle approached. It increased its speed.

Kelly was trying to find the safety. The gun was bouncing. Everything was bouncing. Her fingers touched the safety, slid off. She reached again. She was going to have to use two hands, and that meant letting go of Sarah—

"Get ready!" Sarah shouted.

"But I can't—"

"Now! Do it! Now!"

Sarah swerved the bike, coming alongside the raptor. They were now just three feet away. Kelly could smell the animal. It turned its head and snapped at them. Kelly fired. The gun bucked in her hands; she grabbed Sarah again. The raptor kept running.

"What happened?"

"You missed!"

Kelly shook her head. "Never mind!" Sarah shouted. "You can do it! I'll get closer!"

She angled the bike toward the raptor again, moving closer. But this time was different: as they came alongside, the raptor abruptly charged them, butting at them with its head. Sarah howled and twisted the bike away, widening the gap. "Smart bastards, aren't they!" she shouted. "No second chances!"

The raptor chased them for a moment, then suddenly turned, changing direction, racing away across the plains.

"It's going for the river!" Kelly shouted.

Sarah gunned the engine. The bike shot forward. "How deep?"

Kelly didn't answer.

"How deep!"

"I don't know!" Kelly shouted. She was trying to remember how the raptors looked when they crossed the river. She seemed to remember they were swimming. That meant it must be at least—

"More than three feet?" Sarah said.

"Yes!"

"No good!"

They were now ten yards behind the raptor, and losing ground. The animal had entered an area marked with thick Benettitalean cycads. The rough trunks scratched at them. The terrain was uneven; the bike bounced and jolted over the bumps. "Can't see!" Sarah shouted. "Hold on!" She angled left, moving away from the raptor, heading for the river. The animal was disappearing in the grass.

"What're you doing?" Kelly shouted.

"We have to cut him off!"

Shrieking, a flock of startled birds rose up in front of them. Sarah drove through flapping wings, and Kelly ducked her head. The rifle thunked in her hand.

"Careful!" Sarah shouted.

"What happened?"

"It went off!"

"How many shots do I have?"

"Two more! Make 'em good!"

The river was up ahead, shimmering in the moonlight. They burst out of the grass and came onto the muddy bank. Sarah turned, the motorcycle swerved, slipped, and the bike shot away. Kelly fell, hitting the cold mud, Sarah landing hard on top of her. Immediately Sarah jumped up, running for the bike, shouting, "Come on!"

Dazed, Kelly followed her. The rifle in her hands was thick with mud. She wondered if it would still work. Sarah was already on the bike, gunning the engine, waving her forward. Kelly jumped on, and Sarah headed up the riverbank.

The raptor was twenty yards ahead of them. Approaching the water. "It's getting away!"

Thorne's Jeep crashed down the hillside, out of control. Palms slapped against the windshield; they could see nothing at all, but they felt the steepness of the incline. The Jeep fished sideways. Levine yelled.

Thorne gripped the steering wheel, tried to turn the car back. He touched the brake; the Jeep straightened and continued down the hill. There was a gap in the palms—he saw a field of black boulders looming directly ahead. The raptors were scrambling over the boulders. But maybe if he went left—

"No!" Levine shouted. "No!"

"Hang on!" Thorne yelled, and he twisted the wheel. The car lost traction and slid downward. They hit the first of the boulders, shattering a headlight. The car swung up at an angle, crashed down again. Thorne thought that had finished the transmission but somehow the car was still going, angling down the hillside, moving off to the left. The second headlight smashed on a tree branch. They continued down in darkness, through another layer of palms, and then abruptly they banged down on level ground.

The Jeep tires rolled across soft earth.

Thorne brought the car to a stop.

Silence.

They peered out the windows, trying to see where they were. But it was so dark, it was hard to see anything. They seemed to be at the bottom of a deep gully, a canopy of trees overhead.

"Alluvial contours," Levine said. "We must be in a streambed."

As his eyes adjusted, Thorne saw he was right. The raptors were running down the center of the streambed, which was lined with big boulders on both sides. But the bed itself was sandy, and it was wide enough for the car to pass through. He followed them.

"You have any idea where we are?" Levine said, staring at the raptors.

"No," Thorne said.

The car drove forward. The streambed widened, opening out into a flat basin. The boulders disappeared; there were trees on both sides of the river. Patches of moonlight appeared here and there. It was easier to see.

But the raptors were gone. He stopped the car, rolled down the window, and listened. He could hear them hissing and growling. The sound seemed to be coming from off to the left.

Thorne put the car in gear, and left the streambed, moving off among ferns and occasional pine trees. Levine said, "Do you suppose the boy survived that hill?"

"I don't know," Thorne said. "I can't imagine."

He drove forward slowly. They came to a break in the trees, and saw a clearing where the ferns had been trampled flat. Beyond the clearing, they saw the banks of the river, moonlight glinting on the water. Somehow they had returned to the river.

But it was the clearing itself that held their attention. Within the broad open space, they saw the huge pale skeletons of several apatosaurs. The giant rib cages, arcs of pale bone, shone in the silver light. The dark hulk of a partially eaten carcass lay on its side in the center, clouds of flies buzzing above it in the night.

"What is this place?" Thorne said. "It looks like a graveyard."

"Yes," Levine said. "But it's not."

The raptors were all clustered to one side, fighting over the remains of Eddie's carcass. At the opposite side of the clearing they saw three low mud mounds; the walls were broken in many places. Within the nests they saw crushed fragments of eggshells. There was the strong stench of decay.

Levine leaned forward, staring. "This is the raptor nest," he said.

In the darkness of the trailer, Malcolm sat up, wincing. He grabbed the radio. "You found it? The nest?"

The radio crackled. Levine said, "Yes. I think so."

"Describe it," Malcolm said.

. . .

Levine spoke quietly, reporting features, estimating dimensions. To Levine, the velociraptor nest appeared slovenly, uncared for, ill-made. He was surprised, because dinosaur nests usually conveyed an unmistakable sense of order. Levine had seen it time and again, in fossil sites from Montana to Mongolia. The eggs in the nest were arranged in neat concentric circles. Often there were more than thirty eggs in a single nest, suggesting that many females cooperated to share a single mud mound. Numerous adult fossils would be found nearby, indicating that the dinosaurs cared communally for the eggs. At a few excavations, it was even possible to get a sense of the spatial arrangement, with the nests in the center, the adults moving carefully around the outside, so as not to disturb the incubating eggs. In this rigid structure, the dinosaurs were reminiscent of their descendants the birds, which also displayed precise courtship, mating, and nest-building patterns.

But the velociraptors behaved differently. There was a disorderly, chaotic feeling to the scene before him: ill-formed nests; quarreling adults; very few young and juvenile animals; the eggshells crushed; the broken mounds stepped on. Around the mounds, Levine now saw scattered small bones which he presumed were the remains of newborns. He saw no living infants anywhere in the clearing. There were three juveniles, but these younger animals were forced to fend for themselves, and they already showed many scars on their bodies. The youngsters looked thin, undernourished. Poking around the periphery of the carcass, they were cautious, backing away whenever one of the adults snapped at them.

"And what about the apatosaurs?" Malcolm asked. "What about the carcasses?"

Levine counted four, all together. In various stages of decomposition.

"You have to tell Sarah," Malcolm said.

But Levine was wondering about something else: he was wondering how these big carcasses had gotten here in the first place. They hadn't died here by accident, surely all animals would have avoided this nest. They couldn't have been lured here, and they were too large to carry. So how did they get here? Something was tickling the back of his mind, some obvious thought that he wasn't—

"They brought Arby," Malcolm said.

"Yes," Levine said. "They did."

He stared at the nest, trying to figure it out. Then Thorne nudged him. "There's the cage," he said, pointing. At the far side of the clearing, lying on the ground, partially hidden behind fronds, Levine saw the glint of aluminum struts. But he couldn't see Arby.

"Way over there," Levine said.

The raptors were ignoring the cage, still fighting over Eddie's carcass. Thorne brought out a Lindstradt rifle, snapped open the cartridge pack. He saw six darts. "Not enough," he said, and snapped it shut. There were at least ten raptors in the clearing.

Levine rummaged in the back seat, found his knapsack, which had fallen to the floor. He unzipped it, came out with a small silver cylinder the size of a large soft-drink bottle. It had a skull and crossbones stenciled on it. Beneath, lettering read: CAUTION TOXIC METACHOLINE (MIVACURIUM).

"What's that?" Thorne said.

"Something they cooked up in Los Alamos," Levine said. "It's a nonlethal area neutralizer. Releases a short-acting cholinesterase aerosol. Paralyzes all life forms for up to three minutes. It'll knock all the raptors out."

"But what about the boy?" Thorne said. "You can't use that. You'll paralyze *him*."

Levine pointed. "If we throw the canister to the right of the cage, the gas'll blow away from him, toward the raptors."

"Or it may not," Thorne said. "And he may be badly injured."

Levine nodded. He put the cylinder back in the knapsack, then sat, facing forward, staring at the raptors. "So," Levine said. "What do we do now?"

Thorne looked over at the aluminum cage, partially blocked by ferns. Then he saw something that made him sit up: the cage moved slightly, the bars shifting in the moonlight.

"Did you see that?" Levine said.

Thorne said, "I'm going to get that kid out of there."

"But how?" Levine said.

"The old-fashioned way," Thorne said.

He climbed out of the car.

Sarah accelerated, racing the motorcycle up the mud banks of the river. The raptor was just ahead, cutting diagonally toward them, heading for the water.

"Go!" Kelly shouted. "Go!"

The raptor saw them and changed course, angling farther ahead. It was trying to get distance on them but they were moving faster on the open banks. They came abreast of the animal, flanking it, and then Sarah left the banks, heading back onto the grassy plain. The raptor moved right, deeper into the plain. Away from the river.

"You did it!" Kelly shouted.

Sarah maintained her speed, moving slowly closer to the raptor. It seemed to have given up on the river, and now had no plan. It was just running up the plain. And they were steadily, inexorably gaining. Kelly was excited. She tried to wipe the mud off her rifle, preparing to shoot again.

"Damn!" Sarah shouted.

"What?"

"Look!"

Kelly leaned forward, stared past Sarah's shoulder. Directly ahead, she saw the herd of apatosaurs. They were only fifty yards from the first of the enormous animals, which bellowed and wheeled in sudden fear. Their bodies were green-gray in the moonlight.

The raptor streaked directly toward the herd.

"It thinks it's going to lose us!" Sarah gunned the bike, moving closer. "Get it now! Now!"

Kelly aimed and fired. The gun bucked. But the raptor kept going.

"Missed!"

Up ahead, the apatosaurs were turning, their big legs stomping the ground. Their heavy tails whipped through the air. But they were too slow to move away. The raptor raced forward, heading directly beneath the big apatosaurs.

"What do we do?" Kelly shouted.

"No choice!" Sarah yelled. She pulled parallel to the raptor just as they passed into shadow, racing beneath the first animal. Kelly glimpsed the curve of the belly, hanging three feet above her. The legs were as thick as tree trunks, stamping and turning.

The raptor ran on, darting among the moving legs. Sarah swerved, followed. Above them, the animals roared and turned, and roared again. They were beneath another belly, then out into moonlight, then in shadow again. Now they were in the middle of the herd. It was like being in a forest of moving trees.

Directly ahead, a big leg came down with a *slam!* that shook the ground. The bike bounced as Sarah swung left; they scraped against the animal's flesh. "Hang on!" she shouted, and swerved again, following the raptor. Above them, the apatosaurs were bellowing and moving. The raptor dodged and turned, and then broke clear, racing out the back of the herd.

"Shit!" Sarah said, spinning the bike around. A whiptail swung low, narrowly missing them, and then they too were free, chasing the raptor again.

The motorcycle raced across the grassy plain.

"Last chance!" Sarah shouted. "Do it!"

Kelly raised the rifle. Sarah was driving hard and fast, pulling very close to the running raptor. The animal turned to butt her, but she held her position, punched it hard in the head with her fist. "Now!"

Kelly shoved the barrel against the flesh of the neck, and squeezed the trigger. The gun snapped back hard, jolting her in the stomach.

The raptor ran on.

"No!" she shouted. "No!"

And then suddenly the raptor fell, tumbling end over end in the grass, and Sarah swung the bike away and pulled to a stop. The raptor was five yards away, flopping in the grass. It snarled and yelped. Then it was silent.

Sarah took the rifle, snapped open the cartridge pack. Kelly saw five more darts.

"I thought that was the last one," she said.

"I lied," Sarah said. "Wait here."

Kelly stayed by the bike while Sarah moved cautiously forward through the grass. Sarah fired one more shot, then stood waiting for a few moments. Then she bent down.

When she came back, she was holding the key in her hand.

In the nest, the raptors were still tearing at the carcass, off to one side. But the intensity of the behavior was diminishing: some of the animals were turning away, rubbing their jaws with their clawed hands, drifting slowly toward the center of the clearing.

Moving closer to the cage.

Thorne climbed into the back of the Jeep, pushing aside the canvas cover. He checked the rifle in his hands.

Levine slid into the driver's seat. He started the engine. Thorne steadied himself in the back of the Jeep, gripped the rear bar. He turned to Levine.

"Go!"

The Jeep raced forward across the clearing. By the carcass, the raptors looked up in surprise as they saw the intruder. By then the Jeep was past the center of the clearing, driving past the enormous dead skeletons, the broad ribs high over their heads, and then Levine was swinging the car left, pulling alongside the aluminum cage. Thorne jumped out, and grabbed the cage in both hands. In the darkness he couldn't tell how badly Arby was hurt; the boy was turned face down. Levine climbed out of the car; Thorne yelled for him to get back in, as he lifted the cage high and swung it onto the back of the Jeep. Thorne jumped into the back, next to the cage, and Levine shoved the car in gear. Behind them, the raptors snarled and raced forward in pursuit, running among the skeletal ribs. They crossed the clearing with stunning speed.

As Levine stepped on the gas, the nearest raptor leapt high, landing up on the back of the car, and grabbing the canvas tarp in its teeth. The animal hissed and held on.

Levine accelerated, and the Jeep bounced out of the clearing.

In darkness, Malcolm sank back into morphine dreams. Images floated in front of his eyes: fitness landscapes, the multicolored computer images now employed to think about evolution. In this mathematical world of peaks and valleys, populations of organisms were seen to climb the fitness peaks, or slide down into the valleys of nonadaptation. Stu Kauffman and his coworkers had shown that advanced organisms had complex internal constraints which made them more likely to fall off the fitness optima, and descend into the valleys. Yet, at the same time complex creatures were themselves selected by evolution. Because complex creatures were able to adapt on their own. With tools, with learning, with cooperation.

But complex animals had obtained their adaptive flexibility at some cost—they had traded one dependency for another. It was no longer necessary to change their bodies to adapt, because now their adaptation was behavior, socially determined. That behavior required learning. In a sense, among higher animals adaptive fitness was no longer transmitted to the next generation by DNA at all. It was now carried by teaching. Chimpanzees taught their young to collect termites with a stick.

Such actions implied at least the rudiments of a culture, a structured social life. But animals raised in isolation, without parents, without guidance, were not fully functional. Zoo animals frequently could not care for their offspring, because they had never seen it done. They would ignore their infants, or roll over and crush them, or simply become annoyed with them and kill them.

The velociraptors were among the most intelligent dinosaurs, and the most ferocious. Both traits demanded behavioral control. Millions of years ago, in the now-vanished Jurassic world, their behavior would have been socially determined, passed on from older to younger animals. Genes controlled the capacity to make such patterns, but not the patterns themselves. Adaptive behavior was a kind of morality; it was behavior that had evolved over many generations because it was found to succeed—behavior that allowed members of the species to cooperate, to live together, to hunt, to raise young.

But on this island, the velociraptors had been re-created in a genetics laboratory. Although their physical bodies were genetically determined, their behavior was not. These newly created raptors came into the world with no older animals to guide them, to show them proper raptor behavior. They were on their own, and that was just how they behaved—in a society without structure, without rules, without cooperation. They lived in an uncontrolled, every-creature-for-himself world where the meanest and the nastiest survived, and all the others died.

The Jeep picked up speed, bouncing hard. Thorne held on to the bars, to keep from being thrown out. Behind him, he saw the raptor swinging back and forth in the air, still clinging to the tarp. It wasn't letting go. Levine drove back onto the flat muddy banks of the river, and turned right, following the edge of the water. The raptor hung on tenaciously.

Directly ahead, lying in the mud, Levine saw another skeleton. Another skeleton? Why were all these skeletons here? But there was no time to think—he drove forward, passing beneath the row of ribs. Without lights, he leaned forward and squinted in the moonlight, looking for obstacles ahead.

In the back of the car, the raptor scrambled up, released the tarp, clamped its jaws on the cage, and began to pull it out of the back of the Jeep. Thorne lunged, grabbed the end of the cage nearest him. The cage twisted, rolling Thorne onto his back. He found himself in a tug of war with the raptor—and the raptor was winning. Thorne locked his legs around the front passenger seat, trying to hold on. The raptor snarled; Thorne sensed the sheer fury of the animal, enraged that it might lose its prize.

"Here!" Levine shouted, holding a gun out to Thorne. Thorne was on his back, gripping the cage in both hands. He couldn't take the gun. Levine looked back, and saw the situation. He looked in the rearview mirror. Behind them, he saw the rest of the pack still in pursuit, snarling and growling. He could not slow down. Thorne could not let go of the cage. Still driving fast, Levine swung around in the passenger seat, and aimed the rifle backward. He tried to maneuver the gun, knowing what would happen if he accidentally shot Thorne, or Arby.

"Watch it!" Thorne was shouting. "Watch it!"

Levine managed to get the safety off, and swung the barrel straight at the raptor, which was still gripping the cage bars in its jaws. The animal looked up, and in a quick movement closed its jaws over the barrel. It tugged at the gun.

Levine fired.

The raptor's eyes popped wide as the dart slammed into the back of its throat. It made a gurgling sound, then went into convulsions, toppling backward out of the Jeep—and yanking the gun from Levine's hands as it fell.

Thorne scrambled to his knees, and pulled the cage inside the car. He looked down inside it, but he couldn't tell about Arby. Looking back, he saw the other raptors were still pursuing, but they were now twenty yards back, and losing ground.

On the dashboard, the radio hissed. "Doc." Thorne recognized Sarah's voice.

"Yes, Sarah."

"Where are you?"

"Following the river," Thorne said.

The storm clouds had now cleared, and it was a bright moonlit night. Behind him, the raptors still continued to chase the Jeep. But they were now falling steadily behind.

"I can't see your lights," Sarah said.

"Don't have any."

There was a pause. The radio crackled. Her voice was tense: "What about Arby."

"We have him," Thorne said.

"Thank God. How is he?"

"I don't know. Alive."

The landscape opened out. They came back into a broad valley, the grass silvery in the moonlight. Thorne looked around, trying to orient himself. Then he realized: they were back on the plain, but much farther to the south. They must still be on the same side of the river as the high hide. In that case, they ought to be able to make their way up onto the ridge road, somewhere to the left. That road would lead them back to the clearing, and the remaining trailer. And safety. He nudged Levine, pointed to the right. "Go there!"

Levine turned the car. Thorne clicked the radio. "Sarah."

"Yes, Doc."

"We're going back to the trailer on the ridge road."

"Okay," Sarah said. "We'll find you."

Sarah looked back at Kelly. "Where's the ridge road?"

"I think it's that one up there," Kelly said, pointing to the spine of the ridge, on the cliffs high above them.

"Okay," Sarah said. She gunned the bike forward.

The Jeep rumbled across the plain, deep in silvery grass. They were moving fast. The raptors were no longer visible behind them. "Looks like we lost them," Thorne said.

"Maybe," Levine said. When he had pulled out of the streambed, he had seen several animals dart off to the left. They would now be hidden in the grass. He wasn't sure they would give up so easily.

The Jeep was roaring toward the cliffs. Directly ahead he saw a curving switchback road, running up from the valley floor. That was the ridge road, he felt sure.

Now that the terrain was smoother, Thorne crawled back between the seats and crouched over the cage. He peered in through the bars at Arby, who was groaning softly.

Half the boy's face was slick with blood, and his shirt was soaked. But his eyes were open, and he seemed to be moving his arms and legs.

Thorne leaned close to the bars. "Hey, son," he said gently. "Can you hear me?"

Arby nodded, moaning.

"How you doing there?"

"Been better," Arby said.

The Jeep ground onto the dirt road, and headed upward along the switchbacks. Levine felt a sense of relief as they moved higher, away from the valley. He was finally on the ridge road, and he was going to be safe.

He looked up, toward the crest. And then he saw the dark shapes in the moonlight, already at the top of the road, hopping up and down.

Raptors.

Waiting for him.

He pulled to a stop. "What do we do now?"

"Move over," Thorne said grimly. "I'll take it from here."

At the Edge of Chaos

Thorne came up onto the ridge, and turned left, accelerating. The road stretched ahead in the moonlight, a narrow strip running between a rock wall to his left, and a sheer cliff falling away on the right. Twenty feet above him, on the ridge, he saw the raptors, leaping and snorting as they ran parallel to the Jeep.

Levine saw them too.

"What are we going to do?" he said.

Thorne shook his head. "Look in the tool kit. Look in the glove compartment. Get anything you can find."

Levine bent over, fumbling in darkness. But Thorne knew they were in trouble. Their gun was gone. They were in a Jeep with a cloth top, and the raptors were all around them. He guessed he was probably about half a mile from the clearing, and the trailer.

Half a mile to go.

Thorne slowed as he came into the next curve, moving the car away from the plunging drop of the cliff. Rounding the curve, he saw a raptor crouched in the middle of the road, facing them, its head lowered menacingly. Thorne accelerated toward it. The raptor leapt up in the air, legs raised high. It landed on the hood of the car, claws squealing as they raked metal. It smashed against the windshield, the glass streaking spiderwebs. With the animal's body lying against the windshield, Thorne couldn't see anything. On this dangerous road, he slammed on the brakes.

"Hey!" Levine shouted, tumbling forward.

The raptor on the hood slid off to the side. Now Thorne could see again, and he stamped on the gas. Levine fell back again as the car moved forward. But three raptors were charging the car from the side.

One jumped onto the running board and locked its jaws on the side mirror. The animal's glaring eye was close to Thorne's face. He swung the wheel left, scraping the car along the rocky face of the road. Ten yards ahead a boulder protruded. He glanced at the raptor, which continued to hold on tenaciously, right to the moment when the boulder smashed into the side mirror, tearing it away. The raptor was gone.

The road widened a little. Thorne had more room to maneuver now. He felt a heavy thump, and looked up to see the canvas top sagging above his head. Claws slashed down by his ear, ripping through the canvas.

He swung the car right, then left again. The claws pulled out, but the animal was still up there, its body still indenting the cloth. Beside him, Levine produced a big hunting knife, and thrust it upward through the cloth. Immediately, another claw raked downward, slashing Levine's hand. He yelled in pain, dropping the knife. Thorne bent over, reaching down to the floor for it.

In the rearview mirror, he saw two more raptors in the road behind him, chasing the Jeep. They were gaining on him.

But the road was broader now, and he accelerated. The raptor on the roof peered over the top, looking in through the broken windshield. Thorne held the knife in his fist and jabbed it straight up with full force, again and again. It didn't seem to make any difference. As the road curved, he jerked the wheel right, then back, the whole Jeep tilting, and the raptor on the roof lost its grip and rolled backward off the top. It tore most of the canvas roof away as it went. The animal bounced on the ground and hit the two pursuing raptors. The impact knocked all three over the side; they fell snarling down the cliff face.

"That does it!" Levine shouted.

But a moment later, another raptor jumped down from the cliff and ran forward, only a few feet from the Jeep.

And lightly, almost easily, the raptor leapt up into the back of the Jeep.

In the passenger seat, Levine stared. The raptor was fully inside the Jeep, its head low, arms up, jaws wide, in an unmistakable attack posture. The raptor hissed at him.

Levine thought, *It's all over.*

He was shocked: his entire body broke out in sweat, he felt dizzy, and he realized in a single instant there was nothing he could do, that he was moments from death. The creature hissed again, snapping its jaws, crouching to lunge—and then suddenly white foam appeared at the corners of its mouth, and its eyes rolled back. Foam bubbled out of its jaws. It began to twitch, its body going into spasms. It fell over on its side in the back of the car.

Behind them he now saw Sarah on the motorcycle, and Kelly holding the rifle. Thorne slowed, and Sarah pulled alongside them. She handed the key to Levine.

"For the cage!" she shouted.

Levine took it numbly, almost dropped it. He was in shock. Moving slowly. Dumbly. I nearly died, he thought.

"Get her gun!" Thorne said.

Levine looked off to the left, where more raptors were still racing along, parallel to the car. He counted six, but there were probably more. He tried to count again, his mind working slowly—

"Get the damned gun!"

Levine took the gun from Kelly, feeling the cold metal of the barrel in his hands.

But now the car sputtered, the engine coughing, dying, then coughing again. Jerking forward.

"What's that?" he said, turning to Thorne.

"Trouble," Thorne said. "We're out of gas."

Thorne popped the car into neutral, and it rolled forward, losing speed. Ahead was a slight rise, and beyond that, across a curve, he could see the road sloped down again. Sarah was on the motorcycle behind them, shaking her head.

Thorne realized his only hope was to make it over the rise. He said to Levine, "Unlock the cage. Get him out of there." Levine was suddenly moving quickly, almost panicky, but crawled back, and got the key in the lock. The cage creaked open. He helped Arby out.

Thorne watched the speedometer as the needle fell. They were going twenty-five miles an hour . . . then twenty . . . then fifteen. The raptors, running alongside, began to move closer, sensing the car was in trouble.

Fifteen miles an hour. Still falling.

"He's out," Levine said, from the back. He clanged the cage shut.

"Push the cage off," Thorne said. The cage rolled off the back, bouncing down the hill.

Ten miles an hour.

The car seemed to be creeping.

And then they were over the rise, moving down the other side, gaining speed again. Twelve miles an hour. Fifteen. Twenty. He careened around the curves, trying not to touch the brakes.

Levine said, "We'll never make it to the trailer!" He was screaming at the top of his lungs, eyes wide with fear.

"I know." Thorne could see the trailer off to the left, but separated from them by a gentle rise in the road. They could not get there. But up ahead the road forked, sloping down to the right, toward the laboratory. And if he remembered correctly, that road was all downhill.

Thorne turned right, away from the trailer.

He saw the big roof of the laboratory, a flat expanse in the moonlight. He followed the road past the laboratory, down around the back, toward the worker village. He saw the manager's house to the right, and the convenience store, with the gas pumps in front. Was there a chance they might still have gasoline?

"Look!" Levine said, pointing behind them. "Look! Look!" Thorne glanced over his shoulder and saw that the raptors were dropping back, giving up the chase. In the vicinity of the laboratory, they seemed to hesitate.

"They're not following us any more!" Levine shouted.

"Yeah," Thorne said. "But where's Sarah?"

Behind them, Sarah's motorcycle was nowhere to be seen.

Trailer

Sarah Harding twisted the handlebars, and the motorcycle shot forward over the low rise in the road ahead. She crested and came down again, heading toward the trailer. Behind her, four raptors snarled in pursuit. She accelerated, trying to get ahead of them, to gain precious yards. Because they were going to need it.

She leaned back, and shouted to Kelly, "Okay! This has to be fast!"

"What?" Kelly shouted.

"When we get to the trailer, you jump off and run in. Don't wait for me. Understand?"

Kelly nodded, tensely.

"Whatever happens, don't wait for me!"

"Okay."

Harding roared up to the trailer, braked hard. The bike skidded on the wet grass, banged into the metal siding. But Kelly was already leaping off, scrambling up toward the door, going into the trailer. Sarah had wanted to get the bike inside, but she saw the raptors were very close, too close. She pushed the bike toward them and in a single motion stepped up and threw herself through the trailer door, landing on her back on the floor. She twisted her body around and kicked the door shut with her legs, just as the first of the raptors slammed against it.

Inside the dark trailer, she held the door shut as the animals pounded it repeatedly. She felt for a lock on the door, but couldn't find one.

"Ian. Does this door lock?"

She heard Malcolm's voice, dreamy in the darkness. "Life is a crystal," he said.

"Ian. Try and pay attention."

Then Kelly was alongside her, hands moving up and down. The raptors thumped against the door. After a moment she said, "It's down here. By the floor." Harding heard a metallic click, and stepped away.

Kelly reached out, took her hand. The raptors were pounding and snarling outside. "It'll be okay," Harding said reassuringly.

She went over to Malcolm, still lying on the bed. The raptors snapped and lunged at the window near his head, their claws raking the glass. Malcolm watched them calmly. "Noisy bastards, aren't they?" By his side, the first-aid kit was open, a syringe on the cushion. He had probably injected himself again.

Through the windows, the animals stopped throwing themselves against the glass. She heard the sound of scraping metal, from over by the door, and then saw that the raptors were dragging the motorbike away from the trailer. They were hopping up and down on it in fury. It wouldn't be long before they punctured the tires.

"Ian," she said. "We have to do this fast."

"I'm in no rush," he said calmly.

She said, "What kind of weapons have you got here?"

"Weapons . . . oh . . . I don't know. . . ." He sighed. "What do you want weapons for?"

"Ian, please."

"You're talking so fast," he said. "You know, Sarah, you really ought to try to relax."

In the darkened trailer, Kelly was frightened, but she was reassured at the no-nonsense way Sarah talked about weapons. And Kelly was beginning to see that Sarah didn't let anything stop her, she just went and did it. This whole attitude of not letting other people stop you, of believing that you could do what you wanted, was something she found herself imitating.

Kelly listened to Dr. Malcolm's voice and knew that he would be of no help. He was on drugs and he didn't care. And Sarah didn't know her way around the trailer. Kelly did; she had searched the trailer earlier, looking for food. And she seemed to remember . . .

In the darkness, she pulled open the drawers quickly. She squinted, trying to see. She was sure she remembered one drawer, low down, had contained a pack marked with a skull and crossbones. That pack might have some kind of weapons, she thought.

She heard Sarah say, "Ian: try and think."

And she heard Dr. Malcolm say, "Oh, I have been, Sarah. I've had the most wonderful thoughts. You know, all those carcasses at the raptor site present a wonderful example of—"

"Not now, Ian."

Kelly went through the drawers, leaving them open so she would know which ones she had already checked. She moved down the trailer, and then her hand touched rough canvas. She leaned forward. Yes, this was it.

Kelly pulled out a square canvas pack that was surprisingly heavy. She said, "Sarah. Look."

Sarah Harding took the pack to the window, where moonlight shone in. She unzipped the pack and stared at the contents. The pack was divided into padded sections. She saw three square blocks made of some substance that felt rubbery. And there was a small silver cylinder, like a small oxygen bottle. "What is all this stuff?"

"We thought it was a good idea," Malcolm said. "But now I'm not sure it was. The thing is that—"

"What is it?" she said, interrupting. She had to keep him focused. His mind was drifting.

"Nonlethals," Malcolm said. "Alexander's ragtime band. We wanted to have—"

"What's this?" she said, holding up one of the blocks in front of his face.

"Area-dispersal smoke cube. What you do is—"

"Just smoke?" she said. "It just makes smoke?"

"Yes, but—"

"What's this?" she said, raising the silver cylinder. It had writing on it.

"Cholinesterase bomb. Releases gas. Produces short-term paralysis when it goes off. Or so they say."

"How short?"

"A few minutes, I think, but—"

"How does it work?" she said, turning it in her hand. There was a cap at the end, with a locking pin. She started to pull it off, to get a look at the mechanism.

"Don't!" he said. "That's how you do it. You pull the pin and throw. Goes off in three seconds."

"Okay," she said. Hastily, she packed up the medical kit, throwing the syringe inside, shutting the lid.

"What are you doing?" Malcolm said, alarmed.

"We're getting out of here," she said, as she moved to the door.

Malcolm sighed. "It's so nice to have a man around the house," he said.

．．．

The cylinder sailed high through the air, tumbling in the moonlight. The raptors were about five yards away, clustered around the bike. One of the animals looked up and saw the cylinder, which landed in the grass a few yards away.

Sarah stood by the door, waiting.

Nothing happened.

No explosion.

Nothing.

"Ian! It didn't work."

Curious, one raptor hopped over toward where the cylinder had landed in the grass. It ducked down, and when it raised its head, it held the cylinder glinting in its jaws.

She sighed. "It didn't work."

"Oh, never mind," Malcolm said calmly.

The raptor shook its head, biting into the cylinder.

"What do we do now?" Kelly said.

There was a loud explosion, and a cloud of dense white smoke blasted outward across the clearing. The raptors disappeared in the cloud.

Harding closed the door quickly.

"Now what?" Kelly said.

With Malcolm leaning on her shoulder, they moved across the clearing in the night. The gas cloud had dissipated, several minutes before. The first raptor they found in the grass was lying on its side, eyes open, absolutely motionless. But it wasn't dead: Harding could see the steady pulse in the neck. The animal was merely paralyzed. She said to Malcolm, "How long will it last?"

"Have no idea," Malcolm said. "Much wind?"

"There's no wind, Ian."

"Then it should last a bit."

They moved forward. Now the raptors lay all around them. They stepped around the bodies, smelling the rotten odor of carnivores. One of the animals lay across the bike. She eased Malcolm down to the ground, where he sat, sighing. After a moment, he began to sing: "I wish

I was in the land of cotton, old times there are not forgotten, look away . . ."

Harding tugged at the motorcycle handlebars, trying to pull the bike from beneath the raptor. The animal was too heavy. Kelly said, "Let me," and reached for the handlebars. Harding went forward. Without hesitating, she bent over and put her arms around the raptor's neck, and pulled the head upward. She felt a wave of revulsion. Hot scaly skin scraped her arms and cheek. She grunted as she leaned back, raising the animal.

"In Dixie land . . . duh-duh-duh-duh . . . to live and die in Dixie . . ."

She said to Kelly, "Got it?"

"Not yet," Kelly said, pulling on the handlebars.

Harding's face was inches from the velociraptor's head and jaws. The head flopped back and forth as she adjusted her grip. Close to her face, the open eye stared at her, unseeing. Harding tugged, trying to lift the animal higher.

"Almost . . ." Kelly said.

Harding groaned, lifting.

The eye blinked.

Frightened, Harding dropped the animal. Kelly pulled the bike away. "Got it!"

"Away, away . . . away down south . . . in Dixie . . ."

Harding came around the raptor. Now the big leg twitched. The chest began to move.

"Let's go," she said. "Ian, behind me. Kelly, on the handlebars."

"Away . . . away . . . a-way down south . . ."

"Let's go," Harding said, climbing on the bike. She kept her eyes on the raptor. The head gave a convulsive jerk. The eye blinked again. It was definitely waking up. "Let's go, let's go. Let's go!"

Village

Sarah drove the motorcycle down the hill toward the worker village. Looking past Kelly, Sarah saw the Jeep parked at the store, not far from the gas pumps. She braked to a stop, and they all climbed off in the moonlight. Kelly opened the door to the store, and helped Malcolm inside. Sarah rolled the motorcycle into the store, and closed the door.

"Doc?" she said.

"We're over here," Thorne said. "With Arby."

By the moonlight filtering in through the windows, she could see the store looked very much like an abandoned roadside convenience stand. There was a glass-walled refrigerator of soft drinks, the cans obscured by mold on the glass. A wire rack nearby held candy bars and Twinkies, the wrappers speckled green, crawling with larvae. In the adjacent magazine rack, the pages were curled, the headlines five years old.

To one side were rows of basic supplies: toothpaste, aspirin, suntan lotion, shampoo, combs and brushes. Alongside this were racks of clothing, tee shirts and shorts, socks, tennis rackets, bathing suits. And a few souvenirs: key chains, ashtrays, and drinking glasses.

In the center of the room was a little island with a computer cash register, a microwave, and a coffee maker. The microwave door hung wide; some animal had made a nest inside. The coffee maker was cracked, and laced with cobwebs.

"What a mess," Malcolm said.

"Looks fine to me," Sarah Harding said. The windows were all barred. The walls seemed solid enough. The canned goods would still be edible. She saw a sign that said "Restrooms," so maybe there was plumbing, too. They should be safe here, at least for a while.

She helped Malcolm to lie down on the floor. Then she went over to where Thorne and Levine were working on Arby. "I brought the first-aid kit," she said. "How is he?"

"Pretty bruised," Thorne said. "Some gashes. But nothing broken. Head looks bad."

"Everything hurts," Arby said. "Even my mouth."

"Somebody see if there's a light," she said. "Let me look, Arby. Okay, you're missing a couple of teeth, that's why. But that can be fixed. The cut on your head isn't so bad." She swabbed it clean with gauze, turned to Thorne. "How long until the helicopter comes?"

Thorne looked at his watch. "Two hours."

"And where does it land?"

"The pad is several miles from here."

Working on Arby, she nodded. "Okay. So we have two hours to get to the pad."

Kelly said, "How can we do that? The car's out of gas."

"Don't worry," Sarah said. "We'll figure something out. It's going to be fine."

"You always say that," Kelly said.

"Because it's always true," Sarah said. "Okay, Arby, I need you to help now. I'm going to sit you up, and get your shirt off. . . ."

Thorne moved off to one side with Levine. Levine was wild-eyed, his body moving in a twitchy way. The drive in the Jeep seemed to have finished him off. "What is she talking about?" he said. "We're trapped here. Trapped!" There was hysteria in his voice. "We can't go anywhere. We can't do anything. I'm telling you, we're all going to d—"

"Keep it down," Thorne said, grabbing his arm, leaning close. "Don't upset the kids."

"What difference does it make?" Levine said. "They're going to find out sooner or—Ow! Take it easy."

Thorne was squeezing his arm hard. He leaned close to Levine. "You're too old to act like an asshole," he said quietly. "Now, pull yourself together, Richard. Are you listening to me, Richard?"

Levine nodded.

"Good. Now, Richard, I'm going to go outside, and see if the pumps work."

"They can't possibly work," Levine said. "Not after five years. I'm telling you, it's a waste of—"

"Richard," Thorne said. "We have to check the pumps."

There was a pause. The two men looked at each other.

"You mean you're going outside?" Levine said.

"Yes."

Levine frowned. Another pause.

Crouched over Arby, Sarah said, "Where are the lights, guys?"

"Just a minute," Thorne said to her. He leaned close to Levine. "Okay?"

"Okay," Levine said, taking a breath.

Thorne went to the front door, opened it, and stepped out into darkness. Levine closed the door behind him. Thorne heard a click as the door locked.

He immediately turned, and rapped softly. Levine opened the door a few inches, peering out.

"For Christ's sake," Thorne whispered. "Don't lock it!"

"But I just thought—"

"Don't lock the damn door!"

"Okay, okay. I'm sorry."

"For Christ's sake," Thorne said.

He closed the door again, and turned to face the night.

Around him, the worker village was silent. He heard only the steady drone of cicadas in the darkness. It seemed almost too quiet, he thought. But perhaps it was just the contrast from the snarling raptors. Thorne stood with his back to the door for a long time, staring out at the clearing. He saw nothing.

Finally he walked over to the Jeep, opened the side door, and fumbled in the dark for the radio. His hand touched it; it had slid under the passenger seat. He pulled it out and carried it back to the store, knocked on the door.

Levine opened it, said, "It's not lock—"

"Here." Thorne handed him the radio, closed the door again.

Again, he paused, watching. Around him, the compound was silent. The moon was full. The air was still.

He moved forward and peered closely at the gas pumps. The handle of the nearest one was rusted, and draped with spiderwebs. He pulled the nozzle up, and flicked the latch. Nothing happened. He squeezed the nozzle handle. No liquid came out. He tapped the glass window on the pump that showed the number of gallons, and the glass fell out in his hand. Inside, a spider scurried across the metal numerals.

There was no gas.

They had to find gas, or they'd never get to the helicopter. He frowned at the pumps, thinking. They were simple, the kind of very reliable pumps you found at a remote construction site. And that made sense, because after all, this was an island.

He paused.

This was an island. That meant everything came in by plane, or boat. Most times, probably by boat. Small boats, where supplies were offloaded by hand. Which meant . . .

He bent over, examining the base of the pump in the moonlight. Just as he thought, there were no buried gas tanks. He saw a thick black PVC pipe running at an angle just under the ground. He could see the direction the pipe was going—around the side of the store.

Thorne followed it, moving cautiously in the moonlight. He paused for a moment to listen, then moved on.

He came around to the side and saw just what he expected to see: fifty-gallon metal drums, ranged along the side wall. There were three of them, connected by a series of black hoses. That made sense. All the gasoline on the island would have had to come here in drums.

He tapped the drums softly with a knuckle. They were hollow. He lifted one, hoping to hear the slosh of liquid at the bottom. They needed only a gallon or two—

Nothing.

The drums were empty.

But surely, he thought, there must be more than three drums. He did a quick calculation in his head. A lab this large would have had a half-dozen support vehicles, maybe more. Even if they were fuel-efficient, they'd burn thirty or forty gallons a week. To be safe, the company would have stored at least two months' supply, perhaps six months' supply.

That meant ten to thirty drums. And steel drums were heavy, so they probably stored them close by. Probably just a few yards . . .

He turned slowly, looking. The moonlight was bright, and he could see well.

Beyond the store, there was an open space, and then clumps of tall rhododendron bushes which had overgrown the path leading to the tennis court. Above the bushes, the chain-link fence was laced with creeping vines. To the left was the first of the worker cottages. He could see only the dark roof. To the right of the court, nearer the store, there was thick foliage, although he saw a gap—

A path.

He moved forward, leaving the store behind. Approaching the dark gap in the bushes he saw a vertical line, and realized it was the edge of an open wooden door. There was a shed, back in the foliage. The other door was closed. As he came closer, he saw a rusted metal sign, with flaking red lettering. The letters were black in the moonlight.

PRECAUCION
NON FUMARE
INFLAMMABLE

He paused, listening. He heard the raptors snarling in the distance, but they seemed far away, back up on the hill. For some reason they still had not approached the village.

Thorne waited, heart pounding, staring forward at the dark entrance to the shed. At last he decided it wasn't going to get any easier. They needed gas. He moved forward.

The path to the shed was wet from the night's rain, but the shed was dry inside. His eyes adjusted. It was a small place, perhaps twelve by twelve. In the dim light he saw a dozen rusted drums, standing on end. Three or four more, on their sides. Thorne touched them all quickly, one after another. They were light: empty.

Every one, empty.

Feeling defeated, Thorne moved back toward the entrance to the shed. He paused for a moment, staring out at the moonlit night. And then, as he waited, he heard the unmistakable sound of breathing.

Inside the store, Levine moved from window to window, trying to follow Thorne's progress. His body was jumpy with tension. What was Thorne doing? He had gone so far from the store. It was very unwise. Levine kept glancing at the front door, wishing he could lock it. He felt so unsafe with the door unlocked.

Now Thorne had gone off into the bushes, disappearing entirely from view. And he had been gone a long time. At least a minute or two.

Levine stared out the window, and bit his lip. He heard the distant snarl of the raptors, and realized that they had remained up at the entrance to the laboratory. They hadn't followed the vehicles down, even now. Why not? he wondered. The question was welcome in his mind. Calming, almost soothing. A question to answer. Why had the raptors stayed up at the laboratory?

All kinds of explanations occurred to him. The raptors had an atavistic fear of the laboratory, the place of their birth. They remembered the cages and didn't want to be captured again. But he suspected the most likely explanation was also the simplest—that the area around the laboratory was some other animal's territory, it was scent-marked and demarcated and defended, and the raptors were reluctant to enter it. Even the tyrannosaur, he remembered now, had gone through the territory quickly, without stopping.

But whose territory?

Levine stared out the window impatiently, as he waited.

"What about the lights?" Sarah called, from across the room. "I need light here."

"In a minute," Levine said.

At the entrance to the shed, Thorne stood silently, listening.

He heard soft, snorting exhalations, like a quiet horse. A large animal, waiting. The sound was coming from somewhere to his right. Thorne looked over, slowly.

He saw nothing at all. Moonlight shone brightly over the worker village. He saw the store, the gas pumps, the dark shape of the Jeep. Looking to his right, he saw an open space, and clumps of rhododendron bushes. The tennis court beyond.

Nothing else.

He stared, listening hard.

The soft snorting continued. Hardly louder than a faint breeze. But there was no breeze: the trees and bushes were not moving.

Or were they?

Thorne had the sense that something was wrong. Something right before his eyes, something that he could see but couldn't see. With the effort of staring, he began to think his eyes were playing tricks on him. He thought he detected a slight movement in the bushes to the right. The pattern of the leaves seemed to shift in the moonlight. Shift, and stabilize again.

But he wasn't sure.

Thorne stared forward, straining. And as he looked he began to think that it wasn't the bushes that had caught his eye, but rather the chain-link fence. For most of its length, the fence was overgrown with an irregular tangle of vines, but in a few places the regular diamond pattern of links was visible. And there was something strange about that pattern. The fence seemed to be moving, rippling.

Thorne watched carefully. Maybe it *is* moving, he thought. Maybe there's an animal inside the fence, pushing against it, making it move. But that didn't seem quite right.

It was something else. . . .

Suddenly, lights came on inside the store. They shone through the barred windows, casting a geometric pattern of dark shadows across the open clearing, and onto the bushes by the tennis court. And for a moment—just a moment—Thorne saw that the bushes beside the tennis court were oddly shaped, and that they were actually two dinosaurs, seven feet tall, standing side by side, staring right at him.

Their bodies seemed to be covered in a patchwork pattern of light and dark that made them blend in perfectly with leaves behind them, and even with the fence of the tennis court. Thorne was confused. Their concealment had been perfect—too perfect—until the lights from the store windows had shone out and caught them in the sudden bright glare.

Thorne watched, holding his breath. And then he realized that the leafy light-and-dark pattern went only partway up their bodies, to mid-thorax. Above that, the animals had a kind of diamond-shaped crisscross pattern that matched the fence.

And as Thorne stared, the complex patterns on their bodies faded, the animals turned a chalky white, and then a series of vertical striped shadows began to appear, which exactly matched the shadows cast by the windows.

And before his eyes, the two dinosaurs disappeared from view again. Squinting, with concentrated effort, he could just barely distinguish the outlines of their bodies. He would never have been able to see them at all, had he not already known they were there.

They were chameleons. But with a power of mimicry unlike any chameleon Thorne had ever seen.

Slowly, he backed away into the shed, moving deeper into darkness.

"My God!" Levine exclaimed, staring out the window.

"Sorry," Harding said. "But I had to turn on the lights. That boy needs help. I can't do it in the dark."

Levine did not answer her. He was staring out the window, trying to comprehend what he had just seen. He now realized what he had glimpsed the day Diego was killed. That brief momentary sense that something was wrong. Levine now knew what it was. But it was quite beyond anything that was known among terrestrial animals and—

"What is it?" she said, standing alongside him at the window. "Is it Thorne?"

"Look," Levine said.

She stared out through the bars. "At the bushes? What? What am I supposed to—"

"*Look*," he said.

She watched for a moment longer, then shook her head. "I'm sorry."

"Start at the bottom of the bushes," Levine told her. "Then let your eyes move up very slowly. . . . Just look . . . and you'll see the outline."

He heard her sigh. "I'm sorry."

"Then turn out the lights again," he said. "And you'll see."

She turned the lights out, and for a moment Levine saw the two animals in sharp relief, their bodies pale white with vertical stripes in the moonlight. Almost immediately, the pattern started to fade.

Harding came back, pushed in alongside him, and this time she saw the animals instantly. Just as Levine knew she would.

"No shit," she said. "There are two of them?"

"Yes. Side by side."

"And . . . is the pattern fading?"

"Yes. It's fading." As they watched, the striped pattern on their skins was replaced by the leafy pattern of the rhododendrons behind them. Once again, the two dinosaurs blended into invisibility. But such complex patterning implied that their epidermal layers were arranged in a manner similar to the chromatophores of marine invertebrates. The subtlety of shading, the rapidity of the changes all suggested—

Harding frowned. "What are they?" she asked.

"Chameleons of unparalleled skill, obviously. Although I'm not sure one is entirely justified in referring to them as chameleons, since technically chameleons have only the ability—"

"What are they?" Sarah said impatiently.

"Actually, I'd say they're *Carnotaurus sastrei*. Type specimen's from Patagonia. Two meters in height, with distinctive heads—you notice the short, bulldog snouts, and the pair of large horns above the eyes? Almost like wings—"

"They're carnivores?"

"Yes, of course, they have the—"

"Where's Thorne?"

"He went into that clump of bushes to the right, some time ago. I haven't seen him, but—"

"What do we do?" she said.

"Do?" Levine said. "I'm not sure I follow you."

"We have to do something," she said, speaking slowly, as if he were a child. "We have to help Thorne get back."

"I don't know how," Levine said. "Those animals must weigh five hundred pounds each. And there are two of them. I told him not to go out in the first place. But now . . ."

Harding frowned. Staring out, she said, "Go turn the lights back on."

"I'd prefer to—"

"Go turn the lights back on!"

Levine got up irritably. He had been relishing his remarkable discovery, a truly unanticipated feature of dinosaurs—although not, of course, entirely without precedent among related vertebrates—and now this little musclebound female was barking orders at him. Levine was offended. After all, she was not much of a scientist. She was a naturalist. A field devoid of theory. One of those people who poked around in animal crap and imagined they were doing original research. A nice outdoor life, is all it amounted to. It wasn't science by any stretch—

"On!" Harding shouted, looking out the window.

He flicked the lights on, and started to head back to the window.

"Off!"

Hastily, he went back and turned them off.

"On!"

He turned them on again.

She got up from the window, and crossed the room. "They didn't like that," she said. "It bothered them."

"Well, there's probably a refractory period—"

"Yeah, I think so. Here. Open these." She scooped up a handful of flashlights from one of the shelves, handed them to him, then went and got batteries from an adjacent wire rack. "I hope these still work."

"What are you going to do?" Levine said.

"We," she said, grimly. "We."

.   .   .

Thorne stood in the darkness of the shed, staring outward through the open doors. Someone had been turning the lights on and off inside the store. Then, for a while they remained on. But now suddenly they went off again. The area in front of the shed was lit only by moonlight.

He heard movement, a soft rustling. He heard the breathing again. And then he saw the two dinosaurs, walking upright with stiff tails. Their skin patterns seemed to shift as they walked, and it was difficult to follow them, but they were moving toward the shed.

They arrived at the entrance, their bodies silhouetted against the moonlight beyond, their outlines finally clear. They looked like small tyrannosaurs, except they had protuberances above the eyes, and they had very small, stubby forelimbs. The carnivores ducked their squarish heads down, and looked into the shed cautiously. Snorting, sniffing. Their tails swinging slowly behind them.

They were really too big to come inside, and for a moment he hoped that they would not. Then the first of them lowered its head, growled, and stepped through the entrance.

Thorne held his breath. He was trying to think what to do, but he couldn't think of anything at all. The animals were methodical, the first one moving aside so the second could enter as well.

Suddenly, from along the side of the store, a half-dozen glaring lights shone out in bright beams. The lights moved, splashed on the dinosaurs' bodies. The beams began to move back and forth in slow, erratic patterns, like searchlights.

The dinosaurs were clearly visible, and they didn't like it. They growled and tried to step away from the lights, but the beams moved continuously, searching them out, crisscrossing over their bodies. As the lights passed over their torsos, the skin paled in response, reproducing the movement of the beams, after the lights had moved on. Their bodies streaking white, fading to dark, streaking white again.

The lights never stopped moving, except when they shone into the faces of the dinosaurs, and into their eyes. The big eyes blinked beneath their hooded wings; the animals twitched their heads and ducked away, as if annoyed by flies.

The dinosaurs became agitated. They turned, backing out of the shed, and bellowed loudly at the moving lights.

Still the lights moved, relentlessly swinging back and forth in the night. The pattern of movement was complex, confusing. The dinosaurs bellowed again, and took a menacing step toward the lights. But it was half-hearted. They clearly didn't like being around these moving sources. After a moment, they shuffled off, the lights following them, driving them away past the tennis courts.

Thorne moved forward.

He heard Harding say, "Doc? Better get out of there, before they decide to come back."

Thorne moved quickly toward the lights. He found himself standing beside Levine and Harding. They were swinging fistfuls of flashlights back and forth.

They all went back to the store.

Inside, Levine slammed the door shut, and sagged back against it. "I was never so frightened in my entire life."

"Richard," Harding said coldly. "Get a grip on yourself." She crossed the room, and placed the flashlights on the counter.

"Going out there was insane," Levine said, wiping his forehead. He was drenched in sweat, his shirt stained dark.

"Actually, it was a slam dunk," Harding said. She turned to Thorne. "You could see they had a refractory period for skin response. It's fast compared to, say, an octopus, but it's still there. My assumption was that those dinosaurs were like all animals that rely on camouflage. They're basically ambushers. They're not particularly fast or active. They stand motionless for hours in an unchanging environment, disappearing into the background, and they wait until some unsuspecting meal comes along. But if they have to keep adjusting to new light conditions, they know they can't hide. They get anxious. And if they get anxious enough, they finally just run away. Which is what happened."

Levine turned and glared angrily at Thorne. "This was all your fault. If you hadn't gone out there that way, just wandering off—"

"Richard," Harding said, cutting him off. "We need gas or we'll never get out of here. Don't you want to get out of here?"

Levine said nothing. He sulked.

"Well," Thorne said, "there wasn't any gas in the shed anyway."

"Hey, everybody," Sarah said. "Look who's here!"

· · ·

Arby came forward, leaning on Kelly. He had changed into clothes from the store: a pair of swimming trunks and a tee shirt that said "InGen Bioengineering Labs" and beneath, "We Make The Future."

Arby had a black eye, a swollen cheekbone, and a cut that Harding had bandaged on his forehead. His arms and legs were badly bruised. But he was walking, and he managed a crooked smile.

Thorne said, "How do you feel, son?"

Arby said, "You know what I want more than anything, right now?"

"What?" Thorne said.

"Diet Coke," Arby said. "And a lot of aspirin."

Sarah bent over Malcolm. He was humming softly, staring upward. "How is Arby?" he asked.

"He'll be okay."

"Does he need any morphine?" Malcolm asked.

"No, I don't think so."

"Good," Malcolm said. He stretched out his arm, rolling up the sleeve.

Thorne cleaned the nest out of the microwave, and heated up some canned beef stew. He found a package of paper plates decorated in a Halloween motif—pumpkins and bats—and spooned the food onto the plates. The two kids ate hungrily.

He gave a plate to Sarah, then turned to Levine. "What about you?"

Levine was staring out the window. "No."

Thorne shrugged.

Arby came over, holding his plate. "Is there any more?"

"Sure," Thorne said. He gave him his own plate.

Levine went over and sat with Malcolm. Levine said, "Well, at least we were right about one thing. This island was a true lost world—a pristine, untouched ecology. We were right from the beginning."

Malcolm looked over, and raised his head. "Are you joking?" he said. "What about all the dead apatosaurs?"

"I've been thinking about that," Levine said. "The raptors killed them, obviously. And then the raptors—"

"Did what?" Malcolm said. "Dragged them to their nest? Those animals weigh hundreds of tons, Richard. A hundred raptors couldn't drag them. No, no." He sighed. "The carcasses must have floated to a bend in the river, where they beached. The raptors made their nest at a source of convenient food supply—dead apatosaurs."

"Well, possibly . . ."

"But why so many dead apatosaurs, Richard? Why do none of the animals attain adulthood? And why are there so many predators on the island?"

"Well. We need more data, of course—" Levine began.

"No, we don't," Malcolm said. "Didn't you go through the lab? We already know the answer."

"What is it?" Levine said, irritably.

"Prions," Malcolm said, closing his eyes.

Levine frowned. "What're prions?"

Malcolm sighed.

"Ian," Levine said. "What are prions?"

"Go away," Malcolm said, waving his hand.

Arby was curled up in a corner, near sleep. Thorne rolled up a tee shirt, and put it under the boy's head. Arby mumbled something, and smiled.

In a few moments, he began to snore.

Thorne got up and went over to Sarah, who was standing by the window. Outside, the sky was beginning to lighten above the trees, turning pale blue.

"How much time now?" she said.

Thorne looked at his watch. "Maybe an hour."

She started to pace. "We've got to get gas," she said. "If we have gas, we can drive the Jeep to the helicopter site."

"But there's no gas," Thorne said.

"There must be some, somewhere." She continued to pace. "You tried the pumps. . . ."

"Yes. They're dry."

"What about inside the lab?"

"I don't think so."

"Where else? What about the trailer?"

Thorne shook his head. "It's just a passive tow-trailer. The other unit has an auxiliary generator and some gas tanks. But it went over the cliff."

"Maybe the tanks didn't rupture when it fell. We still have the motorcycle. Maybe I can go out there and—"

"Sarah," he said.

"It's worth a try."

"Sarah—"

From the window, Levine said softly, "Heads up. We have visitors."

Good Mother

In the predawn light, the dinosaurs came out of the bushes and went directly toward the Jeep. There were six of them, big brown duckbills fifteen feet high, with curving snouts.

"Maiasaurs," Levine said. "I didn't know there were any here."

"What are they doing?"

The huge animals clustered around the Jeep, and immediately began to tear it apart. One ripped away the canvas top. Another poked at the roll bar, rocking the vehicle back and forth.

"I don't understand," Levine said. "They're hadrosaurs. Herbivores. This aggressiveness is quite uncharacteristic."

"Uh-huh," Thorne said. As they watched, the maiasaurs tipped the Jeep over. The vehicle crashed over on its side. One of the adults reared up, and stood on the side panels. Its huge feet crushed the vehicle inward.

But when the Jeep fell over, two white Styrofoam cases tumbled out onto the ground. The maiasaurs seemed to be focused on these cases. They nipped at the Styrofoam, tossing chunks of white around the ground. They moved hurriedly, in a kind of frenzy.

"Something to eat?" Levine said. "Some kind of dinosaur catnip? What?"

Then the top of one case tore away, and they saw a cracked egg inside. Protruding from the egg was a wrinkled bit of flesh. The maiasaurs slowed. Their movements were now cautious, gentle. They honked and grunted. The big bodies of the animals blocked their view.

There was a squeaking sound.

"You're kidding," Levine said.

On the ground, a tiny animal moved about. Its body was pale brown, almost white. It tried to stand, but flopped down at once. It was barely a foot long, with wrinkled folds of flesh around its neck. In a moment, a second animal tumbled out beside it.

Harding sighed.

Slowly, one of the maiasaurs ducked its huge head down, and gently scooped the baby up in its broad bill. It kept its mouth open as it raised its head. The baby sat calmly on the adult's tongue, looking around with its tiny head as it rose high into the air.

The second baby was picked up. The adults milled around for a moment, as if unsure whether there was more to do, and then, honking loudly, they all moved off.

Leaving behind a crumpled, shattered vehicle.

Thorne said, "I guess gas is no longer a problem."

"I guess not," Sarah said.

Thorne stared at the wreckage of the Jeep, shaking his head. "It's worse than a head-on collision," he said. "It looks like it's been put in a compactor. Just wasn't built for those sorts of stresses."

Levine snorted. "Engineers in Detroit didn't expect a five-ton animal to stand on it."

"You know," Thorne said, "I would have liked to see how our own car stood up under that."

"You mean, because we beefed it up?"

"Yes," Thorne said. "We really built it to take fantastic stresses. Huge stresses. Ran it through computer programs, added those honeycomb panels, the whole—"

"Wait a minute," Harding said, turning away from the window. "What are you talking about?"

"The other car," Thorne said.

"What other car?"

"The car we brought," he said. "The Explorer."

"Of course!" she said, suddenly excited. "There's another car! I completely forgot! The Explorer!"

"Well, it's history now," Thorne said. "It shorted out last night, when I was coming back to the trailer. I ran it through a puddle and it shorted out."

"So? Maybe it still—"

"No," Thorne said, shaking his head. "A short like that'd blow the VR. It's an electric car. It's dead."

"I'm surprised you don't have circuit breakers for that."

"Well, we never used to put them in, although on this latest version . . ." He trailed off. He shook his head. "I can't believe it."

"The car has circuit breakers?"

"Yes. Eddie put them in, last minute."

"So the car might still run?"

"Yes, it probably would, if you reset the breakers."

"Where is it?" she said. She was heading for the motorcycle.

"I left it on that side road that runs from the ridge road down to the hide. But Sarah—"

"It's our only chance," she said. She pulled on her radio headset, adjusted the microphone to her cheek, and rolled the motorcycle to the door. "Call me," she said. "I'm going to go find us a car."

They watched through the windows. In the early-morning light, she climbed onto the motorcycle, and roared off up the hill.

Levine watched her go. "What do you figure her odds are?"

Thorne just shook his head.

The radio crackled. "Doc."

Thorne picked it up. "Yes, Sarah."

"I'm coming up the hill now. I see . . . there's six of them."

"Raptors?"

"Yeah. They're, uh . . . Listen. I'm going to try another path. I see a—"

The radio crackled.

"Sarah?" She was breaking up.

"—sort of a game trail that—here—think I better—"

"Sarah," Thorne said. "You're breaking up."

"—do now. So just—ish me luck."

Over the radio, they heard the hum of the bike. Then they heard another sound, which might have been an animal snarl, and might have been more static. Thorne bent forward, holding the radio close to his ear. Then, abruptly, the radio clicked and was silent. He said, "Sarah?"

There was no answer.

"Maybe she turned it off," Levine said.

Thorne shook his head. "Sarah?"

Nothing.

"Sarah? Are you there?"

They waited.

Nothing.

"Hell," Thorne said.

.   .   .

Time passed slowly. Levine stood by the window, staring out. Kelly was snoring in a corner. Arby lay next to Malcolm, fast asleep. And Malcolm was humming tunelessly.

Thorne sat on the floor in the center of the room, leaning back against the checkout counter. Every so often, he'd pick up the radio and try to call Sarah, but there was never any answer. He tried all six channels. There was no answer on any of them.

Eventually he stopped trying.

The radio crackled. "—ate these damned things. Never work right." A grunt. "Can't figure out what—things—damn."

Across the room, Levine sat forward.

Thorne grabbed the radio. "Sarah? *Sarah?*"

"Finally," she said, her voice crackling. "Where the hell have you been, Doc?"

"Are you all right?"

"Of course I'm all right."

"There's something wrong with your radio. You're breaking up."

"Yeah? What should I do?"

"Try screwing down the cover on your battery pack. It's probably loose."

"No. I mean, what should I do about the car?"

Thorne said, "What?"

"I'm at the car, Doc. I'm there. What should I do?"

Levine glanced at his watch. "Twenty minutes until the helicopter arrives," he said. "You know, she just might make it."

Dodgson

Dodgson awoke, aching and stiff, on the floor of the concrete utility shed. He got to his feet, and looked out the window. He saw streaks of red in a pale-blue sky. He opened the door to the utility shed, and went outside.

He was very thirsty, and his body was sore. He started walking beneath the canopy of trees. The jungle around him was silent in the early morning. He needed water. More than anything, he needed water. Somewhere off to his left, he heard the soft gurgle of a stream. He headed toward it, moving more quickly.

Through the trees, he could see the sky growing lighter. He knew that Malcolm and his party were still here. They must have some plan to get off the island. If they could get off, he could too.

He came over a low rise, and looked down at a gully and a flowing stream. It looked clear. He hurried down toward it, wondering if it was polluted. He decided he didn't care. Just before he reached the stream, he tripped over a vine and fell, swearing.

He got to his feet, and looked back. Then he saw it wasn't a vine he had tripped over.

It was the strap of a green backpack.

Dodgson tugged at the strap, and the whole backpack slid out of the foliage. The pack had been torn apart, and it was crusty with dried blood. As he pulled it, the contents clattered out among the ferns. Flies were buzzing everywhere. But he saw a camera, a metal case for food, and a plastic water bottle. He searched quickly through the surrounding ferns. But he didn't find much else, except some soggy candy bars.

Dodgson drank the water, and then realized he was very hungry. He popped open the metal case, hoping for some decent food. But the case didn't contain food. It was filled with foam packing.

And in the center of the packing was a radio.

He flicked it on. The battery light glowed strongly. He flicked from one channel to another, hearing static.

Then a man's voice. "Sarah? This is Thorne. Sarah?"

After a moment, a woman's voice: "Doc. Did you hear me? I said, I'm at the car."

Dodgson listened, and smiled.

So there was a car.

In the store, Thorne held the radio close to his cheek. "Okay," he said. "Sarah? Listen carefully. Get in the car, and do exactly what I tell you."

"Okay fine," she said. "But tell me first. Is Levine there?"

"He's here."

The radio clicked. She said, "Ask him if there's any danger from a green dinosaur that's about six feet tall and has a domed forehead."

Levine nodded. "Tell her yes. They're called pachycephalosaurs."

"He says yes," Thorne said. "They're pachycephalo-somethings, and you should be careful. Why?"

"Because there's about fifty of them, all around the car."

Explorer

The Explorer was sitting in the middle of a shady section of the road, with overhanging trees above. The car had stopped just beyond a depression, where there had no doubt been a large puddle the night before. Now the puddle had become a mudhole, thanks to the dozen or so animals that sat in it, splashed in it, drank from it, and rolled at its edges. These were the green dome-headed dinosaurs that she had been watching for the last few minutes, trying to decide what to do. Because not only were they near the mudhole, they were also located in front of the car, and around the sides of the car.

She had watched the pachycephalosaurs with uneasiness. Harding had spent a lot of time on the ground with wild animals, but usually animals she knew well. From long experience, she knew how closely she could approach, and under what circumstances. If this were a herd of wildebeest, she would walk right in without hesitation. If it were a herd of American buffalo, she would be cautious, but she'd still go in. And if it was a herd of African buffalo, she wouldn't go anywhere near them.

She pushed the microphone against her cheek and said, "How much time left?"

"Twenty minutes."

"Then I better get in there," she said. "Any ideas?"

There was a pause. The radio crackled.

"Levine says nobody knows anything about these animals, Sarah."

"Great."

"Levine says a complete skeleton has never been recovered. So nobody has even a guess about their behavior, except that they're probably aggressive."

"Great," she said.

She was looking at the situation of the car, and the overhanging trees. It was a shady area, peaceful and quiet in the early-morning light.

The radio crackled. "Levine says you might try walking slowly in, and see if the herd lets you through. But no quick movements, no sudden gestures."

She stared at the animals and thought: They have those domed heads for a reason.

"No thanks," she said. "I'm going to try something else."

"What?"

In the store, Levine said, "What'd she say?"

"She said she was going to try something else."

"Like what?" Levine said. He went to the window and looked out. The sky was growing lighter. He frowned. There was some consequence to that, he thought. Something he knew in the back of his mind, but wasn't thinking about.

Something about daylight . . .

And territory.

Territory.

Levine looked out at the sky again, trying to put it together. What difference did it make that daylight was coming? He shook his head, gave it up for the moment. "How long to reset the breakers?"

"Just a minute or two," Thorne said.

"Then there might still be time," Levine said.

There was static hiss from the radio, and they heard Harding say, "Okay, I'm above the car."

"You're where?"

"I'm above the car," she said. "In a tree."

Harding climbed out on the branch, moving farther from the trunk, feeling it bend under her weight. The branch seemed supple. She was now ten feet above the car, swinging lower. Few of the animals below had looked up at her, but the herd seemed to be restless. Animals sitting in the mud got up, and began to turn and mill. She saw their tails flicking back and forth anxiously.

She moved farther out, and the branch bent lower. It was slippery from the night's rain. She tried to gauge her position above the car. It looked pretty good, she thought.

Suddenly, one of the animals charged the trunk of the tree she was in, butting it hard. The impact was surprisingly forceful. The tree swayed, her branch swinging up and down, while she struggled to hold on.

Oh shit, she thought.

She rose up into the air, came down again, and then she lost her grip. Her hands slipped on wet leaves and wet bark, and she fell free. At the last moment, she saw that she would miss the car entirely. Then she hit the ground, landing hard in muddy earth.

Right beside the animals.

The radio crackled. "Sarah?" Thorne said.

There was no answer.

"What's she doing *now?*" Levine began to pace nervously. "I wish we could see what she's doing."

In the corner of the room, Kelly got up, rubbing her eyes. "Why don't you use the video?"

Thorne said, "What video?"

Kelly pointed to the cash register. "That's a computer."

"It is?"

"Yeah. I think so."

Kelly yawned as she sat in the chair facing the cash register. It looked like a dumb terminal, which meant it probably didn't have access to much, but it was worth a try anyway. She turned it on. Nothing happened. She flicked the power switch back and forth. Nothing.

Idly, she swung her legs, and kicked a wire beneath the table. She bent over and saw that the terminal was unplugged. So she plugged it in.

The screen glowed, and a single word appeared:

LOGIN:

To proceed further, she knew she needed a password. Arby had a password. She glanced over and saw that he was still asleep. She didn't want to wake him up. She remembered that he had written it down on a piece of paper and stuck it in his pocket. Maybe it was still in his clothes, she thought. She crossed the room, found the bundle of his wet, muddy clothes, and began going through the pockets. She found his wallet, the keys to his house, and some other stuff. Finally she found a piece of paper in his back pocket. It was damp, and streaked with mud. The ink had smeared, but she could still read his writing:

VIG/&*849/

Kelly took the paper and went back to the computer. She typed in all the characters carefully, and pressed the return key. The screen went blank, and then a new screen came up. She was surprised. It was different from the screen she had seen earlier, in the trailer.

She was in the system. But the whole thing looked different. Maybe because this wasn't the radionet, she thought. She must be logged into the actual laboratory system. It had more graphics because the terminal was hard-wired. Maybe they even ran optical pipe out here.

Across the room, Levine said, "Kelly? How about it?"

"I'm working on it," she said.

Cautiously, she began to type. Rows of icons appeared rapidly across the screen, one after another.

She knew she was looking at a graphic interface of some kind, but the meaning of the images wasn't obvious to her, and there were no explanations. The people who had used this system were probably trained to know what the images meant. But Kelly didn't know. She wanted to get into the video system, yet none of the pictures suggested anything to do with video. She moved the cursor around, wondering what to do.

She decided she'd have to guess. She picked the diamond-shaped icon on the lower left, and clicked on it.

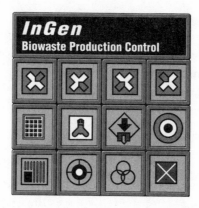

"Uh-oh," she said, alarmed.

Levine looked over. "Something wrong?"

"No," she said. "It's fine." She quickly clicked on the header, and got back to the previous screen. This time she tried one of the triangular-shaped icons.

The screen changed again:

That's it, she thought. Immediately the image popped off, and the actual video images began to flash up on the screen. On this little cash-register monitor, the pictures were tiny, but now she was in familiar territory, and she moved around quickly, moving the cursor, manipulating the images.

"What are you looking for?" she said.

"The Explorer," Thorne said.

She clicked the screen. The image zoomed up. "Got it," she said.

Levine said, "You do?" He sounded surprised.

Kelly looked at him and said, "Yeah, I do."

The two men came and stared at the screen over her shoulder. They could see the Explorer, on a shaded road. They could see the pachycephalosaurs, lots of them, milling around the car. The animals were poking at the tires and the front fender.

But they didn't see Sarah anywhere.

"Where is she?" Thorne said.

Sarah Harding was underneath the car, lying on her face in the mud. She had crawled there after she fell—it was the only place to go—and now she was staring out at the animals' feet milling all around her. She said, "Doc. Are you there? Doc? Doc." But the damned radio wasn't working again. The pachys were stamping and snorting, trying to get at her under the car.

Then she remembered that Thorne had said something about screwing down the battery pack. She reached behind her back, and found the pack, and twisted the cover shut tight.

Immediately, her earpiece began to crackle with static.

"Doc," she said.

"Where are you?" Thorne said.

"I'm under the car."

"Why? Did you already try it?"

"Try what?"

"Try to start it. To start the car."

"No," she said, "I didn't try to start it, I fell."

"Well, as long as you're under there, you can check the breakers," Thorne said.

"The breakers are under the car?"

"Some of them. Look up by the front wheels."

She twisted her body, sliding in the mud. "Okay. I'm looking."

"There's a box right behind the front bumper. Over on the left."

"I see it."

"Can you open it?"

"I think so." She crawled forward, and pulled at the latch. The lid came down. She was staring at three black switches. "I see three switches and they are all pointing up."

"Up?"

"Toward the front of the car."

"Hmmm," Thorne said. "That doesn't make sense. Can you read the writing?"

"Yes. It says '15 VV' and then '02 R.'"

"Okay," he said. "That explains it."

"What?"

"The box is in backward. Flip all the switches the other way. Are you dry?"

"No, Doc. I'm soaking wet, lying in the damn mud."

"Well then, use your shirtsleeve or something."

Harding pulled herself forward, approaching the bumper. The nearest pachys snorted and banged on the bumper. They leaned down and twisted their heads, trying to get to her. "They have very bad breath," she said.

"Say again?"

"Never mind." She flipped the switches, one after another. She heard a hum, from the car above her. "Okay. I did it. The car is making a noise."

"That's fine," Thorne said.

"What do I do now?"

"Nothing. You better wait."

She lay back in the mud, looking at the feet of the pachys. They were moving, tramping all around her.

"How much time left?" she said.

"About ten minutes."

She said, "Well, I'm stuck under here, Doc."

"I know."

She looked at the animals. They were on all sides of the car. If anything, they seemed to be growing more active and excited. They stamped their feet and snuffled impatiently. Why were they so worked up? she wondered. And then, suddenly, they all thundered off. They ran toward the front of the car, and away, up the road. She twisted her body and watched them go.

There was silence.

"Doc?" she said.

"Yeah."

"Why'd they leave?"

"Stay under the car," Thorne said.

"Doc?"

"Don't talk." The radio clicked off.

She waited, not sure what was happening. She had heard the tension in Thorne's voice. She didn't know why. But now she heard a soft scuffling sound, and looking over, saw two feet standing by the driver's side of the car.

Two feet in muddy boots.

Men's boots.

Harding frowned. She recognized the boots. She recognized the khaki trousers, even though they were now caked with mud.

It was Dodgson.

The man's boots turned to face the door. She heard the door latch click.

Dodgson was getting in the car.

Harding acted so swiftly, she was not aware of thinking. Grunting, she swung her body around sideways, reached out with her arms, grabbed both ankles, and pulled hard. Dodgson fell, giving a yell of surprise. He landed on his back, and turned, his face dark and angry.

He saw her and scowled. "No shit," he said. "I thought I finished you off on the boat."

Harding went red with rage, and started to crawl out from under the car. Dodgson scrambled to his knees as she was halfway out, but then she felt the ground begin to shake. And she immediately knew why. She saw Dodgson look over his shoulder, and flatten himself on the ground. Hurriedly, he started to crawl under the car beside her.

She turned in the mud, looking down along the length of the car. And she saw a tyrannosaurus coming up the road toward them. The ground vibrated with each step. Now Dodgson was crawling toward the center of the car, pushing himself close to her, but she ignored him. She watched the big feet with the splayed claws as they came alongside the car, and stopped. Each foot was three feet long. She heard the tyrannosaur growling.

She looked at Dodgson. His eyes were wide with terror. The tyrannosaur paused beside the car. The big feet shifted. She heard the animal somewhere above, sniffing. Then, growling again, the head came down. The lower jaw touched the ground. She could not see the eye, just the lower jaw. The tyrannosaur sniffed again, long and slow.

It could smell them.

Beside her, Dodgson was trembling uncontrollably. But Harding was strangely calm. She knew what she had to do. Quickly, she shifted her body, twisting around, moving so her head and shoulders were braced against the rear wheel of the car. Dodgson turned to look at her just as her boots began to push against his lower legs. Pushing them out from beneath the car.

Terrified, Dodgson struggled, trying to push back, but her position was much stronger. Inch by inch, his boots moved out into the cold morning light. Then his calves. She grunted as she pushed, concentrating every ounce of her energy. In a high-pitched voice, Dodgson said, "What the hell are you doing?"

She heard the tyrannosaur growling. She saw the big feet move.

Dodgson said, "Stop it! Are you crazy? Stop it!"

But Harding didn't stop. She got her boot on his shoulder, and pushed once more. For a while Dodgson struggled against her, and then suddenly his body moved easily, and she saw that the tyrannosaur had his legs in its jaws and was pulling Dodgson out from under the car.

Dodgson wrapped his hands around her boot, trying to hold on, trying to drag her with him. She put her other boot on his face and kicked hard. He let go. He slid away from her.

She saw his terrified face, ashen, mouth open. No words came out. She saw his fingers, digging into the mud, leaving deep gouges as he was pulled away. And then his body was dragged out. Everything was strangely quiet. She saw Dodgson spin around onto his back, and look upward. She saw the shadow of the tyrannosaur fall across him. She saw the big head come down, the jaws wide. And she heard Dodgson begin to scream as the jaws closed around his body, and he was lifted up.

Dodgson felt himself rise high into the air, twenty feet above the ground, and all the time he continued to scream. He knew at any moment the animal would snap its great jaws shut, and he would die. But the jaws never closed. Dodgson felt stabbing pain in his sides, but the jaws never closed.

Still screaming, Dodgson felt himself carried back into the jungle. High branches of trees lashed his face. The hot breath of the animal whooshed in snorts over his body. Saliva dripped onto his torso. He thought he would pass out from terror.

But the jaws never closed.

. . .

Inside the store, they stared at the tiny monitor as Dodgson was carried away in the jaws of the tyrannosaur. Over the radio, they heard his tinny distant screams.

"You see?" Malcolm said. "There is a God."

Levine was frowning. "The rex didn't kill him." He pointed to the screen. "Look, there, you can see his arms are still moving. Why didn't it kill him?"

Sarah Harding waited until the screams faded. She crawled out from beneath the car, standing up in the morning light. She opened the door and got behind the wheel. The key was in the ignition; she gripped it with muddy fingers. She twisted it.

There was a chugging sound, and then a soft whine. All the dashboard lights came on. Then silence. Was the car working? She turned the wheel and it moved easily. So the power steering was on.

"Doc."

"Yes, Sarah."

"The car's working. I'm coming back."

"Okay," he said. "Hurry."

She put it in drive, and felt the transmission engage. The car was unusually quiet, almost silent. Which was why she was able to hear the faint thumping of a distant helicopter.

Daylight

She was driving beneath a thick canopy of trees, back toward the village. She heard the sound of the helicopter build in intensity. Then it roared overhead, unseen through the foliage above. She had the window down, and was listening. It seemed to move off to her right, toward the south.

The radio clicked. "Sarah."

"Yes, Doc."

"Listen: we can't communicate with the helicopter."

"Okay," she said. She understood what had to be done. "Where's the landing site?"

"South. About a mile. There's a clearing. Take the ridge road."

She was coming up to the fork. She saw the ridge road going off to the right. "Okay," she said. "I'm going."

"Tell them to wait for us," Thorne said. "Then come back and get us."

"Everybody okay?" she said.

"Everybody's fine," Thorne said.

She followed the road, hearing a change in the sound of the helicopter. She realized it must be landing. The rotors continued, a low whirr, which meant the pilot wasn't going to shut down.

The road curved off to the left. The sound of the helicopter was now a muted thumping. She accelerated, driving fast, careening around the corner. The road was still wet from the rains the night before. She wasn't raising a cloud of dust behind her. There was nothing to tell anyone that she was here.

"Doc. How long will they wait?"

"I don't know," Thorne said, over the radio. "Can you see it?"

"Not yet," she said.

Levine stared out the window. He looked at the lightening sky, through the trees. The streaks of red were gone. It was now a bright even blue. Daylight was definitely coming.

Daylight . . .

And then he put it together. He shivered as he realized. He went to the window on the opposite side, looked out toward the tennis court. He stared at the spot where the carnotauruses had been the night before. They were gone now.

Just as he feared.

"This is bad," he said.

"It's only just now eight," Thorne said, glancing at his watch.

"How long will it take her?" Levine said.

"I don't know. Three or four minutes."

"And then to get back?" Levine said.

"Another five minutes."

"I hope we make it that long." He was frowning unhappily.

"Why?" Thorne said. "We're okay."

"In a few minutes," Levine said, "we'll have direct sun shining down outside."

"So what?" Thorne said.

The radio clicked. "Doc," Sarah said. "I see it. I see the helicopter."

Sarah came around a final curve and saw the landing site off to her left. The helicopter was there, blades spinning. She saw another junction in the road, with a narrow road leading left down a hill, into jungle, and then out to the clearing. She drove down it, descending a series of switchbacks, forcing her to go slow. She was now back in the jungle, beneath the canopy of trees. The ground leveled out, she splashed across a narrow stream, and accelerated forward.

Directly ahead there was a gap in the tree canopy, and sunlight on the clearing beyond. She saw the helicopter. Its rotors were beginning to spin faster—it was leaving! She saw the pilot behind the bubble, wearing dark glasses. The pilot checked his watch, shook his head to the copilot, and then began to lift off.

Sarah honked her horn, and drove madly forward. But she knew they could not hear her. Her car bounced and jolted. Thorne was saying, "What is it? Sarah! What's happening?"

She drove forward, leaning out the window, yelling "Wait! Wait!" But the helicopter was already rising into the air, lifting up out of her view. The sound began to fade. By the time her car burst out of the jungle into the clearing, she saw the helicopter heading away, disappearing over the rocky rim of the island.

And then it was gone.

"Let's stay calm," Levine said, pacing the little store. "Tell her to get back right away. And let's stay calm." He seemed to be talking to himself. He walked from one wall to the next, pounding the wooden planks with his fist. He shook his head unhappily. "Just tell her to hurry. You think she can be back in five minutes?"

"Yes," Thorne said. "Why? What is it, Richard?"

Levine pointed out the window. "Daylight," he said. "We're trapped here in daylight."

"We were trapped here all night, too," Thorne said. "We made it okay."

"But daylight is different," Levine said.

"Why?"

"Because at night," he said, "this is carnotaurus territory. Other animals don't come in. We saw no other animals at all around here, last night. But once daylight comes, the carnotaurus can't hide any more. Not in open spaces, in direct sunlight. So they'll leave. And then this won't be their territory any more."

"Which means?"

Levine glanced at Kelly, over by the computer. He hesitated, then said, "Just take my word for it. We have to get out of here right away."

"And go where?"

Sitting at the computer, Kelly listened to Thorne talking to Dr. Levine. She fingered the piece of paper with Arby's password on it. She felt very nervous. The way Dr. Levine was talking was making her nervous. She wished Sarah was back by now. She would feel better when Sarah was here.

Kelly didn't like to think about their situation. She had been holding herself together, keeping up her spirits, until the helicopter came. But now the helicopter had come and gone. And she noticed neither of the men was talking about when it would come back. Maybe they knew something. Like it wasn't coming back.

Dr. Levine was saying they had to get out of the store. Thorne was asking Dr. Levine where he wanted to go. Levine said, "I'd prefer to get off this island, but I don't see how we can. So I suppose we should make our way back to the trailer. It's the safest place now."

Back to the trailer, she thought. Where she and Sarah had gone to get Malcolm. Kelly didn't want to go back to the trailer.

She wanted to go home.

Tensely, Kelly smoothed out the piece of damp paper, pressing it flat on the table beside her. Dr. Levine came over. "Stop fooling around," he said. "See if you can find Sarah."

"I want to go home," Kelly said.

Levine sighed. "I know, Kelly," he said. "We all want to go home." And he walked away again, moving quickly, tensely.

Kelly pushed the paper away, turning it over, and sliding it under the keyboard, in case she should need the password again. As she did so, her eye was caught by some writing on the other side.

She pulled the paper out again.

She saw:

SITE B LEGENDS

EAST WING	WEST WING	LOADING BAY
LABORATORY	ASSEMBLY BAY	ENTRANCE
OUTLYING	MAIN CORE	GEO TURBINE
CONVENIENCE STORE	WORKER VILLAGE	GEO CORE
GAS STATION	POOL/TENNIS	PUTTING GREENS
MGRS HOUSE	JOG PATH	GAS LINES
SECURITY ONE	SECURITY TWO	THERMAL LINES
RIVER DOCK	BOATHOUSE	SOLAR ONE
SWAMP ROAD	RIVER ROAD	RIDGE ROAD
MTN VIEW ROAD	CLIFF ROAD	HOLDING PENS

She realized at once what it was: a screen shot from Levine's apartment. From the night when Arby had been recovering files from the computer. It seemed like a million years ago, another lifetime. But it had really been only . . . what? Two days ago.

She remembered how proud Arby had been when he had recovered the data. She remembered how they had all tried to make sense of this list. Now, of course, all these names had meaning. They were all real places: the laboratory, the worker village, the convenience store, the gas station. . . .

She stared at the list.

You're kidding, she thought.

"Dr. Thorne," she said. "I think you better look at this."

Thorne stared as she pointed at the list. "You think so?" he said.

"That's what it says: a boathouse."

"Can you find it, Kelly?"

"You mean, find it on the video?" She shrugged. "I can try."

"Try," Thorne said. He glanced at Levine, who was across the room, pounding on the walls again. He picked up the radio.

"Sarah? It's Doc."

And the radio crackled. "Doc? I've had to stop for a minute."

"Why?" Thorne said.

Sarah Harding was stopped on the ridge road. Fifty yards ahead, she saw the tyrannosaur, going down the road away from her. She could see that he had Dodgson in his mouth. And somehow, Dodgson was still alive. His body was still moving. She thought she could hear him scream.

She was surprised to find she had no feeling about him at all. She watched dispassionately as the tyrannosaur left the road, and headed off down a slope, back into the jungle.

Sarah started the car, and drove cautiously forward.

At the computer console, Kelly flicked through video images, one after another, until finally she found it: a wooden dock, enclosed inside a shed or a boathouse, open to the air at the far end. The interior of the boathouse looked in pretty good shape; there weren't a lot of vines and ferns growing over things. She saw a powerboat tied up, rocking against the dock. She saw three oil drums to one side. And out the back of the boathouse there was open water, and sunlight; it looked like a river.

"What do you think?" she said to Thorne.

"I think it's worth a try," he said, looking over her shoulder. "But where is it? Can you find a map?"

"Maybe," she said. She flicked the keys, and managed to get back to the main screen, with its perplexing icons.

Arby awoke, yawned, and came over to look at what she was doing. "Nice graphics. You logged on, huh?"

"Yeah," she said. "I did. But I'm having a little trouble figuring it out."

Levine was pacing, staring out the windows. "This is all well and good," he said, "but it is getting brighter out there by the minute. Don't you understand? We need a way out of here. This building is single-wall construction. It's fine for the tropics, but it's basically a shack."

"It'll do," Thorne said.

"For three minutes, maybe. I mean, look at this," Levine said. He walked to the door, rapped it with his knuckles. "This door is just—"

With a crash, the wood splintered around the lock, and the door swung open. Levine was thrown aside, landing hard on the floor.

A raptor stood hissing in the doorway.

A Way Out

Sitting at the console, Kelly was frozen in terror. She watched as Thorne ran forward from the side, throwing the full weight of his body against the door, slamming it hard against the raptor. Startled, the animal was knocked back. The door closed on its clawed hand. Thorne leaned against the door. On the other side, the animal snarled and pounded.

"Help me!" Thorne shouted. Levine scrambled to his feet and ran forward, adding his weight.

"I told you!" Levine shouted.

Suddenly there were raptors all around the store. Snarling, they threw themselves at the windows, denting the steel bars, pushing them in toward the glass. They slammed against the wooden walls, knocking down shelves, sending cans and bottles clattering to the floor. In several places, the wood began to splinter on the walls.

Levine looked back at her: *Find a way out of here!*

Kelly stared. The computer was forgotten.

"Come on, Kel," Arby said. "Concentrate."

She turned back to the screen, unsure what to do. She clicked on the cross in the left corner. Nothing happened. She clicked on the upper-left circle. Suddenly, icons began to print out rapidly, filling the screen.

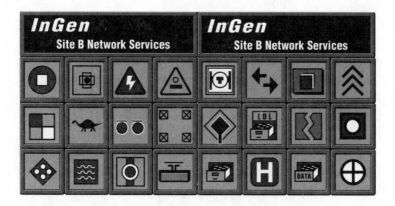

"Don't worry, there must be a key to explain it," Arby said. "We just need to know what—"

But Kelly was not listening, she was pressing more buttons and moving the cursor, already trying to get something to happen, to get a help screen, something. Anything.

Suddenly, the whole screen began to twist, to distort.

"What did you do?" Arby said, in alarm.

Kelly was sweating. "I don't know," she said. She pulled her hands away from the keyboard.

"It's worse," Arby said. "You made it worse."

The screen continued to squeeze together, the icons shifting, distorting slowly as they watched.

"Come on, kids!" Levine shouted.

"We're trying!" Kelly said.

Arby said, "It's becoming a cube."

Thorne pushed the big glass-walled refrigerator in front of the door. The raptor slammed against the metal, rattling the cans inside.

"Where are the guns?" Levine said.

"Sarah has three in her car."

"Great." At the windows, some of the bars were now so deeply dented that they broke the glass. Along the right-hand wall, the wood was splintering, tearing open big gaps.

"We have to get out of here," Levine shouted at Kelly. "We have to find a way!" He ran to the rear of the store, to the bathrooms. But a moment later he returned. "They're back there, too!"

It was happening fast, all around them.

On the screen, she now saw a rotating cube, turning in space. Kelly didn't know how to stop it.

"Come on, Kel," Arby said, peering at her through swollen eyes. "You can do it. Concentrate. Come on."

Everyone in the room was shouting. Kelly stared at the cube on the screen, feeling hopeless and lost. She didn't know what she was doing any more. She didn't know why she was there. She didn't know what the point of anything was. Why wasn't Sarah here?

Standing beside her, Arby said, "Come on. Do the icons one at a time, Kel. You can do it. Come on. Stay with it. Focus."

But she couldn't focus. She couldn't click on the icons, they were rotating too fast on the screen. There must be parallel processors to handle all the graphics. She just stared at it. She found herself thinking of all sorts of things—thoughts that just came unbidden into her mind.

The cord under the desk.

Hard-wired.

Lots of graphics.

Sarah talking to her in the trailer.

"Come on, Kel. You have to do this now. Find a way out."

In the trailer, Sarah said: *Most of what people tell you will be wrong.*

"It's important, Kel," Arby said. He was trembling as he stood beside her. She knew he concentrated on computers as a way to block things out. As a way to—

The wall splintered wide, an eight-inch plank cracking inward, and a raptor stuck his head through, snarling, snapping his jaws.

She kept thinking of the cord under the desk. The cord under the desk. Her legs had kicked the cord under the desk.

The cord under the desk.

Arby said, "It's important."

And then it hit her.

"No," she said to him. "It's not important." And she dropped off the seat, crawling down under the desk to look.

"*What are you doing?*" Arby screamed.

But already Kelly had her answer. She saw the cable from the computer going down into the floor, through a neat hole. She saw a seam in the wood. Her fingers scrabbled at the floor, pulling at it. And suddenly the panel came away in her hands. She looked down. Darkness.

Yes.

There was a crawlspace. No, more. A tunnel.

She shouted, "Here!"

The refrigerator fell forward. The raptors crashed through the front door. From the sides, other animals tore through the walls, knocking over the display cases. The raptors sprang into the room, snarling and ducking. They found the bundle of Arby's wet clothes and snapped at them, ripping them apart in fury.

They moved quickly, hunting.

But the people were gone.

Escape

Kelly was in the lead, holding a flashlight. They moved, single file, along damp concrete walls. They were in a tunnel four feet square, with flat metal racks of cables along the left side. Water and gas pipes ran near the ceiling. The tunnel smelled moldy. She heard the squeak of rats.

They came to a Y-junction. She looked both ways. To the right was a long straight passageway, going into darkness. It probably led to the laboratory, she thought. To the left was a much shorter section of tunnel, with stairs at the end.

She went left.

She crawled up through a narrow concrete shaft, and pushed open a wooden trapdoor at the top. She found herself in a small utility building, surrounded by cables and rusted pipes. Sunlight streamed in through broken windows. The others climbed up beside her.

She looked out the window, and saw Sarah Harding driving down the hill toward them.

Harding drove the Explorer along the edge of the river. Kelly was sitting beside her in the front seat. They saw a wooden sign for the boathouse up ahead.

"So it was the graphics that gave you the clue, Kelly?" Harding said, admiringly.

Kelly nodded. "I just suddenly realized, it didn't matter what was actually on the screen. What mattered was there was a lot of data being manipulated, millions of pixels spinning there, and that meant there had to be a cable. And if there was a cable, there must be a space for it. And enough space that workmen could repair it, all of that."

"So you looked under the desk."

"Yes," she said.

"That's very good," Harding said. "I think these people owe you their lives."

"Not really," Kelly said, with a little shrug.

Sarah shot her a look. "All your life, other people will try to take your accomplishments away from you. Don't you take it away from yourself."

The road was muddy alongside the river, and heavily overgrown with plants. They heard the distant cries of the dinosaurs, somewhere behind them. Harding maneuvered around a fallen tree, and then they saw the boathouse ahead.

"Uh-oh," Levine said. "I have a bad feeling."

From the outside, the building was in ruins, and heavily overgrown with vines. The roof had caved in in several places. No one spoke as Harding pulled the Explorer up in front of a pair of broad double doors sealed with a rusted padlock. They climbed out of the car and walked forward in ankle-deep mud.

"You really think there's a boat in there?" Arby said doubtfully.

Malcolm leaned on Harding, while Thorne threw his weight against the door. Rotten timbers creaked, then splintered. The padlock fell to the ground. Harding said, "Here, hold him," and put Malcolm's arm over Thorne's shoulder. Then she kicked a hole in the door wide enough to crawl through. Immediately she went inside, into darkness. Kelly hurried in after her.

"What do you see?" Levine said, pulling planks away to widen the hole. A furry spider scurried up the boards, jumping away.

"There's a boat here, all right," Harding said. "And it looks okay."

Levine pushed his head through the hole.

"I'll be damned," he said. "We just might get out of here, after all."

Exit

Lewis Dodgson fell.

Tumbling through the air, he dropped from the mouth of the tyrannosaur, and landed hard on an earthen slope. The breath was knocked out of him, his head slammed down, and he was dizzy for a moment. He opened his eyes, and saw a sloping bank of dried mud. He smelled a sour odor of decay. And then he heard a sound that chilled him: it was a high-pitched squeaking.

He got up on one elbow, and saw he was in the tyrannosaur nest. The sloping mound of dried mud was all around him. Now there were three infants here, including one with a piece of aluminum wrapped around its leg. The infants were squeaking with excitement as they toddled toward him.

Dodgson scrambled to his feet, unsure of what to do. The other adult tyrannosaur was on the far side of the nest, purring and snorting. The one that had brought him was standing over him.

Dodgson watched the babies moving toward him, with their downy necks and their sharp little jaws. And then he turned to run. In an instant, the big adult brought his head down, knocking Dodgson over. Then the tyrannosaur raised its head again, and waited. Watching.

What the hell is going on? Dodgson thought. Cautiously, he got to his feet again. And again, he was knocked down. The infants squeaked and came closer. He saw that their bodies were covered in bits of flesh and excrement. He could smell them. He got up on all fours, and began crawling away.

Something grabbed his leg, holding him. He looked back and saw that his leg was in the jaws of the tyrannosaur. The big animal held it gently for a moment. Then it bit down decisively. The bones snapped and crunched.

Dodgson screamed in pain. He could no longer move. He could no longer do anything but scream. The babies toddled forward eagerly. For a few seconds they kept their distance, heads darting forward to take quick bites. But then, when Dodgson did not move away, one hopped up on his leg, and began to bite at the bleeding flesh. The second jumped on his crotch, and pecked with razor-sharp jaws at his waist.

The third came right alongside his face, and with a single snap bit into his cheek. Dodgson howled. He saw the baby eating the flesh of his own face. His blood was dripping down its jaws. The baby threw its head back and swallowed the cheek, and then turned, opened its jaws again, and closed over Dodgson's neck.

SEVENTH CONFIGURATION

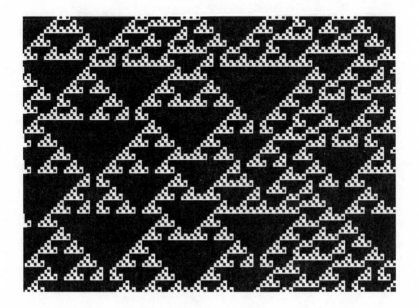

"Partial restabilization may occur after eliminating
destructive elements. Survival partly determined by
chance events."

IAN MALCOLM

Departure

The boat left the jungle river behind, and moved into darkness. The walls of the cave echoed the throb of the engines as Thorne steered the boat through the swift tidal current. To their left, a waterfall splashed down, a ray of light on cascading water. And then they burst out, moving beyond the high cliff wall and the crashing surf, into the open ocean. Kelly gave a cheer, and threw her arms around Arby, who winced and smiled.

Levine looked back at the island. "I have to admit, I never thought we'd make it. But with our cameras in place, and the uplink working, I expect we can continue to gather the data, until we finally get our answer about extinction."

Sarah Harding stared at him. "Maybe we will, and maybe we won't."

"Why not? It's a perfect Lost World."

She stared at him in disbelief. "It's nothing of the sort," she said. "Too many predators, remember?"

"Well, so it may appear, but we don't know—"

"Richard," she said. "Ian and I checked the records. They made a mistake on that island, many years ago. Back when the lab was still in production."

"What mistake?"

"They were manufacturing infant dinosaurs, and they didn't know what to feed them. For a while they gave them goat's milk, which was fine. It's very hypoallergenic. But as the carnivores grew, they fed them a special animal-protein extract. And the extract was made from ground-up sheep."

Levine said, "So? What's wrong with that?"

"In a zoo, they never use sheep extract," she said. "Because of the danger of infection."

"Infection," Levine repeated, in a low voice. "What kind of infection?"

"Prions," Malcolm said, from the other side of the boat.

Levine looked blank.

"Prions," Harding said, "are the simplest disease-causing entities known, even simpler than viruses. They're just protein fragments. They're so simple, they can't even invade a body—they have to be passively ingested. But once eaten, they cause disease: scrapie, in sheep; mad-cow disease; and kuru, a brain disease in human beings. And the dinosaurs developed a prion-disease called DX, from a bad batch of sheep protein extract. The lab battled it for years, trying to get rid of it."

"You're saying they didn't?"

"For a while, it seemed as if they did. The dinosaurs were flourishing. But then something happened. The disease began to spread. The prions are excreted in feces, so it is possible—"

"Excreted in feces?" Levine said. "The compys were eating feces. . . ."

"Yes, the compys are all infected. The compys are scavengers; they spread the protein over carcasses, and other scavengers became infected. Eventually, all the raptors were infected. Raptors attack healthy animals, not always successfully. One bite, and the animal becomes infected. And so, bit by bit, the infection spread through the island again. That's why the animals die early. And the rapid die-off supports a much larger predator population than you would expect—"

Levine was visibly anxious. "You know," he said, "one of the compys bit me."

"I wouldn't worry," Harding said. "There may be a mild encephalitis, but it's usually just a headache. We'll get you to a doctor in San José."

Levine began to sweat. He wiped his forehead with his hand. "Actually, I don't feel very good at all."

"It takes a week, Richard," she said. "I'm sure you'll be fine."

Levine sank back in his seat unhappily.

"But the point," she said, "is that I doubt this island will be able to tell you very much about extinction."

Malcolm stared back at the dark cliffs for a moment, and then began to speak. "Maybe that's the way it should be," he said. "Because extinction has always been a great mystery. It's happened five major times on this planet, and not always because of an asteroid. Everyone's interested in the Cretaceous die-out that killed the dinosaurs, but there were die-outs at the end of the Jurassic and the Triassic as well. They were severe, but they were nothing compared to the Permian extinction, which killed eighty percent of all life on the planet, on the seas and on the land. No one knows why that catastrophe happened. But I wonder if we are the cause of the next one."

"How is that?" Kelly said.

"Human beings are so destructive," Malcolm said. "I sometimes think we're a kind of plague, that will scrub the earth clean. We destroy things so well that I sometimes think, maybe that's our function. Maybe every few eons, some animal comes along that kills off the rest of the world, clears the decks, and lets evolution proceed to its next phase."

Kelly shook her head. She turned away from Malcolm and moved up the boat, to sit alongside Thorne.

"Are you listening to all that?" Thorne said. "I wouldn't take any of it too seriously. It's just theories. Human beings can't help making them, but the fact is that theories are just fantasies. And they change. When America was a new country, people believed in something called phlogiston. You know what that is? No? Well, it doesn't matter, because it wasn't real anyway. They also believed that four humors controlled behavior. And they believed that the earth was only a few thousand years old. Now we believe the earth is four billion years old, and we believe in photons and electrons, and we think human behavior is controlled by things like ego and self-esteem. We think those beliefs are more scientific and better."

"Aren't they?"

Thorne shrugged. "They're still just fantasies. They're not real. Have you ever seen a self-esteem? Can you bring me one on a plate? How about a photon? Can you bring me one of those?"

Kelly shook her head. "No, but . . ."

"And you never will, because those things don't exist. No matter how seriously people take them," Thorne said. "A hundred years from now, people will look back at us and laugh. They'll say, 'You know what people used to believe? They believed in photons and electrons. Can you imagine anything so silly?' They'll have a good laugh, because by then there will be newer and better fantasies." Thorne shook his head. "And meanwhile, you feel the way the boat moves? That's the sea. That's real. You smell the salt in the air? You feel the sunlight on your skin? That's all real. You see all of us together? That's real. Life is wonderful. It's a gift to be alive, to see the sun and breathe the air. And there isn't really anything else. Now look at that compass, and tell me where south is. I want to go to Puerto Cortés. It's time for us all to go home."

Acknowledgments

This novel is entirely fiction, but in writing it, I have drawn on the work of researchers in many different fields. I am especially indebted to the work, and the speculations, of John Alexander, Mark Boguski, Edwin Colbert, John Conway, Philip Currie, Peter Dodson, Niles Eldredge, Stephen Jay Gould, Donald Griffin, John Holland, John Horner, Fred Hoyle, Stuart Kauffman, Christopher Langton, Ernst Mayr, Mary Midgley, John Ostrom, Norman Packard, David Raup, Jeffrey Schank, Manfred Schroeder, George Gaylord Simpson, Bruce Weber, John Wheeler, and David Weishampel.

It remains only to say that the views expressed in this novel are mine, not theirs, and to remind the reader that a century and a half after Darwin, nearly all positions on evolution remain strongly contended, and fiercely debated.

A NOTE ON THE TYPE

The text of this book was set in Electra, a typeface designed by W. A. Dwiggins (1880–1956). This face cannot be classified as either modern or old style. It is not based on any historical model, nor does it echo any particular period or style. It avoids the extreme contrasts between thick and thin elements that mark most modern faces, and it attempts to give a feeling of fluidity, power, and speed.

Composed by Merri Ann Morrell,
Chester, Connecticut
Printed and bound by Quebecor Printing,
Martinsburg, West Virginia
Computer graphics by David Nakabayashi
Dinosaur illustrations on endpapers by Gregory Wenzel
Endpaper map by David Cain
Designed by Virginia Tan